CALIFORNIA THIRST

The California Water War
of the 1920s

James R. Morris

California Thirst

Copyright © 2025 James R. Morris

ISBN 979-8-9985320-0-9

This is a work of historical fiction. Apart from the well-known actual people of the time, events, and locales, all names, characters, organizations, places, and events are either products of the author's imagination or are used fictitiously. Any resemblance to current events, locales, or living persons is purely coincidental.

CALIFORNIA THIRST

CHAPTER 1   DO YOU KNOW THE WAY TO L.A.?

Spring 1927.   Alongside the Los Angeles Aqueduct, near the town of Independence, 230 miles north of Los Angeles

"You sure he's dead?" the woman asked.

"Gotta be," her husband said as he gingerly felt the man's neck for a pulse. In the moonlight, the right side of the face was pasty white, and the left side was dark mush from her close-up shotgun blast.

The tall rancher grasped the dead man's arms and pulled the heavy body to the edge of the truck's bed. He stepped back and gazed at the stars. Looking at the stars usually calmed him. But tonight, it was hard to stay calm with the still-warm body in the bed of his pickup.

"What are you waiting for?"

"Okay, here we go," he said as he grabbed the body by the armpits and pulled. The corpse hit the ground with a hollow-sounding whump. He struggled to drag it across the rough ground to the waterway. It was slow going. His wife grabbed the legs and helped drag the cadaver to the edge of the Los Angeles Aqueduct.

The man scanned the desert landscape to be sure they were alone. While he stalled, his wife bent down and pushed. With a splash, the body disappeared into the dark water flowing south to the thirsty city.

The lady straightened up and brushed her hands together, signifying the completion of the task. "Maybe we should have weighted him down."

"Too late now," the man said as he climbed into the pickup.

CHAPTER 2   OFFER

Four years earlier, in the Summer of 1923.

Near the town of Independence

Riding back to their ranch after visiting the Schaffers farther down the valley, Alice Lukin turned in her saddle and spoke to her husband, Fred, riding beside her. "You think the Schaffers will be able to keep their spread?"

Fred wiped the sweat from his face with his handkerchief and shrugged. "Don't figure there's much chance. They're just like all the others driven from the valley. That damned DWP takes the water, and you got no choice but to watch your ranch dry out."

At the top of a sagebrush-covered rise, Fred halted his horse. He leaned forward, resting his forearms on the saddle horn, and watched a car speeding down the lane toward their ranch house in the distance. Who'd be in such a hurry to get to their place? He lightly spurred his horse.

When they reached their farmyard, a new model Chevrolet sedan idled near the barn with a man behind the wheel. Their dog faced the car in a crouch, like he was daring a cow to make a move.

The man rolled down his window. "Hey, can you call off your dog? He won't let me out of my car."

Fred gave a shrill two-fingered whistle and commanded, "Here, Tinker!" The dog strutted to him with his head erect as though he were immensely proud of keeping that metal cow from making a move.

A stocky man wearing a Homburg, a bow tie, and a business suit stepped out of the car. His jacket appeared stretched to its limit to house his stout arms and broad shoulders. He reminded Fred of pictures he'd seen of muscular prizefighters. More likely, he was just a salesman, a dude from the city. Either way, he had a belligerent face that would be easy to dislike.

The man strode toward Fred. "Are you Frederick Lukin?"

"Yeah. Who might you be?" the lanky rancher asked as he swung down from his saddle. Removing his hat, he smoothed his unruly, thinning hair, and slapped his sweat-stained Stetson against his thigh to get rid of the dust.

The man extended his hand. "Earl Magon. I'm the new District Acquisition Manager for the City of Los Angeles Department of Water and Power."

Towering over the man, Fred looked down at the hand as if it were foul and didn't offer his own. He knew full well what the man wanted, but asked, "What does the DWP want with us?"

Magon slowly lowered his hand.

Fred had heard the DWP had brought in a new man to speed up the acquisition of water rights for Los Angeles. They bought the ranches in the Owens Valley for their water, drying out the land and letting it return to desert so the rapidly growing metropolis down south would have something to drink. Over the last few years, most of DWP's water acquisitions had been around Bishop, at the valley's north end. But during the current drought, that wasn't enough. Now, they were buying more land and water in this south end. The DWP would soon own everything, and there would be nothing left but desert.

"I'd like to talk some business with you. It's hot out here." Magon nodded toward the house. "Can we go inside?"

Fred shook his head. "No. Got work to do. What do you want?"

Magon turned his gaze toward the fields. "I want to buy your ranch with its water rights, including your Lower Owens Irrigation Ditch shares."

Fred spat on the ground. "Not for sale." He turned to help Alice off her horse.

"This attractive little lady must be Mrs. Lukin." With a slight bow, he said, "I'm Earl Magon."

She looked him up and down. "I heard you the first time."

Magon was momentarily silent, then glanced from wife to husband with a smile that belied the hostility in his eyes. "The DWP will pay top dollar, and you can leave this godforsaken desert and live like a king in Los Angeles, the land of the future. You shouldn't pass it up."

Alice glared at Magon. "What's godforsaken to one person is heaven to another. We'll keep our land and water."

Magon stepped closer, arms akimbo and head thrust forward like a schoolyard bully. "Look, folks, you need a dose of reality. It makes no sense for you to struggle to raise a few head of cattle. You use the water to run a small herd and just barely scrape by. That same water in Southern California is twenty times as productive and earns twenty times as much as it does here. We can afford to pay a good price for your water, carry it in our aqueduct over two hundred miles south through the desert to L.A., and still have money left over. You must know the saying that money talks and money wins. We have the money, and we will win. If you don't work with me, others will, and we'll still get the water. You'll be left with nothing."

Fred's voice shook with anger. "You bastards! You think because you have money, you can come here and suck us dry. We don't want your money." He pointed at Magon's car and raised his voice, "Now get off our property."

Magon shrugged and walked to his car. As he opened the door, he looked back at the couple and exclaimed, "It's strange how unfortunate things happen to people who refuse to work with me."

Fred watched the DWP man's car kick up dust as it bounced and fishtailed down the dirt road toward town. He scanned the landscape as the dust settled. With the majestic Sierra Nevada towering ten thousand feet over the valley like a granite sentinel to the west and the sere Inyo Mountains enclosing it on the east, the

Owens Valley's narrowness made Fred feel protected from the rest of the world. But he knew the protection was an illusion. The land was being stolen away, just like his pioneer ancestors had wrested it from the native Paiutes and Shoshones not so many years before. Now, Los Angeles was seizing control of the valley for its water. He had heard other ranchers had done well selling out to the DWP. Maybe it was a lost cause, but damned if he would sell this land his family had homesteaded over fifty years ago.

CHAPTER 3   DITCH DEFENSE

A couple of weeks after the DWP man's visit, Fred and the owner of the neighboring ranch, Murphy Hamhurst, were working together on a section of the Lower Owens Irrigation Ditch. The canal drew water from the Owens River and carried it to the six ranches that owned shares in the small cooperative ditch company. Members of the cooperative maintained the ditch, clearing the silt and weeds, repairing bank cave-ins, and servicing the gates controlling the flow.

"Hey, Fred," Murphy shouted from farther down the ditch. "What should we do about this gate that feeds your south field? The wood's darn near rotten and needs replacement. Wanna do it now?"

"Lemme take a look, Murph," Fred hollered to the short, rotund rancher who invariably had a cigar hanging out of his mouth. Fred joined Murphy and inspected the planks. "Not now. It'll last this season, and I can fix it later. If you want some water to reach your spread, we need to concentrate on clearin' the weeds plugging things up."

Murphy leaned on his shovel. "Yeah, what with the drought and weeds, I'm not gettin' a decent flow. But you know what really burns me up? Seems like you, me, Slim, and Henry are the only ones ever do any work to keep it goin'. I ain't seen Boyd or Stevens out here doin' anything for months. We do the work, and they get the water."

"Ahh, Stevens's gettin' pretty old," Fred said. "It's hard on him, but damn, I think Boyd's just plain lazy. He drinks and lets his place go t' hell. With the river level droppin', we need everybody to chip in to keep our water flowin'."

"We always seem to get the hind tit," Murphy complained. "The drought's playin' hell on everything, and the DWP's takin' more all the time."

"Yeah, keeps goin' like this, and we'll all be bone dry and forced to give up."

The rapid thudding of hooves interrupted their exchange, and they both turned to watch Slim Berks, another of the six ranchers depending on the ditch, rein up in front of them.

"There's a bunch of men diggin' a bypass channel up by our ditch intake," the stout rider gasped, out of breath as though he had been the one galloping instead of the horse.

"What do you mean?" Fred asked.

"They was digging a new ditch across that U-bend in the river, like to bypass the headgate. We'll be left dry."

"Damn! Who was it?" Murphy asked.

"Ain't seen none of 'em before. They was a tough-lookin' bunch, more like a gang of hoodlums than a crew of ditch diggers. One fella had a rifle."

"Bet it's the work of that DWP acquisitions jackass that threatened me a couple of weeks ago," Fred said.

"Yeah," Murphy replied. "A while back, I heard a DWP crew tried to dig a bypass up by Big Pine. Russ Harper had to chase 'em out at the end of a rifle. Probably what we'll have to do."

Fred gazed in the direction of the canal's intake as he thought it over. "Those sons-a-bitches! Slim, how about drivin' into town and get Jake and his guys to help. Murph, get your rifle. Let's meet in the trees by the intake."

Fred got his rifle from the house and trotted along the ditch to the intake on the Owens River. From a copse of cottonwoods and locusts, he watched a crew of men digging a new ditch across the U-bend as Slim had described. If they finished the channel, it would bypass the headgate of the ranchers' cooperative canal. Without the water, the spreads on the ditch would dry up and be the next ranches to be abandoned to return to desert, just what the DWP wanted.

Fred hollered across the river. "What the hell do you think you're doing? You got no business there. Get away from my land."

A man he immediately recognized as Earl Magon stepped from behind a tall sagebrush with a Winchester 30-30 pointed at

Fred. "This ain't your land, Lukin. Your land stops at the top of the bend where you're standing. This is none of your concern, so get away."

"The hell it isn't my concern. My property's on the river, and I've got a legal claim for that water. You can't reroute it."

"This is Department of Water and Power business," Magon shouted. "And just so you won't do something stupid, my men are armed and can handle a rifle better than a shovel."

Murphy joined him, but Fred figured he still needed more rifles to scare the ditch diggers away. After waiting half an hour, he worried that no help would show up. Suddenly, the sand exploded at the base of the tree, followed instantly by the sharp crack of a shot. He scooted behind the tree and looked back to see that Murphy was okay. His neighbor was hunched down behind a rock and waved.

"Don't shoot yet," Fred said, sotto voce. "Wait till Slim and Jake get here with more men."

As he said it, he spotted Jake running full-tilt, leading eight men. Slim jogged behind, struggling to keep up. Each man carried his deer rifle, looking determined to defend the water supply.

"Cover them," Fred yelled to Murphy. "Make those bastards keep their heads down till Jake finds cover. Don't hit nobody."

Murphy opened fire over the heads of the digging crew as Fred ran to greet his brother-in-law with a slap on the shoulder. "Jake, damn glad you made it. Thanks."

"What now?" Jake asked.

"I'd like to settle this without more shooting. I don't want a war, but it may come to that."

"Who are they?"

"The crew chief is that DWP dude who came to the ranch," Fred replied. "He must've brought a bunch of thugs up from L.A. to do the City's dirty work."

A volley of shots erupted from across the river, accompanied by the sounds of slugs whapping into the tree trunks.

"Everybody okay?" Fred yelled.

"Yeah," his men answered in unison.

"Back off now," shouted the DWP crew leader with the Winchester. "We're not on your land and we're going to finish this channel."

"No!" Fred shouted. "Get out."

Magon's head and shoulders showed above the edge of the fresh ditch. An image of the enemy in the trenches in France five years earlier flashed through Fred's mind. 'Don't hit nobody' he had said, but he couldn't resist. *Ok, maybe just a scratch.* He steadied his rifle on a log as he had in 1918. This time, it was more personal – his home, his land, his water. Steady. Steady. He slowly squeezed the trigger. The rifle bucked with a bang.

Magon screamed and grabbed his shoulder as he fell back into the ditch. "Shoot them! Shoot the bastards!"

There was a roar as the DWP crew shot all at once. Bullets whistled and splatted into trees with no apparent damage. Fred and his men answered with their own volley, kicking up dirt at the edge of the new ditch.

"How'd they get out here?" Jake asked. "I doubt they walked."

Fred scanned the area around the diggers and gestured with his chin. "Bet they have a truck parked outta sight, over that hill. Got an idea." He pointed north. "Take your men and wade across upstream and flank them from the top of the rise. You'll have clear shots, and the DWP thugs 'll have to give up."

Jake ran through the trees and explained the plan to his men. They circled out of the DWP crew's sight, waded the shallow river, and took position behind the crest of a hill. As soon as Fred figured they were in place, he shot over the heads of the digging crew as the signal. Jake's flankers opened fire down the length of the unfinished ditch, trying not to hit the diggers but showing their exposure.

After a few shots into the dirt at their feet, Magon's thugs placed their rifles on the ground and raised their hands.

Fred stood. Motioning for Murph and Slim to follow, he walked to the riverbank with his rifle aimed at the diggers. Jake led his men down the hill. As they surrounded the DWP crew, Fred, Murphy, and Slim forded the river. "Throw their weapons in the river," he directed his men.

"Hey, you can't do that. Those are our rifles," Magon yelled, standing with one hand holding his wounded shoulder.

"Not anymore," Fred answered. "You dug that ditch; now get your shovels and fill it up. Then get outta here."

The filling went faster than the digging, but it was late afternoon by the time the ditch was filled.

Fred's shot had only grazed Magon, and Jake told him where to find Doc Woodin, the only doctor in town.

Before Magon left, he shouted, "Lukin, you'll pay for this."

Heading back to his ranch house, Fred reviewed the day. He had fought and won this minor battle. It felt pretty good, but it settled nothing. He knew the DWP would keep pushing until it had driven all the ranchers from their land and taken every drop of the valley's water for Los Angeles.

CHAPTER 4   MORNING COFFEE

Standing on the wooden sidewalk in front of his general store the next morning, Jake Shapiro watched a Model T flatbed, loaded with hay bales, race by, kicking up a cloud of dust. Waiting for the dust to settle, the short, slight merchant scanned up and down the street. With just eight blocks from one end of town to the other, he loved the intimacy of Independence, where he knew most everything about the town and everyone in it. It was so different from San Francisco, where he had grown up and left after the earthquake. The big city had every sort of store and service imaginable, but the essentials were here: his general store, with groceries, clothing, and sundries; King's drug store and fountain on the corner, Doris's Inyo Cafe across the street, plus the handful of other small-town businesses. The one thing most towns this size didn't have was that magnificent county courthouse across the street. The new three-story Greek Revival structure, with a white façade and imposing columns, was the pride of the county. It contrasted sharply with that eyesore at the southwest edge of town: the district headquarters of the Los Angeles Department of Water and Power. For Jake, everything about the DWP was unappealing, especially their policy of buying all the land and water rights. On the other hand, they were the largest employer and the area's lifeblood, keeping businesses like his alive.

Jake crossed the street to join his friends for their morning coffee at Doris's Inyo Cafe. As he entered, he took off his fedora and placed it on the hat rack. Two morning regulars already sat at the table by the front window.

"Morning, Ed… George," Jake said as he pulled up a chair.

Appearing instantly with a pot in her hand, the tall, middle-aged proprietress began pouring. "Ready for coffee, Jake?"

"Thanks, Doris. I need it this morning."

She laughed. "From what I heard and how you look, you need something stronger than coffee."

"Hard to get anything stronger unless you make it yourself," Jake replied.

"Sounds like you had quite a battle out at Fred's place yesterday," George King, the pharmacist, said. "Everybody in town is already talking about it. Some of what they're sayin' might even be true. What happened?"

As Jake began his account, Doris pulled a chair up to the table and sat down as though she were one of the morning coffee crew. "I gotta hear this, too."

"Well, just after the lunch hour, Slim comes barreling into the store— " Before he could finish the sentence, Fred stepped through the doorway.

"Here's our other warrior," Doris announced as she got up to get another cup.

The rancher nodded to the group as he hung his sweat-stained hat on the hat rack. Doris poured him a cup and sat back down. She gestured with the coffeepot. "Jake, here, was just telling us what happened yesterday. Go on, Jake?"

"Fred can tell it better than I can."

Fred stirred some sugar into his coffee, blew on it, stared out the window for a moment, and then recounted the previous day's events.

"You didn't really throw their rifles into the river, did you?" Ed Walters asked.

Fred laughed. "Sure did. Be tough to use them now."

"Wow!" Ed said. "That must be a fortune rusting away in the river. Bet I could fix them up if I could find them."

"Take care if you try," Fred warned. "Bet that bunch of thugs will be sneakin' around out there trying to recover 'em first chance they get."

"They'll be itching for a fight now," Jake said.

"I'm ready for a fight," Fred responded. "If we don't fight back, L.A. will take every drop of water in the valley. I'm fed up with them running us over. With this drought, they're taking more from the river than originally agreed twenty years ago. Now they're drilling wells, pumping us dry, and buying up our ditches and shutting them down. That new DWP man, Magon, asked me to sell.

When I refused, he threatened me. Then yesterday, he started digging that bypass. Can't say I'm sorry I shot him."

Ed laughed. "You win the marksmanship prize."

Doris raised her coffee pot. "More coffee before it's cold?" Nobody responded, but she topped off their cups anyway and said, "You know, they'll keep pushing to force people to sell. Prices will go up, and everyone will sell if the price is high enough. L.A. can afford it because the water is a lot more valuable down there than it is up here."

Jake chuckled. "Leave it to the women to know what something is worth. My Betty keeps our books. She's always after me for charging the wrong price."

"Damn right," Doris said. "If we don't step in, you men are sure to make a mess of things."

Before anyone could speak in defense of men, the sound of the door opening interrupted them. They all turned to see Inyo County Sheriff Charlie Cole enter the cafe.

"Mornin', Charlie," Fred said.

"Morning." The meticulously uniformed sheriff removed his white Stetson from his mostly bald head, pulled a chair to the table, and spun it around to straddle it with his arms resting on the back.

Everyone looked expectantly at the sheriff, waiting to see what he would say about the gun battle.

"Damn it, Doris, where's my coffee?"

"Hold your horses, you old coot," Doris said as she fetched another cup.

Cole took a Bull Durham bag out of his pocket and tore a paper from the front of the bag. Holding the paper in one hand, he folded it into a trough and, with his other hand, slowly poured a trail of tobacco along the fold. He looked around the table, lifted the paper to his lips, and ran his tongue along its length. With the paper wetted, he rolled the cigarette and lit it with a match he struck on the sole of his boot. He took a drag on the cigarette and looked at Fred.

"So, Fred! I hear tell that you shot up a crew of DWP workers yesterday out by your place. What the hell is going on?"

Once again, Fred recounted his story.

"You can't just take pot-shots at folks diggin' a ditch in the desert," the sheriff said. "Sounds like they weren't on your property, so it's not like they were burglars taking stuff out of your house."

"*The hell*! They intended to take both my property and the property of our ditch co-op. Water law says I have a right to use the water flowing by my land. Somebody can't just come along and divert the river and deprive me of it, even if it is the City of Los Angeles."

Cole stubbed his cigarette in an ashtray. "Dammit, Fred, you don't need to lecture me on the law. I know the law, and the law says you can't shoot at people."

"Then you also know that the law allows me to defend my property when they're trying to steal it. Besides, they shot first.

Murphy and Slim can back me up on that, and Jake here can confirm the rest."

"That may be," Cole answered, "but the crew chief and his men will probably say you opened fire without warning." He turned to Shapiro. "Jake, you was there. How did it start?"

"I wasn't there when it started. I don't think anyone was really aiming to hit anybody, only to scare the other side off."

"Somebody was aiming," the Sheriff said. "Their crew chief, that new fella, Magon, was shot in the shoulder and had to be patched up by Doc Woodin."

"It wasn't much of a wound—not much more than a scratch," Jake responded.

Fred gestured at Cole with his coffee cup. "Those people are thieves and thugs. They'll destroy us all if we let them, and you know it, Charlie."

"Yeah, I think I do. That's why I'm sitting here having coffee with you. I know what's going on, and I don't like L.A. taking our water any more than you do. But my job is to cool things down before they get out of hand." He took a swallow of coffee and spat it back in the cup. "Dammit, Doris, this coffee is cold."

"It wouldn't get cold if you drank it instead of wasting time getting after one of our own," Doris snapped as she got up to get a fresh pot.

Cole looked at the ceiling. "I hope the day never comes when I have to arrest that woman."

George King chuckled. "Yeah, you'd be in trouble, Charlie. She'd kick you out of the house and lock you up in your own jail,"

"I heard that, and damned right I would," Doris called from behind the counter.

CHAPTER 5   LEAVING THE PROMISED LAND

While Fred argued with the sheriff at the cafe, Paul Schaffer worked to start the water pump on his ranch southeast of town. He opened a valve and the steam engine began to push the flywheel. The big wheel turned slowly at first, then picked up speed, the long rods reciprocating up and down, driving the pump. Give it time, and maybe it will bring enough water. Finally, a little came out. In normal times, what began as a trickle would build to a steady flow. But today was worse than yesterday. Just dribbles, not near what his fields and livestock needed. This late in the season, the alfalfa should be tall and ready to cut. Instead, the few hardy plants that had survived the hot, dry summer were only about a foot high, not even tall enough to cut. And, without more water, there wasn't enough left in the troughs to keep the livestock going for more than a few days. Maybe he could sell the few remaining head.

He heard a car drive into the farmyard. That would be Mr. Hanson from the Federal Land Bank. Paul trudged back to the house, where he and Marie invited the FLB man to join them at the kitchen table.

After some initial small talk, Hanson got to the point. "I am so sorry, Paul, but I have no choice. You haven't made a payment for eleven months now, and we have strict orders from the Washington office to collect or foreclose. In fact, it's worse than that. We can't make any new loans in Owens Valley because L.A.'s actions in the valley have killed the market for ranch land. It'll make it easier for everybody if you voluntarily sign over the title, and we won't have to go through a formal foreclosure."

Paul shuffled the papers sitting on the table. He knew the end had come, but felt compelled to resist the inevitable and spoke words he knew weren't true. "But Mr. Hanson, if I can sell this alfalfa crop and a few of our steers, we will pay. We just need some more time."

Hanson shook his head. "Paul, that's what you said in the spring. I looked at your alfalfa when I drove in today. I doubt you could bale it, much less sell it. And your cattle look as bad as your alfalfa. The longer we wait to resolve this, the worse it will get. Every day without water, your spread's value goes down. It's better to do it now." He stood his hands clasped behind his back and gazed out the kitchen window. After a moment, he turned back. "Tell you what I can do. We take title to the ranch property now. You keep the livestock and stay long enough to sell them. That will give you some funds to get started elsewhere."

Marie reached over and gently grasped his wrist. "Paul, Paul, let it go. It's wearing you down. This was once a beautiful ranch… a beautiful valley, but no more. The water's gone, and it won't come back. Like Mr. Hanson says, tomorrow the ranch will be worth less than it is today and keep going down. We can start over in Visalia near my relatives. There's water over there that L.A. will never get."

A few weeks later, Paul and Marie stood on the loading platform of the Southern Pacific station four miles east of Independence. The low building, with its weathered mustard-yellow clapboard siding and wide overhanging eaves, looked identical to all the other SP stations serving rural towns throughout the West. However, this one looked lonelier than most, plopped amid the sagebrush without a single tree nearby.

A small cluster of well-wishers surrounded the couple waiting for the train to Mojave, where they would change trains and head west over the southern Sierras to start a new life in the central valley.

Fred put his hand on Paul's shoulder. "God, Paul, I hate to see you folks leave. A few more families leave, and there won't be none left."

"We hate it more 'n you do." He slapped his thigh. "Hell, we don't even have a car to leave in. The dealer took it back."

"You sure about this?" Henry Olivera asked. "You could stay here, maybe get a job with the DWP. Even stay at our house till you find something."

Marie's lips tightened into a thin line. "Henry, there is no way I would let Paul work for the DWP after what they've done. I think we would both rather starve."

"Well, I wish Isabel would forbid me to work," Henry joked.

"I should let you starve," answered his wife, Isabel, standing next to him. "You're getting a little paunchy. Pretty soon, you won't be able to get on your horse."

Henry chuckled. "Not my fault. It's your enchiladas."

"We'll miss your enchiladas, Isabel," Marie said.

Alice gave Marie a hug. "They'll have enchiladas over there. Why did you pick Visalia?"

"My brother has property over there," Marie replied. "They'll let us stay with them till we can get settled."

"Nice country," Paul said, more to reassure himself than to explain to his friends. "Plenty of water. Good land. I can get a job 'till I can afford some land for a cattle spread." He shook his head. "Just never thought I'd have to leave here. Born here and thought of this as the promised land. Now look at it."

"Yeah, coulda been a paradise," Fred said. "They used to haul tons of produce out of here. Now, farms and ranches are dryin' up and everybody's leaving. I'm wondering when my turn will come."

"If it does, you can always come over the mountains and stay with us," Paul replied.

Fred laughed. "Thanks. Who knows, we may be on the next train."

A piercing whistle interrupted the awkward banter. The narrow gauge 'Slim Princess' locomotive, puffing white clouds of steam from its piston boxes and acrid, black smoke from its smokestack, pulled into the station trailing four freight cars and one lonely passenger coach. As soon as the train came to a halt, the conductor jumped down to the platform and shouted, "All aboard!"

The women took turns hugging Marie, and the men shook hands with Paul.

"Come on, Helen. Time to go," Paul called to his teen-aged daughter, sitting alone on a bench by the station house.

She slowly stood and walked toward the train like a convict trudging toward the scaffold. With tears streaming down her cheeks, the girl followed her parents up the steps into the passenger car.

The whistle shrilled again, and the chug-a-chug of the engine drowned out the farewells as the well-wishers waved goodbye.

CHAPTER 6   PARTY

Fred stood on the SP loading platform with the rest of the well-wishers, watching the train puff its way south. His friends were gone, and his world was drying up and shrinking.

He glanced at Alice and her sister, Betty Shapiro, standing together. Some people said the petite sisters were hard to tell apart, but he thought Alice was prettier despite being three years older. Both ladies had their dark brown hair cut in the currently popular marcelled bob they had seen in the Sears Roebuck catalog. And, aside from different fabrics for their shirt-waist dresses, the only other visible differences were their eyes. Alice's deep azure eyes were shaded by a straw hat with a broad flat brim, and Betty, who wore no hat, squinted her large brown eyes in the sun's glare.

As the farewell-wishers turned to leave the platform, Alice remarked to no one in particular, "This is just too depressing. Everybody's leaving the valley."

Betty's face lit up. "We need some cheering up. Let's have a party!"

"A party? Now?" asked Grace Berks, Slim's stout wife.

"Sure, why not?" Alice replied. She grabbed Fred's arm. "Everyone needs cheering up. Grace, Betty, and I decided we'll have a party." Before Fred could respond, she announced loudly, "Hey, everybody. We're having a cheer-up party. We have some quail and doves in the icebox that Fred shot yesterday. I'm sure the rest of you can figure out something to bring. Go home, get your food and drinks, and come to our place this evening."

The women huddled together and made quick plans for the spur-of-the-moment gathering.

The men looked at Fred. He spread both hands and shrugged. "Guess we gotta do what they say. I imagine we can find something to drink."

"I got some new whiskey from Canada," Henry said.

"And I have a new batch I made last month," Slim added.

In the pleasantly warm summer evening, the cheer-up party got underway at the Lukin's ranch house with guests arriving from town and nearby ranches. While the women congregated in the kitchen, the men clustered in front of the barn, where Fred directed the assembly of tables from boards laid across saw horses. Homebrew and bootleg liquor appeared in an amazing variety as each man trotted out his prohibited homemade libation.

"Hey, Slim, your latest grog isn't bad," Jake called as he raised his glass.

"Made it from feed oats," Slim answered.

"You mean the oats you feed your horses?"

"Yeah. No different from what you cook on the stove. Besides, the alcohol kills anything that ain't good for you."

"Good for you?" Charlie Cole asked. "As Sheriff of Inyo County, I'm duty-bound to assess its health benefits." He poured a shot and downed it in one swig. He coughed, and his eyes teared up. "Potent stuff, Slim. It must be medicinal." The sheriff poured some more and raised the glass. "As the legal authority for the county, I pronounce this liquid beneficial to your health and only slightly illegal."

In the kitchen, Alice hefted her big iron Dutch-oven from her stove and lifted the lid. Aromatic steam wafted through the room.

"That smells *sooo* good," Grace lauded. "You must give me your recipe."

"I don't really have a recipe," Alice said. "Just do what I saw my mother do—cover the dove or quail with onions, thick cream, and a little spice, then bake them for two hours or more. I started these as soon as I got home from the station. Okay, Betty," she called to her sister, "the oven's clear. You can warm your venison stew."

Betty slid her pot into the oven and remarked, "My heart broke watching the Schaffers leave. It would be so painful to leave your friends and the land where you grew up."

"It's sad," Agnes Brice said from her seat at the kitchen table. "So many families are being forced to leave because they lost their water. Over the last two years, our school has lost thirteen kids because their families moved away. In our small school, that's a lot."

Doris swallowed a slug of bootleg booze and coughed from the sting. "Thirteen?" she croaked. "That doesn't sound like many."

"With only seventy-eight kids in all the grades, it's devastating," Agnes replied. "I had four leave last year in my fourth and fifth-grade classroom. At this rate, pretty soon, we won't have enough kids to keep the school open."

"Yeah," Doris agreed. "Charlie says that the county tax revenue is declining due to people leaving. The county will have to cut budgets. He says some smaller schools, like Aberdeen and Keeler, will have to close."

Isabel Olivera paused her enchilada preparation and glanced at Alice. "How do you think Schaffer's move will affect Helen and your son's engagement plans?"

"I've asked myself the same question," Alice replied. "After Carl graduated last year, they planned on getting engaged as soon as Helen graduated next spring. He hasn't said anything to me or Fred, and I've wondered if it was still on. I've been skeptical it would last after Jake got him that construction job in San Francisco. I'm not convinced that absence makes the heart grow fonder."

"They'll be nearer to each other with Helen in Visalia," Isabel said. "Maybe they'll see each other more often."

"Who knows?" Alice said.

The kitchen gossip and banter continued as the ladies finished their preparations. When the food was warmed and ready, Alice led the parade of the women out to the tables, each carrying her culinary contribution: wild game, fried chicken, pork sausage, and, of course, beef. Most every household had its own garden and the banquet overflowed with dishes of freshly harvested vegetables.

Chairs, benches, and every conceivable seating device appeared, and everyone found a place. Some sat on hay bales dragged out of the barn. The conversation got louder as people competed to be heard while others shouted for a tray of food to be passed.

Amid the camaraderie, Fred's neighbor, Murphy Hamhurst, drove into the farmyard, making a dusty stop in front of the diners. "Hey, Fred, hey Fred," he yelled as he exited his truck.

"Hey to you, Murph," Fred called. "You're late; there may not be any food left. Where's Clara Mae?"

"Not comin'," Murphy answered breathlessly. "Fred, you got some cattle down."

"What do you mean, down?"

"On the ground, dead-like. Saw some staggerin' too. In your south field, by the water trough close to the canal."

"Let's go," Fred said. He ran to his pickup with Murphy at his side. Most of the other men abandoned their meals and took to their cars to follow. In moments, Fred bounced over the rutted track through his fields, leading a caravan of fellow ranchers and townspeople.

"There," Murphy pointed.

Fred skidded to a stop and jumped from his pickup. In the fading evening light, he saw collapsed cattle scattered across the field. There were a few still standing with their heads hanging like they were waiting for death. He ran from one carcass to another, lifted a head, and eased it gently back to the ground. A standing yearling gave him a look as if begging for release from torture. Fred patted its back, and it collapsed on the ground. Its legs jerked, spasmed, and went still. Fred surveyed the field of dead and dying cattle. This was his life, his livelihood. He bent over with his hands on his knees and struggled not to lose his dinner and drinks.

"Murph, how many you think are down?" Slim asked.

"Hard to tell in the dark." Murphy pointed from one dark shape to another. "I count twenty-three down and see three still standin'. Could 'a missed some, though." He turned to Fred and put his hand on his friend's shoulder. "How many you have in this field?"

The rancher unfolded a handkerchief and wiped his face. "Thirty-two, almost half of my herd. I drove them in here three days ago."

"See anything wrong then?"

"Didn't notice anything. What would I see, anyway?"

"Don't know. Just askin'." Murphy peered at the scattered carcasses. "What do we do now?"

Fred gazed at the field of dead and dying cattle. He pointed at the few that were still standing. "Don't know what's wrong, but we need to end their suffering."

Murphy grimaced. "Want me to shoot 'em?"

"Yeah. Would you? I can't do it."

"I'll help," Slim said. "I'll get my rifle."

Sheriff Cole walked from one dead animal to another. He squatted down beside a steer. Its tongue lolled out of the mouth, black and swollen. Cole pushed back an eyelid and inspected the eye. He stood and gazed around the pasture. He walked to the fence and grabbed a handful of hay from one of many small piles spread along the fence line. In the dim light, he sorted through it, extracted a few tufts of plant and smelled, then looked up in the night sky. "Damn," he said quietly. He held out his hand with bits of the hay. "Fred, know what this is?"

Fred shrugged. "What?"

"Look close and smell it."

Fred took some from Cole's hand and examined it. He placed it close to his nose, then stared at the sheriff. "Jimson weed?"

"Yeah, I think so," Cole said. "Jimson's poison but probably wouldn't kill all of them. I think something else might be there, too." He pointed toward the small piles of hay along the fence. "You put that there?"

"No," Fred said as he grabbed another handful and turned it over in his hand. "Hadn't noticed it before."

The other men watched and listened to this exchange. Each one grabbed a handful and examined it. They talked excitedly as they showed each other what they found in the hay.

"This hay's along the fence like it was thrown from the other side," the sheriff said. "You sure you didn't put it there?"

"Absolutely," Fred replied. "I bring my bales in the pickup and put them by the water trough, not along the fence." Fred turned and looked at his dead cattle in the field. "I'll kill that S.O.B.!" he shouted to the sky.

"Now don't go sayin' and doin' stupid stuff, Fred," Cole warned. "We don't know who mighta done this."

"It was that DWP bastard, *Magon*, sure as hell," Fred growled.

"You don't have any proof."

"Proof?" Fred exclaimed. "By the time we get proof, my whole herd 'll be dead."

CHAPTER 7   TALKING REVENGE

Fred looked at his dead cattle scattered across the pasture. It had to be Magon. He was the one who said that unfortunate things happen to people who refuse to work with him. Then, the thug said Fred would pay when he resisted the attempt to divert the river to bypass the co-op irrigation ditch. Fred kicked at the ground. Revenge played through his mind as he walked to his truck.

At the house, the rest of the party guests anxiously waited to hear what had happened. The story was told in hushed, funereal tones as the men returned from the field.

Sitting disconsolately at the makeshift table, Fred jerked at the sound of a shot from his south pasture where Murphy and Slim were tending the grisly task of putting the poisoned steers out of their misery. Alice, sitting close, put her arm across his shoulders and leaned her head against his. More shots. With each blast, he jerked like he was the victim. The guests stood in small clusters and listened, each person counting the shots. No one said a word. They stared with sad eyes, thinking how that could have been their herd.

Cole sat down next to Fred, and Doris set glasses in front of the two friends. She grabbed a bottle from the middle of the table and filled both glasses.

Fred gazed at the glass like he didn't quite know what it was. Hesitantly, he reached for it, drained half, and coughed. "I'll get that son-of-a-bitch," were his first words since leaving the field.

"Now, don't jump to conclusions," Cole said. "Like I said earlier, we don't know who did it or even if it was intentional."

"Baloney!" Fred thundered. "Out there, you jumped to a conclusion. We all know who did this, and it wasn't accidental. I told you Magon threatened me when I refused his offer to buy me out. He tried to dig that bypass and now my cattle turn up dead."

"Maybe Charlie's right," George King said from across the table. "It might not have been Magon. I heard that something like this occurred up in Big Pine last spring. A guy refused a DWP offer, and pretty soon his horses got sick and one died. And that was before Magon came up here from L.A."

Henry reached for a bottle and topped off his glass. "Magon or not, it was still the DWP."

"Whoever did it, you have to do it according to the law," Cole said.

"According to the law?" Fred groused. "The law hasn't done us any good so far."

"Yeah, how much law do we have to take from that damned DWP?" Henry asked. "They run over people and nothing happens. We need to do something about it ourselves. Teach them a lesson."

"How would you do that?" Someone from farther down the table asked.

Fred set his empty glass on the table. "It wouldn't be hard. A little dynamite in the aqueduct and boom, the water flows back to the river instead of L.A. That should be a good lesson."

George pointed at Fred with his fork. "That's crazy. Start doing stuff like that, and pretty soon, you've got a war on your hands. And guess who'll win. It won't be anybody sitting here."

From his perch on a hay bale at the end of the table, Jake spoke up. "George, I've probably lost a third of my customers. I bet your drug store has lost almost as much business as I have. The DWP is driving people out of the valley. It wouldn't hurt my feelings to see the Department of Water and Power suffer a bit."

George shook his head. "I don't see how damaging the aqueduct gets our customers back."

From the kitchen porch came Doris's voice. "Hey, Charlie, time to go. I gotta get up early to open the cafe."

"Be right there," Cole shouted. "Gentlemen, my boss commands me to leave, but you guys better stop this drunken talk." He placed his hand on his dejected friend's shoulder. "Fred, I know how you must feel. I'd feel the same way, but you can't solve it by doing something stupid. Gotta go now."

Murphy and Slim returned from their grisly work in the pasture to what started as a party but had turned into a wake. They each pulled a chair to the table. Without saying anything, Slim grabbed a bottle from the middle of the table and filled an empty glass. He handed the bottle to Murphy.

Slumped at the table, Fred broke the silence. "I counted eleven shots. What happened?"

Murphy lowered his glass, and his voice shook. "The ones that were still standing when you were there were done for, so we put them down. Found others further out in the field, and some of those that were already down were still alive but suffering, so we shot them. You said thirty-two, so there must be some that we couldn't find in the dark."

"What'll you do with the carcasses?" Slim asked.

Fred shrugged. "Hadn't thought about it."

"Butcher 'em, maybe?" Slim queried.

"Nope, can't take the chance. Layin' there all night, they won't be fresh. Besides, can't feed poisoned meat to folks. Could bury them, though."

"It'd take one hell of a hole for that many cows," Slim said. "How about burning them?"

Murphy let out a soft whistle. "Jesus! What a stench. It would fill the entire valley."

"Might just smell like a big barbecue," Jake remarked.

"Not with all those guts in the fire," Murphy answered.

"What we ought to do is take them over to the DWP office and burn them on the steps," Henry said.

Fred reached for a bottle. "I don't want to think about dead cows. I'll figure it out tomorrow." He poured himself another shot of bootleg whiskey and stared at his glass. After a long silence, he slurred, "I like the idea of blowing up the aqueduct. If a person had dynamite and kept quiet about it, it should be pretty easy."

CHAPTER 8   BONFIRE

The next morning, Fred knew if he opened his eyes, the room would spin, and he would gag from his dry tongue that felt three times too big for his mouth. But if he didn't get up, he might pee the bed. He opened his eyes, and just as he expected, the room spun, and his stomach lurched. He forced himself to sit up and, with effort, resisted his stomach's attempt to rebel.

The room wobbled, tilted, and spun faster when he stood. With one hand on the wall, he negotiated a trip to the bathroom. After staggering back to bed, he stared at the ceiling and thought about his dead cattle. Almost half of his herd. Damned the Department of Water and Power. They want everything. If you don't give it to them, they'll destroy you. Maybe he should give in and sell. Others had sold and done very well. But this ranch was his life. He didn't want to live anywhere else. But damn, he burned to get back at Magon and the DWP. Especially Magon. He's the one who said bad things happened if you refused to work with him. Hell would have to freeze over before Fred worked with that bastard.

Alice's voice at the door snapped his train of thought. "Breakfast is ready if you're able to eat, which, from the look of you, I doubt."

He forced himself to get up again, struggled to the bathroom, and splashed water on his face. He retched at the feel of the toothbrush in his mouth and struggled not to puke. Straining to stay upright, he walked slowly to the kitchen, where he slumped into his chair.

One look at the scrambled eggs and he rushed for the bathroom. When he got back to the kitchen, Alice had replaced the eggs with some toast and coffee. *Bless her heart.*

Alice sat down across the table and watched him struggle to choke down the toast. "What now—aside from not drinking that much?"

He stared at his plate. "Definitely not drink that much."

"I know you planned on selling the yearlings this fall," she said. "Will we have any left to sell?"

"Not many. Most of those in the lower field were the ones I planned to market. That would've helped to see us through the winter. We may have to dip into our savings at the bank."

Alice got up and lightly kissed the small bald spot on top of his head. "We'll make it one way or another."

Fred forced down the last of his breakfast and walked outside. The day matched his mood—overcast and depressing. He hoped the cool early morning air might help clear his head. He watched

Tinker cavort back and forth, always happy. Dogs seemed never to worry. It would be great to feel like that all the time. But then, they didn't drink bootleg booze.

He thought about the dead cattle. Through the fog in his mind, he recalled last night talking about what to do with them. He sure couldn't leave them in the field to rot, and there were too many to bury. Burning them seemed like the only solution. That would be hard. They were mostly water. But they also had lots of fat. If the fat caught fire it should work. There was some gasoline in the barn. Use that to get them started.

He trudged to the barn. A few minutes later, he walked out of the barn holding a three-gallon gas can in each hand and was surprised when a short caravan of a truck and two cars pulled into the farmyard.

Slim stepped out of his beat-up pickup. "A good morning to you, neighbor."

"Not much good about it," Fred groused. "What makes you so damned chipper after a miserable night shooting cows and drinkin' your awful booze?"

"He's immune to his homemade firewater," Murphy said as he got out of his car. "We figured you'd need some help with that mess in your field. Even brought some gas."

Fred gazed at the men, Murphy, Slim, and Henry. Three neighbors to help with a sickening task. Friends like them were one reason he loved living here. "Thanks. Help's welcome. I figured I'd drag the carcasses together, pour gas on, and light 'em up."

"Like I said last night, we should burn them on the steps of the DWP office," Henry said.

Fred shook his head. "A tempting idea, but hard to get 'em over there. Plus, Charlie'd probably arrest us on some trumped-up charge."

"Nah, he'd light the first match," Henry said.

Murphy laughed. "Yeah, then he'd arrest us."

Fred motioned toward the barn. "There's some ropes hangin' by the saddles. Grab those to drag the cows behind the cars into a pile."

Driving his old, war surplus pickup, Fred led the procession to the south pasture. As soon as they drove through the gate, Tinker jumped from the truck bed. Barking excitedly, the dog raced toward the dark humps scattered across the field. Crows and vultures flapped into the sky to escape the rude disturbance, and two coyotes trotted away.

Fred parked next to a cluster of carcasses. The smell of death and beginning rot reminded his stomach of its uneasy condition. As he got out of the truck, he gagged and struggled to keep his breakfast down.

"Whoo," Slim groaned as he waved his hand in front of his face. "Didn't think they would go bad this fast."

"It was hot last night. Can't last long in the heat," Murphy remarked.

"Let's get started," Fred said. "Lash a cow to each car and drag them to the middle of the field. Pile them up if we can, maybe in four or five stacks. Then see if we can light them up."

The impromptu crew dragged the cadavers together and pulled and pushed the smaller ones to the top. By mid-morning, the dead cattle were stacked into five large pyres, ready for the torch.

Fred poured gasoline over the first pile. "Stand back," he yelled and threw a match. The gas caught with a whoosh, and the air filled with the smells of burning hair and gasoline. Then the hides began burning, followed by layers of fat. Flames rose into the morning sky, and a weak breeze took the smoke south and west toward town. As soon as the first mound was fully flaming, Fred threw matches on the other gas-soaked piles of carcasses. In moments, the heaps were ablaze with a heat that could melt metal.

The men stood silently, staring into the bonfire, each knowing that part of Fred's livelihood was going up in smoke.

Slim broke the silence. "The DWP should pay for this."

"Yeah, but it will never happen," Fred said. "I can't never prove it was them."

"I don't mean that kind of pay. I mean like we was talking last night—revenge pay," Slim replied.

"You had the right idea," Murphy said. "Hit 'em where it hurts. Blow up the aqueduct."

Fred stepped farther back from the scorching fire and the others followed suit. "Have to admit, it would feel good to see them suffer. Specially Magon, but Charlie's right, we gotta follow the law. Can't act like a bunch of anarchists blowin' things up."

"Baloney!" Slim thundered. "They don't care about the law. They abide by the law only when it suits them."

"They piss all over us and get away with it," Henry added.

Fred stared into the bonfire of cows. "Have to admit, I'd like to throw Magon on there."

The beep of a horn from the direction of the barn interrupted their chatter.

"Looks like your brother-in-law couldn't stay away," Henry observed.

Jake parked his black Durant sedan beside the pasture fence and climbed between the barbed wire strands. "I came to see what was going on. That stench will drive everybody out of the county. It's worse in town than here."

"Good. I hope Magon chokes on it," Fred grumbled.

"He won't choke," Jake replied, "but it will suffocate the rest of us for sure."

"Henry's right," Murphy declared, "we're just lettin' the City piss all over us. We gotta show them we won't stand for it."

"I'd like to get back at them, but there's too much at stake," Fred said. "Get caught doing something stupid and I'd end up losing the ranch or going to jail. Charlie's right. Let the law take care of it."

"For Christ's sake, Fred," Murphy roared. "You were all for it last night. This was done to you, and now you go all soft."

"Yeah, well, I had too much to drink last night. I've lost enough already. With fewer steers to sell this season, we'll barely be able to pay our bank loans. We watched Paul Schaffer leave. I don't want to follow him."

CHAPTER 9   MAGON'S VISIT

Mid-morning the day after burning his dead cattle, Fred stood in his south pasture poking his shovel at the still smoldering pile of partially burned carcasses. This was a big part of his income for the season – going up in foul-smelling smoke. He raised the shovel above his head and swung down on the disgusting pile. "Damn. Damn. Damn them," he hollered.

Magon did this. Poisoning cattle—the coward's way. God, he wanted some payback. Murph and Slim had both said he should retaliate. They'd think he was soft if he didn't. No, he wasn't soft, just sensible. His first duty was to protect his family – think about Alice and Carl. But, oh God, he needed to strike something and swung the shovel again at the smoking pile. 'Whack!' It hit a solid, unburned pelvis, and the shock reverberated painfully up his arm. Somehow, the physical pain was a relief, mirroring the pain he felt inside. He leaned against the shovel handle and contemplated the smelly heap. What didn't burn, he would have to bury. Better get some more gasoline.

As he turned toward the barn, he saw a car bumping along the rutted track along the fence. It looked like the new model Chevrolet Magon drove. Why would that bastard come out here after what he did?

The car stopped and sure enough, it was the DWP acquisitions manager. Dressed in blue jeans, a red plaid shirt under a loose, unbuttoned sack coat, and a new western-style cowboy hat. Fred figured he must be trying to convince the locals that he was one of them, but he looked even more out of place than when Fred first saw him.

"Ah, I found you. Good morning, Mr. Lukin," Magon said cheerfully. As he squeezed between the strands of barbed wire, his coat gapped open to reveal a gun in a shoulder holster under his coat. "I heard about your cattle. I am sorry for such a tragedy," the DWP agent said unctuously. He pointed at the smoldering mound. "That them?"

Fred glared at the intruder, seething in anger. He wanted to strike in the worst way but reminded himself of what he told his friends: there was too much at stake—his family, his ranch — and he should let the law take care of it.

Magon continued. "I'll come right to the point. I know how important it is to sell some of your stock each season." He nodded toward the field. "Clearly, you can't take those poor beasts to market, and your finances must be stretched to the limit. I thought, perhaps…with this unfortunate turn of events…that you might reconsider selling your ranch and its water rights. When we spoke earlier, I said we could offer you a more than generous price. You would be well fixed for years to come."

Forgetting any thought of letting the law take care of it, the rancher's face hardened with rage. "You son-of-a-bitch. You think you can kill my cattle and force me out? Here's my answer." He stepped forward and put all his weight into a straight jab at Magon's jaw.

Magon stepped lightly aside and Fred's fist caught only air. Magon danced forward like a trained boxer and smashed his fist into Fred's face, knocking him flat on his back. Fred's world spun, and he saw two fuzzy Magon images standing over him. "Not many men walk away after trying that. I won't kill you… this time… but you will pay," said a low, gruff voice, sounding as though it was echoing through a long tunnel.

The spinning slowed as Fred watched his assailant walk back toward his car.

At the fence, Magon pushed a strand of barbed wire down with his boot, lifted another strand, and squeezed through. At his car, with one foot on the running board, he turned back. "Mr. Lukin, you don't understand your situation. You are outmatched. A basic rule of war is to know your opponent." He paused and smiled malevolently. "Before refusing to consider an offer, think very carefully about your family. I am sure you want nothing to happen to them." He slid behind the wheel, backed around, and slowly drove down the track the way he had come.

CHAPTER 10   HARD DRIVIN'

Alice checked her wallet to make sure she had enough cash for everything on her shopping list. She stuck her head out the front door and called to her husband, working in the barn. "Fred, Fred, today is Saturday. Remember, you said you'd drive me to town. Can we go now?"

He pulled his pocket watch out and glanced at it. "I'm busy."

Alice was silent for a moment. He'd been awfully touchy lately. He hardly talked to anybody and it seemed like he was mad at something all the time. She didn't want to stir up his anger but hoped to draw him out of his shell. "It's been over a month since the cattle were poisoned. It's time you let it go. Come to town with me."

"I've got work to do. You can drive the Ford."

She shook her head in frustration and walked to the car. She didn't like to drive. It scared her, but she could do it when push came to shove. Luck was with her, and she got it started on the first try and had no problems handling the Ford as it bounced and shook down the washboard dirt road toward town.

She parked in front of Shapiro's General Store, adjusted her hat and entered the store. At the counter, Betty Shapiro was carefully counting change to a thickly built man in a dark coat, standing by the cash register with his back to Alice.

Betty looked up. "Where's Fred?"

The customer turned slowly. Alice did a double-take. It was Magon. His eyes narrowed as though he were a wolf assessing his prey. He picked up his grocery bag and, without a word, walked out the door, with his eyes boring into Alice as he passed.

A cold shiver went down Alice's back. She felt weak and a little shaky with a dread that she had seldom experienced.

"What's wrong?" Betty asked.

"That Magon. He's so scary."

"He sure stared at you when I asked about Fred. So, where is he?"

"Home. Still dejected about losing those cattle. Fred says he's too busy to come to town, but I think he just doesn't want to see or talk to anybody. He's positive that it was Magon who poisoned them and talks about nothing but getting back at him."

Betty nodded. "Everybody in town thinks so, too."

"I keep telling Fred to put it behind him, but I have to admit, it would be good to get a little payback."

"I can think of a lot of ways to do it." Betty paused and laughed. "…but they're all illegal."

"Well, he broke the law when he poisoned our cattle. Seems only fair to get even."

"Maybe another day. But you didn't come to town to talk about Magon."

"You're right." Alice laughed. "Housewives are only allowed to talk about children, cooking, and shopping." She handed a paper to her sister. "Here's my grocery list."

The two women traded news and gossip as Betty picked items from the shelves lining the wall behind the counter and placed them in Alice's shopping basket.

With her shopping complete and no other customers in the store, the sisters sat on the bent-wood chairs by the window and continued their conversation. When another customer arrived, Alice said goodbye, loaded the groceries in the car, and headed for home.

As the car bounced over the ruts and bumps in the dirt road, Alice looked worriedly at the deep gully on the right, then glanced in the rear-view mirror. A pickup truck was coming fast from behind. The truck swerved around her as though to pass. She slowed down and moved a bit to the right to let the truck get by on the one-lane road. When the truck was almost past, it swerved sharply toward her. She jerked the wheel hard to avoid hitting him and her car sailed into the air. She screamed. When the car hit the sandy bottom of the gully, her head whacked the steering wheel, the door sprang open, and she was thrown out.

After an unmeasured period of time, the petite lady wondered why she was lying prone with two bright, fuzzy suns spinning in the sky. She reached out with her right hand and felt the ground. Coarse sand. She tried to reach with her other hand and screamed in pain. She couldn't move her arm, but the pain brought her to her senses. She recalled crashing the car. She glanced to her side. The car was about ten feet away with its front bumper buried in the sand and the driver's door open. She tried again to flex her left arm. A few inches off the ground was all she managed before the pain became too much. She feared her arm might be broken.

It was too hot to stay long in the bright sun surrounded by sagebrush, rabbit brush, and cactus. She tried to stand but was too weak and shaky to get up. Maybe she could crawl over to the car to get some shade. When she tried to crawl on all fours, she screamed in pain when she put any weight on her left arm. It was awkward with just one arm, but she was able to crawl slowly to the car and pull herself into the driver's seat. Still hot, but not as bad as lying in the sand with the sun beating down. A few minutes' rest, and she didn't feel so weak. Time to get some help.

She rummaged around the car and found an old towel. That would do for a sling for her injured arm. With her arm tied up, she struggled up the embankment to the road. She looked toward home and then back to town. It was maybe just a bit under two miles to the ranch and more than that to town. She began walking home. She hadn't gone far when she saw a cloud of dust being kicked up by a car coming toward her. That might be the guy who ran her off the road. She stepped off the road, hid behind a large sagebrush, and watched. When it came into view, she recognized Slim Berks' car, and she waited on the side of the road.

Slim pulled up beside her. "Alice! What are you doing out here?

With her good arm, she pointed to her car down in the gully. "I was run off the road." Then she gestured at the arm in a sling. "Can you take me to see Doc Woodin?"

"Sure. Get in. You want to get Fred to go with you?"

"Yes, please. I guess I can wait a little longer for the doctor."

Slim turned the car around and headed for the Lukin ranch.

Fred was in the barn stacking hay bales when he heard a car drive into the farmyard. He looked out the door to see Slim with Alice in the car.

"Look what I found on the road," Slim said.

"Where's your car? Are you okay?" he asked Alice.

Alice pointed to her arm in her improvised sling and briefly told what had happened.

Fred swore as he listened to her account. When she finished, he got her seated in his pickup, thanked Slim for the help, and drove for the doctor's office.

On the way to town, he asked, "Did you see the other car?"

"Just a glimpse. It all happened so fast."

"Familiar? Seen it before?"

"Not sure, but it looked like the kind of pickup you see around DWP construction."

"Recognize the driver?"

"I didn't get a look at him."

"Did it seem intentional?"

"Sure seemed like it. He was going pretty fast and swerved into me. Even if it wasn't intentional, he had to know he forced me into the gully, and he kept going!"

"Damned! That son-of-a-bitch did it."

"Who?"

He was silent with his jaw clenched.

She stared at him. "Fred, who is a son-of-a-bitch?"

"Magon. Magon! I didn't want to worry you, but when we got in that fight, he said my whole family was at risk."

"Fred Lukin!" she snapped. "You didn't want to worry me and didn't warn me?" Grimacing, she held up her injured arm. "Now look what happened. I think I will never forgive you."

After a long silence, Alice reached with her good arm and patted her husband's hand. He lifted her hand and kissed it.

Fred fidgeted while he sat beside Alice in Dr. Woodin's surgery, a clean, white room next to the kitchen at the back of the doctor's house. The room closed in on him as images of the combat hospital in France flooded his mind—men screaming as they were brought on stretchers from the trenches with limbs blown off—him biting his lip till it bled to keep himself from screaming while the doctors complained of the morphine shortage as they operated on his leg torn up by German bullets—and watching men die in the beds all around him while his wounds healed. But this was worse. Alice was injured. He would willingly relive all that if he could abolish her pain.

The doctor held her wrist in both hands. "Now, this might hurt a bit." He gave her arm a quick jerk.

Alice screamed, and the room spun drunkenly around Fred. He feared he would pass out and bent his head between his knees like they had taught him in the army. The doctor's wife stuck an ammonia ampoule under his nose to keep him conscious.

When the doctor finished applying plaster over the bandage on her lower arm, Alice took Fred's hand. "Time to go home, dear."

Alice was wound up and talked nervously at a mile a minute on the drive to the ranch. "Goshen and glory, that truck was awful careless. Do you really think it was Mr. Magon? Maybe he didn't intend to hit me? No one would do a thing like that. Not even that man." She held up her injured arm. "I won't be able to do a thing wearing this cast. Doctor Woodin said I'll have to wear it for six weeks. Do you think we could afford to hire Maggie from the reservation to help around the house? How will we be able to pay the doctor bill? Maggie was really good that other time we used her. She works a couple of days a week for Edna King and Edna swears by her...." And she continued without rest.

Fred glanced sideways at his wife and smiled, thankful that she would be okay. She was wound up and needed time to calm down. Best let her chatter. After all, she didn't pause long enough for him to answer. In any case, he wasn't listening. His mind was too busy thinking about revenge. Magon poisoned the cattle and attacked his wife. What a coward—kill helpless beasts and strike at a man's family. One way or another, that cockroach would pay.

CHAPTER 11   BOXING DAY

"Thanks, Woody," Fred said to the auto repairman the morning after Alice's car wreck. "It'll be hell to get the car out of that gully. I looked it over on my way in, but couldn't tell how bad it might be. I'll see you later. I got something I gotta do here in town."

Fred drove his pickup two blocks to the DWP office on the southwest edge of town. The office wasn't open yet. He parked across the street and watched employees streaming into the building for the start of their day pushing paper. Poor bastards. Farmers, ranchers, and others driven from their land or businesses by the DWP and now working for it. How could they do it? He hadn't seen Magon enter, but Fred figured he must be in there by now. The rancher got out of his truck and walked across the street to the entrance.

"Good morning, Fred," the receptionist said cheerily as he came through the door. "I heard about Alice. How's she doing?"

"Morning, Hazel. She's doing okay, but with only one good arm, she'll need some help for a while. Where's Magon?"

"Back in his office," the receptionist said. "Is he expecting you?"

"No, just point the way."

She pointed. "Straight down that corridor, but I better take you."

"No, stay here," he said and marched down the hall.

"Fred, Fred," she called after him. "You can't just barge in."

"Stay there, Hazel!" he ordered.

The door with 'District Manager of Property Acquisitions' stenciled in gold lettering on the glass was slightly ajar. Fred shoved the door. It smashed against the wall with a bang. Magon looked up from his desk with his mouth open and eyes wide. With a smooth, practiced motion, he drew a revolver from a desk drawer and pointed it at the invader. "Hey, Clyde, get in here. We got a guest."

A stout man built like a gorilla stepped into Magon's office from an adjacent room and closed the door.

"Hold him," Magon ordered.

Like lightning, the gorilla grabbed Fred and yanked his arms into a double hammerlock that felt like his shoulders were being pulled from their sockets.

"Let go! Let me go, dammit!" Fred yelled as he struggled in vain to escape the gorilla's grasp.

"Shut up," the gorilla growled and tightened his grip.

Before he could shout again, Magon punched him hard in his solar plexus, knocking his wind out. Before Fred could catch his breath, Magon slapped him hard across the face with his open hand, then pulled a handkerchief from a pocket and crammed it into Fred's mouth. Without taking his eyes off his muffled victim, Magon removed his coat and set it carefully on his chair. He rolled both shoulders and rotated his neck like a boxer loosening up for a fight. He danced around, jabbing the air with his fists. "I haven't done this since I left L.A." He smiled cruelly. "It'll give me a chance to practice my moves."

Fred's foot lashed out and caught Magon's knee.

The acquisitions boss yowled and glared as he stepped into his punch and buried his fist in Fred's solar plexus again.

Someone pounded on the door. "Mr. Magon, Mr. Magon, is everything all right?"

Magon opened the door just a crack. "Everything's fine. Go back to work." He shut and locked the door and took a few more jabs at the air. "Okay, Clyde, hold tight." He danced back and forth and began pummeling Fred's midsection without mercy. Barely conscious through a fog of pain, Fred's last memory was a fuzzy image of the stocky acquisitions manager drawing his right arm back and his fist flying in slow motion at Fred's face.

Pain dominated Fred's being, and he strained to open his eyes. He was outdoors, lying on the sandy ground, looking straight up at the sky. A crowd of people stared down at him. Sheriff Cole stood in the middle with a disgusted expression, shaking his head.

"Okay, Daggett, help me get him up," the sheriff said. The two men grabbed Fred's arms and stood him up. Deputy Daggett pulled his arms behind his back and snapped handcuffs on his wrists. "Let's get him down to the office and book him," Cole said. They dragged their limp prisoner to the car and shoved him into the back seat. A man poked his head in the open window and patted his shoulder. "We're behind you, Fred."

"Don't encourage him. He's in enough trouble as it is," came the sheriff's exasperated voice.

Three blocks to the courthouse seemed like a lifetime, with the sheriff ranting at him all the way. Cole leaned over the front passenger seat and thundered. "You stupid dolt! I warned you, but you wouldn't listen. Now look at you, beaten up with blood all over and under arrest. Magon wants you charged for trespassing on City property and attacking a public servant. From the looks of you, he must have put up a whale of a defense. You know he won't let this drop, and it will probably have to go to trial. How dumb can you get? It was stupid! What'll happen to Alice if you go to jail?"

When they got to the sheriff's office, it was a relief to stumble out of the car and not have to listen to Cole.

"Get him washed up, then book him," Cole told Daggett.

In the restroom, Fred stared at the face in the mirror. It looked worse than something out of Jake Shapiro's butcher case. The splash of cold water on his face simultaneously stung and soothed as it dripped crimson into the washbowl. He winced as he unbuttoned his shirt and inspected his belly. It was already black and blue—one massive bruise that screamed in pain when touched. The pain turned to frustration and rage when he thought about Alice injured, his cattle poisoned, himself beaten half to death, and he was the one going to jail. The man had said, "Money talks, and money wins." He wouldn't swallow that without a fight.

CHAPTER 12   COURT

After an excruciating night on the hard jail cot, Fred woke to the sound of the cell door being unlocked.

"The Sheriff says to take you upstairs," Deputy Daggett said as he opened the cell door.

Fred sat up and groaned. The movement hurt more today than it did the day before. "I gotta pee first," he mumbled through swollen lips.

"You can stop on the way." Daggett held up a pair of handcuffs. "Sorry, I have to do this. We cuff all prisoners when we take them to court."

Every part of his body screamed with pain. This seemed worse than his wounds in France. He stooped in agony as he followed Daggett to the courtroom. When he stepped through the door, the capacity crowd erupted with cheers and applause.

Judge Daley pounded his gavel and called for order. The crowd quieted. Fred spotted Alice in the front row of the gallery, surrounded by friends. Alice managed a desolate smile as Daggett led Fred before the judge.

Judge Daley's mouth dropped as he scanned the prisoner. "The purpose of this hearing is to hear the charges against this prisoner and to set bail. Sheriff Cole, I want to hear what happened to this man. In my many years on this bench, I have seen very few prisoners who looked as badly beaten as Mr. Lukin."

Cole stepped before the judge. "Your honor, yesterday morning, I was called about a disturbance at the local office of the Los Angeles Department of Water and Power. When Deputy Daggett and I arrived at the scene, we found Mr. Lukin lying unconscious in the street in front of the DWP office building." He turned and pointed at Magon, who sat in the front row of the gallery on the opposite side of the room from Fred's partisans. "Mr. Magon, the DWP's District Acquisitions Manager, said Mr. Lukin trespassed and attacked him without cause, and he wanted the man arrested. I arrested the accused and jailed him."

"Was he in this condition when you arrested him?" the judge asked.

"Yes, your honor, except he's had the opportunity to wash up."

The room erupted with shouts against Magon. "Order, order," the judge commanded, and the room quieted. "Mr. Magon, please tell the court what happened."

Magon stood. "Thank you, your honor. This man trespassed in the Department of Water and Power building and invaded my office. He was like a wild man and attacked me. To protect myself, I hit him. Then I asked my assistant to take him outside. Someone in the office called the sheriff when the disturbance began. My assistant had just taken the man out the door when the sheriff arrived. I want to commend the sheriff for his prompt action."

The room filled with more angry shouts, and the judge called for order. "Mr. Magon. You say you hit him. How many times did you hit him?"

"Once… that I recall."

"Did anyone else hit him?"

"No, your honor. Not that I remember."

Judge Daley's eyebrows rose. "Once that you recall? Not that you remember? Surely, if you were there, you would remember you or someone else hitting him!" The judge turned to Fred, who had remained standing. "Mr. Lukin, what is your memory of your… your… ah… exchange with Mr. Magon?"

Fred strained to stand straight and mumbled through his swollen lips. "Sir, I mean Your Honor, I entered Magon's office as he said, but I did not act like a wild man. As soon as I went through the door…" Fred paused and coughed. Blood-red spit splashed on the floor.

"Sheriff," the judge said, "please bring the prisoner a chair."

"Your Honor, it is easier to stand than to sit," Fred said.

"Very well. Continue."

Fred struggled to speak without coughing. "When I entered Magon's office, he pulled a gun from his desk and called his bodyguard. I never had a chance to say anything."

"Gun? Bodyguard?" the judge said as he looked accusingly at Magon. "Why didn't you say anything?"

"The guard grabbed me, and Magon stuffed a cloth in my mouth. The guard held me and Magon started hitting me."

"Started hitting you?" the judge asked. "But he said he hit you once… that he recalls. How many times did he hit you?"

"I don't know. I didn't count. He pounded my stomach. The last I remember was when he hit my face."

Angry shouts filled the courtroom.

"Order! Order!" the judge commanded as he pounded his gavel. "The way your face looks, it must have been quite a blow. What about your stomach? Does that look like your face?"

"It doesn't look as bad as it feels."

"Perhaps you could show me."

With his wrists still in handcuffs, Fred clumsily lifted his shirt to reveal his belly covered with black, blue, and red bruises.

The judge's eyes widened and his jaw dropped. He glared at Magon, and shouts engulfed the room. The judge pounded his gavel. "Order. Quiet. Be quiet, or you will be removed from the courtroom." When the shouting stopped, the judge said, "Mr. Hess, please approach the bench."

District Attorney Hess walked to the judge's bench. "Yes, Your Honor?"

Judge Daley leaned over and spoke quietly. "By his own admission, Mr. Lukin invaded Mr. Magon's office. However, his trespass in a municipally owned office did not warrant the extreme physical punishment that he received. The beating he took far outweighs his transgression. I think it would be fitting to drop the charges."

"That's okay by me, but this DWP guy may raise a stink."

"Let him. But he needs to be reminded that, given the condition of Mr. Lukin, it would be appropriate for him to be charged with assault and battery."

The D.A. resumed his place at the prosecution table and faced the judge. "Your Honor, the County would like to drop the trespassing charges against Mr. Lukin."

The courtroom exploded in cheers, and the judge banged his gavel. "Order. Order." The room quieted. "Very well. Sheriff Cole, please remove the prisoner's handcuffs and release him. I recommend he see a doctor immediately." He raised his gavel to end the proceedings, but before the gavel banged down, Magon shot up from his seat, waving his hands.

"Your Honor. Your Honor," he called, but the spectators' cheers drowned his voice.

Fred limped to Alice, who, in tears, tried to embrace him with her good arm. He recoiled in pain when she touched him. People crowded around, congratulating him and wishing him a quick recovery. He glanced toward the back of the room and saw Magon gesture with one hand slicing across his throat as he stepped through the doorway.

CHAPTER 13   BANKER WATSON

In his office, Doctor Woodin told Fred he had cracked ribs and wrapped his chest. That brought some relief, but it still hurt like heck to breathe or move.

He leaned on Alice as he shuffled out of the doctor's office to where Jake Shapiro waited by his car to drive them home. Fred's pickup was still parked in front of the DWP, and Murphy agreed to drive it back to the ranch.

Pain stabbed like a knife in his ribs every time the car hit a bump. At home, every part hurt as he got out of the car. Alice steadied one shoulder, and Jake held the other as they guided him into the house.

"Take him into the bedroom," Alice directed.

"No, just let me sit down here in the kitchen for a while. I could use a glass of water. No, better yet, some of Slim's homemade stuff."

Alice gave him her patented look of disapproval. "Not when you're sick."

"I'm hurt, not sick. The hooch might help."

"If you're not sick now, you will be when you drink Slim's poison." In spite of her objections, she got a jar of the booze, poured some into a glass, and handed it to him.

He took a couple of swallows. He closed his eyes and leaned back with his long legs stretched out under the table. His mind drifted and filled with nightmare images of dead cattle, Magon dancing like a prizefighter with his fists flashing, Alice at the bottom of the gully screaming for help while Magon stomped on her arm, and then he was throwing Magon's limp body on the blazing pyre of burning cows.

Alice's dreamt screams turned into her gentle voice. "Fred, Fred, wake up. You fell asleep right here at the table. I fixed some soup. You think you'll be able to eat?"

He looked around. It took a moment to realize he was home, sitting at the kitchen table. He gently felt his lips and jaw. It would be hard to open his mouth wide enough to eat. "No. Maybe later," he mumbled.

"I'll help you get to bed," Alice said.

Getting undressed and into bed was agony. He quickly succumbed to sleep that was haunted, once again, by images of burning cattle and Alice screaming in pain while Magon danced around with a crew of evil thugs from the big city.

When he got up the next morning, his head pounded, his bruised belly screamed, and his ribs raged with pain when he moved. Alice set a bowl of hot Wheatena cereal at his place as he sat down. After a few spoonfuls of the warm cereal, opening his mouth got easier. What a pleasure something as simple as a plain breakfast could be.

After eating, he went outside and hobbled around the farmyard, inspecting and running his hand over the ranch equipment. He wondered about the car. Woody said he would tow it out of the gully. It must be in pretty bad shape. He hoped insurance would cover some of it. He had made such a mess of things. Maybe he should sell to the DWP. Sell out? No! Not a chance. After the cattle were killed, he thought about it and rejected the idea. Now, he was even more determined and would rather die than deal with the DWP and its hired thug, Magon.

All morning, Fred puttered around the barn until Alice called him in for lunch.

"This is the soup I made yesterday," Alice said as she spooned it into a bowl. "It should be easy enough to eat."

"You said you were going to get Maggie Begay to help around the house while your arm mended," Fred said as he crumbled some crackers into his soup. "Have you been able to do anything about that?"

She looked at him like he was out of his mind, and her voice rose to an exasperated pitch. "And when would I have time to do that?" She raised her arm in a sling. "I not only have a broken arm, but I had to go to court to see if my husband was going to jail."

He stared at his soup. Anything he said would bury him deeper.

"Will we have enough to pay for some help?" she asked in a softer tone.

"Yeah, but it'll be a tight fall and winter," he replied. "The fall cattle sales are coming up soon, and we only have twenty-eight yearlings left to sell. Losing the others really put us in a pinch, and prices have been going down lately. Maybe they'll bounce back, but I doubt it." He slapped the table. "Thirty-one dead. That's how many bullets I want to put in Magon."

"Fred Lukin!" she snapped. "You stop talking like that. Your place is here, not jail."

She was right. He had to put it behind him and play the hand he had been dealt. Get back to business: sell the yearlings, scrape through the winter, and work at rebuilding his herd. He rose from his chair and folded his arms around his wife. "I'm lucky to have you."

She laughed. "Yes, you are." returning his hug with her one good arm.

"Ow! That hurts."

"Sorry. I forgot. But don't you forget that you're lucky to have me. Now eat your soup."

He laughed lightly. "What a pair. You with a broken arm and me with broken ribs."

He sat down and had taken a few spoons of soup when there was a sharp rap on the door.

"I'll get it," Alice said.

When she opened the door, Fred recognized their guest – Mark Watson, the tall, handsome owner of the Inyo Bank. As usual, the man's distinguished mustache was perfectly manicured, and he wore an impeccably tailored navy-blue suit. Fred had dealt a bit with the man while negotiating loans but didn't know much else about him except that he led the opposition to the DWP in the Bishop area. The word was he was a leader in the Bishop Ku Klux Klan and also was widely known for his philandering.

The banker's eyes pored over Alice, and Fred got a fleeting image of a wolf eyeing its prey.

"You must be Mrs. Lukin. I'm sorry I haven't met you before. I am Mark Watson of the Inyo Bank." He smiled and took her hand in both of his while his gaze lingered. He held her hand for what Fred thought was too long. Alice frowned and jerked her hand back.

With the way Watson looked at Alice, Fred struggled to suppress his impulse to slug him. Instead, he stood and tried to hide his pain as he limped to the door and extended his hand.

The banker gaped at Fred's bruised face, paused, and offered his hand. "Hello, Fred. I haven't seen you for a spell. I heard about your run-in with the DWP. I had to come down here to check up on our Independence branch office, so I thought I'd stop by to see how you're doing and ask if there is anything I can do to help."

Fred hesitated. Help? Bankers didn't come calling except to foreclose, and so far, they were still up to date on their loan payments. They might have some difficulty later this winter, but it was too early for the banker to show up. "You heard about it up in Bishop already? That is fast. Come in." He gestured to a chair at the table. "Please have a seat. Can we offer you some coffee?"

Watson waved his hand as he sat down at the kitchen table. "Oh, no, no. I don't want to be any trouble for your beautiful wife. It looks like you were eating. Please go ahead."

Standing by the sink, nervously massaging a tea towel, Alice asked, "What did you hear about Fred up in Bishop?"

"The word traveling faster than the telegraph is that the DWP acquisitions agent down here beat you in his office while his goon held you. What happened?"

Fred grimaced and told his story through swollen lips.

As he listened, Watson absent-mindedly pulled at his mustache and silently stared at Fred's bruises. "This Magon sounds like a thug," the banker said when Fred finished retelling his ordeal. "They must have sent him up here to break a few heads. Until now, their only violence was when they recently dynamited a rancher's ditch north of Bishop. As far as I know, they haven't beaten anyone up before. This is a new stage of their water war against the valley."

Fred stood and arched his back. "I need to stretch. Hurts if I sit too long." He gently rubbed the small of his back and straightened up. "Mr. Watson, I am curious what prompted you to visit us. Is it our loan you are worried about?"

Watson waved his hand, indicating no concern. "No, no, not at all. But what happens to the people of the valley affects my bank. If the ranchers and merchants fail, ultimately, my bank fails. I am concerned about what the DWP is doing. The City of Los Angeles is pushing all of us over the same cliff. When the City began its water and land acquisitions twenty years ago, it focused on our north end of the valley around Bishop. Until recently, they hadn't pushed into this southern section. Now, with a couple of dry years, they are pressuring you and others down here. And, with this new guy, Magon, it appears they are turning to strong-arm tactics. They are expanding their war against the valley, and that has me worried."

Alice had made herself busy at the sink while the two men talked. She turned to face the banker. "Mr. Watson, perhaps I am speaking out of turn, but…"

"No, you are not speaking out of turn, Mrs. Lukin. Please… speak your mind."

Placing the dish towel on the counter, she stood with her arms folded. "Very well. I have heard that you lead the opposition to the DWP in Bishop and Big Pine. Now you show up here after Fred was beaten and arrested. We have enough trouble here without someone coming in to rile up folks and make more trouble. I don't need to have my husband in jail."

Fred glanced uneasily at the banker. "Alice, I don't think he is trying to rile up folks, are you, Mr. Watson?"

The banker nervously chuckled. "I wouldn't say rile up, but I would like to get people organized. Look what happens if they aren't organized—divide and conquer. The DWP picks them off one at a time. That's what happened here. They go after you, just one person, and when you defend yourself, you get beaten up and jailed. None of this would have occurred if twenty ranchers had shown up in Magon's office. If people act together, we can mount a defense. They can't put us all in jail."

"Well, they held my husband and beat him. He is injured. I don't want him involved," Alice said.

Fred squirmed with embarrassment. Alice seldom made a secret of her views, and her low opinion of Mark Watson was uncomfortably plain, at least to him. Hopefully, it wasn't quite that apparent to their guest. He struggled to fill the silence. "Alice, he's right. They will keep picking us off one by one if we don't fight back."

"Fight back?" she said, her voice rising in anger. "You fought back and can barely walk." She turned and stalked out, slamming the door as she headed for her garden.

The banker looked amused as he watched her exit. "Mrs. Lukin is very forthright. I should leave now. I need to visit the branch office in town." He stood and looked at Fred for a moment.

"Before I go, if you are okay to walk, perhaps you could show me around your ranch."

As the two men walked slowly into the farmyard, Watson commented, "Mrs. Lukin is very beautiful. You are a lucky man,"

Fred's eyes narrowed when he glanced at the banker. What did he mean by that? Men generally didn't make comments about another man's wife, and this guy had a reputation for chasing every skirt in the valley. But not wanting to seem rude, he replied, "Thank you. We've known each other since grade school." He was silent as they continued to the center of the farmyard, then stopped and explained the layout of the ranch. When he turned toward his south pasture, his voice caught and wavered as he pointed. "That's where my cattle were poisoned."

Watson nodded and then turned and pointed northeast. "Your cooperative ditch connects to the river up there?"

"Yeah. My land runs along the edge of the river, and the head-gate where we divert water is on my land. The ditch channel flows through my property before it reaches any of the other ranches in our co-op."

"Ahh, now I get it. That's why you're the DWP's current target. If they get your ranch, they get control of the head-gate. Who has the controlling share of the co-op ownership?"

"No one guy has control. I have the largest share because my acreage is the largest. I have two shares, and the other five guys each have one share."

"Who are the others?"

"Besides me, Murphy Hamhurst, Slim Berks, Henry Olivera, Russell Boyd, and Clay Stevens."

"Seven shares and it takes four to control? They get yours and only need two more to take over?"

"Yeah. They get control and close the ditch down. That kills six ranches in one blow and takes our water to L.A."

"That's what they've been doing up around Bishop and Big Pine—getting control of as many irrigation canals as they can. Each one they get pushes several ranches over the edge. They don't even have to buy all the ranch property. They take the water and the ranch returns to sagebrush. That's why I have been pushing to organize the Owens Valley Irrigation District. The irrigation district buys each individual's shares and merges them into one entity. We can deal with the DWP with one voice."

Fred lifted his hat and ran his hand through his hair. "The DWP's not going to get my ditch shares or this property. They'll have to kill me first."

"I wouldn't be surprised if they try that, too. To stop them, you guys down here need to organize an irrigation district of your own…or join ours."

"Sounds complicated."

"Not really," Watson answered. "Of course, you need an attorney to set it up, but it's not hard. The irrigation district borrows money by issuing bonds and then uses the money to buy the ranchers' shares in the ditch. That way, the ranchers get some immediate cash in the bank, and it keeps the DWP off their backs. The district earns the money to pay the bonds by selling the water back to the ranchers. Our members like the arrangement."

"I'd have to think about it and talk it over with the others. I wouldn't want to lose control of our water."

"None of us wants to lose control," Watson said. "These problems are not yours alone. You're just the latest target. If we want to survive, we need to fight with one voice. Your wife was right. I have been working to organize opposition to the DWP. I thought that because you have been mistreated, you might be interested in joining us."

Fred eyed Watson. He had an uncomfortable feeling about the man. He sure didn't like the way he had looked at Alice. But it didn't seem like there was much of a downside to joining the banker to fight the DWP. He sure wasn't winning by going it alone and if he didn't do something, they would eventually crush him. "What do you have in mind?"

"Organize! People from all the towns need to speak with one voice so the DWP can't continue using its 'divide-and-conquer' approach to beat us down, as it has for twenty years. I'd like you to be part of it, and it'd be help if you could recruit others from Independence. This Friday, a group of us will get together to discuss the next steps. We'll meet after dark at Keough Hot Springs south of Bishop. I hope two or three from Independence can make it. That will give us a few from each town. It's a start."

Fred stared at his south pasture and in his mind, saw ghost pyres of dead cattle. "I'll ask around and see if anyone's interested."

CHAPTER 14   WATSON'S MEETING

The next morning, Fred limped into the Inyo Cafe for coffee with the usual gang. It was heartening to hear them shout their greetings when he came through the door. Then, he saw Charlie Cole at the table and thought of turning around and going home. But no, he wasn't going to turn tail. *Let that bastard be the one to leave.* He grabbed a chair and joined his friends.

Henry Olivera lifted his coffee cup in a toast. "To one tough guy. You're looking good, Fred."

"Yeah, specially for a guy that just got beaten up," Murphy added. He gestured with his thumb at Charlie Cole, seated next to him. "And jailed by our righteous sheriff here."

Everybody around the table laughed, except Fred and Cole.

"Dammit, Murph," Cole growled, "you elected me to enforce the law. I got a call about a trespasser." He nodded at Fred. "I found this yahoo lying in the street with the DWP guy yelling that he had invaded the office and attacked him. I went by the book and arrested him."

A clamor erupted as the men denounced the arrest. The sheriff continued, "And Fred, I'm sorry about what happened, but that's what the situation called for, and I can't play favorites."

"No, Charlie," Jake said, "but you could get more of the story before you arrest a local who's passed out on the ground and can't defend himself against some thug from out of town, who nobody knows, making wild accusations."

Cole's face turned crimson. He smacked his coffee cup down and stood, sending his chair crashing to the floor. "God dammit! The law's the same for locals and outsiders." He slammed the door as he stormed out.

"Hey, Charlie, I told you not to slam my door," Doris yelled at the top of her voice from behind the counter. She stepped to the table and gently put her hand on Fred's shoulder. "Go easy on Charlie. He's eating himself up about your arrest. He talked most of last night about quitting and returning to San Francisco. He was a cop there before he moved here after the earthquake. Anyway, he hates the DWP as much as anybody here, but he's going crazy worrying how to keep the peace between the locals and the City."

"Easy on him?" Fred exclaimed. "He threw me in his cell with broken ribs. It's hard to forget that."

"Give it some time. I think he'd give his life for any of you guys." She looked around and waved the coffeepot in the air. "Anybody need more coffee?"

They all shook their heads.

Jake stood up. "I have to get back to the store."

"I'll go with you. Alice wants me to get some things," Fred said as he followed Jake out the door. Outside, he leaned against his pickup parked in front of the cafe. "I wanted to talk to you without Charlie or Doris listening. Mark Watson came out to my place yesterday and invited me to a meeting up at Keough's about organizing opposition to the City. He said to bring a couple of others who shared their dislike of the DWP. I thought of you and Murph."

"Yeah, I've heard he's been organizing up around Bishop," Jake said. "I'd like to see what's going on. But I'm not sure I should go. I was told he's mixed up with the Ku Klux Klan."

"I've heard he's one of their big shots," Fred said, "but I think they are probably harmless."

"For you, maybe, but not for me," Jake replied. "They hate Jews like me more than they hate Catholics."

"We'll leave fast if there's any sort of problem."

The following night, the air was crisp, and the Sierras to the west were a towering black silhouette against the inky blue sky when Fred and Murphy rode with Jake to attend Watson's meeting. Murphy pointed to the turnoff ahead. "Jake, that's the road to Keough's."

"I know the way," Jake said impatiently. "I bring my kids swimming up here all the time. They love the hot pool." He turned off the highway toward a stand of trees a little less than a mile to the west. The car bumped along the rutted dirt road and pulled in beside others parked in front of the weathered green building surrounding the hot springs swimming pool.

Fred got out of the car, rubbed his lower back, and stretched. Every muscle still ached from the beating. One way or another, he would get back at Magon. But for now, he'd find out what Watson had up his well-tailored sleeve. Fred scanned the gathering—maybe thirty or so men standing in small clusters, talking and gesturing in the dim light of kerosene lanterns hanging from the low branches of cottonwood trees. He recognized several of the ranchers from the north end of the valley and some of the merchants from Big Pine and Bishop.

Jake nodded toward a cluster of men dressed in white robes with tall, pointed hats gathered beneath a large locust tree. "Those are the crazies I was talking about the other day."

"I'll be damned. KKK!" Murphy said. "What in God's name are those guys doing here?"

Jake pulled his jacket tighter against the cool evening air. "They sure make me nervous, me being a Jew and all."

"Relax," Fred said. "It should be okay. I see Rob Lamm and John Morris in the crowd. They're Jews. Probably some others here, too."

Mark Watson and another man walked toward them. "Fred, Jake, Murphy, pleased you could make it." He gestured to the large, beefy man at his side. "This is Jeff Keough. Owns this place."

"We all know Jeff," Murphy remarked as they shook hands.

"You're the last ones," the banker said.

Watson climbed on a hay bale overlooking the waiting men. "Let's get started," he hollered. The buzz of conversation died and men gathered in front of the respected banker. Silently, he gazed at his audience. Then, in a full voice, he boomed, "Do you want to defeat the City of Los Angeles?"

The crowd erupted with shouts of "Yes!" "Yeah!" "Damn right" "For sure!"

"Okay!" Watson hollered. "That's why we're here. I called this meeting to organize opposition to the high-handed methods of the DWP. For too long, they have bullied us with divide-and-conquer tactics to get hold of our water and drive this valley to oblivion. They have pushed people down and driven them from the valley. Our valley! By now, you've probably all heard about the DWP crews blowing up a dam on the Round Valley ditch. That shows the lengths they will go to knock us down. But it gets worse. Down in Independence a few days ago, their new acquisitions agent, a guy named Magon, had his goon hold Fred Lukin while they beat him unmercifully and then pressed charges against him."

Angry shouts filled the air.

He pointed. "Fred is here with us tonight. He is still carrying the bruises and enduring the pain of broken ribs. This is a man who courageously faced the horrors of fighting in the trenches of the Great War and came home a hero. But here, in his homeland, a hoodlum from LA held him at gunpoint while another thug hit him. You can't fight back when you are alone like that."

Fred squirmed with discomfort. He turned to Jake and Murphy, standing at his side. "I didn't come for this. Let's get out of here." The three men squeezed through the crowd and walked toward Jake's car.

"Hey, Fred, where you going?" Watson yelled.

"I came here to oppose the DWP," he shouted back, "but I sure as hell didn't expect to be no freak-show exhibit."

"Come on back. I apologize. I didn't mean it like that. There's not a man here that doesn't respect you."

The air filled with voices. "Come on back. That could happen to any of us."

"Yeah, we can at least listen," Murphy said, and the three of them turned and stood at the back of the audience.

Watson continued in his booming voice. "Toughness and courage are not the issues. You all have that. But no one can fight them alone, no matter how tough or how much courage you have. They will destroy each of you one by one if you go that route. If we don't want to be beaten up at gunpoint, we have to organize and speak with one voice."

Shouts of agreement and outrage echoed off the buildings.

He continued. "I believe it is time to take action."

"What kind of action?" someone yelled.

"What do you do if someone takes what is yours?" he shouted back. "What do you do if someone punches you in the nose?"

"Punch back!" came a shout.

"Yes! You retaliate! You hit them where it hurts," he hollered. "Water is the only thing they understand. We stop the water and they will yell bloody murder. That's what we want—for them to howl to the whole state and nation. The louder they scream, the more people will know what is happening here—how they're trying to destroy us. When that happens, we can get some outside help, and they'll deal fairly with us."

"You think anything will come of this?" Jake asked from behind the wheel as he drove home from the meeting later that night.

Fred stared across the dark desert from the back seat of Jake's car. "A heck of a long meeting. It's past eleven, but it doesn't seem like much really happened—mostly just talk. Watson wound everybody up and said strong words about fighting the DWP but didn't have plans to actually do anything."

"It's got to start somewhere," Jake said. "They're just getting organized."

"Everything's about Bishop," Murphy complained. "They talked about irrigation ditches up there and even a little about Big Pine, but nothin' about Independence and Lone Pine. They hardly know we're alive down in our south end. Fred's right. We was only there for display—extras to give Watson something to talk about."

"I don't know what they're goin' to do," Fred said, "but Watson's right, the only thing the DWP understands is water. If you want to hit them, you have to go after the water. But something about Watson rubs me the wrong way. He seems too slick, and my gut says I shouldn't trust him. Alice doesn't like him, and she's a pretty good judge. Plus, I don't know what those KKK guys were doing there. They never said anything, but I don't want to get mixed up with that crowd. We should go our own way."

"I worry about them too," Jake said. "But the people around Bishop think Watson's great. Wait and see what happens."

Fred frowned and shook his head. "Wait? If we wait, nothing will ever happen."

"When your cows were killed, you were all for blowing up the aqueduct," Murphy said. "I say, let's do it."

"Murph, that was a bunch of drunks talking," Jake replied.

"Even drunks are right sometimes," Fred said.

CHAPTER 15   FIREWORKS

A few weeks later, Fred sat on a hay bale in his barn, absent-mindedly rubbing saddle soap on a bridle while he shot the bull with Slim and Murphy. "I heard that Frank Lopez, down by Manzanar, sold his spread to the DWP."

"I heard it too," Slim said. "The DWP took all the water from George's crick and is pumping the ground dry. He wasn't getting enough to keep a cactus alive."

"He was part of that group suing for an injunction to stop their pumping," Murphy added. "The City's payin' top price to buy those guys out so their suit never goes to trial."

Slim chuckled. "Maybe we should sue them and see what we can get."

Fred set the bridle down and looked disgusted. "That just plays into their hands and gives them what they want. They just keep stalling till the other side gives up."

"You think anything will come of Watson's plans?" Murphy asked. "At that meeting at Keough's, he talked big about organizing resistance, but as near as I can tell, he's not actually done much."

"And I don't think he ever will," Slim said. "He's just a lot of talk, and the City keeps buying more land and water and forcing people out of the valley."

"Like they say, if you want something done, you gotta do it yourself," Slim said.

"When I had our party and everybody drank too much, we talked about blastin' the aqueduct," Fred said. "I think we should do it. Plant dynamite, light it up and get the heck out."

"You know how to handle that stuff?" Murphy asked. "Mess around with it and you blow yourself up if you don't know what you're doin'."

"I learned a little in the war," Fred replied. "I know it takes more than putting dynamite alongside the ditch. You have to place it so it's contained, like inside the concrete, so the explosion breaks it. But I don't know enough to do it right."

"Must be somebody around who knows how to do it," Slim said.

Fred thought about it a moment. "There's Floyd Lee, lives out by Aberdeen. He was the explosives man in my company during the war. He would know about as much as anyone."

"But he works for the DWP, don't he?" Slim asked.

"He may work for the City, but that don't mean he likes it," Fred replied. "They drove his family off their land and he took a job with the DWP. I think he hates them as much as anyone."

"I heard he's a big drinker," Slim commented.

"I'm sure he'd stay sober for us," Fred replied.

"And where would we get enough dynamite for something like that?" Slim asked.

"My brother-in-law works at the vanadium mine west of Bishop," Murphy answered. "They use a lot of dynamite, and he says they're pretty careless about security. I think he could get us some. But where would we do it?"

"Not too close," Fred said. "Maybe between here and Lone Pine. North of Lone Pine, the aqueduct goes along the side of the Alabama Hills. If the downhill side—the east side—of the ditch was blown, the water would flood out into the valley. It would be hard to stop the flow and repair it."

Shortly after midnight, a few nights later, two vehicles turned off the highway onto a faint track leading west toward the aqueduct, skirting the edge of the rocky Alabama Hills. Fred stopped his pickup and waited for the second car, driven by Jake, to pull up beside him. He leaned out the window and spoke. "Okay, Jake, like we planned. Toss that barbed wire across the phone lines above you to short out the line."

With his headlights off, Fred scanned the landscape, lit up by the just-past-full moon. He hadn't thought about the moon. He chided himself for missing that detail. At the very least, he should have picked a moonless night. On the other hand, in the crisp spring air, the rocky desert was beautiful. With the bright moon washing out the colors, it was all sharp contrasts in black and white. The sage and rabbit brush were sparse here, fighting for space among the large boulders that dominated the Alabama Hills. Alice always said the boulders looked like giant potatoes standing on end. Up ahead, the rounded hills were black silhouettes against the background of the towering Sierra escarpment, silver in the bright moonlight.

When Jake finished placing the wire, they bumped and rattled in low gear through the sagebrush toward the aqueduct. "You sure this leads to the right spot?" he asked Murphy, riding with him in the cab.

"Positive. Scouted it out. There's some big rocks up ahead we can park behind so we're out of sight from the highway and close to the aqueduct."

The truck jerked. Whomp! "Damn! You said the track was clear," Fred complained.

"It is if you drive around the rocks, not over them," Murphy replied.

Fred stuck his head out the window to question his explosives man, who rode in the truck bed with the bags of dynamite. "Hey, Floyd, you sure these bumps won't set the dynamite off?"

"Nuttin' to worry about," the explosives man answered. "This shtuff won't blow just 'cause of a few bumps."

Fred shook his head, and hoped the damned sot was sober enough to do it. Fred stared across the sagebrush at the aqueduct ahead. This scheme was a stupid idea. Maybe they should call it off.

"What ya waitin' for?" Murphy asked.

Fred took a deep breath. They'd gone this far. Might as well get to it. He eased the truck behind a rock outcropping and hoped it couldn't be seen from the highway.

When the truck stopped, Floyd slid off the truck bed. He stood a moment, then staggered and fell to the ground.

"You're drunk!" Fred growled in exasperation.

"Only a little." He reached his hand up. "Here, help me up." When he stood, he pulled a silver flask from his coat and held it out. "Anybody want some?"

"Damn!" Fred exclaimed and slapped at the flask, sending it flying into the sagebrush.

"You din't need t' do that," the drunk slurred as he staggered across the sand, looking for the flask.

"Leave it," Fred said with a snarl. "We'll get it later."

Floyd staggered and steadied himself against the pickup fender. "I can still light a fuse."

Fred closed his eyes and fought the urge to slug the guy. He glanced at the others. "Still want to do it?" They nodded in unison. "Okay, just like we planned. Murph and I will each carry two bags of dynamite. Henry will stand guard."

Fred grabbed two bags and trudged up the incline to the edge of the aqueduct, with the others following. He stood at the rim of the concrete-lined channel and watched the dark water flow slowly south to Los Angeles. He wondered how much of the valley's water flowed to the city each day. The canal looked to be about thirty feet wide, and he figured it was about ten to twelve feet deep, with the water coming a couple of feet from the top. He knew they measured flow in cubic feet per second, but the math escaped him. He just knew that it was a lot — enough to meet the needs of the fast-growing city.

He looked at the drunken explosives man. "Floyd, think you can show us where to place it?"

"Sure. Shtick with me 'n get 'er done right," the explosives man said. He squatted on his heels and lit a cigarette while he appraised his target.

"Hey, don't smoke. We're holding dynamite," Jake whispered.

"Harder t' ignite than that." Floyd stood unsteadily and flipped his cigarette into the water. "Hope some Angeleno chokes on that." Taking faltering steps along the bank, he watched the ground. "You guys help me. By each joint in the concrete, there should be a weep pipe that drains leakage. A vertical pipe that vents the weep should poke out of the ground up here along the edge of the ditch. We'll put the dynamite in the vent." He bent down and pushed a small bush aside. "Here's one." He appraised the vent pipe. "We can put bundles of about twelve sticks, four clusters with three sticks taped together, down this pipe. The trick is to have 'em all blow at once, so we cut fuses all the same length for each bundle. Fred, help me cut the fuses."

The two men squatted on the ground and cut fuses all the same length to burn for, what Floyd said, was fifteen minutes—long enough to get away and on the road home. The explosives man's hands shook as he inserted fuses in the dynamite and bound the bundles with adhesive tape.

"Okay, put 'em down the pipe, light up, and get out," Floyd said.

Holding each bundle with a string, Fred lowered them down the pipe one after another, with the fuses snaking out of the top of the pipe. He looked at his co-conspirators. "Ready?" They all nodded. He struck a match on the sole of his boot and touched the bundle of fuses and watched for a few seconds to see that they were all burning. "Okay, let's go." As he turned to escape, he glanced to see Floyd bend over the edge of the canal with his hands on his knees. The drunk retched and puked into L.A.'s drinking water. He straightened and looked skyward. His arms windmilled in the air. He hollered incomprehensibly and toppled over the edge into the dark water.

"Help! Hey, gemme outta here! I can't swim," came his shouts as he splashed, attempting to stay afloat.

The saboteurs ran to the edge and looked over to see the man flailing in the water as the current slowly carried him south toward Los Angeles.

"We oughta throw him a rock to hold on to," groused Slim.

"Lead us not into temptation," Fred quoted. He glanced at the blazing fuses. Should he yank them out? Throw water on them? They still had almost fifteen minutes. If they couldn't pull the fool out in time, maybe they could still drown the fuses. He stripped off his shirt as he trotted along the bank, keeping pace with the drunk. "Gimme your shirt," he told Slim. He quickly tied the sleeves together and was poised to toss one end to the flailing man when Henry's shout stopped him.

"Wait! Here, let's use this," Henry yelled, holding a long two-by-four board. "I found it in the brush. Probably left from construction."

Henry and Slim held the board out to the flailing man and pulled him to the concrete embankment.

Fred groaned in pain from his still-healing ribs when he bent down to grab Floyd's wrist and pull him up over the lip of the aqueduct. "How much time left?"

Jake glanced at his pocket watch. "A little less than ten minutes."

"Come on, let's get out of here," Fred said, already sliding down the incline toward the cars, followed by the others. He hurled himself into his truck.

Murphy pushed Floyd onto the truck bed and ran to the front of the truck. "Ready?, he softly called.

Hit it," Fred called back.

Murphy pulled the truck's starting crank, and their collective prayers were answered when it started immediately. Murphy leaped into the front. Fred turned the truck around and glanced to see that Jake was ready to follow.

The two vehicles bounced through the brush to the highway and turned north. They had covered a few miles on the highway when Fred slowed almost to a stop.

"Watchya doin'?" Murphy screamed.

"The flask," Fred exclaimed. "That stupid drunk's flask. I just remembered. It's still out there. I gotta go back."

"No!" Murphy howled. "Don't. No time. We gotta get away."

The words were barely out of Murphy's mouth when a bright flash lit up the sky, followed seconds later by the sound of a thunderous explosion. Fred glanced back and saw a cloud of dust billowing into the moonlit sky. He stepped on the gas and kept his truck chugging at a steady pace on the unpaved highway toward Independence.

"Jesus, that explosion probably woke everybody in town," Fred said. "We better get off the highway so nobody sees us driving into town at this strange hour." At the edge of town, he waved his arm out the window to signal Jake to turn right. Both vehicles pulled in behind Woody's gas station with their lights off. Fred rolled his window down to talk to Jake and parked next to him.

"Let's wait here for a while to see what happens. For sure, Charlie will have heard that and head down as soon as he can. Watch for his car to pass, and then we can go home."

CHAPTER 16   SUSPICION

At the sound of the blast, Charlie was instantly awake in his house in Independence. What the heck was that? Sure sounded like dynamite. He glanced over at Doris. Still sound asleep. She could sleep through anything. He slid out of bed and threw on his robe as he hurried to the door. From his porch, everything looked quiet and normal except for the lights coming on in a few neighbors' windows. The blast sounded like it came from the south, but it was hard to tell from inside the house, especially when he was asleep.

"What was that, Charlie?" his neighbor called from his open door.

"Don't know, Otto," Cole replied. "Some sort of explosion. Sounded a long way off. Could you tell which direction? Maybe from the south?"

"Yeah, south. I was awake, and it sure sounded like it came from the south."

"Thanks. I'll drive out and see what happened."

Cole hurried back into the house, made a quick trip to the bathroom, and then threw on his sheriff's uniform. As he dressed, he silently cursed the county. There was no deputy on duty this time of night. With his minimal budget, the county allowed him one deputy and a part-time constable for each town. Not enough to man the sheriff's office for twenty-four hours. Whatever that explosion was, no one was in the sheriff's office to answer a call for help. Daggett should have a home phone, but the deputy insisted he didn't get paid enough to afford the luxury, and Cole sure didn't want everybody in the county to have his home number. He'd have to check out the explosion himself. It wasn't cold, so the black and white Nash started on the first try, and he was soon on his way down the highway to find what might have happened.

A few miles south of Independence, a stream of water surged across the highway, carving a channel across the sandy, unpaved road. He stopped and watched for a moment. His eyes followed the water through the sagebrush and up the hill to its source. In the moonlight, he saw a dark gap where water poured out a ragged break in the side of the aqueduct.

Looking across the flooding water, he saw the lights from a line of cars coming up the highway from Lone Pine, a few miles down the road. He looked back toward Independence and saw more cars coming from the north. *God in heaven, we don't need a bunch of onlookers interfering.* But it would be hard to keep them away.

He got back in his car and slowly drove through the brush toward the damaged aqueduct that skirted the edge of the rocky

Alabama Hills. When he parked, he saw the dark silhouette of a man standing at the edge of the ditch. Cole trudged up the slope. At the top, Cole recognized Sam Porter, the watchman for Alabama Gates, the aqueduct's overflow spillway a mile to the north.

"Sheriff Cole, I tried to call your office, but nobody answered," Sam said.

"Yeah, nobody on duty at this hour." Cole gestured at the water pouring down the hill. "So what happened here?"

Sam pointed at the gash in the aqueduct. "Pretty clear somebody blasted the ditch."

"You see anything?"

"No. I was asleep up at the house. Felt like the place was coming apart— like an earthquake, except noisier. I came down here as fast as I could. When I saw what happened, I went back and called your office, then tried to get hold of Mr. Laird, the DWP boss for the valley. He didn't answer, so I called Mr. Magon, their water acquisitions man. Then came back here. There's not much I can do except watch."

Cole stared at the chasm the explosion had carved into the waterway. He shook his head. Did these people think that sabotaging the big ditch would make the DWP pack up and go home? That was just plain stupid.

The image of Fred Lukin popped into his mind. He thought of that party at Fred's place a few months ago. He could still hear Fred saying, 'A little dynamite and boom, the water flows back to the river instead of L.A.' Sure enough, there it was — water flowing back toward the Owens River. Motive? There was plenty of that. Cole ticked off the list in his head. First, Fred said Magon had threatened him. Second, there were Magon's men digging the bypass of Fred's co-op irrigation ditch. Third, Fred's cattle were poisoned. Then, his wife was driven off the road and injured. No real evidence, but Fred insisted it was the DWP thug, Magon. Cole had to admit that he'd probably think and act the same way. He spat on the ground in disgust. This was going to be a mess for everyone — not the least of which was himself and that damned Fred. They'd been friends for many years, but now what? He looked down the hill and saw cars turning off the highway and coming up toward the aqueduct break. *Dammit, now the trouble starts.*

At the south end of Independence, Fred and his accomplices had waited just a few minutes when the sheriff's car sped past. Moments later, a stream of cars followed. Fred thought it looked like half the town was driving south in the middle of the night to see what had happened.

"Ok, we can go home now", Fred said.

"Ya know," Murphy responded, "we'll be more noticeable by our absence than if we go back down there. Wanna follow the crowd?"

"Can't take him," Fred said, gesturing with his thumb at Floyd in the back.

"Jake's house is just down the street," Murphy replied. "We can dump him there till we get back, and then we can take him back to Aberdeen."

After dropping off Floyd, Fred, Muphy, Jake, Slim, and Henry retraced their earlier route south to join the spectators at the blast site. When Fred encountered the water cutting across the highway, he turned west off the road toward the aqueduct. When they got closer, they parked among the other cars parked willy-nilly in the sagebrush. They walked up the incline and joined the onlookers gathered at the edge of the big ditch. There looked to be well over thirty spectators, all staring, pointing, and jabbering about the water pouring through the sagebrush toward the mostly dry Owens River. Shattered pieces of concrete littered the ground. Fred glanced across the stream of escaping water to see Sheriff Cole's eyes boring into his. The sheriff shook his head with a disgusted expression that Fred guessed meant, 'Won't you ever learn?'

Magon stood beside the sheriff. As soon as he spotted Fred, he pointed and yammered at Cole. It was impossible to hear over the roar of the water and the sounds of the crowd, but Fred could imagine the accusations the DWP agent was throwing his way.

Cole stepped on pieces of broken concrete to cross the flood. With spectators watching, he stood inches from Fred and said in his deep bass voice, "Mr. Lukin, do you know anything about this act of criminal vandalism?"

Men squeezed close to hear.

Fred looked steadily into Cole's eyes. "Charlie, why would I know anything about it? I just got here."

Cole's angry glare swept over Murphy, Slim, Henry, and Jake. "Where have you gentlemen been all night?"

Before they could answer, an angry murmur spread through the crowd, and shouting erupted.

"Leave them alone, Sheriff."

"Fred's one of us."

"He was with me."

"I saw him at the Masonic Lodge."

"Quiet!" Cole bellowed over the clamor. "This is a matter for the law."

When the hollering stopped, a man stepped forward and pointed at Magon, standing beside the sheriff. "How do we know he didn't do it?"

"He mighta done it to frame Fred," another yelled.

"We know he beat Fred at the point of a gun," yet another exclaimed.

"Yeah. He's the one that needs a beating."

Shouted accusations and threats filled the air, directed at Magon. His bulging eyes moved across the faces of the men surrounding him. Sweat beaded on his forehead, and he shrank back behind the sheriff.

Cole pointed his pistol in the air. The ear-splitting boom of his gun echoed from the rocky hills. Not a sound came from the circle of men. He looked like an angry bear as he eyed each man. "Step back," he ordered. "You men all know better than to act like a mob. Now get in your cars and go home."

Fred and his friends turned with the rest of the spectators and returned to their cars parked below the blasted waterway. The escaping water now flowed under and around the parked cars. It spilled over Fred's boots as he waded to get into his car. A wave of relief swept over him when he squeezed behind the wheel and waited for Murphy to crank the motor to life.

"I figured he'd stop us when we left," Murphy said as they fell in with the parade of cars heading back to the highway and home.

"I'd probably be on my way to jail by now if all those guys hadn't started yelling," Fred replied. "Now we have to do something about Floyd."

"Shoulda let him drown," Murphy said.

"Gotta get him back home, quick," Fred said. "I can't do it 'cause Charlie might come to check on me. Maybe you and Slim?" Fred asked.

"Slim can take him. I might kill the drunken idiot if he is with me."

CHAPTER 17   HOME FIRES

Fred pulled up to Murphy's house and looked at his friend in silence for a moment. "You and Jake will see Floyd gets home first thing tomorrow?"

"Said I would."

"Murph, sorry about this. If I get caught, I'll try to keep it away from you."

"Same here."

A dim light glowed in the kitchen window when he drove into his farmyard. Alice was likely awake. He'd hoped she had gone to bed and was asleep. He eased the kitchen door open as quietly as he could. She was asleep at the kitchen table with her head resting on her arm. He carefully tiptoed into the room, but the floor squeaked with his first step. He grimaced.

She lifted her head and looked at him with bleary eyes. "What time is it?"

He pulled his pocket watch from his Levis. "Three-twenty."

She looked him up and down. "Your boots are wet."

Damn! He'd forgotten he waded through the runoff from the ditch. Without saying anything, he sat down and positioned the boot jack he kept by the door. Dry boots were hard enough to get off, but wet ones were a real struggle. Maybe she wouldn't say anything if he busied himself with the boots.

Alice stood and watched. "I heard that explosion."

"Yeah? Me too."

"I can imagine. Hope it hurt your ears." Without another word, she headed to the bedroom.

He watched her go. Not what he had expected. No explosion. Maybe her silence was worse. He gave another pull, and his foot popped from the first boot.

The next morning, Fred picked at the bacon and eggs that Alice put in front of him. She had not said a word to him since he woke up. She acted as if she was placing breakfast in front of a statue. She poured him a second cup of coffee, sat down, and watched him eat. It was hard to eat with someone silently watching like that.

"I hope Carl's getting along okay in San Francisco."

She nodded. No frown. No smile.

There was a scraping at the door and then a knock. Alice walked to the door and opened it. "Hello, Charlie. Nice to see you."

"Is Fred here?" came the sheriff's familiar, deep voice.

Fred turned around and watched Cole remove his hat and step into the kitchen. He motioned to a chair. "Have a seat, Charlie."

"Thanks. I'll stand. It's not a social call."

"What can I do for you, Sheriff?"

Cole looked from husband to wife. "Alice, I need to speak to Fred alone."

Alice forced a metallic smile. "You can talk here. There are no secrets in this family."

The sheriff raised his eyebrows and shrugged. "Okay. I'll get right to it. Fred, where were you before I saw you at the aqueduct last night?"

Before he could answer, Alice said, "Why, Charlie, he was here all evening until we heard that explosion." She stood next to her husband with her hand on his shoulder. "Isn't that right, dear?"

Fred turned and gazed at her in wonder and nodded. "Of course, *dear*." She never failed to surprise him.

Disgust and frustration flashed across Cole's face. "Alice," he said as though he was scolding a delinquent student, "you know that perjury is a crime, don't you?"

Alice gave him her most solicitous smile. "Of course, Sheriff Cole, but it's not perjury if it's the truth."

His eyes rolled toward the ceiling, and he pursed his lips. He angrily slapped his hat on and, without a word, stormed out the door.

Fred turned and looked at her for a long moment, then whispered, "You're amazing. Thank you."

She stood with her hands on her hips. "Fred Lukin, you stupid ox! If you ever do anything like that again, I'll just let you go to jail where you belong. Now tell me what happened."

Later that afternoon, Fred stood beside his pickup, massaging the small of his back with both hands. Damn these ribs, they still hurt, especially as he bent side-to-side. He didn't think he was old, but there were times like this when he thought maybe he was getting too old to heft hay bales onto the truck. As he stretched, he took in the view of the Sierras to the west. Every season, winter, spring, summer, or fall, is always spectacular, always different. He never got tired of the view of the chiseled, silvery granite escarpment carved by eons of wind, water, and snow. But this spring, the snow cover was thinner than the previous two or three seasons. Less water for everyone. The DWP would push, plot, and cheat to take a greater share of the water to slake L.A.'s insatiable thirst. Each year, less remained for the valley. Was blasting the aqueduct the right thing to do? Would that make them think about what they were doing to the people in the valley and deal with them more fairly and honestly? He knew the answer was no. He and his friends risked themselves, their families, and their livelihoods for nothing. His gaze shifted from the mountains to the valley. No, nothing had been accomplished except risking jail. There was no view from jail. He couldn't help agreeing with Alice: he'd been a stupid ox.

Looking toward town, he noticed a rooster tail of dust spraying into the air from a car coming down the lane.

The rancher stood by his truck, half-loaded with hay bales, and watched Mark Watson pull up. What was he doing here? It was easy to dislike the banker. It wasn't just that he tried to take over and run everything, but the memory of the way he looked at Alice that last time he was here floated to the top whenever the banker came to mind, setting his blood to a boil.

Looking distinguished, as always, the banker strode forward with his hand out. "Fred. Glad to see you. I hope you are well-rested. I've heard you had a busy night." He chuckled good-naturedly. He looked at the cloudless blue sky. "Gorgeous day. Last evening must have been a great night for fireworks."

Jesus, Fred thought, how could the rumor travel that fast? Was it all over the valley already? Even if he had been innocent, with everyone in the valley thinking otherwise, he didn't have a chance. He was as good as in jail already. "How can I help you, Mr. Watson?" he asked with a note of impatience.

"Don't worry, I'm neither the police nor the DWP. I heard about the blasting of the aqueduct and came down to see what happened. I was just out there. Quite a job. One side of the ditch blown and water pouring out. They already have a crew trying to fix it. I talked to the foreman. He said they'll have to stop the flow at the intake out by Aberdeen. It'll take a few days for the repairs. That guy Magon drove up when I was there. He ranted and raved about you doing it, then ran me off."

"He's crazy! I had nothing to do with it," Fred insisted. "He'd accuse me of anything just to get me off this ranch."

Watson flashed his car salesman smile. "Of course, I know you weren't involved, and I'm sure everyone else does, too. However, a few things I'd like to point out." He held his fingers up and spoke deliberately, counting off his items. "First, my congratulations to those who were involved—whoever they were. It gets things started, kind of like the Boston Tea Party. Second, I'm disappointed they didn't work with my group. As I noted at that recent meeting, we can accomplish more by working together. Plus, if everyone is involved, they can't put us all in jail. Third, I am very concerned about the dynamite. I own the vanadium mine. A substantial amount of explosives was stolen from there a few days before this attack. That dynamite is registered and can be traced to my business. Further, it was unnecessary. If we were working together, I am sure that an explosive like that could be gotten in a way that was not so traceable. Fourth, to show the advantage of working together, if there are legal problems, my attorney in Bishop will be available to help. Whoever did it needs only to let me know. They don't need to be in this by themselves."

The rancher stared at the banker, not knowing what to say. Finally, he found his tongue. "Ah… ah, that is generous of you, Mr. Watson. Perhaps I can pass the word around so the men involved will hear."

Watson slapped Fred's shoulder like a buddy. "You do that. Oh, I almost forgot to tell you. This already hit the L.A. papers, and the City is sending police and detectives up here to sort things out. The L.A. City Council is offering a ten-thousand-dollar reward for the arrest of the perpetrators. That should make it interesting." He glanced at his pocket watch. "I better get back to Bishop. You look like you could use some sleep," and laughed as he got back in his car.

As he watched the banker drive away, Fred rubbed his shoulder as though to brush away Watson's touch. Each time he saw him, his dislike grew. Watson mentioned a reward. Fred's stomach twisted. Ten thousand dollars? It would take him several good years to earn anything close to that. What next?

CHAPTER 18   CITY COPS

The next night, Fred couldn't sleep and tossed and turned, replaying the attack and wondering what would happen next. In the morning, despite knowing he should keep a low profile, with all that had happened, morning coffee with the guys at Doris's seemed a necessity. After wrapping up the early morning chores and checking the livestock, he drove to town. When he got to the cafe, the tables and counter were filled. Doris bustled from one table to another with her coffeepot. The regulars sat at their accustomed table by the window, looking glum. Tough-looking men he didn't know occupied the other tables.

After hanging his hat on the stand and taking an empty chair, Fred glanced questioningly at each of his friends, who sat silently nursing their coffees. He gestured with his chin at the strangers in the cafe. "What's going on?"

Jake managed a wry smile and spoke quietly. "Cops from L.A., along with some big city newspaper reporters. They pulled into town early this morning."

"What about Charlie? He been around?"

As he asked, Doris stepped up with her coffeepot in one hand and a cup and saucer in the other.

"I'm runnin' ragged. Think I'll sit." She set the cup in front of Fred, pulled up an extra chair and handed the pot to Fred. "Here, pour your own." She let out an exhausted sigh. "Heard you ask about Charlie. At the crack-a-dawn, those guys" —she gestured with her thumb— "pounded on our door, demandin' to see the sheriff. Charlie talked to them. When they left, he was mad enough to kill. Guess they called him a hick sheriff, a country bumpkin, and every other insult they could think of. Still, he agreed to take them out to the scene of the crime a little later. But he said it'd be a cold day in hell before they learned anything more from him." She laughed and looked at Fred. "I guess whoever did the deed is unlikely to have Charlie on his back."

"Think they know any of us?" Jake asked.

"Nah. To them, you're just a bunch of country bumpkin farmers."

"Hey, girl, bring some more coffee," a raspy voice demanded from a table occupied by the out-of-town cops.

Doris stood. "Gotta get back to work. At least I oughta make some money off these big city cops."

Later that morning, Sheriff Cole rode in the passenger seat as Deputy Daggett drove the sheriff's Nash to the site of the blasted aqueduct. The L.A. cops followed in a short caravan of three police cars, with reporters for Southern California newspapers bringing up the rear. Twelve miles south of Independence, Daggett turned off the highway onto a bumpy track through the sagebrush and stopped by an outcropping of large boulders below the aqueduct.

Cole got out and gazed at the clear, azure sky and the mountains to the west, then watched the cops unload. What a screw-up, he thought. A beautiful day, sure to be ruined by a bunch of city cops here to make trouble. Why did Fred and his cronies have to do it? Whatever happened to being a county sheriff in a peaceful backwater? Sure, maybe he was a country bumpkin sheriff. Nothin' wrong with that. After all, that's why he gave up being a city cop in San Francisco.

He walked to the new gully where water had poured out of the blasted aqueduct. A DWP crew had stopped the flow and now the gully was just damp desert sand. He trudged up to the edge of the aqueduct. While he watched the DWP crew working to repair the damage, L.A. Detective Lieutenant Dodson walked up beside him.

"Thanks, you can go now. We'll take it from here," the lieutenant said.

Cole stepped back a few yards and motioned to Daggett, still standing beside their car. The deputy joined him, carrying a thermos of coffee, and poured each of them a cup. Without a word, the two local cops stood at the edge of the empty aqueduct, drinking their brew and watching.

The L.A. cops talked and pointed at the slabs of concrete blown out of the side of the canal. The lieutenant climbed down into the now mostly dry channel and talked to the work crew placing wood forms for new concrete.

"We've seen enough," Cole said to Daggett. "Now we know how to be cops. Let's go."

"Don't you want to hear this?" Daggett asked as he pointed over his shoulder with his thumb.

Behind him, the police lieutenant had taken a photogenic stance at the edge of the aqueduct. The reporters immediately crowded around with cameras flashing. "I'm Lieutenant Dodson, and I can give you a statement now." The air filled with shouted questions. The cop waved his hands, and they quieted. "It looks pretty clear to me. The evidence shows that about forty men were involved in staging this attack. Most likely, they were communist agitators or members of the Industrial Workers of the World—the Wobblies. As you all know, the Wobblies have been making trouble in Los Angeles, and they probably came up here to spread their treason. It won't take us long to round them up and put them away."

Shouting erupted among the reporters, who competed to get their questions answered.

Cole shook his head and told his deputy, "I'm glad not to be a city cop and have to deal with reporters."

When Cole turned away, a reporter stepped from the troop and trotted over with his pencil poised over his notepad. "Are you the sheriff? Can you make a statement? Have you seen any agitators around trying to get people riled up?"

Cole struggled to maintain a serious expression. "No, don't know as I have. But I'm sure the lieutenant must be right." He turned to Daggett, whose mouth hung open in surprise. "You see any treasonous strangers around, deputy?"

Daggett blinked and shook his head. "Ah, ah… Nope, I don't think so. There was some travelers driving through here a couple a days ago, heading north. Wasn't nobody that looked familiar."

"Yeah, you can never tell about some folks that drive through here," Cole said. "But we're real pleased that the detectives could clear this up so fast. I hope you have a pleasant stay here. Maybe write about what's happening to the valley — ranches losing their water and folks moving away."

As the two local lawmen returned to their car, Daggett asked, "Why do you think the lieutenant said there were forty men?"

Cole paused and pointed at the ground. "See all those tire tracks? Must 'a been at least forty people involved."

"But—those are tracks from everybody who came out here after the blast the other night, plus the City work crew that's repairing it."

Cole chuckled. "Right. But the city cops know what they are doing."

CHAPTER 19   F.L.

Sheriff Cole sat at his desk reading the latest edition of the *Inyo Independent*. The article on the front page of the weekly newspaper reported the aqueduct bombing and noted the ten-thousand-dollar reward for an arrest. An awful lot more than his pathetic sheriff's salary and much greater than most of the locals earned in several years. That should bring some interesting stories to the surface.

The sound of the door opening interrupted his reading. It was Dodson, the L.A. cop who had called him a hick sheriff the day before.

"Sheriff Cole," the man began, "I have several leads that we need to follow up. I'd like to get your help."

Cole resisted the temptation to remind the pompous bastard that a hick sheriff wouldn't be of much use to city cops, but he made a small jab. "I thought you concluded it was Wobbly agitators."

"Might be, but we still need to check things out." He held up a silver flask. "One of our guys found this in the sagebrush by the blast site. It's clean enough that it coulda been dropped recently, maybe during the attack." He handed it to the sheriff. "See the inscription? Know anybody with initials F. L.?"

Cole turned it over in his hand. Initials—F.L. *Damn that stupid Fred.* "Can't say as I do."

"You must know everyone—especially the hard cases, radicals, and ne'er-do-wells. That's where we start." The lieutenant handed a small notebook to the sheriff. "Here, write them down."

Cole frowned, and his jaws tightened. He didn't want to spend his time with this ass. *Get rid of him. Send him on a wild goose chase.* He looked at the ceiling, jotted a name, looked at the ceiling again, jotted another name, and then a couple more. He handed the notebook back. "These are the ones I can think of. Check these out."

The city cop ran his eyes down the page. "Frank Lopez, Felton Lynn, Felix Lewis, Floyd Lee. Not much of a list."

The sheriff shrugged. "Not many with those initials that I could think of, offhand."

"Any reason to suspect any of them? Any of them communists or anarchists?"

"No. They have the initials but no radicals or hard cases."

"We can start with the closest one. Who is that?"

Cole scrunched his face in concentration and looked at the ceiling. "None very close. Floyd Lee's a little strange but harmless. Lives out by Aberdeen, a small village a few miles north. Turn at the Aberdeen sign by the highway and ask anyone in the village. Should be easy to find."

"Be easier if you show me the way."

"You guys are detectives. Oughta be able to find your own way."

"I'd appreciate it if you'd come along. Help with questioning."

Damn, there goes my afternoon. In a huff, Cole grabbed his hat off the rack. "Come on. I'll drive."

He wasn't sure where Floyd's house was, only that he lived in Aberdeen. He pulled up to the first house in the hamlet.

The woman who answered his knock frowned at the mention of Floyd Lee. "Don't know how that guy keeps a job. Always half-drunk. Anyway, down to the end of this street, take that track east about a mile up the canyon. Not far. A little rock house just before you get to the spring."

After bouncing up the steep track, Cole parked in front of a low, run-down rock hovel that looked like it hadn't an ounce of care since some luckless prospector had thrown it up years ago. A worn-down Model T parked by the side was the only sign that someone lived there. He bent down and rubbed dirt from a small window. But it was still too grimy to see into the dark interior. He knocked on the door. No response. A harder pound jarred the door open.

Cole stepped inside, pausing for his eyes to adjust to the gloom. The stench of stale sweat and pee permeated the place.

Floyd Lee, clothed in a dirty undershirt and Levis, was sprawled face-up on the stained mattress with arms spread wide.

"Hey, Floyd, Floyd Lee, wake up," the sheriff called, getting no reaction. He shook his shoulder. "Wake up."

The man jerked and curled into a fetal ball with his hands over his head. "No, don't. Please, please, don't do it," he mumbled.

Cole gently nudged him again. "Don't do what, Floyd?"

He scrunched into a tighter ball. "Don't let them get me. Keep them back."

"Keep who back?"

Floyd squirmed and pointed toward the ceiling. "Them! Oh, no. Here they come," and screamed.

Cole lifted the man to a sitting position and gently shook him. "It's okay. Nobody will hurt you."

Floyd's eyes opened wide with a look of terror. "Are you a German?"

"No. I'm Sheriff Cole. You know me."

The groggy man ran his hand over his face, rough with two days' stubble. "What 'd'ya want?"

"You got company." Cole pointed toward the man standing in the doorway. "This is Detective Dodson from Los Angeles. He wants to talk to you."

Dodson stepped forward with the silver flask. "Mr. Lee, I'm looking for the owner of this. You recognize it?"

Floyd took it, turning it over in his hand. "Hey, I used to have one just like this. Even had my initials. Where'd you get it?"

"The question is, where'd you lose it?"

"Don't know. I dreamed I lost it and then found it."

"Where was the dream?" Dodson asked.

"Out in the desert, I think. But there was a lot of water. None of that in the desert."

"Who was with you?"

"The bunch from my squad. Sergeant Bates and others—Bob Cornelius, Bill Wellman, Ray Obert, Fred Lukin, Jim Sawyer, and other guys I don't remember. We went over the top, and the Germans shot us up somethin' terrible. Some of those Bosch was flying around like bats. I remember Fred went down, howling mad 'cause he couldn't get up."

The mention of Fred's name got Cole's attention, but he said nothing and let the city cop continue.

"Were you fighting the Germans in the desert?" Dodson asked incredulously.

"No, no. What gave you that idea?"

"You said your dream was in the desert with a lot of water."

"That's crazy. Weren't no desert. The water was in the trenches."

"Where'd you lose the flask?"

"What flask? I didn't have no flask."

Dodson held up the flask. "This one—with your initials on it."

"Lemme see." He reached, but Dodson pulled it back. "Hey, give it to me. It's mine. I need a drink."

"It's evidence. I have to keep it," the cop said.

"Evidence of what?"

"That you blew up the aqueduct."

"Sure, we hit it. The sergeant ordered us to. It was full of supplies for the Germans. You shoulda seen that blast. Must 'a been full of ammo—went sky high."

"You mean the aqueduct?"

"No. Aqueducts aren't full of ammunition."

Dodson rolled his eyes and headed to the door. "Come on, this is a waste of time."

"Hey, gimme my flask," Floyd yelled as the cop left.

As they drove away, Dodson asked, "What do you think? Is it his?"

"I doubt it," Cole replied. "Floyd's confused. Been that way since the war. He works as a general laborer for the DWP when he's sober. Hard to figure why they keep him on."

"I don't know about his work, but I can't imagine him blowing up an aqueduct," the cop said. "Guess we have to talk to some other F.L.s. Who's next on the list?"

Cole looked at his pocket watch. "It's kinda late. How about tomorrow?"

CHAPTER 20   A LOTTA KICK

Cole fidgeted at his desk the next morning while he waited for Dodson. The last thing he wanted was to waste time babysitting the city cop, looking for the owner of a liquor flask. But that might be the quickest way to get the LA cops to leave town. It was strange that Dodson didn't ask questions. Cole thought that if he were investigating in an unknown town, being driven around by the sheriff, he'd ask lots of questions. But this guy was silent. That was okay. Cole didn't want to talk to him, either.

The office door opened. It was Dodson. "Hot today. Didn't expect it this early in the season."

Cole shrugged. "Gets pretty hot here. Ready for the next guy on the list?"

"My plans changed. After we got back yesterday, I spoke with Mr. Magon at the DWP. He is certain that one of the local ranchers," he paused and glanced at his notepad, "by the name of Fred Lukin, is responsible for the attack on the aqueduct. Fred Lukin–F.L. You failed to mention him."

"Didn't think of him. Probably missed some others, too."

"Mr. Magon said the man attacked him. He might be an agitator or a communist. I need to check it out. I'd like you to accompany me to his ranch."

Cole figured he'd better go, if for no other reason than to keep Fred from doing something stupid. He carefully fitted his hat in place. "My car's in back."

"I'll follow you. I have two other agents waiting in my car."

Cole called down the hall, "Hey, Ray, we're going out to the Lukin ranch. You drive."

At the north edge of town, the sheriff's car turned east toward Fred's ranch. "Speed it up," Cole said. "Those guys are worried about agitators. Let's agitate them a little."

Daggett stepped on the gas and accelerated down the sandy, two-track road.

The sheriff looked back and chuckled to see their car bouncing and fishtailing over the washboard lane. He pictured them grabbing and holding on as they bounced around. They probably have better roads in L.A.

When they pulled up in front of Fred's house, the dog rushed the cars, barking and growling. "Easy, Tinker," Cole said as he exited the car and offered his hand for the dog to sniff. Tinker wagged his tail and sat back on his haunches. "Wait here," the sheriff said to Daggett and the L.A. cops, "I'll see if he's home."

Alice answered his knock. "Charlie, what are you doing out here? Who's that with you?"

"Cops from L.A. They want to talk to Fred. Is he here?"

Her face fell. Cole noticed the tremor in her hands. "I'll get him. Wait here."

Fred came slowly to the door. "What's going on, Charlie?"

The sheriff gestured with his chin toward the car. "There's some cops that want to talk to you."

The rancher forced a nervous smile. "What about?"

"Now that there's a real mystery, isn't it, Fred? After that aqueduct bombing, I can't imagine why detectives would drive all the way up here from L.A. A real mind stumper."

"Okay, I'll talk to them."

Cole motioned to the cops, who approached as though ready to attack. They stopped a few feet in front of the porch. "Are you Mr. Lukin?" Dodson asked.

"What do you want?"

"I'm Detective Lieutenant Dodson of the Los Angeles Police Department." He held up the flask. "This yours?"

"No, never seen it before."

"No matter," Dodson said. "Mr. Magon of the DWP says you are the perpetrator of the bombing of the Los Angeles aqueduct earlier this week. He ordered your arrest." He turned to Cole. "Sheriff, I want you to arrest this man. We will take custody and drive him to Los Angeles."

"What's your evidence to support the charge?" Cole asked.

"Mr. Magon's testimony."

Fred's eyes narrowed, and his face reddened in anger. "Magon? I don't know much law, but I know that you can't arrest me simply because that thug tells you to."

"He's right," Cole said. "I'm not going to arrest a man based solely on someone's word."

The L.A. cop stepped closer. "Mr. Magon represents the Department of Water and Power of the City of Los Angeles. If you won't arrest this guy, we will." He took a pair of handcuffs from his belt. "Gimme your hands, Lukin."

Cole stepped between the two men. "Back off," he roared. "You can't arrest anyone in this county. You have no legal jurisdiction here and neither does your Mr. Magon. Now get in your car and get out."

The two other L.A. cops drew their pistols and held them on Cole.

"Get out of the way, you stupid yokel," Dodson growled.

Cole's eyes narrowed. "You think you can shoot me and make it out of the county alive?"

Dodson drew his gun from a holster behind his back. "For sure. We have three guns and yours is still in your belt."

"Look behind you," Cole said.

The cops turned to see Daggett shielded behind the sheriff's car with his pistol trained on them.

"And don't forget me," came Alice's voice. They all looked toward the sound. A double-barreled shotgun pointed from the corner of the house, with Alice squinting over the sight from the other end.

"She's a pretty good shot," Fred said.

Cole smiled. "With that double-barreled shotgun, she doesn't have to be. Now, if you gentlemen would carefully place your guns on the ground, you can be on your way."

The cop glared at Cole and shook his head. "We're not giving up our guns. We'll leave for now and be back with enough evidence to hang this guy." Still holding his gun on Cole, he backed a step at a time toward his car, followed by his two acolytes. They piled into their car and turned around to head out of the farmyard.

Before the car was ten yards away, the air split with a deafening boom from the corner of the house, followed by whacks and pings of shot chewing pockmarks into the paint of the escaping car.

Fred, Cole, and Daggett turned as one and stared with shock at the diminutive lady lying on her back with the shotgun at her side.

Fred ran to her. "You okay?"

Alice managed a shaky smile. "I never shot both barrels before. A lotta kick."

CHAPTER 21   WANTED

The next afternoon, Jake Shapiro stood behind his dry goods counter, listening to his customer.

"Jake, I know I'm a little behind on my bills. But I need those boots."

"I know, Harold," Jake said. "Lots of ranchers are having a hard time. But so am I. I grant credit but people can't pay. It's like I'm giving the stuff away. Suppliers are after me, and I'm gettin' behind on my bills too. Pretty soon, I'll have to close my doors and leave the valley like all the others."

Harold pulled up the leg of his jeans to show his old boots. "These ones are worn down so nothin's left. I'm just walkin' in my socks. If I can get through this season with a good crop of alfalfa, I'll be able to pay you."

"How's your crop looking?" Jake asked, knowing full well that Harold's alfalfa was practically dead.

"Truth be told, awful. Can't get enough water. The water level in my well's been droppin', and I can't pump enough to do much good. But maybe we'll get a good rain."

"Harold, how many good rains have you seen in the last three seasons?"

"Yeah, it's been dry, for sure, but a guy's gotta have hope. My wife says that if you hope and pray, the Lord will provide. I surely am hopin', and she does the prayin'. I may even start goin' to church. You oughta go too."

"You know I'm Jewish, and we don't have a synagogue here. Besides, we both know you're not going to go to church."

"Yeah, the missus complains about that all the time. Anyhow, about these boots. I'll pay as soon as I sell some more hay."

Jake rolled his eyes. "Okay, Harold. Maybe your hoping and her praying will do some good. We're all due for some luck."

Harold's face lit up, and he stuck out his hand to shake. "Thanks, Jake. Put it on my ticket. I'm good for it."

After Harold left with his boots, the store was empty, so Jake stepped outside for some fresh air. He sat on the bench in front of the store, leaned back with his legs stretched out on the plank sidewalk, and took stock of the town. Such a comfortable village, but business was slow. Down the street, George King complained that he had trouble covering the small payroll for his drugstore and fountain, and a block in the other direction, the shelves in the hardware store were almost as bare as Jake's.

The sound of a squeaking door interrupted his thoughts. He glanced to see Betty coming out of the store. Married almost thirteen years with two kids, he thought she looked better than ever—petite and trim, with just a few budding streaks of gray in her dark hair. But her look of exasperation warned of trouble. She stepped over his legs, blocking the sidewalk, and took the seat beside him. He sat quietly, watching across the street at nothing in particular, waiting to find out what was on her mind.

After an icy silence, she ran her hands over her skirt, straightening it, and without looking at him, spoke. "When I was going over the books in the office, I heard you talking to Harold Pressey. Surely, you didn't just sell him a three-dollar pair of boots on credit?"

"That I did."

"Heavens to Betsy, Jake, he already owes us twenty-eight dollars. You keep doing this and it's like giving the merchandise away. Those were our best Chippewa boots. Can't he at least take some cheaper ones?"

"He's good for it. He'll pay when he can."

She frowned. "That's what everybody in town says, but they never do. Pretty soon, we won't be able to pay our own bills. We're behind on our bank loan, and need I remind you of what we owe to the Eibeschutzs? We won't be able to keep the store if this continues."

"I can't just ignore people who are having a hard time. I came here from San Francisco after the earthquake with nothing and couldn't have made it without some help. We've got to help each other when we can."

Betty pursed her lips and frowned. "I've heard all that before, but pretty soon we will be the ones in trouble, and who's going to help us then? And what about Lester and Estella? What will we leave our kids if we give everything to other people?"

He ran his hand over his thinning hair. "Darn it, Betty! You worry too much. *We'll manage!* Things will turn around and business will improve."

"How? The City's buying every ranch and water right they can. People who owe us are leaving the valley. They won't pay because they can't, and we'll end up losing everything." She rose and stomped back into the store, slamming the door behind her.

He waited a few minutes until he thought the coast was clear and went back inside. He busied himself straightening up the merchandise on the shelves behind the counter. The mindless task of arranging cans on the shelves helped divert his mind from their financial worries.

Suddenly, his attention was drawn back to the present by a racket outside. It sounded like someone was hammering on the wall of the building. He stepped out to see what was going on. Two large men wearing identical three-button sack coats stood on the sidewalk, with one taking a sheet of paper to the clapboard front of the store.

"Hey, you can't do that," he protested. "This is my building. Stop it."

The guy without the hammer looked down at the small merchant and spoke with a grating voice. "I'm Lieutenant Dodson of the L.A. police. We're putting up reward posters." He held up a sheet with large print.

REWARD: $10,000 FOR INFORMATION LEADING TO THE ARREST AND CONVICTION OF PERSON OR PERSONS GUILTY OF BLASTING THE LOS ANGELES AQUEDUCT

"Let me see that," Jake said as he grabbed the page. He scanned the notice. It went on to give the known details of the attack. His guts felt like they were quivering. He had already heard about the reward. Most likely, everybody in the valley had. He was one of the 'persons', and the poster brought it home that there was a price on his head. "Get that off my building," he ordered as he ripped the notice from the wall, wadded it up, and threw it on the ground.

Dodson pulled a pistol from inside his coat and held it on Jake. "This is official police business. It's a crime to interfere." The man glanced up and quoted the sign across the front of the store. "Shapiro's Groceries and Merchandise. You Shapiro?"

"Yes, Jacob Shapiro."

The cop slid his gun back under his coat and eyed Jake like he was trying to figure out how to deal with a strange animal. "General store, eh? You probably know everybody in town. Maybe you can help us with this case. There's a big reward."

"I doubt I could help." Jake gestured at the man's handful of posters. "I wouldn't have any idea who might do that sort of thing. I heard you guys say it was some outside agitators. You're likely right. Somebody from L.A."

"Yeah, we thought so at first, but we have new information. Here's something I want you to look at." He reached into his back pocket and pulled out the silver liquor flask. "Know who this might belong to?"

The color drained from Jake's face, and he labored to control the tremor in his hand as he reached for it. He turned it over in his hand, examining it as though it was the strangest thing he'd ever seen. "No, never seen it before. Where'd you get it?"

The cop stared down at the merchant, eyeing him skeptically. "We found it out by the blast site. Look at the initials. What do they say?"

"F L."

"Know any F L's around here?"

"Must be a lot of F L's."

"You know a guy named Fred Lukin?"

He wasn't about to say Fred was his brother-in-law, but it didn't hurt to know him. "Sure. Everybody knows Fred."

"His initials are F L, right?"

"Yeah."

"Think this Lukin was involved?"

"No. He's lived here all his life, and he's a decorated veteran of the Great War – a law-abiding citizen. I can't imagine him doing anything like that." He handed the flask back.

"That's all … for now." The cop took a few steps down the sidewalk, turned back, and looked steadily at Jake. "Shapiro, right?"

Jake nodded.

"Sounds like a Jew name. You a Jew?"

Jake glared at the man. "What difference does that make?"

"Maybe none," the cop replied. "But a lot of communist agitators are Jews."

"Take your posters and flask and get away from here," Jake snarled.

The cops marched down the street and stopped in front of King's drug store. One began tacking a poster to the front of the store. In moments, George King rushed out the door, yelling and waving his arms. The two cops talked briefly to the druggist. King gestured for the men to get away.

Jake watched as they approached an old man the locals called Crazy Benny. The man was harmless—he mostly sat on the edge of the sidewalk like he was doing now. They showed him the poster and talked, but Jake couldn't make out the words. Then they handed the old man the 'F L' flask. He crouched on his knees and held the flask inches from his face and, with his other hand, slapped his forehead a couple of times. He stood up and waved his hands as he spoke. He pointed across the street toward the cafe. The cop shook his head and reached for the flask.

Benny pulled the flask close and stepped back. "No!" he screamed. "It's mine. It's mine."

A cop grabbed the old man and snatched at the flask. In the struggle, Benny fell to the sidewalk and howled in pain. At the sounds of the struggle, people rushed out of neighboring stores to the scene of two husky L.A. cops manhandling the emaciated old man who now lay howling on the sidewalk, clutching the silver flask like it was his last, treasured possession.

"Hey, leave the old man alone!" someone yelled.

"Get outta town, you thugs!" another hollered.

The cops looked nervously around as a small crowd of townspeople gathered around them.

From behind Jake, Betty rushed out of the store and down the sidewalk like she was ready to battle the out-of-town gendarmes. Gently helping the old man up, she scowled at the cops and solicitously led Benny, still clutching the flask, back toward the store.

Clapping erupted from the spectators, followed by more shouting at the cops.

"Go back to L.A.!"

"Give back our water!"

"Go chase the criminals in your own city!"

"They *are* the criminals," came a shout, followed by laughter.

"Come on. Let's get out of here. Everybody in this town is crazy," the lieutenant muttered as he and his assistant retreated toward their car parked across the street in front of the courthouse.

Angry shouts rained on their car as they drove away.

CHAPTER 22   JURISDICTION

The Inyo Cafe was filled to capacity with a breakfast crowd of locals celebrating what someone called the 'Battle of Benny' the day before. Benny was accorded a seat of honor at the window table with the morning regulars. He sat straight and beamed with his celebrity status as he devoured a stack of pancakes and gulped coffee.

Doris trotted from table to table, pouring coffee and delivering breakfast platters.

"You look frazzled," Alice said as Doris poured her another cup. "How can we help?"

"Long as you're willin', help serve." Doris handed Alice a stack of orders. "Here. Pick up the platters from Gong Loy in the kitchen. Each ticket says which table. Tell 'em what's on a plate. Everybody knows what they ordered."

Alice called to her sister. "Come on, Betty, you can carry some plates."

"We can do something too," Isabel Olivera said as she stood up and pulled Grace with her.

"You guys go help Gong Loy. He's fallin' behind."

Doris watched the ladies pitch in. "I got me some free help. Time to retire."

Alice laughed. "You retire, and you'd have to stay home and take care of Charlie."

"I just changed my mind," Doris answered.

"You could run for sheriff," Jake called.

"She'd win for sure," Charlie responded from his place next to Fred at the window table.

The laughter that echoed through the cafe halted abruptly when the door banged open and a squad of eight L.A. cops rushed in, pistols drawn. All eyes focused on the intruders.

Detective Dodson stood with his feet apart, pointing his pistol at Fred, sitting between Benny and Charlie. "Fred Lukin, you are under arrest for—"

The loud crash and clatter of plates breaking on the floor interrupted him. Alice, eyes wide with shock, stood empty-handed, with shattered plates scattered around her feet. The room erupted in pandemonium, with everyone yelling at the out-of-town cops.

Dodson raised his gun and shot through the ceiling. "Silence!" he shouted.

"Hey!" Doris screamed. "You damn well better pay to fix that."

Sheriff Cole stepped in front of the L.A. cop. "Dodson, I told you before that you have no jurisdiction in this county. You can't arrest anyone."

Dodson wiggled his gun. "This gives me jurisdiction."

"If you try to take Mr. Lukin at the point of a gun, I will charge you with kidnapping."

The L.A. cop pointed his revolver at Cole. "Get out of the way, you stupid bumpkin. We're taking Lukin to Los Angeles where he will be charged." Keeping his eyes and gun on Cole, he commanded his deputies, "Cuff him."

The lieutenant and the rest of the squad held the crowd at bay with their guns while a burly cop held his pistol to Fred's head and another quickly snapped handcuffs on his wrists. They roughly pushed their captive outside while the rest of the cops kept their pistols trained on the diners as they backed out the door.

Alice pressed through the throng of friends to the window and watched the City police shove her husband into a car parked down the street. The cops loaded up, and their three-car caravan sped south out of town.

"Alice, don't worry," Cole said. "We'll get him back." He jumped up on a chair and rasped out his orders. "Those guys have a head start, and they'll be in Lone Pine in twenty minutes. We need to stop them before they go that far. I'll call my constable down there and get him moving. Jake, get on your phone and call anyone in Lone Pine that might help. Tell them to join the constable to set up a roadblock north of town and stop those guys. Any of you who want to help as a volunteer posse, get your guns. Meet me in front of the courthouse in five minutes."

Alice stepped in front of the chair where Cole stood. "What can we do, Sheriff?"

"Stay here. Help Doris clean up. This is a job for men. We'll bring Fred back safe. I promise."

Twenty minutes later, Cole squinted through the windshield of his black and white police car at three L.A. police cars angled across the highway about a quarter-mile ahead.

"Okay, that's them," he said to Deputy Daggett at the wheel. "Stop here. Park the car across the road as a shield."

Daggett slowed to a halt, and five cars filled with the citizen posse followed suit.

The sheriff stepped out of the car and yelled toward the last car in the cavalcade. "Hey, Murph, park your car to block the road behind us so nobody blunders into this disaster." He surveyed the situation. The L.A. cops had been arrayed behind their cars, facing the Lone Pine contingent barricading the road farther south. But now the out-of-town cops had to face both directions, likely confused as to which was the greater threat.

Cole looked at the dry, boulder-strewn Alabama Hills to the west. How ironic. The invading cops had set up for their siege downhill from the site of the aqueduct blast a few days before, and the channel cut by the rogue water crossed the unpaved road between the two opponents.

"Stay behind your cars," Cole directed the posse. "Cover them, but don't shoot."

He watched Dodson jerk Fred out of a car and, with a gun pointed at his captive's head, the L.A. cop shouted at Cole. "This man is our lawful prisoner. If you want him to live, call your men off and let us pass."

"Legitimate police don't threaten to shoot their prisoners," Cole yelled back. "That's what kidnappers do. Release him and you can be on your way."

"No! Either he goes with us to stand trial in Los Angeles, or he dies right here."

"Look how many of us there are on both sides of you," Cole shouted. "If anything happens to Mr. Lukin, not one of you will leave this valley alive. Let him go."

The two men shouted threats back and forth with neither side yielding. No shots were fired, but Cole worried that if this standoff went on too long, someone would get trigger-happy and set off a battle that could get Fred and others killed. He racked his brain for a way to ease the tension when he heard what sounded like a fleet of cars approaching from the north. Probably tourists. They'd just have to wait 'til this falderal was over.

The sound of car doors slamming was followed by shouts from his posse.

"What're you doin' here?"

"You don't belong here; go home."

"This is no place for women."

God save us. What now? Cole wondered as he glanced back. A whole flock of women. It looked like half the female population of Independence was marching in his direction, bringing to mind those suffrage marches of a few years earlier. Leading the parade were the two formidable sisters, Alice Lukin and Betty Shapiro. And damn! There was Doris, too! What was going on?

The women gathered in front of Cole, and Alice looked up at him. "Sheriff, have you got my husband free yet?"

"No, Alice. It will probably take a little longer. You ladies have to get away. Go back to town. There might be some shootin' here."

"If there is shooting, then Fred will be the first target. That's the only way you men can ever think to solve problems."

"No. We will get him out and safe. Just give us a while."

"Nonsense," Alice insisted. "He won't have a while when you guys get through." She turned to the other women. "Come on, let's go."

The swarm of women flowed forward. The men at the barricade grabbed at their wives, but most dodged and the female tide flowed past them into the no-man's-land between the locals and the city cops.

Shock and worry stabbed at Cole as this vulnerable group of small-town housewives marched toward the eight L.A. cops holding Fred.

The women walked straight toward the cops. When they got there, Alice stepped in front of the lieutenant holding a gun to Fred's head.

"Alice, get away from here right now," Fred commanded.

She ignored him and addressed the cop politely. "Sir, how should I address you?"

The man answered equally formally. "I am Senior Detective Lieutenant Dodson of the Los Angeles Police. And you are?"

With exaggerated courtesy, she replied, "I am most disappointed you do not remember me from our ranch. I, sir, am Mrs. Frederick Lukin, wife of this fine gentleman you are holding by force. I would be most appreciative if you would release him." She smiled. "If you like, I can vouch for his good behavior."

The police officer nodded. "Oh, yes. I remember—the lady with the shotgun. We're not letting him go. He's our prisoner to be tried in Los Angeles."

With her arms spread, Alice spun around, indicating the women who had accompanied her. "These ladies came to help me retrieve my husband. As you can see, there are quite a few of us— many more than there are of you and we have you surrounded.

Release Fred and we will leave so you may safely return to your city of angels."

Holding Fred with one arm, with his gun in his other hand, Dodson gestured at the other city cops. "Lady, with my squad of trained officers, I am sure we will be able to—" The press of Alice's pistol barrel at his ear stopped him mid-sentence. Each of the women had quickly drawn a pistol from her purse or skirt and pointed it at one of his crew.

He began to bring his pistol back to bear on Fred, but he froze at the sound of Alice's revolver hammer clicking back.

"Please drop your gun," she said politely. "I can't miss with my gun cocked at your ear."

He glanced sideways at her. "Be calm. I'll put it on the ground." He bent down. Before he let go of the gun, he spun to get a shot off.

Two shots exploded simultaneously.

Alice stared at the wounded man sitting on the ground with blood pouring from the side of his head where part of his earlobe was missing. She bent down and took his gun and slipped it into her purse. She felt around in her purse, then glanced down and ran her finger across a small hole in the side. She pulled her make-up compact out. His bullet was stuck in the metal case.

Cole and his citizen posse came running. They quickly surrounded the L.A. cops and allowed them to help their lieutenant to his feet. One of the cops handed his commander a handkerchief to stop the blood from spreading a dark stain down the front of his blue serge coat.

With a shaky smile, Alice threw her arms around Fred.

"That was really stupid, you know," Fred whispered in her ear.

"Maybe," she whispered back.

God, what a mess now, Cole thought. Eight captive cops, one with a wounded ear. He just wanted them to leave and all this to go away. The last thing he wanted was a bunch of big-city cops in his jail. But he needed to play it out, if nothing else, to keep his self-respect and maintain independence from L.A. He stood in front of the L.A. cops who were corralled at gunpoint into a tight circle by his posse. "You are all under arrest for the attempted kidnapping of Fred Lukin."

Holding a cloth to his ear, the lieutenant leaned toward one of his men and shouted. "What'd he say?"

The other cop repeated Cole's words into his commander's good ear.

"Sheriff, you can't arrest us," the lieutenant shouted. "That man is guilty of destroying city property. We have every right to arrest and take him to Los Angeles."

"Stop shouting," Cole said. "I told you before, you have no standing as police in this county. Here, you are ordinary citizens. In front of many witnesses, you took a man at gunpoint. That is kidnapping."

The cop pointed at Alice walking with Fred back to their car. "Yes, and that witch just shot me." He pulled the cloth away from his ear. "Look at this. My ear's a mess and I can't hear anything but ringing. She should be arrested and charged alongside her husband."

"What I saw, as did all these witnesses, was that you were illegally holding a gun on her husband and then tried to shoot her and she defended herself. I doubt any jury would find her guilty of anything but self-defense."

"You can't arrest us for doing our job," the lieutenant shouted. "If you try to hold us in your pathetic, dinky jail, our lawyers will be all over you. You'll be tied up for years in court, and when it's done, we'll own the county."

Damn it, they already do, Cole thought. "Meanwhile, you'll still be in our dinky jail," he replied.

The city cops were squeezed into separate cars and driven back to the sheriff's office in Independence. While Dr. Woodin worked in Cole's office to patch up the lieutenant's mangled ear, the posse helped herd the other L.A. cops to the cells.

"Hey, you can't put us all in here," one cop blared as he was being forced with three others into one of the two small cells.

"Sure, we can," Daggett said. He gave the guy a push on his back. "Get in there and be quiet."

The cop spun around with eyes blazing and shouted, "Keep your hands off me, you yokel!"

The men of the posse backing Daggett stepped menacingly forward, the cop obediently stepped into the cell, and the deputy shut and locked the door.

After the posse left, Daggett and the sheriff stood outside the cells packed with the L.A. policemen. Holy God, Cole thought, how much trouble did he have on his hands now? One cop shot by a local housewife, and his cells filled with this gang of city gendarmes. Every day brought more trouble than the day before.

"What are we going to do with them, Sheriff?" Daggett asked. "We've never had this many prisoners all at once. And, we've never had cops as prisoners."

"A problem, for sure," Cole replied. "This jail wasn't built for that many. This is supposed to be a peaceful county with no need for a big jail. Maybe we could send a couple up to the Mono County jail in Bridgeport. I'd like to see them rot in jail, just not my jail."

"How will we feed 'em?" Daggett asked.

"Same as we do with any prisoners. Get it from the cafe. Probably the best food any of them had in a while. Damned trouble is, it'll bust our food budget. Go over and tell Doris we'll need eight dinners tonight."

"Ahh, boss, she'll scalp me. Wouldn't it be better if you told her?"

Cole ran his hand over the top of his balding head. "She can't scalp me, but she might cut something else off. Just remind her how much she'll get paid."

CHAPTER 23   FINE

Late the next afternoon, Cole sat at his desk, sorting through meaningless mail with his mind occupied with the crowded jail cells down the hall. God, he'd be glad to get rid of those prisoners. The sound of the door opening pulled his thoughts away from his captives. He looked up at a well-dressed man standing in the doorway. "May I help you?"

"I am Clarence Lynch from the City Attorney's office in Los Angeles. You must be the sheriff. I have come for your prisoners." He held out a paper. "This is my demand for the immediate release of the Los Angeles police officers who you are holding illegally."

"I am Sheriff Cole." He took the paper and ran his eyes down the page. He wanted to get rid of the prisoners, but he didn't want to make it easy for this guy from L.A., and it had to be by the book. "Mr. Lynch, I assume you know that this must be brought before the judge for a hearing."

"Yes, of course. A judge in Los Angeles approved it."

"You must think the sheriff of a hayseed county is a yokel who will roll over when a big city lawyer waves a paper in his face. But it doesn't work that way. Up here, you have to follow the rules just like down south." He counted off with his fingers. "First, a judge in a distant county has no jurisdiction here, so this paper is worthless. Second, even if the venue was proper, I see no indication of a judge's decision written on the petition. Third, it does not specify which prisoners are the object of the petition. It says only that prisoners who are Los Angeles policemen must be released." He handed back the petition. "I suspect that when Judge Daley looks at it tomorrow, he will tell you the petition has no authority in this county."

"I can't wait that long," Lynch said. "I want them released now."

"They are charged with the felony crime of kidnapping. I will not release them without the judge's order. I am sure that you will be able to present the petition tomorrow. Now, if you will excuse me, I am closing the office. I will be here tomorrow morning."

The next day, Sheriff Cole stood in his office and looked down to inspect his uniform. He wanted to look good for the upcoming court appearance, and this was the freshly pressed outfit he kept for such occasions. He looked pretty good.

A woman poked her head through the doorway. "Charlie, the bail hearing's ready to start. Time for the prisoners. It looks like the whole valley's here."

"Thanks, Wilma. I'll be right up. Hey Daggett," he called down the hall. "They're ready upstairs. Let's go." He took a shotgun from the rack, shoved three shells in the magazine, another in the chamber, and joined his deputy in front of the cells. "Okay, I'll cover them while you let them out one at a time and cuff them. Good thing there aren't more. We wouldn't have enough cuffs."

One of the prisoners chuckled derisively. "What a pathetic excuse for a police force, barely enough cuffs for the prisoners."

"But we have plenty of shotgun shells to handle all sorts of problems," Daggett responded as he held out the cuffs for the first prisoner.

They got the eight prisoners cuffed and chained together in single file. With Cole leading the parade and Daggett guarding the rear, they marched the men down the hall and up the stairs to the courtroom, where they were seated in the front row behind the bar.

The sheriff scanned the crowded room. Most of the seats were taken. Fred and Alice were in the back row, surrounded by their friends—their cheering section. He wondered how word of the hearing had spread so fast and so far. Not only were the Independence folks here, but he recognized people from the other valley towns, Lone Pine, Big Pine, and even Bishop. He hadn't expected that. Cole turned and faced Judge Daley at the bench.

"Sheriff, I understand you met Mr. Lynch yesterday," the judge said.

Cole nodded at Lynch, standing in front of the judge's bench beside Walt Hess, the Inyo County District Attorney.

The judge got right to it. "Mr. Lynch represents the policemen who you arrested at the roadblock between here and Lone Pine. He is petitioning the court to release these individuals. I want you and Mr. Hess to explain your reasons for the charges and for holding them in the county jail."

Cole didn't want to keep eight out-of-town cops in the two small cells next to his office, but he didn't want to make it easy for the arrogant City lawyer, either. "Your Honor, those men kidnapped Mr. Lukin in front of more than a dozen witnesses. They are a danger to the community and must remain imprisoned for the safety of our citizens."

"Nonsense," the L.A. attorney responded. "Your Honor, those men are not common criminals. They are veteran police officers— loyal and conscientious public servants sent here to investigate the despicable attacks on our aqueduct that supplies water to over five hundred thousand citizens in Los Angeles. They were doing their duty to enforce the law as they understood it. They thought they had the authority to arrest people who had attacked and vandalized the property of the City of Los Angeles. Granted, they may have overstepped their bounds, but they were acting in what they thought was a lawful manner."

"Enforcing the law?" District Attorney Hess said with a note of exasperation. "That's nonsense. Sheriff Cole warned them in front of many witnesses that they had no standing as police in this county and would be breaking the law if they took Mr. Lukin. They ignored the warning and took Mr. Lukin at gunpoint. Their act was kidnapping, pure and simple. That is a felony and as policemen, they knew it."

"Those men are no danger to the community," the L.A. attorney replied. "It would not serve any legitimate purpose for them to be jailed. As police officers, they are not a flight risk, and the Los Angeles Police Department can guarantee that they would appear in court when required."

"Your Honor," Hess said, "if we release these individuals, we will have no way to make them appear for court. They will undoubtedly return to Los Angeles, over two hundred miles away and beyond the jurisdiction of this court. Besides, even if bail is posted, it will be paid by a rich city that would be indifferent to forfeiting it. The people of Inyo County request that we hold them here until trial."

"Your Honor," Lynch said, "if we cannot agree on bail, let me offer a compromise. What if they plead guilty to a lesser charge and pay a fine, and we can all go home?"

Judge Daley glanced at the county D.A. "Mr. Hess, would that be satisfactory?"

"Absolutely not. We can't allow police from another jurisdiction a free hand to come up here and arrest our citizens at will. They broke the law, and they must stand trial for it."

"Mr. Hess," Lynch said. "If you persist in this, I can guarantee that we will tie you up with hearings for years to come. You can feed and house our police officers indefinitely and the trial will never occur."

"Okay, how about a fine of... five thousand dollars per prisoner?" Hess said.

"Enough!" the judge interjected. "Given the situation, I think a fine is a good solution. And, given the gravity of their actions, a fine equal to one year's salary for each man is justified. Mr. Lynch, how much does each of your policemen earn?"

"I'm not sure of the exact number for these specific men. I think it is about eighteen hundred per year." He bent down and jotted on a paper, then faced the judge. "Your honor, that's over fourteen thousand dollars for all eight men. That's not reasonable and is far more than the City can afford in a case like this. A fine of, say, one hundred dollars per man would be fair."

"That's boloney," Hess growled. "Surely, L.A. can pay a fine for their own officers who, you say, were acting in the line of duty when they kidnapped one of our citizens."

"Each of you makes a valid point, and there is room for compromise," the judge said. "Here's my decision. Mr. Lynch, the sheriff will release your men after they each plead guilty to a charge of disturbing the peace and pay a fine equal to one-half of their annual salary."

CHAPTER 24   TABLE TALK

A few months after his attack on the aqueduct, Fred sat in his parlor reading the *Inyo Independent* while he waited for dinner. It was a rare treat to get off his feet and catch up on the valley's news.

"Did you read Carl's letter yet?" Alice called from the kitchen.

"Yeah. Sounds like he's doing okay and likes working in San Francisco."

"He sounds so grown up."

"I'm glad Jake helped him get the job. Working in construction is good experience."

"He's probably a little homesick, and I'm disappointed he won't be able to come home for a while."

"Ahh, it'll do him good," Fred said.

"Easy for you to say. When you were young, you never left home until you joined the army…. Dinner will be ready in just a few minutes."

Fred turned his attention back to the newspaper and stared at the front page picture of William Mulholland inspecting the construction of his new dam in the San Francisquito Canyon north of Los Angeles. The resulting reservoir at the end of the aqueduct would store enough Owens Valley water to meet the city's needs for over a year. Looking at Mulholland's picture made his blood boil. *He takes our water for orange groves and swimming pools in L.A. and drives our valley back to desert.* He wadded up the weekly paper, walked into the kitchen, and threw it in the trash.

"Why did you do that? I haven't finished reading it," Alice said.

"Nothin' in it except stuff about Mulholland and his new dam."

"Did you see the ad for the latest model Ford? It says their newest touring car costs two hundred and ninety-five dollars. They let you pay over several months. We sure could use a new one. The old one's a wreck."

"You're the one that says we can't afford a new one."

"I know," Alice replied. "But even if we can't get a new car, at least we can get out and see a movie. Did you see that ad for a new Harold Lloyd movie? They're showing *Safety Last* next week at the Legion Hall. God knows we could stand a few laughs."

It seemed like a long time since he had laughed, and he didn't feel much levity now. It was hard to work up any enthusiasm for watching some idiot do stupid things on the screen while the DWP was destroying their way of life, but Alice would enjoy getting out. "Yeah, okay. Maybe we can go."

Alice took her apron off. "Dinner's ready. Fried chicken and boiled squash are on the stove. Get a plate and help yourself."

Fred filled his plate and sat down. When Alice took her seat, she sat silently for a moment, watching Fred as he took a bite of chicken.

"Okay," Fred said. "I can tell you're ready to bust if you don't say whatever's on your mind. Out with it."

"You know, this morning when I was in town, Betty told me that everyone is talking about another attack on the aqueduct. The rumor is that there are lots in on it, men from all the towns."

Fred grunted and continued eating.

"You know how stupid that is?" she said, with her voice rising. "It didn't accomplish anything last time except almost get you jailed, and a cop shot in the ear – *by me*! It took the women to save your bacon. You might not be so lucky next time."

Fred issued another grunt. It was hard to think of anything to say. He stabbed another bite of chicken.

"Betty and I talked about it. Then, Grace and a couple of other women came into the store, and they'd heard about it, too. Seems like everybody knows a new attack is planned. Not many secrets in this town. I imagine that half the employees at the DWP office know."

Fred mumbled through a mouthful of chicken, "News to me."

Alice slammed her fork and knife on the table. "Fred Lukin, don't you lie to me! You are no good at it. You're a great rancher, but a terrible liar, so don't even try."

He laughed. "Alice, I love you. We need to go see that movie."

"And don't change the subject! I love you, too, but it's no good if you do something stupid and end up in jail, or worse."

"This is really good chicken."

It was her turn to laugh. "You're not going to get off that easy. Look, you guys are going about this all wrong. You're simply flailing like a cornered animal. A trapped bear snarls and fights, and all it ever gets is dead."

Fred leaned back in his chair and contemplated his wife. "You have a better idea?"

"Yes. Betty and I talked about it. You can't get rid of the DWP by poking it with a sharp stick, and that's what aqueduct blasts are, pokes with a sharp stick. What you need is help from the outside. If the rest of the state knew what was happening here, they would support us. Plus, maybe the DWP would change the way they treat us. You have to get the story out to the rest of the world."

"Okay, but how do we do that?"

"You won't get any place if people view you as anarchists. You have to show that you are ordinary, good citizens. The way to do that is to get everybody, men and women, involved in getting our story out without blowing things up."

"Get everybody involved? Involved in what? Being good citizens and doing nothing will get us nowhere."

"Is there a way to stop the water without blasting and destroying the aqueduct?"

Fred tilted his head back and looked at the ceiling. "Maybe. We could close the gates at the intake up north by Aberdeen. But I think they have guards posted there now."

"Can you cut the flow anywhere else?"

"Lemme think about it."

A week later, Fred sat across the table from Mark Watson in a Bishop coffee shop. He had just finished summarizing Alice's ideas to get men and women from throughout the valley involved. He didn't like the pompous banker and didn't want to work with him, but Watson was the recognized leader of the DWP opposition in the Bishop area, and they needed his participation to get people from the north end of the valley to join in.

"How can we stop the water without a blast?" Watson asked.

"Open the spillway at Alabama Gates."

"Alabama Gates?"

"The floodgates on the aqueduct at the north end of the Alabama Hills between Independence and Lone Pine, about a mile north of that blast in May. We open the floodgates, and the water will flow from the aqueduct east across the valley to the Owens River instead of Los Angeles. If we can hold it open for a few days,

L.A. will howl. It will make the newspapers all over the state. Then we might get favorable action from politicians in Sacramento."

Watson sipped his coffee. "I like the idea, but not sure why we need to have women and families involved."

"It shows the world that we are not a small bunch of radical anarchists. We are regular, law-abiding families who are being mistreated."

Watson rubbed his palms together. "Yeah. That sounds good. It should work." He stood up. "I'll recruit people from this area. Give my regards to your pretty wife."

CHAPTER 25   ALABAMA GATES

On a cold Sunday morning in mid-November, with Murphy in the passenger seat, Fred drove his pickup at the head of a caravan of cars heading south. There were over twenty vehicles with men from all the valley towns. This was like replaying his drive in May to blast the big ditch. But this time, about a mile north of the site of the earlier attack, he turned west off the highway to follow the short track up to Alabama Gates. He had driven past here many times, but he had never been to the gatehouse.

The structure looked like a covered bridge spanning two arched spillways. With its red-tiled roof and four arched windows across a stucco facade, it reminded him of a picture he'd seen of a small Roman building, but one that had been dropped into the sere, rocky landscape of the Alabama Hills. This was where they would open the floodgates, diverting the aqueduct water down the spillways to cascade across the desert back to the Owens River.

Cajoling his old pickup up the road in low gear, he led the procession onto a flat parking area at the aqueduct's edge. As planned, as soon as the caravan stopped, men sprang out of their cars and ran to the gatehouse.

The gatekeeper stood in the doorway, facing the invaders. "What're you guys doing here? You can't come in here."

"Sam, we're takin' over," Fred said.

"No, don't. I'll get in a heap of trouble."

Mark Watson stepped forward. "Stand aside. Even the City doesn't expect you to fight off several dozen men."

The gatekeeper scanned the faces. "I know practically every one of you. I'll have to tell my boss who was here."

"He'll find out anyway," Fred said, "and we'll say that you tried to hold us back."

"Don't do it. As soon as word gets out, a bunch of city cops will come shootin'."

"We're ready for that," Murphy said. "If shootin' starts, you keep your head down."

Sam frowned and shook his head. "You guys are crazy." He went back inside, sat down at a small table and thumbed through the *Police Gazette* magazine he had been reading before the interruption.

The raiders crowded into the small, one-room building. Fred looked at the two huge wheels. "How do you work these, Sam?"

The man stubbornly folded his arms. "You're on your own. I ain't gonna give you instructions."

Standing beside Fred, Murphy said, "Must be like any other valve. Turn clockwise to close and counterclockwise to open. Here, let me try." He grabbed the wheel and grunted with the effort but couldn't make it budge. Fred and another man joined and failed.

"You guys are hopeless," the gatekeeper said disgustedly from his seat. "There's a little locking ratchet behind the wheel. Pull that back first."

Fred laughed. "Thanks, Sam." He felt behind the wheel. "Ah, there it is. Try now."

The wheel turned easily, winding the chains to open the gate. Soon, the sound of water roaring down the spillway drowned the sounds of the men cheering. Another man unlocked the second wheel and opened the other gate. Fred stepped to the window overlooking the spillway. Two huge spouts of water shot east toward the almost-dry bed of the Owens River running south down the center of the valley toward the landlocked Owens Lake.

"You have a phone?" Fred asked.

"Right there." Sam pointed.

Fred got connected to King's Drug Store in Independence. "Hi, Edna. This is Fred. Is Alice there?" A moment later, he said, "We did it. Tell the others to come on down a little later." He paused and listened. "No, nobody was hurt. No trouble. Okay, see you in a while." He hung up and stepped aside for the next guy to make his call. When the last one hung up, Fred said to the gatekeeper, "Okay, Sam, your turn if you have to call somebody at the DWP office."

As Sam stepped to the phone, Murphy, standing at a gatehouse window, exclaimed, "Hey, look at this. "Hardly a drop's goin' down the aqueduct for L.A."

Cheers filled the gatehouse.

About an hour after Sam called the DWP office in Independence, Sheriff Cole and Deputy Daggett arrived at the gatehouse in the sheriff's black and white Nash. They got out of the car, walked to the edge of the spillway, and watched the huge gush of water pour down the spillway into the desert. Cole turned and his eyes swept over the men. "I guess you guys know this is against the law and that you have to close those floodgates."

"We won't do that, Charlie," Fred said. "The water belongs to the people of the valley."

"Fred, that's nonsense, and you know it. The City bought and paid for that water. None of you may like how they got it, or the things they've done since, but your action here is illegal. You are committing trespass, theft, and several other crimes. Either stop this now or I will take your names and charge you." He turned to Daggett. "Deputy, get a notebook out of the car and take names." He paused. "Better bring one for each of us." Within minutes, with a pencil poised over a notebook, Cole scanned the crowd and announced each name as he wrote it down.

Men gathered around him, vying for recognition.

"Hey, sheriff, don't forget me, Vic Carrasco, in Lone Pine."

"Me too, Sid Hart, from Manzanar."

"Put my name down … Paul Walters ."

"Slow down, slow down. We'll get to you," Cole hollered.

He was hurriedly writing names when he spotted a line of cars turning off the highway toward the gatehouse. He lifted his hat and smoothed his sparse hair. What now?

In moments, the cars parked near the spillway. Women and even a few kids poured from the cars, most lugging baskets. People congregated and chattered like it was a holiday celebration. Women spread blankets on the ground and laid out meals that looked enough to feed hundreds. A cold November day. What a strange time for a community picnic, he thought.

"Oh, Lord, don't tell me," Cole said to himself when he spotted Doris with a picnic basket, walking with Alice Lukin and Betty Shapiro, accompanied by Betty's kids, Lester and Estella, and Slim's wife, Grace.

Doris waved to him and set out her picnic in the midst of all the others. "Come on, Charlie. You need to eat something too."

Laughter rippled through the crowd.

He spread his open hands in a gesture of resignation. "Oh, hell, might as well," he said and walked toward Doris's picnic. "Hey Daggett," he called, "go get Sam to join us." Applause and cheers erupted from the picnickers.

Cole was working over a piece of fried chicken when a murmur spread through the crowd. People stood looking toward the highway. He couldn't see what was going on and walked to where a cluster of people were excitedly chattering and pointing. A parade of cars looking like a military convoy turned off the highway in his direction. He guessed they were L.A. guards or police sent to protect the floodgates. *This could get messy.* He'd better intercept them before they get to the gatehouse. He walked down the road, chewing a drumstick.

"Need some company, sheriff?" Mark Watson called.

"No. Stay there," he ordered. "I don't want a war."

He stood in the middle of the road chewing his chicken, waiting for the caravan. The lead car stopped with its bumper inches from his knees. The sheriff tossed his drumstick into the sagebrush and wiped his mouth with his sleeve.

A man in a dark suit and black fedora got out of the car and walked slowly up to him. "You the sheriff?"

"Yes. Sheriff Cole. You are?"

"Agent Raymond Shaw of the Pinkerton Agency."

"Pinkertons, eh? What are you guys doing up here?"

"We're working for the Los Angeles Department of Water and Power and deputized by the Los Angeles Sheriff's Department." The agent gestured with his thumb at the cars behind him. "That's my crew. Two dozen of 'em. We was sent up here when we got word the anarchists was planning to blast the aqueduct again. Good thing we came. It looks like quite a bunch up there."

"That 'bunch' includes women and children, besides men from throughout the valley. My job is to prevent bloodshed, so I want—"

The Pinkerton interrupted. "It doesn't matter what you want. Your job is to enforce the law. Those guys are breaking it and are traitors. I want them all arrested and charged. If you won't do it, we will."

"No!" Cole barked. "I'm going to defuse this situation so no one, including you, gets hurt. You must know what happened when City cops tried to arrest someone up here. One of them got shot — by a woman, no less! I don't want that to happen again."

"What you want doesn't matter. Get out of our way."

Cole turned and looked up the hill. Men now stood shoulder-to-shoulder along the edge of the parking area, most holding rifles. "There are at least sixty well-armed men up there. You may think you can handle them, but, believe me, they want a fight more than you do. For you, this is a job. For them, it's their home, their families, and their lives. I know these people, and know that if you start a battle, not one of you will get out of the valley alive. My best advice is for you to pull back and let this play out. Please turn around so I can work on it." He turned and trudged back up the hill. When he topped the rise, he looked back to witness the Pinkerton's cars turning around and heading down the hill. Applause and cheers echoed from the rocky Alabama Hills.

"Where's Doris's fried chicken? I didn't get to finish my lunch." More cheers filled the air. He had barely sat down when he heard someone say, "Here comes Laird."

Cole watched the district DWP boss park at the bottom of the hill and walk up the road.

The overweight man panted for breath when he reached the top and gasped, "Sheriff."

"Paul. Your goons just left," Cole said.

"I saw them. They'll be available in case they're needed."

"You armed?"

"No, do I need to be?" Laird opened his coat. "See." He scanned the gathering. "Who's in charge here?"

Fred walked up beside the sheriff and said, "We're all in charge. The entire valley's behind us."

"You know," Laird said, "the water you're wasting belongs to the City. It's not hurting a soul going down our ditch to L.A. If we don't take it, it just flows into Owens Lake and dries up."

"What do you mean, 'not hurting a soul'?" Fred demanded. "You've pumped the valley dry and driven people from their farms and homes."

Another man stepped close and stabbed his finger at Laird's chest. "You tell Mulholland that we're gonna stay here 'till they settle with us."

With each poke at his chest, the district DWP boss's eyes widened in fury. He grabbed the man's offending index finger and bent it back until there was an audible 'crack'. The man yowled in pain and fell to his knees.

Men immediately circled and grabbed at Laird. From the crowd came shouts of "Hang him." Others took up the yell with "String him up." and "I'll get a rope." Someone else hollered, "No, throw him in his ditch."

"Get away," Sheriff Cole shouted.

"Let him go," Fred hollered as he joined the fray to help the sheriff extract Laird from the mob.

Finally, Cole yanked the DWP boss loose. "You okay, Paul?"

Laird straightened his coat and dusted off his slacks. "Yeah, I guess so. Thanks."

"You better leave 'til this simmers down," the sheriff said.

"I'm leaving. But they've got to close the gates and go home, or there's going to be hell to pay. You tell them that."

"We're gonna stay here until you settle with us," Fred said.

"Settle? What's to be settled? What is it you're after here? I doubt any of you even know what you want."

"We know," Fred said. "So do you. Straight, honest dealing, and stop drying up the valley. Peaceful negotiations get us nowhere. The water will keep running until you deal with us straight."

Laird faced Cole. "If you can't stop this lawlessness, I'm sure the state militia can." He turned and walked down the hill.

"You know what a mess this'll be if the governor sends the militia?" the sheriff said.

"Maybe that's what we need," Fred replied. "Let's beat Laird to the punch and ask for the militia ourselves. State militia makes it a state affair, instead of just a dispute between L.A. and an obscure valley. We want the governor, state legislature, and Aunt Jane to know what's going on here. If we can do that, maybe it'll put enough pressure on the City to deal fairly with us. Besides, right now, we're sitting ducks for their rent-a-cop Pinkertons and any other thugs they hire. The militia may serve as a shield."

Cole's voice rose in exasperation. "You're crazy. You don't know which side the governor or the militia are on. If it goes wrong, a lot of people can get hurt. You've made your point. Now it's time to go home."

"Sorry to make your job so hard, Charlie, but we're not giving up."

Cole pursed his lips in disgust. "How long's this gonna last?"

"Not sure," Fred replied. "We have a good hand. We'll play it out and see what happens."

Throughout the day, families left and more arrived, making it into an all-day rolling picnic. Late in the afternoon, Fred and Alice stood beside their truck, watching the clusters of people excitedly talking and laughing. Alice stood on her tiptoes and kissed his cheek. "Oh, Fred, this is wonderful—the best social in years."

He put his arm around her. "Yeah. Hope it does some good." He turned toward the mountains. "Sundown. Time for you to go home. I'll stay for the guard watch the first night. You come back tomorrow."

Alice, Betty, Grace, and Betty's two kids squeezed into Betty's car. As they drove away, Mark Watson walked up beside Fred. "A very pretty lady, your wife. You're a lucky man. You staying here tonight?"

"Yeah, I'll probably stay every night."

Watson slapped Fred's shoulder like a buddy. "Guess I gotta head back to Bishop."

CHAPTER 26   HOUSE CALL

Fred had squirmed all night, trying to get comfortable in his sleeping bag. He hadn't slept on the ground like this for years. Despite several saddle blankets on the ground for padding, he lost his battle against the rocks and bumps. It was time to admit defeat and get up. He stood, stretched, and gazed east across the valley at the sky brightening behind the Inyo Mountains. The aroma of frying bacon and boiling coffee filled the crisp morning air. Men stood watching John Callaway prepare breakfast, flipping eggs in an enormous pan of bubbling bacon grease on a stove-top, jerry-rigged over the open campfire.

When Fred joined the breakfast spectators, Slim thrust a steaming cup into his hand. "You look like you need this."

"Thanks." Fred held the tin cup in both hands for warmth. "What with the bootleg hooch last night and sleeping on rocks, I feel like I need a hospital, but the coffee will keep me goin' till then." He edged closer to the fire. "Cold this morning."

Callaway flipped eggs, two at a time, in the bubbling fat. "Good huntin' weather. I got a four-pointer up in Monache. You go this year?"

"Nah," Fred said. "Couldn't get away. That stuff you're cooking ready yet?"

"Grab a plate. The bacon, eggs, and camp-fried potatoes are ready, but you'll have to wait for the biscuits."

Carrying the tin plate piled high with his breakfast, Fred followed Slim over to where Murphy sat eating at the edge of the spillway with his legs hanging over the lip.

"What do ya think'll happen now?" Murphy asked.

"Who knows," Fred replied. "L.A. can't afford to let this go on very long. They gotta do somethin'. Those Pinkertons backed down yesterday, but you can bet they're hangin' back waiting for their chance."

"Seems like they won't do much with a crowd here, 'specially with women," Murphy said.

Fred took a swig of lukewarm coffee from his tin cup and wiped his mouth on his sleeve. "That's what I figured when we planned this, but not so sure after seein' that bunch of hired thugs. When the powerful are threatened, women are just easier targets. Remember, just before the war, there was that massacre of miners and families in Colorado. They shot up entire families with machine guns. And look what happened to the suffrage women who tried to get the vote."

"Think we should call it off?" Slim asked.

"I worry, but we can't back down now," Fred replied. "If they really want to fight it out, we have a heck of a military position here. The main approach is uphill across an open field of fire, and we have a steep, rocky hill behind us. Would like to a had a position like this when we fought the Germans in France. Plus, we got the aqueduct as a hostage."

"Watchya think that is?" Slim asked, gesturing with his chin at a string of cars turning off the highway in their direction. "Think it's the Pinkertons?"

Fred watched for a moment. "Don't look the same as that bunch from yesterday. We'd better get ready just in case."

With two fingers in his mouth, Murphy let loose with a shrill whistle that got everybody's attention.

Fred pointed at the approaching cars and shouted. "Better get ready. Might be cops. But in case they're not, keep your guns outta sight till we need them."

Men lined up at the edge of the parking lot and watched the small convoy struggle up the steep road.

"Let's go see what they want," Fred said as he walked with Slim and Murphy down the road. He waited in the middle of the road about fifty yards down the hill.

The lead car stopped, and a man stuck his head out the window. "Is this where the locals captured the aqueduct?"

"Might be. Who are you?" Fred asked.

The man stuck his hand out the window with his press card. "Jack Webley, L.A. Examiner," he said cheerily. "I'm here to report on the water war."

"Water war, huh? Never thought it was a war." Fred offered his hand. "I'm Fred Lukin. I run a cattle spread near Independence. The rest of these guys reporters, too?"

"The whole bunch—from most of the papers in Southern California."

This is what they were after—get the story out and tell the world what was happening to the valley. "Welcome," Fred said. "Drive up to the flat where the other cars are parked." He stepped aside to let the cars pass.

By the time he had walked back to the top, the newsmen had already begun button-holing the locals. With notepads open, they questioned anyone who looked like they might answer. Most of the valley men had never met a city reporter, much less been interviewed by one, and they stood with serious expressions, nervously answering the deluge of questions.

The reporter from the Examiner spotted Fred and approached with his notepad ready. "Mr. Lukin, you willing to answer a few questions?"

"If I can. Hadn't finished my breakfast when you guys arrived. Wanna join me?"

Webley's eyes lit up. "Sure. We drove all night. Haven't had anything to eat. Got enough for the others?"

"Hey, John, can we feed these guys too?" Fred yelled at the cook.

"Got plenty. Biscuits are ready now."

A cheer erupted from the reporters who lined up alongside their interview subjects for a camp breakfast.

With Webley at his side, Fred stood in line for a second go at breakfast and then resumed his seat at the edge of the spillway.

Webley watched the water cascading freely while he ate. He pointed with his fork. "Lotta water being wasted there, just running into the desert. But it doesn't make exciting reading at the breakfast table."

Fred gave a low chuckle. "This is as much excitement as we want. Small-town people live quiet lives."

"My readers want some action."

"Maybe an old-fashioned gunfight to lighten up the morning paper for somebody in L.A.?"

"Yeah, that's it."

"You and me at dawn?" Fred asked.

"I have a better idea. You and Bill Mulholland at twenty paces."

"No deal. That old crow's too dangerous. He wants all of us dead."

"For sure," the reporter agreed. "He's famous for saying they should hang you all, but there aren't enough trees left in this valley."

"He should know. He's the one that killed the trees," Fred said. "That's what you need to write about–what's happening to the crops and people here."

"Which people?"

Fred pointed. "That's Sid Hart. Raises apples and pears at Manzanar, a few miles up the road. His orchard's almost dead for lack of water. Talk to him, he'll show you around, then you tell the world what you've seen."

Fred and Webley continued talking as they ate breakfast. More people from the towns and ranches drove in to join the crowd. They were just finishing breakfast when Fred felt a familiar touch on his shoulder and looked up. "Mr. Webley, this is my wife, Alice."

Webley stood up and offered his hand. "An honor to meet you, Mrs. Lukin. I write for the Los Angeles Examiner."

"Please sit down. I'll join you," Alice said.

"Thank you, but I should interview some other folks."

After the reporter departed, Alice sat down next to Fred at the edge of the spillway. "Have a comfortable night in your sleeping bag?"

"Great. Soft saddle blankets, better than a feather bed. You?"

"My night was interesting. I hadn't been home long before Mark Watson showed up at our door."

"Watson? What'd he want?"

"You have to ask?" she said in disbelief. "You know his reputation as a Lothario. He thinks every woman he sees is fair game."

"Damn! Sonofabitch!" He slammed his breakfast plate down. "I'll kill the guy."

"Fred, calm down!"

"What happened?"

"I sure as heaven didn't let him in. I kept the door locked and got a shotgun. He finally gave up and went away. I drove into town and spent the night at Betty's house."

With fury etched on his face, he scanned the area and spotted the banker by his car at the lower end of the parking lot, holding court, talking and laughing with a group of people. Fred stalked rapidly in that direction.

"No, Fred, don't! Leave it alone," Alice cried as she chased after him.

It was too late. "You son-of-a-bitch," Fred growled when he reached Watson.

Watson gave a puzzled look. "Fred, what's wrong?"

"You tried to attack my wife," Fred growled as he drew his fist back.

Watson's eyes widened, and his face paled as he held up a hand to shield a blow. "No, no. This is a misunderstanding."

"No misunderstanding!" Fred growled as he swung at Watson's jaw, knocking him back against his car.

Before Fred could swing again, two men grabbed his arms and pulled him back as a crowd quickly gathered to see what the commotion was about.

Watson rubbed his swelling jaw as he straightened up. "You're crazy," he mumbled. "Hold him," he said to the two men, and it was his turn to strike.

The men holding Fred yanked him out of the way and released their grips.

Watson glared at the three men, then noticed the onlookers crowding around. "Did you see this unprovoked attack?" he asked in a resounding voice. "This man is dangerous, a menace to the community. The sheriff should have put him away a long time ago."

Alice stepped next to Fred, put her arm around his waist, and spoke loudly to the crowd. "Fred was not unprovoked. Last night, when Fred spent the night here, this man," pointing at Watson, "tried to get into my house when he figured I was alone. I grabbed a shotgun and made sure he could see it through a window. That's what it took to get rid of him."

A sprinkling of clapping, mainly from the women, spread through the spectators.

The banker glanced around the crowd with eyes wide with fear, and his voice shook. "That's a lie. Yesterday, when I left here, I drove straight to Bishop. I certainly did not go to the Lukin ranch or disturb this woman."

"I do not lie," Alice responded. "He kept shaking the door and yelling for me to let him in."

"Mrs. Lukin misunderstood. I thought Fred was home and wanted to talk some business with him."

"First, you said you didn't go there. Then you say you went there to see Fred. Which is it?" Slim asked while standing behind Fred and Alice.

"Yeah, which is it?" someone shouted from the crowd.

Watson stood straight and lifted his chin, looking every inch the regal aristocrat. "Who are you going to believe? I've served this community all my life, lending you money, supplying you with hardware, and providing jobs. Who is worthy of your trust, me, a respected banker and merchant, or this rag-tag family making wild accusations? This woman shot a policeman."

A man in the crowd shouted, "If she shoots at cops, you oughta know better than to bother her." Laughter rippled through the crowd.

"I believe Alice," Murphy Hamhurst announced.

Henry Olivera stepped up beside Murphy. "So do I. Mark just told us he didn't go to Fred's ranch and then said he did. Doesn't sound very trustworthy to me."

A man stepped forward. "I've trusted Mark Watson and his bank with my money my whole life. There is not a more honest man in this valley."

"Maybe you trust him with your money, but you better not trust him with your wife," another man shouted, followed by more laughter.

The air filled with shouts, pro and con.

"He's a good man," one man shouted.

"And he tries to prove it to every woman in the valley," another answered.

"I'm not going to listen to this," Watson growled. He got in his car and gunned it down the hill toward the highway.

By midday, the furor of the brief fight had died down, and women arranged their contributions to the community buffet on tables hauled in and the tailgates of the pickups.

Reporter Webley took a seat on the ground beside Fred and Alice, watching women exchange recipes and news while men passed bottles of home-brewed beer and bootleg liquor to anyone brave enough to sample it. "My God, look at all that food. I tried to count the number of people here. I got past six hundred and gave up. But this spread could feed twice that number."

"Yep," Fred said, "a good turnout, ranchers, merchants, families, they're all here. Not just a small bunch of radical anarchists like the DWP wants you to think."

The conversation was interrupted when someone shouted, "Here comes Sheriff Cole."

When the sheriff parked and got out of his car, somebody else hollered, "Hey, Charlie, you're late for lunch."

"Not here for the food," he answered. He waved a handful of papers. "I have summons for you scofflaws whose names I took yesterday. They require you to appear in court to answer charges of trespass and damage to the property of the City of Los Angeles. Judge Daley set the court date for your appearance as December first. If you plead guilty, you will be fined. If you plead innocent, you will have a court date set to be tried on the charges. Come and get it when I call your name."

As he handed out the summons to the grumbling recipients, a rancher from Bishop shouted, "Hey, Charlie, watch this." The man held the summons over his head and tore it into pieces, then ceremoniously tossed the bits into the water gushing from the floodgates.

Cole shook his head in exasperation. "Bill, you still have to show up and answer the summons."

Other men copied Bill's action and threw their torn-up summonses into the water.

"Charlie, no hard feelings," a farmer from Big Pine proclaimed. "We know you have to do this."

"That's why you elected me—to arrest you when you deserve it," he shouted back.

"It's those flatlanders from L.A. that should be arrested," a man yelled.

"Could be, but here's other news," Cole answered in his deep voice. "Yesterday, after Ed Laird threatened to call for the state militia to take charge here, Judge Daley and I called his bluff and sent a message to Governor Richardson in Sacramento, appealing for him to send the state militia."

The air filled with invective and accusations.

Cole waved his arms in the air and bellowed. "Quiet, quiet. Listen up." The shouting died down. "The militia will bring the attention of the whole state to our valley. Papers all over California will carry the story, and every family will learn what has been happening here. No longer will the story be told only from L.A.'s point of view. We will appeal to the state for help in dealing with them."

"We won't need help after we get shot up by the militia," someone hollered, and others joined in shouting down the sheriff.

Fred and Alice joined Cole. Fred's voice boomed and the crowd quieted. "The sheriff's right. This is what we're after. Show that we are united, peaceful, law-abiding citizens, not a bunch of radical anarchists, and the militia won't have reason to shoot. Let people all over California know what is happening here—that the City is taking our water and destroying our way of life. If we do it peacefully, we can get the support from the rest of the state, and Los Angeles will back down."

"What will happen when the state militia arrives?" Alice quietly asked her husband.

"Don't know," he replied. "I just hope some trigger-happy fool doesn't do something stupid and have it blow up in our faces."

"When will they get here?"

"Don't know that either," Fred said. "It'll take a while for them to mobilize and get over here." *God, what have we gotten ourselves into?* The image of the Ludlow massacre filtered through his mind. *Can we stop this before disaster takes over, or is this a train with no brakes gaining speed down the tracks?* It was a big risk. His mind jumped to Watson. With him gadding about, he didn't want Alice to be alone. "I think I'll stay home tonight," he said.

"There's no need for that," Alice said. "If you're worried about Watson showing up again, don't. I'll stay at Betty's."

"One night on the ground is enough. I'm ready for my own bed," he replied.

CHAPTER 27   SCOFFLAW CARNIVAL

Camping's overrated, Fred thought as he pulled into the Alabama Gates parking area late the next morning. Sleeping in his own bed with his wife sure beat fighting the rocky ground.

Slim and Murphy, both walking unsteadily, met him as he got out of his pickup. "You missed some good firewater last night," Slim said.

"Good thing. No headache like I get from your homemade stuff. What else happened after I left?"

"Not much," Murphy said. "Deciding who makes the best moonshine, and a lot of talk about Watson."

"I hope it was all bad," Fred said.

"Nah. There was more guys from Bishop. They think he's great, but no one got shot and not even a fight," Murphy said.

"Probably because nobody could stand up after all the booze," Slim said.

"Any sign of city cops or those Pinkertons?" Fred asked.

"No, but there's a guy here from the governor's office. Come on, I'll introduce you," Murphy said.

Murphy led Fred to an older-looking man with gray hair who stood watching the water roar out of the floodgates. "Mr. McClure, this is Fred Lukin, who helped organize this… a… ah… get-together."

McClure extended his hand. "Good to meet you. I'm state engineer, Wilbur McClure. The Governor received a request from Judge Daley and Sheriff Cole for the state militia. He sent me instead. I drove all day yesterday and a good part of the night." The engineer spread his arms. "As you can see, I'm not the state militia. The Governor didn't want to take the drastic step of calling up the state troops unless it was absolutely necessary. I already talked to the judge and sheriff when I came through Independence, then came down here to see for myself."

Fred felt both relief and disappointment. For now, at least, he didn't need to worry about the militia shooting things up, but one state engineer wouldn't bring the news coverage they were after. "Glad you're here. What do you want to see?"

"Governor Richardson wants to know what's going on. The starting point is to meet people and see what's on their minds. Conditions here, what your dispute with Los Angeles is about, and how things can be peacefully resolved. I plan on staying a while, and I'll travel around the valley for a couple of days, talk to people on both sides, and report back to the Governor."

"I'll introduce you around. Later today, there will be lots of food. You have to stay for that." Fred said.

"I plan on it. I understood you were camped here, so I brought my sleeping bag. I'll rough it with everyone else. That'll give me a chance to hear from folks."

The afternoon banquet was well underway when a convoy of cars, buses, and even a horse trailer turned off the highway toward the aqueduct gatehouse. People crowded to the edge of the parking area to watch. Spirited chatter rippled through the crowd and people pointed excitedly at vehicles pulling into the lot with 'Fox Studios' painted on their sides. A chauffeur sprang out of the Packard touring car that led the parade and opened the back door. A tall man dressed in a white, impeccably tailored western-style suit with dark piping on the pockets and a matching tall-crowned western hat, stepped out of the car to the enthusiastic roar of the spectators.

Another man rushed from the other side of the car and shouted in the tones of a circus announcer, "Ladies and gentlemen, Fox Studios presents the biggest movie star in America... Mr. Tom Mix!"

The crowd erupted with cheers that reverberated as if the rocky hills themselves were a giant megaphone.

As soon as the ovation quieted, the announcer continued. "Here in your own Alabama Hills, we are shooting a new picture starring," he paused, "starring the incomparable Tom Mix." There was more shouting, and he waited for it to die down. "For your pleasure, Mr. Mix will perform some of his famous riding tricks on his talented friend, Tony, the Wonder Horse." Tony had been unloaded from the trailer, and his groom led the black horse to the star, who posed with his mount as reporters snapped photos of the famous pair.

The announcer waved his arms for attention. "And… and, for your musical entertainment, Fox Studios presents," he gestured to the bus, "our talented company, The Mexicali Mariachis." Immediately, a string of beautiful young women wearing brightly colored Mexican costumes danced and swayed down the steps of the bus, swinging their full skirts to the polka-like beat of the mariachi band that followed them out of the studio bus.

The music paused, and Tom Mix sprang onto Tony, waving his big hat. The studio crew pushed the crowd back to provide an area for the star to perform his tricks. He trotted to the end of the cleared area, waved his hat again, and, with his horse galloping at full speed, stood straight up on the saddle. The crowd cheered, and he then stood on one leg as the horse continued running. At the end of the short course, with Mix waving from his saddle, Tony took a bow with both front knees on the ground. The pair performed a few more tricks while the band played, and for the closing act, Tony danced in rhythm to the Mexican music.

While the mariachi band strolled through the gathering, the girls swayed and danced. The girls paired off and held each other, dancing among the local spectators. As they passed by Fred and Alice, without missing a beat, one of the dark-haired girls grabbed Fred, and another girl pulled Jake into the crowd. Cheers, applause, and a few whistles filled the air. "Come on, folks, all of you dance!" cried the studio announcer. The other mariachi dancers twirled among the crowd and grabbed more partners, and wives pulled their husbands into the swaying throng and the couples danced or at least tried to give their best imitation.

Fred wasn't sure what to do and tried hard not to step on the pretty girl's toes. He failed and apologized. She laughed. "That's okay. I'm used to it."

Her unaccented native English was a surprise. He assumed she was from Mexico and probably spoke no English. "Where are you from?" he asked.

She giggled lightly. "Glendale, north of Los Angeles. Bet you thought I was Mexican."

He smiled and tried not to step on her toes.

She laughed and did a pirouette. "My parents are from Iowa."

"You sure don't look it."

Another graceful pirouette. "Makeup, wigs, and costumes do wonders. Most of us girls are trying to get into movies. I got this job till I get an acting part. My parents hate it."

Over the girl's shoulder, Fred saw Mark Watson approach Alice, who was standing at the edge of the dance area. Watson said something, and she shook her head. He grasped her arm and pulled her into the dance. She struggled unsuccessfully to pull away.

Fred released the young lady and pushed through the crowd toward Alice and Watson. "Don't you touch my wife!" he thundered and pulled Alice away. He stood with his fists balled, ready in a fighter's stance.

Alice stepped between the two men and, with both hands on his chest, pushed her husband away. "Fred, no. Let it go. This is a party."

Watson stepped back and carefully straightened his tie and thundered to the people who had gathered around and pointed at Fred. "This man is crazy. The lady asked me to dance with her. Of course, I couldn't refuse."

People looked at Alice for her response. She faced the spectators and answered at the top of her voice. "That is not true. I did not ask him to dance. He asked me. When I said no, he grabbed me and forced me." She turned toward her offender. "Mr. Watson, just yesterday you lied about coming to our ranch. Surely, you did not expect everyone to have forgotten that."

"You're imagining things." His mouth twisted into a malignant frown. "I have never been to your ranch."

Fred stepped forward, nose-to-nose with the banker. "You son-of-a-bitch, you can't call my wife a liar," and drew his fists back to strike.

Alice pushed him back again. The movie studio announcer hastened into the no-man's-land between the would-be combatants and hollered. "Ladies and gentlemen, please join us in singing our patriotic rendition of everyone's favorite, 'God Bless America'." He turned, raised both arms in the air, and signaled the rhythm for his mariachi band in the distinctly non-mariachi song.

While people turned toward the band and sang, Alice pulled Fred away from the cluster surrounding Watson. She steered him to his truck and pushed some pots and platters aside on the truck bed. "Sit," she ordered as she pushed him onto the tailgate. "Now, if you will promise not to act like a mad dog and pick a fight, I'll promise not to speak or dance with anyone else for the next ten minutes."

He managed a weak smile. "What happens after ten minutes?"

Alice laughed. "Depends on how you behave. If you're not peaceful, I may just run away with Mr. Watson."

"Yeah? I'm goin' to pound that guy."

"Remember, I said you have to behave. Now eat some of this good food and don't go making big eyes at those cute girls."

"If you expect me to behave, the least you can do is get me some of Slim's hooch."

"If it'll help," she said and trotted off to find Slim and his endless supply of home-distilled liquor.

Sitting on the tailgate, Fred watched the people eating their barbecue and listened to the lively music while the dancers in colorful full skirts bounced and twirled among the diners.

"It's a nice scene, isn't it?" It was the voice of the state engineer, interrupting Fred's thoughts.

"Mr. McClure! You like the party? Have you learned anything about our valley?"

"A lot. What is most apparent is how many people support this..." he swung his arm around, indicating the crowd and the water pouring out of the floodgates, "movement that has been described elsewhere as an insurrection by anarchists and radicals. I've been pleasantly surprised how... ah... normal everyone is. Honest American citizens protesting what they think is unjust treatment by the large metropolis."

"That's a nice way to put it. But you say, 'what they think is unjust treatment'. Do you think we're wrong?"

"I'm going to be here a few more days. I'll talk to more people on both sides and see for myself what is happening and make my report."

"I suppose that's the most we can ask," Fred said. "We recognize that a city as big as L.A. needs water, and we are willing to share what we have. But we need some help to stop them from taking it all."

"That's reasonable. The governor will hear that too." McClure extended his hand to shake. "It was good to meet you."

As McClure walked away, Slim arrived and thrust a fruit jar in front of his face. "Your wife said you needed this to calm you down and keep you from picking a fight."

"I didn't pick a fight," Fred groused. "That son-of-a-bitch picked it when he went after my wife. I'd like to pound him."

"Don't blame you. It's funny, half the folks in the valley think he can do no wrong. The other half think he's Satan, and he's convinced he's God." Slim paused. "But forget about him." He gestured with his chin at the man walking away, "Think McClure will do us any good?"

Fred gazed into the November sky, thinking it over. "Hope so. We just have to wait and see if the Governor will help us slow down L.A."

CHAPTER 28   DITCH SHARES

It had been almost a year since the occupation of Alabama Gates. There had been no action from the governor. Nevertheless, the valley had been relatively peaceful. On a cool, clear Saturday in early fall, Alice felt like she could bubble over with happiness as she walked into Shapiro's General Store.

"Good afternoon, all," she said to the other women waiting in line for Betty to fill their Saturday orders.

Betty glanced up from the cash register where she was ringing up a purchase. "You sound cheery today."

"Of course, I'm cheery. It's such a beautiful day. It's a relief to get a cool day like this. I feel like dancing."

"It's okay for you to dance, but don't let my students see you," Agnes Brice, the woman standing in front of the cash register, said. "When we have nice days like this, the kids can't sit still. I'm constantly telling them to pay attention."

Betty laughed. "Well, I remember when we were in ninth grade, you were always the one Mrs. Cragen had to scold for daydreaming."

"How would you know? You were too busy flirting with Roy Pool to notice," Agnes retorted.

"Speaking of flirting," said Ruby Plack, standing in line behind Agnes, "are Helen Schaffer and Carl still an item?"

"No, I don't think so," Alice replied. "I think they grew apart after Jake got him that job in San Francisco and the Schaffers moved to Visalia. I know he got a couple of letters from her when they first moved. I'm guessing he might have met a girl up there, but he doesn't tell us anything on those rare occasions when he writes."

"So typical of boys not to say anything," Ruby commented.

When Betty finished with the grocery bill, Agnes stepped close to Alice and spoke in a hushed tone. "I've been dying to ask what's going on out where you live. I heard Murphy Hamhurst agreed to sell to the DWP, and others have sold options. Is it true?"

Alice turned pale, her mouth quivered, and her eyes opened wide like saucers. "That can't be true. Where did you hear it?"

"Just gossip going around. I can't believe it either, but thought I'd ask."

After finishing her shopping, Alice drove slowly home, wanting to delay telling Fred about Murphy selling out. His neighbor and close friend selling to the City and not saying a thing. He'd be more than hurt. He'd be furious.

As soon as she entered the house, Alice sat at the kitchen table to unlace her high-heeled shoes and slipped them off with a relieved sigh. In her bare feet, she busied herself putting away the morning dishes left to dry earlier that morning.

Fred sat at the table, watching his wife. "Something bothering you?"

She turned, leaned with her back to the sink, and massaged a tea towel as she often did when nervous. Her lips trembled, the corners of her mouth turned down, and tears filled her eyes. "Agnes Brice told me that Murphy agreed to sell to the City, and others sold options."

"You sure?"

"Betty and Ruby heard her, too. I don't know if it's true."

As the news sank in, Fred's face turned to the high ruddy shade that signaled his fury. He slapped his hand against the table and shouted, "That bastard!" The news of his neighbor selling hit like a body blow. He had trusted Murphy, and his closest neighbor had said nothing. The least he could do was tell him. Rage took hold. It was like the rage he felt back in the war when he wanted to destroy every enemy soldier that came charging across the no-man's-land, intent on killing him.

He slammed the door as he stormed out. Minutes later, his pickup kicked up a cloud of dust as he pulled up in front of Murphy's house.

In response to his pounding, Murphy's wife opened the door.

"Where is that S-O-B?" he demanded before she could say anything.

She stepped back with her hand over her mouth, eyes wide in shock. "Fred, whatever is the matter?" she asked in a frightened voice. "Murphy is out in the barn."

Fred spun around and stalked toward the barn. "You son-of-a-bitch," he growled when he found Murphy stacking hay bales.

"What the hell?" Murphy said, holding onto a hay bale as a shield as he retreated from his enraged neighbor.

"You bastard!" Fred shouted. "You agreed to sell to the DWP without even telling me."

Murphy set the bale down and stared quizzically at Fred. "What in the world are you talking about?"

"I'm talking about you selling out."

"That's crazy. Calm down and tell me what's going on."

Fred stepped back and looked skeptically at his friend. "You're not selling? Really?"

"Of course not! Where'd you get that idea?"

Fred sat down on a hay bale and ran his hand across his face. "Alice heard it at the store. Agnes Brice told her you were selling out."

"That's a lie," Murphy said. "But we need to find out what's going on. If the DWP got my shares and some others, they would be close to voting control. That's what they did to a couple of ditch companies up in Bishop. They got control, closed the ditch, and diverted the water to the aqueduct. That killed every ranch on that canal."

"Do you think any of the others mighta sold?"

"Seems like we would've heard," Murphy replied. "That sort of stuff gets around pretty fast. Hard to keep secrets around here."

The sound of a car arriving interrupted them, and Murphy stuck his head out the barn door. "Hey, Slim, we're in here."

"You look worried," Fred remarked as Slim came through the barn door.

"I am," Slim replied. "Woody at the gas station said he heard Boyd and Stevens sold options on their ditch shares."

"Did he mention me?" Murphy asked.

"No, should he? Don't tell me you're thinkin' of sellin'."

"No, but Alice heard it at the store this morning," Murphy replied.

"Sure strange that these rumors about sales are suddenly going around town *now*," Fred said.

"You sound pretty calm about it," Murphy said. "You were ready to kill me a while ago."

"Yeah. Somebody selling out is bad, but when I heard you sold, I really felt double-crossed."

"Wasn't me, but we need to find out," Murphy said. "Come on, let's go ask Russell Boyd. Go in my pickup."

Slim and Murphy stood back while Fred knocked on Boyd's door. There was a rustling of the curtains in the window and seconds later, the door swung open. "Hi, Etta. Is Russell here?"

The woman positioned herself in the doorway so they couldn't see much beyond her heavy-set frame. Her eyes darted nervously left and right. "Ah, ah, no, Fred, he ain't here. Can I take a message?"

"Where can we find him?"

"He left the house a while ago. I don't know where he went."

The three men got back into the pickup, and as they drove away, Fred glanced back at Boyd's house and saw a face peeking out a window. "Looks like him. Etta was real nervous. He's trying to avoid us."

"If he is, it's as good as telling us he's sellin' out. The bastard!" Slim said. "Shall we go back?"

"Nah, go ahead to Clay's place. See what he says," Fred replied.

Murphy followed the rough dirt road to the last ranch on the ditch and pulled into the farmyard in front of the run-down clapboard house. In response to Fred's knock, Clay Stevens opened the door.

"Hi, Fred, Murph, Slim. Come on in," the elderly rancher said as he stood aside.

All three removed their hats as they entered.

Fred stared at Clay, searching for his words. The old man found his first. "I figure I know why you've come."

"Yeah, why?" Murphy asked belligerently.

"Take it easy, Murph. Hear me out. I'm getting way too old to run this here spread. Me and Mona figured it was time to get out. We don't got no kids to take it over, and with the City's threats hanging over everything, nobody will buy a place like this. The City made a good offer, and we took it. We'll get enough so that with what we got saved in the Inyo Bank, we can get a place in town for the two of us and live it out."

"Damn!" Slim exclaimed.

Fred ran the possibilities through his mind. If he had known that Clay wanted to sell, could he have done anything to keep it out of the City's hands? There was no way he could swing it by himself, and he didn't know about the others. He slapped his hat against his thigh. "Damn, Clay, you shoulda talked to us first. We mighta thought of a way to keep it away from the City."

"I'm sorry about this," Clay said. "I've wrestled with it for a long time. I just can't do the work no more, and Mona's been after me to get out."

"Is it for sure done, or is there still a way to get out of the deal?" Fred asked. "We heard you sold an option on your ditch shares to the City. That doesn't sound too solid."

"I ain't no lawyer, but options give the City the right to buy, and the seller's hog-tied. This is worse. Not an option. I signed to sell—land, water rights, and ditch shares, the whole shebang. It's done."

Fred looked at the floor and shook his head. "What about Boyd? He sell too? The word is, he optioned his ditch shares."

"Hadn't heard that," Clay replied. "Have to ask him."

The three visitors turned without a word and walked back to the pickup. "Back to Boyd's?" Murphy asked.

"Yeah. Russell's there. He's got to face us sometime," Fred replied.

The three ranchers returned to Boyd's farmhouse. In response to Fred's insistent pounding, the lady answered the door again.

"Etta, we know he's here. I saw him peek through the window when we drove away. He's gotta talk to us sometime."

She pursed her lips. "Wait here." The door slammed.

Angry voices flew from the back of the house, and after a short delay, the door opened. A tall man with a day's rough growth of beard and an ample belly hanging over his belt stood in the doorway. "What'd you guys want?" he asked with a drunken slur.

"Russell, you look like hell," Fred said. "Can we come in?"

"No. We can talk here."

"We heard you mighta optioned your ditch shares," Murphy said.

"None of your business," Boyd said.

What a temptation to slug him. "It's a lot of our business," Fred thundered. "We're the other guys with shares in the ditch the City's trying to take over."

"I optioned my one share, big deal! It won't hurt you a bit. The DWP gets one of seven. There's still six shares left, so what are you belly-achin' about?"

"No, dammit!" Slim declared. "Clay just told us he's selling his place to the City, his ditch share along with it."

Boyd's mouth dropped, and he looked dumbstruck. "I... I didn't know." He looked at his fingers like he was counting. "Anybody else?"

"Only five shares left," Fred said, "my two, and one each for Murph, Slim, and Henry Olivera."

Boyd looked relieved. "Look, I never wanted you guys to get hurt by this. The DWP paid good for the option. They may not exercise it, and I still get to keep what they already paid me. What with the price of beef down and all, I can really use the money."

On the way back to the truck, Murphy said, "Wonder what the City will do with two shares."

"They'll do everything they can to get two more for control and drive us all out," Fred replied.

CHAPTER 29   SHRINKING WORLD

Fred watched helplessly through the acrid smoke as Magon laughed, danced, and shadow-boxed around a pile of burning cow carcasses. In slow motion, Fred turned and watched through a window as Mark Watson and Alice walked away, holding hands. He pounded helplessly on the window to call her back. The pounding continued, and as he woke, he realized someone was pounding on the kitchen door. He glanced to see Alice curled on her side, asleep. He slid out of bed, trying not to wake her, slipped on his pants, and headed for the door. In the kitchen, the glowing radium dial on the wall clock showed ten minutes to three.

Grace Berks stood at the door wearing a coat thrown over her robe. Sobbing, with tears streaming down her face, she said, "Fred, you've got to come quick. Slim's collapsed. He's on the floor. I couldn't move him."

"I'll get my coat and tell Alice."

"I'm right here. I heard. I'm coming too," Alice said as she pulled a coat over her flannel nightgown and struggled into her shoes.

"You drive over?" Fred asked.

"Yes."

"We'll go in your car." The three hastened through the frigid January air to the Berks' car. Fred drove with the two women sitting in the back.

"He got up to go to the bathroom," Grace explained between her sobs as they bumped over the rough road to the Berks' ranch. "When he came back, he grabbed his chest and fell down beside the bed. He's too heavy to move. I didn't want to leave him alone, but I had to get help. Hamhursts are closer, but they're away."

"I'm sure he'll be all right," Alice said to reassure her friend as she hugged her.

When they arrived at the ranch house, Slim was sprawled face down on the bedroom floor. The big man groaned as Fred struggled to turn him over. His eyes fluttered open, and he spoke just above a whisper. "I'll be okay, I just need to rest awhile."

"Let's get you into bed," Fred said. "Think you can do it if I help?"

"Don't think so," Slim croaked.

Fred grasped the sick man's shoulders and gently tried to lift. But strong as he was, he knew he couldn't get Slim's substantial bulk onto the bed alone and doubted the two women would be much help. He stood and looked down at his friend. "I'll have to leave you there while I get Doc Woodin. Grace, get some blankets to keep him warm 'till I bring the doctor."

As he drove away in Grace's car, Fred cursed that not a single one of the ranches this far from town had a phone. In town, after his insistent knocking, the sleepy doctor finally opened his door. "Doc, you've got to come," Fred said. "Slim Berks collapsed."

"I'll get my bag and follow in my car."

At the ranch, Fred led the doctor through the house to the bedroom. Alice and Grace sat on the floor beside the still man, hugging each other. Dr. Woodin kneeled, felt for a pulse, and moved his stethoscope around Slim's chest. He sat silently for a moment, looked up at Fred, and gently shook his head. Grace's mouth turned down and trembled as tears silently dripped off her nose.

After the burial ceremony, the mourners assembled at the Masonic Hall for remembrances and refreshments. Fred, Murphy, Henry, and Jake, four of the six-member pallbearer team, sat at a table, eating cake and sipping punch.

"Need some more fortification in your punch?" Henry asked as he waved a jug of Slim's homemade booze in the air. Silently, each man pushed his glass forward.

"This hooch would be pretty good if it wasn't messed up with this God-awful punch," Murphy said.

"Shh," Henry hushed. "The ladies will hear you and somebody'll get her feelings hurt."

"You gotta have the punch. It's required on these occasions," Fred said.

Murphy laughed. "It musta been made by the undertaker's wife—to kill us all so her husband will get more business."

"Damn, that casket was heavy. I worried I might drop it before we got to the grave," Henry said.

"He *was* quite a load," Jake said.

Fred took a swig and struggled to speak past the booze's sting. "Grace is a good cook, and Slim ate well. Maybe a little too well."

"What'll you guys do now about your ditch now that Slim's gone?" Jake asked. "Grace won't be able to help maintain it. Can you keep going?"

Fred chugged some more hooch and coughed. "It's goin' to be tough to keep the water flowin' without Slim's help. Just me, Murph, and Henry to maintain it."

Murphy nodded. "The problem'll be if Grace sells out to someone else who won't do their share, especially if it's the DWP." He tilted his head toward Henry. "It'll be the worst for Henry, squeezed between Slim's place and Boyd and Stevens below him."

Henry's voice shook when he spoke. "Talk about suckin' at the hind tit, that's me. If the DWP gets hold of Slim's spread, I'm as good as dead. They can dry me out in a month."

Two weeks after Slim's funeral, Fred sat with Murphy and Henry at Grace's kitchen table, waiting for her to speak her mind. She restlessly moved the salt and pepper shakers around in front of her, then nodded to herself as though she had finally found her nerve. "You've been such good neighbors, I thought it would help to talk to you about my situation." She paused and wiped her eyes with a handkerchief. "I'm alone now, with no children to take over, and the ranch is too much to manage by myself. Ever since the funeral, I've been thinking about it and concluded I have to sell."

Fred expected this. It was hard enough to lose his long-time friend, but the sale of Slim and Grace's ranch would put their share of the cooperative irrigation ditch in other hands. If it was the DWP, losing control of the ditch was almost inevitable. If only there were a way for her to hold on. "Grace, you must have some savings. Can you live on that if you don't sell?"

"No. I've looked at the figures over and over. All we have besides the ranch is a small account at the Inyo Bank." She sniffled and wiped at her tears again. "That isn't enough to last more than a few months."

"If you sell, will that give you enough to live on?" Henry asked.

"I don't think so. I don't know how much I'd get for the ranch and there's a mortgage to be paid off. I doubt it would leave much to live on."

"We need to find what you can sell it for," Henry said. "We can get a real estate agent from Bishop to give you an estimate."

Fred grimaced and shook his head. "With the DWP the only buyer, the price is whatever they offer."

"That's why I wanted to talk to you," Grace said. "Slim wouldn't want me to sell to them, and I know you don't want them to get my share in the ditch. I'm wondering if one of you is interested in buying me out?"

Fred looked at the ceiling as he thought about it. It would be good to have the additional acreage and more cattle, but he couldn't afford it. Plus, it was hard taking care of what he had, and a bigger spread would be more work than he could handle without Carl here to help. Then, there was the ditch ownership. He had added up the shares hundreds of times, and he totaled them once more. Seven shares, four required for control, and the DWP already had two. If they got Slim's share and then drove Henry out, that would give them their fourth.

Henry was the first to answer. "I know damned well if the DWP gets this spread, they will cut my flow off and dry me out. But I don't see any way I can buy you out."

"Me neither," Murphy said. "I'm just squeakin' by, and all I have is the land and the cattle. Hell, I hardly have enough cash to buy Anna Mae a new dress."

"What if you three went in together?" Grace asked.

Fred nodded. "Maybe. We each take a share of the acreage and cattle and keep it out of the City's hands."

The other two both shook their heads.

"Could we swing a deal to buy her share of the ditch instead?" Henry said.

"Wouldn't be fair to Grace," Fred replied. "Without water from the ditch, nobody would want to buy a dry ranch."

Thoughtful quiet filled the room. After a while, Grace broke the silence. "I know how much you guys want to keep the DWP out of this, but they're the only buyer. I don't know what else I can do but sell to them."

As much as Fred hated the prospect of the DWP getting the property, Grace had enough trouble. Her husband had just died, and she didn't have much money. He didn't want to make it any worse. He reached across the table and put his hand on hers. "Grace, we will understand if you have to sell to them. But if you sell and still can't get by with that money, what will you do?"

"What others do — get a job. I've spent my whole life on a ranch, but I can do something besides be a farm wife. I was fairly good with figures in school, and I managed our money. Maybe I could do something with that."

CHAPTER 30   CONFRONTATION

Fred parked in front of Jake's store on a crisp afternoon in April. When he got out of his pickup, he stood on the sidewalk and gazed at the deep blue, cloudless sky. The Sierras were still covered with snow, and the pastures were turning green in the valley. This prompted a flash of nostalgia for Slim, gone now for almost four months. The big guy had always remarked about the blue skies and gorgeous mountains in the spring. Fred gently shook his head, getting back to the present. He had things to do here in town. He went around the pickup and opened the door for Alice. "I need to get some stuff at the hardware store while you get the groceries. Meet you back here when I'm through."

Alice adjusted her hat and looked over her shopping list, then entered the store. The store was empty except for Betty, counting cash in the cash register.

Betty looked up. "Alice, I'm surprised to see you on Friday. You usually do your shopping on Saturday."

"I needed some things for tonight's dinner." She held out a small sheet of paper. "Here's my list."

Betty looked the list over. "I was just counting up the cash to take to the bank. Let me finish this and I'll get your stuff, then go to the bank. Not much to deposit. Most people say to put it on their tab. We just hope they'll pay."

Alice's eyes flared. "For God's sake, Betty, I'm your sister, and we will pay."

"Don't get all in a tizzy. I didn't mean you."

"Of course you did," Alice snapped.

"You want this stuff or not?"

"Not if you're going to be snotty about it."

Betty turned to the shelves behind the counter and grabbed items on the list, slamming them on the counter by the cash register. "I'm not being snotty. You're the snotty one."

"No. Something's bothering you. Tell me."

Betty leaned with both hands on the counter and began weeping. "I'm so worried about money and the store. It's the same old story. With so many people moving away, business has declined, and people who come in can only buy on credit." She wiped her nose with a handkerchief. "Jake is too nice. He won't refuse anything to anybody. Today, I only have twenty-three dollars to deposit, and that's for the entire week. I just don't know what we are going to do."

Lost for words, Alice walked behind the counter and embraced her sister. They silently held each other.

Betty pulled away. "Let me finish your list." She retrieved the rest of the items without slamming them down. She jotted the items on a pad, and a bell dinged when she entered the total in the cash register. "Five dollars and eighty-three cents for your tab."

"No, no tab. I've got the cash," Alice said as she took coins and a bill from her purse and counted them on the counter.

"You don't need to do that. I didn't mean you guys."

"Please take it," Alice said.

Betty snatched the money, stuck out her tongue at her sister, and added the five-dollar bill to her deposit. "Twenty-eight dollars." Both women laughed.

The two ladies walked to the local branch office of Inyo Bank. When they entered, Alice was surprised to see Grace Berks behind the teller's counter. "Grace, how nice to see you. I didn't know you were working here already."

A pleased smile crossed Grace's face. "I just got hired. Wednesday was my first day. They were so nice to give me the opportunity. I've never worked outside of home before and it feels good to be among other folks. I was so alone ever since Slim died. Now I get to see almost everybody in town."

Betty placed her money on the counter and pushed it forward.

Grace carefully counted it and filled out a deposit slip. "This is only my eighth deposit today, mostly from the merchants."

When Betty's transaction was finished, Alice rummaged through her purse and handed some bills to Grace. "This is for our monthly mortgage payment."

While Grace filled out the proper form, Alice noticed Mark Watson in the back. This was the first time she had laid eyes on him since the incident at Alabama Gates. She didn't want to contend with him now and hoped he didn't spot her. She quickly took the receipt as soon as Grace completed it and grabbed Betty's hand. "We should leave so Grace can do her work," Just as they got to the door, a hand reached for the knob.

"Ladies, please allow me," said the impeccably dressed banker. "I cannot fail to open the door for two such beautiful ladies."

Betty managed an icy smile, and Alice ignored him as she stepped onto the sidewalk.

When they turned toward Shapiro's store, Watson walked beside Alice. "Mrs. Lukin, I want to apologize for any misunderstanding at Alabama Gates. I certainly did not mean to insult you or make you or your husband think I had any dishonorable intent."

Alice's steps quickened, and she pulled Betty along to escape.

Watson's long strides easily kept pace, and he spoke with a honeyed voice as he gazed down at Alice. "I see you want to get back to the store. Perhaps at a later date, you ladies will allow me to treat you to coffee and dessert in Bishop. We have a coffee shop where they have wonderful cream pies I'm sure you would enjoy."

Alice stopped and glared up at him. "Mr. Watson, it would be a cold day in hell before I would join you for anything. Good day."

As she stepped off the curb to cross the street, she tripped, and as she started to tumble, he reached to stop her.

At that moment, Fred, who was walking back from the hardware store, saw Watson reach out as Alice fell. He raced down the street, quickly lifted Alice to her feet, and turned on Watson. Before the banker could react, Fred seized him by the collar and slammed him against the wall of the adjacent building. He lifted the taller man off the ground and held him in the air with his feet dangling.

"If you ever touch or even speak to my wife again, I will beat you into the ground." He pulled the banker back, slammed him against the wall again, and growled, "Do you understand?"

Watson's eyes went wide, his lips trembled, and he didn't speak.

Fred slammed him against the wall again. "Do you understand?" he roared.

The terrified banker nodded, and Fred gave him one last shove and let go.

"You will pay for that," Watson said as he regained his composure. He straightened his coat and tie, then strutted stiffly back to his bank.

CHAPTER 31   BLAST

A few nights later, the sound of a thunderous explosion woke Fred from his sound sleep, immediately followed by Alice shaking his shoulder.

"Fred, Fred, did you hear that? What do you think it was?"

He knew what it was. "A blast."

"It sounded just like that one a few years ago," Alice said.

"I'm through with that stuff." *That damned Murph.* His friend had kept insisting they had to do it again. But Fred hadn't wanted to get involved and told Murph to forget it. But he must have gone ahead despite the warning, and Fred wondered who else was involved. Not much he could do about it now. "Go back to sleep."

He and Alice were finishing breakfast when there was a knock on the door. When he opened the door, it was no surprise to see Sheriff Cole.

"Morning, Charlie. Come on in."

"No thanks. I imagine you know why I'm here."

"I can guess," Fred said. "We heard a blast last night."

"In exactly the same spot and time of night as that blast almost three years ago to the day. A neat coincidence."

"Charlie, I was home all night. Alice can attest to that."

"Wives generally are not reliable witnesses."

Fred's voice rose. "My wife doesn't lie!"

"Fred, I hope to God that you're being straight with me. But dammit, you're the one with the most visible beef with the City, and half the population of the valley figured you were involved that other time."

"They mighta thought that, Charlie, but it proved nothing, and it doesn't make me guilty now."

Cole forced a skeptical smile. "We've been friends for a long time. But if I find you did it, I *will* throw you in the jug."

Fred heard Cole muttering to himself as he walked back to his car.

The sheriff had been gone less than an hour when Murphy drove into the farmyard where Fred was nailing a new board on the side of the barn to replace an old one that was warped and rotting away. The moment Murphy stepped out of his truck, Fred began scolding him. "Dammit, Murph, you just had to do it, didn't you? That was really stupid. I warned you not to. Charlie just left. He's convinced I did it. The damned trouble is, I will end up in jail, and I won't have done it. And it won't do a thing to stop the City."

"Slow down," Murphy said. "If you think I had anything to do with that explosion, you're wrong. I was at home all night. When I was woke up by the blast, I thought maybe it was you. That's why I came over to check."

Fred stared at Murphy. Was he telling the truth? "Charlie said it was the same place as ours three years ago. Who else woulda done it like a copycat?"

"Not me, for sure, and I doubt it was any of our group," Murphy said. "Wouldn't be Henry, not Jake, and we know for certain it weren't Slim."

Fred laughed. "No, not Slim." He paused and smiled. "But then, who knows? Maybe he came back to haunt the DWP."

Murphy chuckled. "Sounds just like him. I wonder if they will find ghosts of his bootleg bottles by the aqueduct." He lit a cigar as he thought about it. "Some of those Lone Pine guys are pretty mad about their suit goin' nowhere to stop the City's pumpin'. Think it mighta been them?"

"Seems unlikely they'd do it when they're still trying to use the courts."

Murphy puffed on his cigar and blew aromatic smoke. "Last time, a lot of people thought maybe Watson and his Bishop crew did it. Maybe it was them this time."

"My gut says no. Why would they come clear down here when they could do it closer to home?"

"Ya know, I wouldn't be too surprised if it was a set-up by Magon. He still has it out for you, and he sure wants our ditch."

"Maybe," Fred said. "Sounds like something he'd do. But they're tryin' to squeeze Henry out, and if they get his land, they get control. They can keep squeezin' and wait. They wouldn't need to frame me by blowin' up their own aqueduct."

"But that's forgettin' that, for Magon, control of the ditch is second to getting you."

Fred grimaced. "Maybe."

The next day, Fred was working on his irrigation ditch when Sheriff Cole's black and white Nash drove into the farmyard, followed by two police cars from L.A. Fred stabbed his shovel into the ground and walked to meet them.

Cole and six L.A. cops waited by their cars as he approached. Without a word, he nodded to Cole.

"Fred, this is Detective Jack Drummond of the Los Angeles Police Department," Cole said.

Fred nodded.

The detective got right to the point. "Mr. Lukin, where were you Wednesday night?"

Did he have to answer this guy's questions? He knew from the earlier encounters that L.A. cops had no jurisdiction in Inyo County. He was tempted to walk away but silently looked at Drummond and waited.

"Dammit, Fred," Cole said, "it's easier and quicker if you just answer the question. You told me you were here all night. Was that correct?"

"Sheriff, you are the legal authority in the county, and according to your own words," he gestured toward the cops, "these guys are common civilians with no jurisdiction here. I don't even have to let them on my property, much less answer their questions."

Cole rolled his eyes skyward. "Okay, then I'll ask. Where were you at the time of the blast at the aqueduct on the night of May twelfth, nineteen-hundred-and-twenty-seven?"

"I was… " He paused as eyes swept over the City cops. They shouldn't even be allowed on his ranch and he sure didn't want to cooperate with them, even if it was through Sheriff Cole. "Why are you asking?"

"God in heaven, Fred," Cole thundered. "You told me yesterday you were here. If that's true, just say so."

"I told you the truth. I shouldn't have to keep saying it. If you have other questions, these guys will have to get off my property first."

Drummond walked forward. "Mr. Magon said you did that job three years ago, and this morning, he swore it was you this time, too."

Fred stepped close, with his face inches from the cop, and spoke in a slow growl. "Magon's a stupid hired thug and a liar, and if you believe him, you are as stupid as he is."

The whole police squad instantly surrounded Fred like they were ready to pound him into the ground. Cole grabbed Fred's shoulder and pushed him back. "We better leave," he said to the cops. "And Fred, you're digging a deep hole you won't be able to get out of."

When Cole returned to his office, there was an envelope on his desk, addressed to 'Sheriff Cole'. Inside was a penciled note in handwritten block letters:

YOU WILL FIND SOME INERESTING STUFF ABOUT THE ACWADUCK EXPLOSEN IN FRED LUKINS BARN

Who sent this stupidly written note? He examined both sides of the paper for clues. He held the envelope up to the light. No postmark to indicate where it came from. Someone must have snuck in and put it on his desk when he was at Fred's place.

"Daggett, get in here," Cole hollered.

"Watchya need, Boss?" the deputy asked as he came through the door from his small office cubicle next to the cells.

"You leave the office while I was gone?"

"Nope. Here the entire time. But I went out back. I heard a bunch of yellin' and cussin' out there. Turned out to be a couple of guys acting like they were going to fight. When I walked toward them, they got in a car and drove off. Nothing much I could do, so I came back in."

"Which way did they go?"

"North outta town."

Cole held the note out. "Look at this."

Daggett scanned the brief message. "Where'd you get it?"

"It was on my desk when I got back from Fred's."

"That explains the phony disturbance outside."

"Looks like it," Cole said.

"Want me to go check it out?"

"Gotta see Judge Daley for a search warrant, then we'll both go," Cole said.

When Cole and Daggett drove into the farmyard, the sheriff spotted Fred on horseback in his field, driving some cattle from one field to another.

Cole walked to the barbed wire fence at the edge of the field and shouted. "Hey, Fred, I need to talk to you."

Fred drove the last cow through a gate, then rode back toward the barn. From the back of his horse, he asked, "What'd you want?"

Cole held out the search warrant. "I need to search your barn."

Fred's eyes narrowed. "You son-of-a-bitch. You're just dyin' to pin somethin' on me." He pointed, "There's the barn," and turned his horse back toward the field.

Cole shook his head in frustration and motioned for Daggett to follow him into the barn.

"What are we lookin' for, Chief?" Daggett asked.

"You saw the note—evidence related to the explosion."

In the barn, he looked around, assessing where someone might hide something. The three horse stalls were empty except for hay on the floor. Hay bales were stacked along the north wall, and some loose hay was piled on the loft overhead. The south wall had saddle racks and hooks with bridles and ropes looped over them and cupboards above the tack. A small area near the back served as a workshop with tools and an anvil. The place was orderly with few good hiding places.

With his arms folded, Cole stood in the middle of the barn and turned in a circle. *Where would he hide it? Small? Maybe the cupboards. Large? Behind the hay bales? Maybe, but pretty awkward and time-consuming to re-stack the bales.*

"Daggett, search the haystack. I'll check the cupboards."

Daggett grabbed a hay hook and began pulling bales down. Cole opened cupboards filled mainly with veterinary supplies and leather waxes and oils for the saddles and bridles. He rummaged through bottles, cans, and boxes and found nothing.

"Find anything, Daggett?"

"Just hay," the deputy replied.

Cole looked up at the loft. *Yeah, that's gotta be it.*

"Daggett, climb up to the loft and root around in the hay."

The deputy climbed the rungs nailed to the wall studs to the loft. He pawed through the pile of loose hay. "Found something, Chief," and held up a wooden box.

"Hand it down," Cole said. He climbed partway up the ladder and took the box with 'Hercules Powder' stenciled on the side. Boxes like that were common around the many mining claims in the Inyo Mountains. He set it down, peered inside, and whistled. It was empty except for a coil of fuse, a small empty carton for blasting caps, and a single stick of dynamite.

"Holy Jesus," he gasped. "This is it."

CHAPTER 32   HERCULES

Cole got down on one knee and stared into the wooden box labeled 'Hercules Powder.' *Damn you, Fred. Why in hell would you do this a second time and then be so stupid as to hide this in your own barn? Did you really think I wouldn't look?*

"Daggett, look at this."

The deputy stood looking over Cole's shoulder. "Talk about a smoking gun. Now what? We arrest him?"

"Don't see what else we can do. Seems a little too convenient, but still, pretty powerful evidence. He'll say it's not his. But we have to follow the evidence." Cole stood up and limped in a tight circle. *Damn these knees. Each year, it's harder to bend down.* "Okay, get some handcuffs from the car."

The two lawmen walked into the field. Fred dismounted and waited as they approached.

Cole stood in front of him, hesitant to arrest his friend. Finally, he found his official sheriff's voice. "Fred Lukin, I am arresting you for blasting the Los Angeles aqueduct on May twelfth. Please put out your hands so Deputy Daggett can cuff you."

Fred held the reins of his horse. "Charlie, you're set on pinning this on me, but you know I didn't do it, and you don't have a shred of evidence that I was involved."

"Evidence?" Cole huffed. "You know damned well I have evidence. A box of explosives is pretty good evidence. You're a fool if you didn't expect us to look in your barn."

Fred's eyes narrowed, and his brows furrowed. "What explosives? I don't have no explosives."

"I expected you to say that. Pretty weak when you're dumb enough to hide it in your barn."

"If it's there, you sons-a-bitches planted it."

"No. We arrived empty-handed, and now we have a box labeled Hercules Powder, direct from your barn. Now put out your hands so we don't have to make a fight of it."

Fred gestured back at his horse. "I gotta unsaddle him and tell Alice."

Cole shook his head. "I'll tell Alice and Daggett can take care of the horse."

When they got to town, Daggett locked Fred in a cell while Cole headed to Judge Daley's second-floor office.

At the sound of the rap on his open door, Daley glanced up. "You look unhappy, Charlie. What've you got?"

Cole sagged into a chair in front of the judge's desk. "I am unhappy, Stanley. I just put Fred Lukin in a cell. You know that note? We found a box from Hercules Powder with a stick of dynamite, a fuse, and caps in his barn. Hard not to arrest him."

"I suppose so. But it's not up to me. My job is to preside over trials. Who you arrest is between you and Walt Hess."

Cole nodded at the phone. "Call him in here and we can sort it out."

The judge gave a quick call to the district attorney's office down the hall. A few minutes later, D.A. Walt Hess appeared and took a seat in the judge's office.

"Okay, what's so important?" Hess said irritably.

"Fred Lukin," Dalcy said.

"What'd he do now?"

Cole handed the district attorney the anonymous note. "Somebody left that note on my desk. I found a dynamite box in his barn and arrested him."

"Jeez, I guess it's hard not to," Hess shook the note in the air, "given this. But if you're asking my opinion, I think it smells like a frame—and a poorly done one at that. But…it's enough evidence to hold him until you can sort it out. Who knows, might even bring the real culprit out in the open."

Cole slapped the judge's desk. "Dammit, Walt, I'm not arresting him to be a decoy. I'm arresting him because of the evidence."

"Okay," Hess said. "It's your play. But my advice is to keep your distance from Alice."

Cole shook his head, and an ironic smile crossed his face. "For sure. That lady can be a handful. When she gets going, she can be like a wildcat and a bulldog, all rolled up in a compact and troublesome package. When I have to deal with the likes of her, it makes me think I'd like a job as a sheepherder. Solitary. Nobody to bother me, and sheep are peaceful, quiet creatures. And what's worse is she'll not only recruit Betty, but she'll even get Doris after me."

Hess laughed. "Maybe you can move back to San Francisco."

When Cole got back to his office, four L.A. cops stood outside his door. Inside, Detective Drummond occupied the chair in front of the sheriff's desk

"Make yourself at home," Cole growled when he entered. "What can I do for you, Drummond?"

"Lieutenant Drummond, to you," the man said as he puffed on his cigarette and blew smoke rings.

"Very well, *Lieutenant* Drummond." Cole saluted and clicked his heels.

"What you can do for me," Drummond said, "is release your prisoner so I can take him to L.A."

"Which prisoner is that, Lieutenant?"

"Don't be an ass. You were seen taking him into your jail. I want him."

"We've been down this road before. You have no jurisdiction here. In this county, you are welcome as civilian visitors as long as you obey the law."

"We have jurisdiction because he damaged City of Los Angeles property. Twice!"

"A trial has to be in the venue where the crime was committed, which, as you know, is here in Inyo County, not L.A. Now, if you have evidence to provide, I will include it in the file for our D.A. Otherwise, I do not see a role for you in this process."

The lieutenant stood and sauntered over to the row of guns locked in the rack on the wall. He ran his hand over each weapon. "You'll have to provide me with the evidence you assembled in this case. Of course, you need time to gather it. I'll pick it up tomorrow when we come for the prisoner."

"The prisoner stays here," Cole said and chuckled. "But just to keep things interesting, I will tell the ladies of this little village so when you show up, they can give you the same welcome they gave Officer Dodson when he kidnapped a prisoner. I assume you're aware of that incident."

"I know, and someday you'll all pay for that." He turned and left, followed by his squad that had been waiting by the door.

CHAPTER 33   TAKING CARE OF HERSELF

Cole had just gotten rid of the L.A. cops when Alice came bustling into his office. Stretching to almost five-and-a-quarter feet in her black, lace-up high heels, Alice stood in front of his desk. "Charlie, my husband should not be locked up in your filthy jail like a common criminal. He was home with me the entire night of that blast. He is innocent and you know it. When are you going to let him go?"

"Alice, we arrested him based on evidence we found in your barn. He'll stay in jail until either the judge lets him go or until a trial." His voice rose. "And my jail is not filthy."

She stared daggers at Cole, then turned and marched to the door, where she turned for a last word. "Charlie, you're going to regret this." She spun on her heels and marched out in a huff.

He managed a bitter smile and mumbled to himself, "I already do. I already do."

Alice stalked across the street to the Shapiro store to commiserate with her sister. She slammed her purse down on the counter, grabbed a bent-wood chair, and sat by the window with her arms folded, about to boil over.

"Well, what happened?" Betty asked as she looked up from her position on her hands and knees, picking up macaroni that she had spilled on the floor.

Alice hopped up and paced the open floor between the counters lining each side of the store. She was close to tears recounting her meeting with Cole. "He won't let him go."

"You can stay with us as long as Fred's over there. Murphy can take care of things at the ranch."

"Thanks. I'll need to talk to Murph first, and I have things to do, so I'll stay home tonight, then come to stay tomorrow." Alice spread her arms wide, exasperated. "He's innocent. He was with me all night."

"You've said that before. We need to do more than just keep repeating it."

Alice threw her sister a daggered look. "What do you suggest?" she asked acidly.

"Jake and I have been talking about it. The whole thing was set up to frame Fred. Word is, the explosion didn't do much damage, just enough to rile things up. The note pointing to your barn had to be a plant. We need to figure out who did the blast and who planted the evidence."

Alice stood, looking out the window. "Whoever did it is after Fred, either for revenge or to get him out of the way. That's where we start."

"I keep coming back to Magon," Betty said. "It's gotta be him."

"Probably. He may think that getting Fred out of the way would make it easier to get our property. He doesn't realize that he will still have to deal with me."

"The question is, how do we prove any of this?"

"We need to find who planted the stuff in the barn. Magon wouldn't do it himself," Alice said.

"There's the saying, 'Follow the money'," Betty said. "Whoever did it probably got paid. We need to find out who got a bunch of money around the time all this took place."

"How could we do that?"

"Grace is working in the bank now. Maybe she can help."

So many things to do, Alice thought as she drove home from town. *If they don't release Fred soon, I'll have to run the ranch.* He had always handled everything—the cattle, the irrigation, upkeep, and fixing the equipment and cars. As she ticked off the list of things that needed doing, she figured she could handle most of it. She'd need Murphy's help with the heavy stuff, and she wasn't much good at fixing machinery, but she could handle the rest. Cole,

Magon, and the DWP could all go to hell. She'd be damned if she'd let this frame-up force them off the ranch.

She turned from the lane into the farmyard and was surprised to see a car parked by the house with someone sitting on the fender. Her surprise turned to fury when she recognized Mark Watson. *What is that slimy reptile doing here?* Should she turn around immediately and head back to town? No! She'd just told herself that she could handle things. Surely, she could handle this jackass.

She parked in front of the house, retrieved her bag of groceries from the back seat, and marched toward the front door where Tinker was sprawled, barely awake.

Watson hopped off the fender and, with his long strides, caught up with her. "Good afternoon, Alice. Can I help you carry your groceries?"

Refusing to look at him, she said, "I'm *Mrs. Lukin* to you. And I can carry my own groceries."

"I was sorry to hear about Fred's arrest. With him facing a lengthy jail term, you will be alone and need someone to watch out for you. In spite of our past misunderstandings, I want you to know I'm here for you. I'd like to help any way I can."

She paused and looked at him. "You told him a long time ago that if there were legal problems dealing with the City, your attorney would help. I suggest you drive back to Bishop and put him on the case."

He grasped her arm and stepped in front of her. "Like I say, I would like to help. But if I am generous with you, then I think you should be generous with me. You are a beautiful woman, and I am very attracted to you. If you give me a chance, we can be good friends. Shall we go inside?"

Her eyes widened with fury, and she jerked her arm free. "Don't touch me, you… you…" She pointed down the lane and shouted, "Get off my property!"

At the sound of her distressed voice, Tinker struggled to stand up and advanced toward the invader, growling with fangs bared.

Watson backed slowly toward his car, with the old dog keeping pace until the banker was blocked against his car door. "Call your dog off, Mrs. Lukin," he pleaded with a shaky voice.

She called the dog to her side and said to the banker, "You step on this property again, and I won't hold him back."

The banker spoke as he opened his car door. "I'm going. But you're making a mistake. Don't forget, my bank holds the mortgage on this place and our records show you haven't made a payment in over a year. I imagine we will have to foreclose."

"You will never get this property," she screamed. "I make all our payments on time, and I have receipts to prove it."

Watson looked at her with a lupine smile. "I'm sure you know that forgery is a crime."

Her face burned with rage. God, how she wished she had her shotgun. "Get out!" she howled at the top of her lungs.

Her hands shook as she watched him drive away. She had told Betty she'd stay home by herself, but now she wondered if maybe she should stay in town. *No, dammit. I can take care of myself, and I'll be damned if that guy is going to scare me away.*

CHAPTER 34   BOTHER NOT THE LADY

Fred woke up to the early morning sunshine streaming through the small, barred window. A jail cell. Why was he in a jail cell? It took a moment to remember that Charlie Cole had arrested him and put him here. It didn't make sense. When he'd actually blasted the aqueduct, Cole hadn't arrested him. Now, when he had nothing to do with it, Cole said he had the evidence and locked him up. Fred couldn't prove he didn't do it if he was in a jail cell. Maybe Alice could get some help. He'd need an attorney and that took a lot of money. Would they have to sell the ranch to get enough to pay an attorney? Was this a frame to force the sale of the ranch? If it was, Magon was sure to be behind it. But Cole had always been his friend, so why was he in on it now?

Confusion and anger were echoing through his mind when Deputy Daggett arrived with a breakfast tray and a copy of the *Inyo Independent*. His arrest was the feature article on the front page of the weekly paper. It described the note and the sheriff finding the dynamite box in his barn. The editor questioned the validity of both clues because they were so obvious and doubted they had the right guy. It included comments by Murphy and others praising his character and good citizenship. As he read it, Fred felt a little less helpless, knowing he had his friends in his corner. Even the editor of the paper could see the frame. Why couldn't Charlie Cole?

He had just finished the article when Daggett poked his head through the doorway. "You got a visitor, Fred."

He expected Alice, but when Magon strode through the door as though he was on top of the world, Fred wanted in the worst way to reach between the bars and strangle the thug in the most painful way possible.

"Ah, Lukin, they finally put you where you belong," said the DWP acquisitions agent.

"Get out. I have nothing to say to you," Fred growled.

With his arms folded, Magon leaned nonchalantly against the wall opposite the barred jail cell. "Lukin, you've reached your end. Here you sit in a dirty jail in a nothing town. You're a failure. Our water is still flowing. You can't even figure out how to set your charges. It takes a pretty stupid person to use that much dynamite and not do any damage. The best thing for you is to sell your worthless ranch and get out. If you sell to us, the DWP will drop the charges. You'd be out of this jail in a day, a free man. Save yourself the trouble and expense of a trial, and you'll get your money for the ranch by the end of the month."

"Daggett," Fred shouted, "get this jackass outta here."

"I'm going. I'm going. Think it over, Lukin. You could be out of here and on your way."

Alice had spent a restless night tossing, turning, and worrying about Fred in jail and Watson's harassment. After a quick breakfast, she packed some food and a change of clothes to take to Fred. She paused her packing at the sound of a car driving into the farmyard, quickly followed by Tinker's barking. Surely, Watson hadn't returned.

She didn't want to take any chances. She picked up the loaded pump-action twelve-gauge, ready beside the entrance, and cautiously opened the door. It wasn't Watson. This was worse— Magon. But the man appeared to be confined in his idling car by the snarling dog. A slight smile crossed Alice's face at the memory of that time when Magon had first shown up to buy the ranch, and Tinker had kept him imprisoned in his car. Alice stepped onto the porch with the gun at waist level, pointing at Magon. "What are you doing here?" she shouted.

Magon rolled his window down. "Mrs. Lukin, put the gun down. I mean no harm. I just want to talk to you."

She brought the gun to her shoulder and sighted down the barrel. "I have nothing to say to you. Get off my property."

"Hear me out. You have nothing to lose," he shouted.

Alice took a couple of steps forward, keeping the gun trained on Magon. "You accused Fred of trespassing and beat him when he came to your office. Now, you are trespassing on our land. I have every right to shoot you," she growled.

"With your husband in jail, you are likely to lose this ranch. Isn't it better to sell at a good price first?"

"You will never get this ranch." She raised the barrel so as not to hit him and shot over the roof of his car. "Get out," she screamed.

He revved his engine, and the wheels spun as he made a tight U-turn to head out of the farmyard. As the car came around, Magon aimed a pistol out his open window. His gun boomed, and at the same instant, Alice heard a 'thwack', the sound of his bullet hitting the house.

She pumped another shell into the chamber and took her shot at Magon's car. The car's rear window splintered into a cobweb pattern as it careened away. She rushed back into the house and grabbed a box of shells. Her hands shook, and it took several tries to push fresh shells into the magazine. She would be ready if he came back.

Her hands wouldn't stop shaking. She rarely drank, but a stiff drink might calm her down. She got some of Slim's bootleg from the cupboard and poured a glass half full. Her eyes watered and her throat burned with her first sip. Holding the glass of whiskey, she went outside and inspected the bullet hole in the wall. She put her index finger in the hole. It could have been her head. Back inside, she sat down at the kitchen table and, with hands still shaking, reviewed what had just happened. Maybe she'd been too hasty.

Everything was so complicated—Fred in jail, Watson talking foreclosure, three spreads on the ditch already owned by the DWP, and now Magon threatening her. Up until now, she had let Fred worry about it and she had thought he was too extreme. Maybe he was right, but so far, no one had found a way to fight that didn't lead to more defeat. She picked up her glass for another swig. That calmed her a little. It was time to go to town.

Cole had his revolver dismantled with parts spread on his desk, carefully oiling and wiping each piece as he reassembled it. He jerked with surprise and dropped a small spring on the floor when the door banged open. "Dammit, Magon," he growled. "What do you want?"

"Sheriff, that woman shot at me. I want her arrested."

Cole shook his head. *What now?* There were a lot of people he didn't want to deal with, and Magon was near the top of the list. "Which woman?"

"That Lukin woman. She's dangerous."

Ah, Alice. She's a threat, alright. He tried to stifle a laugh but failed. "Did she hit you?"

"No, but she shot my car."

He couldn't resist. "Guess she needs some target practice. Where was the car?"

"In front of her house."

"What were you doing out there?"

"I went to talk business," Magon said.

Cole leaned back in his chair with his arms folded. "Let me guess. She ran you off."

"She had a shotgun when she answered the door. I just wanted to talk."

"I understand you were in here earlier, talking to Fred in his cell. So you knew she was alone at the ranch, and you're surprised she came to the door with a shotgun?"

Before Magon could respond, the door opened with Alice entering backward, pushing it with her rear-end, her arms loaded with a bag of food and clothes for Fred. She turned and froze, eyes wide, staring at Magon. "You thug!" she screamed. "You shot at me."

Magon turned to Cole. "She shot first and shattered my car window."

A smile crossed Cole's face like he had a personal viewing of a western shoot-'em-up movie, except in this case, it was the lady in distress who might tie the villain to the rails in front of the onrushing train. "Glad nobody was hurt. No one was hurt, were they?"

"No," Magon mumbled while skirting cautiously around Alice to leave the sheriff's office.

"Jesus, Alice," Cole said as soon as Magon was out the door. "We're going to have to take your guns away from you before you shoot up the whole county."

"Let my husband go, and I won't have to shoot anyone, not even you, Charlie."

CHAPTER 35   DETECTIVE GRACE

"Grace, do you think you can take care of things by yourself while I go to lunch?" the manager of the Independence branch of the Inyo Bank asked as he donned his hat.

"Go ahead, Mr. Aigner," Grace said. "I can take care of things here while you're gone." This was the first time Grace would be working alone since starting at the bank, and she had been waiting for a chance to begin her detective work. Alice and Betty had recruited her to search bank records to find who might have been paid to plant evidence against Fred.

This could be exciting, sort of like being a detective solving a case. After the sisters recruited her, she checked out a Sherlock Holmes mystery from the library to sharpen her skills. Of course, Holmes would be much more sophisticated in chasing the fiend who framed Fred. Although Sherlock might be clever, he wouldn't know about the bank like she did.

She glanced at the wall clock and realized she'd better hurry before Mr. Aigner returned from lunch. She searched through recent entries for Earl Magon's deposits and withdrawals. That's where Alice said to start. Going back several months, he'd made deposits of his paycheck from the DWP every two weeks, followed by withdrawals she guessed were his living expenses. She hated telling Alice something so boring and normal for the guy everybody said was a strong-arm thug. But then, you wouldn't expect to catch Professor Moriarty so easily.

Maybe it was someone else. She would look for other unusual account transactions around the time of that aqueduct blast. She ran her eyes down the journal pages, scanning for something different. Most people made a lot less than a hundred and fifty dollars per month, and deposits or withdrawals of more than that were noteworthy. When she found a large transaction, she jotted down the details. She'd follow up on the less obvious entries if they didn't have a simple explanation, such as livestock sales, farm equipment purchases, property sales, and the like.

She ran her finger down a page and paused. Just a few days before the aqueduct blast, a man named Irwin Barr had made a cash deposit of one hundred dollars, adding to his prior balance of five hundred seventy-five. She vaguely knew who he was, but not much else. He was new in town—a loner who kept to himself. She didn't know if he worked but thought not. Without a job, where would he get that much money? She continued down the column. There he was again. A two-hundred-dollar deposit two days after the blast. *Sherlock Holmes would think that was suspicious.* She needed to keep looking and found more. Two days ago, he withdrew over three hundred and fifty dollars. Searching further back in the records, she found that he had opened his account shortly before the aqueduct blast.

The scrape of the door opening interrupted her scrutiny of the bank journal. She slammed the journal shut, looked up, and sighed with relief—it was Edna King from the drugstore, not Mr. Aigner.

"Afternoon, Grace," Edna said cheerily. "Got my regular deposit. Not much today, but it never is. How are you liking your new job?"

"I like it. I loved the ranch, but it got lonely, especially with Slim gone. I like being in town, seeing people, and having something new to do."

"I don't know what I'd do if I never talked to other people," Edna said. "Have you talked to Alice? Everybody thought Fred would be released by now, but no, there he sits in the lockup."

Grace counted the bills for deposit, laying them on the counter like a card dealer. "Alice is convinced the evidence was planted. She and Betty are trying to figure out who might have planted it."

"Yes, most everybody thinks it was a plant and Magon had a hand in it," Edna said. "He's the City's hired muscle, and nobody over in the City offices can stand him."

"I wonder if there are others involved," Grace said. "There's this guy, Irwin Barr, who's new around here. Do you know anything about him?"

"He that hefty, jowly guy?"

"Yeah."

"A strange bird. He was in the drugstore yesterday. I tried to be friendly and talk to him. He just glared at me and paid with bills he peeled from a huge roll of cash and left without a word."

"You have any idea where he works?"

"Nope. He never says anything to anybody."

"I wonder if Charlie knows anything about him," Grace said.

"Charlie usually knows most everything that goes on around here, but now, no one's willing to speak to him since he arrested Fred, so maybe not."

Grace nodded agreement and handed the deposit receipt to her customer just as the branch manager came through the door.

"Good afternoon, Edna," he said as he placed his hat on the rack. "Grace, as soon as you finish helping Mrs. King, I need to talk to you."

Grace's heart fell. Did he know she had been snooping in the accounts? As soon as Edna King was out the door, she walked reluctantly to his desk. "Yes, Mr. Aigner? I hope I've done nothing wrong."

"Oh, no. Not at all. I just wanted to tell you I think you are doing an excellent job, particularly since you haven't been here long. I told Mr. Watson about your good work, and he said we could give you a raise of five cents per hour."

She felt like jumping for joy. "Oh, thank you, Mr. Aigner. I love working here, seeing everybody, and learning about banking. It is so interesting. Thank you, thank you."

"And there is something else I need to mention."

"Yes, Mr. Aigner?" she answered with her voice shaking nervously.

"When I told Mr. Watson about your work, he suggested you could cover for one of his employees in Bishop while she takes some time off. It would be good training for you to work at the head office for a week. Do you think you could do that?"

What a great opportunity. It would be good to get the experience and spend some time away. "Oh, yes, Mr. Aigner. I'd love to. When would this be?"

"Next week. You would substitute for Margaret Collins while she is away. She said you can stay at her house while she goes to see her relatives in the San Joaquin Valley for a week."

Spend a week in Bishop? She hadn't been away from the ranch or Independence for years. This would be fun. "Now that you're back, may I take my lunch break?"

"Of course," the manager said.

She retrieved her purse and sack lunch, donned her hat, and hurried down the street to the general store to tell Betty her good news.

CHAPTER 36   BARR

"Here's the last one from the case," Alice said as she passed a soup can to Betty, who stood on a ladder stacking cans on a shelf along the wall behind the counter.

"Let's do that case of canned peas next," Betty said. "You going to stay with us tonight?"

"Yeah. Murphy said he'd check on things at the ranch for me, and it's pretty lonely out there with Fred locked up and Carl working in San Francisco. Also, I worry Watson will show up again." She slammed a can down on the counter. "That darned Cole. He's gotta know Fred didn't do it."

Grace's voice interrupted their talk as she walked through the door. "Guess what. I'm getting a raise, and I get to spend a week at the bank's head office in Bishop."

"That's nice," Alice said without enthusiasm. "But did you find any suspicious payments by Magon?"

"No, nothing for him, but there's this other guy, Irwin Barr, who made large deposits right before and after the blasts."

"Never heard of him," Alice said.

Grace read her list of Barr's deposits and withdrawals.

"He might be what we're looking for," Betty said from her perch on the ladder. "We need to find out more."

"It'll be hard to find out about a guy nobody knows, so we start with the one person who does know," Alice said.

"Who's that?" Grace asked.

"Mr. Barr, of course," Alice replied. "Where does he live?"

Grace pulled her list close to her chest as though to protect it. "That's confidential bank information. I can't reveal it."

"Don't be silly! You already told us about his deposits." Alice grabbed the list from Grace. "Let me see." She glanced at the paper. "That's on the north edge of town at the end of Clay Street. Let's go."

"You're crazy," Betty said. "You can't just go up to a stranger and ask if he blew up the aqueduct or planted evidence."

"Why not? He won't answer, but we might learn something. Come on."

"Not now. I have to keep the store open," Betty said.

She took Grace by the hand. "Let's go."

"Oh, no, not me," Grace said. "I could get fired for telling you about any of this."

"I'll go alone."

Betty shook her head. "You can't go alone. Wait 'til I close. I'll go with you."

"Okay, but I can't just sit here and wait. I'll be back in a few minutes."

"Where are you going?" Betty yelled as Alice hurried out the door.

Cole looked up from the papers on his desk when Alice stormed into his office. *God save me from the banshee from hell. When she shows up, trouble can't be far behind.*

Before he could say a word, she plopped her purse on his desk and took a seat. "You've got to let Fred go. I know who set that explosion and planted the dynamite box in our barn."

"Knowing and proving are two different things," Cole said.

"You didn't know Fred did anything, but you locked him up."

"I have the dynamite box. That's pretty good evidence."

"Evidence that was planted and you know it. Listen to me," she insisted. "There's this guy Barr. He has lots of cash and made large deposits in a bank account right before the aqueduct explosion and right after."

"Lots of people have cash and make deposits." He paused and stared at her with narrowed eyes. "Anyhow, how would you know about someone's cash and deposits?"

She waved her hand, pushing away the question. "That's beside the point. You have to check on this guy."

Cole knew there were no secrets in this town, especially among the women. Grace Berks takes a job at the bank, and now

Alice is talking about someone's bank transactions. He folded his hands on the desk and leaned forward like a teacher scolding a student. "Alice, it's against the rules for a bank employee to disclose confidential information about a bank client. Whoever told you could lose her job, and maybe even be charged with a crime."

She glared steadily at him. "This man deposited one hundred dollars in his account before the blast and two hundred dollars after the blast. This is someone new to town who nobody knows. You need to do your job and check on it."

Cole stood up, almost knocking his chair over. "I know my job," he thundered as he pointed toward the door. "Now get out of my office."

"Apparently not," Alice said. "If you just sit in this office and do nothing, you're going to look like a fool when I show who did it." She stood, smiled malevolently, and dragged her purse theatrically across his desk, scattering papers and spilling a bottle of ink over the wood surface.

Cole scowled at the ink running across his desk as Alice stormed out. "Alice, damned you," he shouted, "you damned well better buy me a new desk."

But she was gone. This was just what he needed, a middle-aged, busy-body housewife butting into police business and destroying his office. As for this guy Barr, there was probably nothing to it, but the note and the barn evidence *were* suspicious. This Barr put a new twist to it. He had seen the guy around town and thought he knew where he lived. In a town this small, it was hard not to. A couple of unusual bank deposits hardly showed anything wrong. But they *were* pretty big deposits for someone who didn't seem to have a job. It was time to pay him a visit.

"Hey, Daggett," he yelled down the hall, "I'm leaving to check something out. Cover the office while I'm gone. And, for God's sake, clean up this mess on my desk." He grabbed the car keys from the hook by the gun rack and headed out.

He parked in front of the house where he thought Barr lived. It was just like a lot of other small rentals found in any one of the towns in the valley. He could picture the inside—the front door opened into the small living room with a miniscule kitchen behind. On one side, two tiny bedrooms separated by a Jack-and-Jill bath. This place looked like it had been run down for years. Cole whistled at seeing the latest model Hudson touring sedan parked in front. A car like that costs almost fifteen hundred dollars. This guy must be doing okay.

It took a while for his knock to be answered. A hard-faced man of middle age, husky and a little shorter than Cole, opened the door and scowled at the intruder. "What'd ya want?"

"You must be Mr. Barr," Cole said. "We've never met, and I thought it was time that we did." He extended his hand. "I'm Sheriff Cole."

The man kept his hand on the doorknob, and his frown deepened. "I know who you are. Why are you here?"

"May I come in?"

"You got a search warrant?"

"It's not that sort of visit," Cole said as he glanced past Barr and saw the house was just as he imagined. The front room was in mild disarray, as might be expected for a middle-aged bachelor, but it looked clean.

"No warrant, no entry."

Cole dipped his head in acknowledgment. "I was admiring your car when I drove up. I couldn't help wondering what sort of great job you might have to afford it."

"My job is none of your business." He paused. "But if you must know, I gamble. I'm a very lucky gambler."

"This is a strange place for a gambler to live. You can probably find gambling in Reno," Cole said.

"Reno's nice, and I go there a lot, but that's not the only type of gambling." Without another word, he closed the door.

As Cole drove the five short blocks back to his office, he thought about how so many interviews raised more questions than they answered. This was certainly one of those. What was the guy doing here? Fancy car, plenty of money, but no job. He said there were all kinds of gambling. What did he mean? What was his kind of gamble? Cole could kick himself for not finding out about him before this. He'd have Daggett send a telegram to Sacramento to check his police record.

Alice's fury had grown with each step when she stomped out of Cole's office. When she got back to the store, she slammed down her purse that had laid waste to Cole's desk. She shrieked, "I could kill that man!"

"Don't say that. Someone might believe you. You shot one cop already," Betty said, only half in jest.

Alice paced back and forth in the center of the store. "I told him about Barr. He won't listen. He's got Fred and doesn't want to hear anything else."

"Did you expect otherwise?"

Alice stopped pacing and stood with her arms akimbo. "We'll just have to do our own investigation. Hurry up and close this place. We have to meet Mr. Barr."

Later that afternoon, after Betty closed the store, Alice and Betty drove the few blocks and parked in front of the man's house. The two women looked at each other with question marks on their faces. Were they really going to do this?

At the sound of the knock, a husky man with fleshy jowls opened the door and stared at the two ladies. "I don't need a Bible," he said as he started to close the door.

"That's not why we're here. Are you Mr. Barr?" Betty asked.

"Who wants to know?"

"I'm Betty Shapiro, and this is Alice Lukin. We'd like to ask you some questions."

He looked from one to the other. "You gotta be sisters." He gestured toward Betty. "I think I've seen you down at the store." He eyed Alice and frowned. "And you're from that Lukin ranch. What questions?"

The two ladies glanced at each other. They hadn't rehearsed any questions, and Alice blurted out the first thing that came to mind. "Did you put the dynamite box in our barn?"

His face darkened with menace as the door slammed.

They turned and, resisting the urge to run, casually walked away. When they got to the car, they abandoned their nonchalance and piled into the car as fast as they could and sped back to Betty's store.

Alice grinned like she had just found a buried treasure. "His reaction was as good as a confession. He certainly knew about the box."

"Maybe. But we have to prove it and then find the link to Magon," Betty said.

Alice pulled up in front of the Shapiro's general store. "You go ahead in," she said to Betty as she parked. "I need to run to the post office and pick up our mail."

"Hurry up. It's almost their closing time," Betty said.

Alice hastened down the street and got to the post office just as the postmistress was locking the door. She rapped on the glass, and the door opened. "Thanks, Lisa. Sorry to hold you up."

"Hi, Alice. Good thing you got here before I closed up. You received a registered letter today that requires your signature. Come to the window, and I'll get it for you." At the window, the postmistress handed Alice the envelope. "Sign here to show you received it and we can both go home."

"Thanks again," Alice said as she signed. Walking back to the store, she stared at the envelope listing the sender as the Inyo Bank. She hesitated to open it. Why in the world was the bank sending her a registered letter? They usually sent their statements and mortgage bills by regular mail. The store was already locked when she got there. She knocked on the door and waited.

"You look worried," Betty said as she opened the door. "What's the matter?"

Alice held out the envelope when she got inside. "You open it."

Betty locked the door, and they both went into the back office. Betty sat behind the desk and, with a letter opener blade, ceremoniously opened the envelope. Without reading it, she handed it across the desk toward her sister.

Alice pulled her hands close to her chest. "No, you read it."

Betty shrugged and unfolded the sheet. Her eyes widened as she glanced down the page.

"What's it say?"

Betty's voice shook. "The bank's foreclosing on your ranch."

"That… that…that *monster*," Alice shrieked. She grabbed the letter and read. "He says because we haven't made a payment in over a year, they're going to foreclose. That liar! I've made every payment, and I have the receipts to prove it."

"Yeah, I know. I was with you several times when you went to the bank."

Alice's eyes filled with tears. "Out there at the ranch last week, he said those were forgeries."

Betty grabbed the letter and read it again. "It says you have ninety days to bring the account up to date." She took the calendar from the hook on the wall and ran her fingers across the weeks, counting. "Twenty days left in this month. Then June and July add another sixty-one. Nincty takes you to mid-August. That gives you some time to fight. You're going to have to get a lawyer for Fred. Maybe he can help with this, too."

Alice cried softly with tears dripping off the end of her nose. "I don't see how we can pay a lawyer. Oh, everything's going wrong."

CHAPTER 37   ACCOUNTING

Driving to Bishop Monday morning, the crisp spring air made Grace feel like singing. But the only songs she knew were church hymns, and somehow, they didn't fit her elated mood. She would work at the bank's head office for a week. It would be sort of like a vacation getaway, and so exciting to learn more about handling the bank's accounts. Arithmetic was her best subject in elementary school, and she was proud that she was proficient at the bank.

As soon as she arrived, the young Collins woman took her in tow and explained journal and ledger transactions. The pretty redhead seemed barely old enough to be out of high school, but she had attended a women's business college in San Francisco and knew all about the accounts.

In the back room where they kept the bank records, Margaret slid a large leather-bound ring binder from a shelf. "This is where the loans to our clients are recorded. When someone repays a loan, it's recorded in the journal and then transferred to this ledger. Most of your work in Independence involves journal entries, but we keep the ledgers here in Bishop in these big binders." She set the binder on a table and pointed to a page. "See, this is the account for Emory Neikirk. He lives west of town and works at the vanadium mine. This shows the payments and which parts are principal and interest. She ran her fingers across the page. Here's the balance; still a few years to go."

Grace could hardly contain herself. "This is so interesting. You must know about everyone in the valley."

Margaret nodded. "I haven't lived here long enough to know everyone, but I'm learning. We're not supposed to discuss any of this with anyone outside the bank."

"Could we look at my loan?"

"We're not supposed to do that either," Margaret said, paused, and whispered conspiratorially. "But why not? Just don't tell anyone." She thumbed through the pages. "Here it is, Berks."

Grace examined it briefly and pointed. "Is this supposed to be the balance?"

"Yes, that's right. One thousand, three hundred and fifty-five dollars right now. It will go down by the amount of your principal payment next month."

Grace felt the blood drain from her face. There was a tremor in her voice. "That can't be. I sold the property to the City in February."

"Did you get paid then?"

"They gave me a check. Mr. Watson was at the settlement. He had me endorse the check over to him."

"Yes, Mr. Watson sometimes attends settlements and takes the check. He has someone in this office process it—usually me. But I don't remember handling yours."

"He said after they processed it, the bank would deposit the difference between the sale amount and my loan balance in my savings account."

"That's the usual practice. Have you received it yet?" Margaret asked.

"No. He said it would take a while, to be patient. That's why I didn't worry about it or say anything. I figured I just had to wait."

Margaret scrunched her mouth and raised an eyebrow. "It shouldn't take this long."

"Can we trace the check I signed over?"

"If it wasn't deposited here, it wouldn't be in our records. The only account where it would show up would be the DWP's account because they wrote it. It would be on their L.A. bank, and we wouldn't have access to that."

The reality of what had happened to her was sinking in. She had signed the title to her property over to the DWP, but had not a penny to show for it. In the bank's records, there was still a loan balance. She wanted to scream and strike out and hit something. She grabbed the big binder, raised it above her head, and slammed it on the floor. It flew open, and ledger pages flew all over the floor.

She looked at Margaret with tears in her eyes. She glanced around to see if anyone else had seen it.

Margaret patted Grace on the shoulder. "It'll be okay. That check will turn up soon, and we'll get this straightened out."

Grace got down on her hands and knees, gathered pages and handed them to Margaret. "What if it doesn't? What'll I do?"

"Let me look into it. Don't bring it up with anyone else, especially Mr. Watson. I'll find out what happened."

Grace had little choice, and Margaret seemed to know what she was doing, so for now, she would put it aside and concentrate on the instructions about the bank's accounts.

At quitting time, the two women went to Margaret's small cottage, where Grace would stay while she worked in Bishop.

Before work the next morning, Grace dropped Margaret at the Southern Pacific railway station to catch the train to Reno, then over the Sierras to the central valley. When Grace got to the bank, she was on her own and hoped she could remember all that Margaret had taught her. Sitting at the worktable in the back room, Grace jotted numbers into the ledger from the Friday cash reports from each of the branch offices. In the short time she had worked at the Independence office, she had been the one to call the report to the head office. She had read the figures over the phone to Mr. Watson, who, according to Margaret, recorded them in the ledger. Sometimes, he had Margaret record them, as Grace was doing now.

She knew it would eventually become routine and boring, but for now, if she could keep her mind off her missing check, it was interesting, and she felt important, knowing they trusted her to handle these crucial transactions.

She carefully recorded the balance reported from Big Pine and glanced at Watson's entry for Independence. Something was wrong. Mr. Watson's handwriting was hard to read, but she was sure the numbers said $9,657. She had called in the Independence report last Friday and remembered clearly that the balance was $11,657. She stood with the paper in hand to show Watson the error, then hesitated. She didn't want to make a mistake. Maybe there was a good explanation. She'd better be quiet and follow directions until she learned more. But as she totaled the figures, the discrepancy weighed on her mind.

She jerked with surprise when Watson's voice interrupted her concentration. "Grace, how are you faring? Is everything okay?"

"I'm doing well, Mr. Watson. I enjoy the work," she said with a nervous tremor in her voice.

"Just want to make sure you don't need anything. Do you have questions I can help with?"

Had he read her thoughts and come to check on her? She searched her brain for a question and asked the first one that popped up. "What do you do with this cash report when I'm finished with it?" As soon as the question was out of her mouth, she wished she had asked something else to change the subject.

"We are required to file it with the state banking office. They keep track of things to ensure each branch follows the rules and is solvent. Anything else?" he asked.

She shouldn't prolong the discussion of cash, but curiosity got the best of her. "I know we have a target cash balance in Independence of $6,000 and we send the excess up here to Bishop. What happens to the money after that?"

"You *are* a curious one. You know, curiosity killed the cat," Watson said with a chuckle. "But to answer your question, we keep some here to meet our needs and deposit the rest with our correspondent bank in Los Angeles."

"Those must be the bank statements from First National Bank that Margaret showed me."

"Exactly," Watson replied as he turned toward the lobby.

As she watched the bank proprietor walk away, she noticed a man who looked vaguely familiar come through the front door. She did a double-take. It was Barr from Independence. The man spoke to the teller and handed her a slip of paper. The teller turned to a ledger to check something, then handed the slip back and shook her head. Grace couldn't hear but guessed the man was trying to make a withdrawal, but there wasn't enough in the account. They talked animatedly as though they were arguing.

The teller motioned for the customer to follow her and took him back to speak to Watson. From the proprietor's reaction, it was clear that he recognized the man. Grace strained to hear while bending over the ledger, pretending to be busy.

"I told you not to come here," she heard Watson say. With the other man's back to her, mumbling was all she heard of his response. Watson belligerently thrust his face close and growled, "I don't owe you a thing." He pointed toward the door. "Now get out!"

There was more mumbling from the man, then his voice rose, and Grace heard only the last part. "… now, or everybody will hear about it."

"Damn you! You don't get another penny," Watson loudly exclaimed as he grabbed the man's arm and pushed him toward the door.

The man jerked his arm free, seized Watson by his coat collar, and slammed him against the teller's counter. Now, his gravelly voice carried clearly to Grace. "Watson, you're a fool to cross me." He slammed the banker against the counter and stormed out.

Grace studied the ledger in front of her like she was searching for a universal truth while Watson straightened his coat and paced furiously back and forth in the lobby.

She closed the cash ledger and placed it on the shelf. Her next task was to bring the loan balances up to date in the mortgage ledger. She took the heavy volume down from the shelf and began recording payments from a stack of the previous week's receipts. She reminded herself of Margaret's instructions — note the payment, then calculate the principal, interest, and new loan balance. Margaret had explained the calculations and showed her how to use the big Burroughs calculating machine sitting on her right. But all those keys were intimidating, so she did it by hand. That was the part she liked anyhow.

She worked through a few accounts until she felt comfortable. No one was paying any attention, so she checked her own account again. Her stomach turned over when she looked at the page. She had seen it earlier, but it shook her to her core to see a balance when it should be zero. She wanted to ask Watson about it, but Margaret had warned her not to. She stared at the ledger page. With the balance shown as still outstanding and no payments since the sale date, she knew it should be listed as delinquent, but it wasn't. She looked closer. Figures and notations had been erased. Out of the corner of her eye, she saw Watson looking her way and started recording a payment for a different account.

As she sorted through the receipts, she came to the page for Fred and Alice Lukin. There were no payments recorded for the last six months. That was bizarre. Alice seemed so conscientious about such things. In fact, Grace remembered forwarding a payment receipt to this office during her first week on the job. She leaned forward, examining the page up close. Again, someone had written over erased entries.

Her anxiety grew. The check for her ranch sale was missing, and what about the Lukins? If they had made recent payments, it looked like some might have been erased or never recorded. Then there were the discrepancies between the cash balances at the branch offices and those here at the head office. Had Margaret noticed these problems? Was that why she had cautioned her not to question Mr. Watson about the cash balance?

The rest of the week, Grace tended to the various accounts as instructed. When she noticed a discrepancy, she recorded it in a small diary she kept in her purse so she could ask Margaret about them when she returned.

CHAPTER 38   MORNING MAIL

Thursday, two days after the clash between Barr and Watson, Deputy Daggett walked into the sheriff's office from his daily trip to the post office. "Here's today's mail."

"Anything interesting?" Cole asked.

"The usual bunch of bulletins and wanted posters, except this." He held a letter and placed the rest on Cole's desk. "Ya know that inquiry to Sacramento about Barr I made late last week? This is their report."

"What'd they say?" Cole said.

"Lots. More 'n twenty-five years ago, when Barr was in his mid-twenties, he served three years for armed robbery." He glanced down at the sheet. "There's a long list of offenses where he was charged but not convicted and others where he was suspected but not charged. Those include arson, using explosives, and blackmail. More recently, he served four years in San Quentin for extortion and got out two years ago. The guy I talked to in Sacramento included a handwritten note that says this Barr guy works in the background for businesses as a fixer. He intimidates and frames a company's opponents, going after anybody threatening the company's position. Basically, he's a high-priced thug. Does anything for anybody that pays well."

"Just the sort of guy you need if you want to drive somebody off their land. But I have a hard time seeing the DWP hiring him," Cole said.

"Why not?" Daggett asked. "They've been doing some of their own strong-arm stuff."

"That's just it. They do it themselves and probably wouldn't pay well enough to hire a guy like Barr." Cole fanned the stack of envelopes like a deck of cards. "After I look through the rest of this mail, we'll talk to him again and see what we turn up."

Cole sliced open envelopes with his pocketknife, glanced at each paper, and added it to a stack. Daggett was right, the usual stuff. Then, one caught his eye. Addressed to Sheriff Cole in handwritten block lettering that looked familiar. The postmark said it was mailed two days ago from Reno. He extracted a sheet with a one-line message written in pencil with block lettering matching that on the front of the envelope:

WATSON BOT THE ACWADUCK BLAST

AND LUKIN FRAME

The printing rang a bell. It reminds him of another note he'd seen recently. He walked to the file cabinet by the window and dug out the note about the dynamite box in Fred's barn. No wonder it looked familiar. Laid side-by-side, both notes used identical lettering and bad spelling. "Hey, Daggett, look at this."

The deputy's eyes widened in amazement. "I'll be a monkey's uncle." He thought about it for a moment. "You think Fred coulda sent it?"

"How could he? He's in our jail. Besides, Fred wouldn't have planted the first note, and they match perfectly. This had to be sent by the guy who planted the first one."

"Who do you think mighta sent it?" Daggett asked.

"Who has a prison record and has been suspected of arson and using explosives? Who said he went to Reno a lot?"

Daggett looked puzzled. "You think it's Barr? But if the note's truc, why would Watson have it in for Fred? It doesn't make sense."

"Don't forget their fight at Alabama Gates and that confrontation across the street we heard about last month."

Daggett shook his head. "A fight's not enough motive to blast the aqueduct to frame a guy."

"Sure it is. Watson thinks he's the top rooster. For some guy to slug him in the mouth with half the valley population watching is intolerable. He's gotta get revenge."

"But people would have to see him take revenge for him to redeem himself."

"Nah. He's the kind to work behind the scenes and have somebody else do the dirty work. And then there's his taste for the ladies. That was the reason for the fight. He's got an eye for Alice and wants to get Fred out of the way."

"He's got plenty of ladies available," Daggett observed. "He doesn't need to go to the trouble of hiring some high-priced thug from out of town to blast the aqueduct and frame Fred to get some female entertainment."

"Deputy, you just don't understand these things. The prize that is beyond reach is irresistible, especially if it's a woman."

Daggett laughed. "So now you're becoming a philosopher, eh, Chief?"

"My philosophy is that people do stupid things."

"For sure," Daggett agreed. "That's what keeps us employed."

Cole scratched his head. "But why would Barr send the note accusing Watson? Why double-cross Watson, if that's what this is? It can lead back to Barr."

"Revenge," Daggett said. "My turn to be a philosopher. Revenge is the second reason for doing stupid things."

"You're right. Time to visit Mr. Barr again."

Cole and Daggett drove to Barr's house, determined to learn more about him. The new Hudson touring car was gone. Cole knocked on the door and waited a minute, then tried the door—locked. The curtains on the windows thwarted his attempts to see in. The guy had flown the coop. The sheriff should have been more insistent when he had the chance. Maybe he could find something out from the landlord, whoever that might be. "When we get to the office," he said to Daggett, "check with County Records to see who owns this dump. Maybe the landlord knows something about this guy."

When he got back to his office, Cole didn't have long to wait.

"Hey, boss. Guess who owns that place," Daggett said when he returned from County Records.

"If I knew, I wouldn't 'a sent you," the sheriff grumbled.

"Mark Watson!"

Cole stared at the deputy. "You sure?"

"Yeah. Double checked. He got it on a defaulted loan four years ago."

"Now that raises a passel of questions," Cole absent-mindedly doodled on scrap paper while he let his mind run. Was Barr the bomber? How was he linked to Watson? Is he working for Watson, the DWP, or somebody else? Most of the cases he dealt with in this sparsely settled land were simple. Things fit. But nothing about this case seemed to fit. This case smelled and made little sense. He whacked his pencil against the desk. Fred had served as a decoy long enough. It was time to spring him. But first, he had to talk to Watson.

"Daggett, I'm going up to Bishop to talk to Watson. Keep an eye on things here."

Before leaving, Cole called Watson and arranged to meet him at the coffee shop on Bishop's main street.

"Thanks for meeting with me, Mark," Cole said as he slid into the booth.

Mark Watson chuckled. "Always glad to meet with our constabulary, Charlie. I recommend the cherry pie, it's great here."

"I know," Cole said. "But no pie today. Doris says I'm getting pudgy."

The waitress appeared with her pencil poised, ready for the order. "Morning, Mr. Watson… Sheriff. What can I get you gentlemen?"

"Just coffee for me, Nellie," Watson said.

"Make that two," Cole added.

Watson leaned forward as though to hear a secret. "What's on your mind, Charlie?"

Cole eyed the banker speculatively. "I've been looking into some issues that I thought you might shed some light on."

"I'll help any way I can." He glanced up as the waitress arrived with two coffees and set them down. "Thanks, Nellie."

Cole stirred sugar into his coffee. "You see, Mark, I've gotten some information I'd like to check with you."

"Okay, shoot."

"First, do you know a man named Irwin Barr?"

Watson's mouth dropped in surprise. After a short hesitation, he replied. "Never heard of him. Why do you ask?"

Cole laughed to himself. Watson was a worse liar than the sheriff had imagined. "You sure you never heard of him?"

Watson's voice rose. "Of course. If I knew him, I'd say so."

"Well, he's been living in a rental house in Independence that you own. Know anything about that?"

Watson sipped his coffee and stared steadily over the rim of the cup at Cole. "No. I don't handle the rentals. Bruce Aigner, the branch manager down there, takes care of that. What's this about? Is this guy wanted or something?"

"Just someone whose name came up in an investigation."

"What sort of investigation? Does it have anything to do with the bombing of the aqueduct? That's about the only thing that's happened lately."

Cole took a sheet from his coat pocket and slowly unfolded it. "Speaking of that, I got this note you might be interested in."

Watson reached across the table to take the paper, but Cole pulled it back out of the banker's range. He watched Watson's face as he recited the message from memory. "It says, 'Watson bought the aqueduct blast and the Lukin frame'."

Watson's face blanched, and he licked his lips. "That's a lie." His voice rose. "Where'd you get that?" He reached across the table again. "Let me see it."

Cole deliberately slid it slowly back into his pocket, all the while scanning Watson's face and waiting for his next move.

"That's just... just scurrilous innuendo. I ought to sue you for libel."

Cole smiled. "Thanks for joining me for coffee, Mark." He stood, placed a fifty-cent piece on the table, and left the coffee shop.

As he walked to his car, Cole replayed the interview. Bruce Aigner handled the rentals. That needed checking … fast. He hurried to the Bishop sheriff's sub-station to place a call to the Independence branch manager before Watson got to him first.

When Aigner came on the line, Cole began. "Hi, Bruce. This is Sheriff Cole calling from Bishop. I need to check a couple of things. Mark Watson says you tend to the bank's property rentals in Independence."

"That's right," Bruce answered. "What do you need to check?"

"Did you rent a house to a Mr. Barr?"

"Yes. He came here a few weeks ago and said Mr. Watson had sent him. The little house at the end of Clay Street was vacant, and he took it."

"How much was the rent?"

"That's the funny part. I told him fifteen a month. He said that Mr. Watson said there was no charge. I called Mr. Watson in Bishop for confirmation. He said to let Barr take the place and to set up a checking account for him. I gave the guy the keys and have seen him only a couple of times since."

"Did he use the checking account?"

"Yes. A little later, Mr. Watson sent a note directing me to credit funds into Barr's checking account."

"What do you mean, 'credit funds into his account'?"

"That's what we usually do with a loan. Nobody hands dollar bills over for the deposit. We just make a paper entry that puts money in the account and the borrower can spend it."

Cole thought about it and asked, "So, if Watson wants to give money to someone, he just has you make a paper entry? Then the customer can take real money out anytime he wants."

"That's right."

"How much was it?" Cole asked.

"I don't remember the exact amounts, but they were fairly large, like a hundred dollars or more with each deposit."

"Each deposit? Were there several of these transactions?" Cole said. "Could you do me a favor? Check those amounts and dates and give me a list."

After a long pause on the other end, Aigner replied. "I'm sorry, Sheriff, I can't do that without a court order. We're not allowed to disclose a customer's banking information. I shouldn't have told you as much as I have. If Mr. Watson finds out, I'll be in trouble."

"Thank you for telling me this much. It's very helpful."

Now that was an interesting meeting, Cole thought as he drove south out of Bishop. When he was a kid in San Francisco, his teacher had read *Alice in Wonderland* to the class and he recalled Alice saying something was curiouser and curiouser. Well, this case was getting curiouser and curiouser.

He hadn't expected the interview with Watson to lead anywhere, but the banker's evasions screamed that the anonymous note was right. Anonymous? Not really. Sure as anything, Barr had been working for the banker, and Watson arranged the aqueduct blast to frame Fred. If that was right, Barr did the actual work. What crime could Watson be charged with? He'd have to get the D.A.'s opinion. But proving anything would require Barr's testimony. He was gone, and Charlie doubted he'd ever see him again.

As soon as Cole got back to Independence, he headed to the District Attorney's office.

The door was open, with D.A. Walt Hess seated behind his desk, talking to Judge Daley. Without knocking, Cole barged into the office and took the chair next to the judge before either man could say anything.

Daley watched him sit down. "Don't worry about interrupting us, Charlie," he said with a tone of sarcasm.

"Thanks, I won't."

"I'm guessing you have something on your mind," the judge said.

"Yeah, Stanley. Walt was right when he advised me to use Fred as a decoy. Now I'd like to let him go."

"You have my blessing," Walt said. "He's been in there, what, two weeks? I'm glad I'm not the one who has to look him in the face."

"Twelve days, to be exact," Cole said. "Any longer and Alice will be after me with a twelve-gauge and a pistol."

The judge laughed. "You got that right. Why release him now?"

"I think the decoy mighta worked."

"What happened?" Hess asked.

"I got another note." Cole handed it to Hess. "The writing matches the first note that said to look in Fred's barn. It's gotta be the same person, and I think I know who."

The D.A. read the note and handed it to the Judge.

Daley read the note and said, "Don't keep us in suspense. Who?"

"There's this guy, Irwin Barr, who showed up in town a few weeks ago with no apparent job or income. My gut tells me that he wrote both notes and maybe did the aqueduct blast too."

"Gut feel doesn't work in court," the judge remarked.

"No, but it usually puts me on the right track. According to the state police, Barr served time for armed robbery several years ago and has a reputation for working as a strong-arm for businesses. It sure looks like he was working for Watson. He's been living rent-free in a Watson property and getting paid by Watson. This latest note was mailed from Reno, and earlier, Barr told me he goes to Reno a lot. As soon as I started asking questions, he skipped town. I'm guessing he and Watson had some sort of falling out and that's why he sent the second note fingering Watson."

"I have a hard time believing Mark Watson is mixed up in such a mess. But in any case, there are too many questions to justify holding Fred," Hess said.

"Good. I'll let him go and then we can all find someplace to hide from Alice," Cole said as he got up to leave.

Back in his office, he completed the paperwork for the prisoner's release. But he stalled, not wanting to face Fred. He was tempted to give the task to Daggett. But this was someone he'd been friends with for many years. He had to face him. He knew Fred would probably never forgive him. He'd arrested him twice and knew this time was wrong. He wouldn't forgive if it had been him.

He walked down the hall and stood silently in front of the cell door, wishing he had something decent to say. Fred scowled at him from the bottom tier of the bunk bed. Cole unlocked the door, pulled it open, and spoke gruffly to cover his emotion. "You're outta here. Judge Daley ordered your release. You gotta sign some stuff, then you can go."

Fred ran his hand over his rough beard. Without a word, he followed Cole down the hall to the office.

Cole handed him a paper bag. "Here's your stuff." He pointed at a paper on his desk. "Sign here. Daggett can drive you home."

Fred signed. Ignoring the offer of a ride and saying not a word to the sheriff, he walked out the door and headed across the street to Jake and Betty's store.

When Jake pulled up in front of the ranch house, Fred got out of the car and leaned in. "Thanks for driving me home, Jake. I know you gotta get back to the store." He shut the door, slapped the car roof, and turned toward the house. Aside from asking Jake for a ride home when he left the sheriff's office, those were the only words he had uttered since leaving the cell.

He didn't want to scare Alice by barging in when she wasn't expecting him, so he knocked on the door and waited.

When she opened the door, her eyes widened and her mouth dropped in surprise. "Fred," she screamed. She buried her face against his chest and they held each other. Eventually, she stepped back and looked at him with tears flowing down her cheeks.

"You got my shirt wet," Fred said with a broad smile.

"Your shirt needs washing, and you stink," she replied. "Did you escape, or did Charlie let you go?"

"He let me go. Said Daley ordered my release. I guess they dropped the charges but didn't say why."

"Now what?" Alice asked.

"Act like a rancher. There's so many people I'd like to get back at, but there's too much to do around here. I need to get back to work."

Stretching on tiptoes, Alice affectionately patted the top of his head. "Good boy. Forget about those guys and mind our own business." She stood back and looked him up and down. "Now, get out of those stinky clothes and get a bath."

CHAPTER 39   WHAT SHE LEARNED

Grace left work early on Friday, her last day at the Bishop office, and drove to the train station to pick up Margaret. She looked at the big clock above the ticket window in the Southern Pacific station. Three-fifteen. The train from Reno was late and she paced nervously back and forth on the platform, eager to ask Margaret about all those unusual accounting entries. With Margaret back, Grace could return to Independence. It would be good to get home, but she also felt a little sad to leave Bishop. It had been good to get away.

There was the whistle, and a few minutes later, the train pulled into the station. Margaret was the last one to get off. At the bottom of the steps, the two women bussed cheeks, and Grace carried the young woman's suitcase to the car.

Margaret spoke excitedly as they drove toward town. "I've been going crazy waiting to tell you. Guess what I found." She continued before Grace could say a word. "When I was home with my family, I called an old high school friend who works at Pacific

National Bank in L.A., the correspondent where our bank deposits its cash. She told me that Mr. Watson has two accounts there, one for Inyo Bank and another one in his own name. She said that the check for your ranch was endorsed by him and deposited in his personal account. She said it looked like that account was used mostly to pay expenses for his other businesses and his personal expenses and sometimes for investments in the stock market."

Grace thought about it for a moment. "So, he stole my money without paying off my loan. It disappears and never shows on the bank's books." She gave a high-pitched scream and slapped the steering wheel. "Damn him!"

"Yeah. He's using bank funds for his other businesses and playing the stock market. I bet that's against the law," Margaret said.

"How do I get my money back?"

"I don't know," Margaret replied. "I can't tell anyone how I found out or my friend will get fired."

"But I found other stuff in the books that wouldn't involve your friend."

Margaret looked surprised. "What did you find? The only thing I ever saw were minor discrepancies."

"I kept a diary. I'll show you when we get to your place."

At Margaret's cottage, Grace fixed some tea while Margaret washed up and got settled. They sat down at the kitchen table and

Grace explained her diary entries listing the discrepancies in the cash and loan accounts.

Margaret pursed her lips in frustration. "I don't know why I didn't notice any of that. I'm embarrassed that I missed it."

"Why would you?" Grace asked. "I noticed it because I've worked in the two different branches, so I could see the differences. I also know the people, and you're sort of new to the valley. There is no reason you should have known about the payment for my ranch or anything about the Lukin's account."

Margaret sipped her tea and thought about it. "Should we tell the sheriff?"

"Not yet," Grace replied. "We don't know who to trust. Lots of people think Mr. Watson is the valley's savior, so we need to be careful who we talk to. Let me ask Alice and Betty".

Driving back to Independence after leaving Margaret at her cottage, Grace thought of little else but her missing check. That money was all she had, and that crook had stolen it. Did he think she was so stupid that she'd never catch on? He probably thought she was just a dumb farmwife who couldn't understand anything except cooking, sewing, and feeding the chickens. He'd find out otherwise when she put him in his place.

Grace's kitchen was empty of fresh food when she got home Friday evening. She made do with crackers and a bowl of canned soup and turned in for the night. She slept fitfully, tossing and turning, thinking about her money and Watson's deceptions. In the morning, she fixed a quick breakfast of coffee and toast of stale bread and then headed out to the Lukin ranch.

Driving over the bumpy, sandy road, she thought about the hundreds of times she had been over it. Yet, it seemed unfamiliar now. She smiled. She was changing into a city girl after only a few weeks away from the ranch where she and Slim had spent most of their lives. She was nineteen when they got married. It was hard to believe that, after thirty-seven years together, neither he nor the ranch was part of her life.

Before she had a chance to knock, Alice flung the door open. "Grace! I heard you driving up. How nice to see you. Come in. Come in." The two women hugged and bussed cheeks. "I just fixed some tea. Would you like some?"

"Yes, thank you. When I parked, I saw Fred working out in the field. When did they release him?"

"Wednesday," Alice said from the kitchen counter as she poured two cups of tea. "Neither one of us knows for sure why he was released, but at least Charlie came to his senses. How was your stay in Bishop?"

"I learned lots of interesting stuff. That's why I came out here. I have to tell somebody."

"Tell what?"

Grace recounted the disappearance of the payment for her ranch and the discrepancies in the bank's accounts.

When Grace said Alice's recent loan payments were missing, Alice shrieked. "That crook! Right after Fred was arrested, he came out here and propositioned me. When I told him to leave, he threatened me with our mortgage loan. I've made every payment on time, and I have the receipts to prove it, but he sent us a foreclosure notice. It gives us until mid-August to bring it up to date. You either give him what he wants or he will destroy you. I've even thought about giving in to him."

Grace's voice rose. "Alice Lukin! Don't you dare do that! Does Fred know about any of this?"

"No. I haven't had the nerve to tell him. He just got out of jail. I don't want him back in for murder."

"We've got to pull Watson down," Grace said.

"Yeah, but how?" Alice said.

Grace opened her diary. "I took these notes about his deceptions, but I don't know who to tell. I don't know how far he'd go if he faced exposure. He has lots of friends, and I'm scared."

"We certainly aren't on his list of friends. Betty and Jake are coming tomorrow for Sunday dinner. Join us and we can talk it over."

CHAPTER 40   RECORDS

Sunday night, Betty, Jake, Grace, Alice, and Fred sat around the Lukins' table, savoring dessert.

"Alice, that was such a wonderful dinner," Grace said after her last bite of apple pie. "That was one of the best pot roasts I've had in a long time. With Slim gone and me living alone, I don't cook like I used to."

"Grace, you're the best cook I know. I'll let you cook for us to stay in practice," Betty said with an impish smile.

"You couldn't pay enough," Grace responded good-naturedly. "Besides, after a day at the bank, I'm usually too tired to cook for myself."

"Speaking of the bank," Jake said, "Alice told us you found irregularities in the accounts when you were in Bishop. You want to show us?"

Grace dug her diary out of her purse and, as she turned the pages, described some of the problems she found, such as inconsistencies between the cash balance at the local branch and what had been recorded at the Bishop's headquarters. When she got to Alice and Fred's mortgage account, she hesitated and looked questioningly at Alice. Alice gave an almost imperceptible negative shake of her head and Grace skipped to another account.

Fred looked from Alice to Grace and back. "What was that about?"

Alice sighed. "We might as well tell him. He's gotta know about it eventually."

Grace explained how the Lukin loan payments were not recorded on the mortgage ledger.

"Bastard!" Fred thundered. Then thought about it for a moment. "There's something more. What didn't you want to tell me?"

Everyone looked at Alice, waiting. She stared at her empty dinner plate, pushed her silverware around on the table, picked up some crumbs, and put them on her plate.

"What don't you want me to know?" Fred demanded.

Alice took a deep breath. "Now Fred, if you promise not to go wild, I'll tell you."

"Out with it!"

Another deep breath. "When I came home from town the day they put you in jail, Watson was waiting. He offered to provide his attorney for you if I would, as he put it, be generous with him, and we could be good friends. When I told him to get off the property, he said we hadn't made our mortgage payments, and he was going to foreclose."

Fred slapped the table. "I'll kill that guy!"

"You promised not to go wild," Alice said.

"I'm not wild," he loudly insisted. He looked at Alice. "Did he leave?"

"Yes. I got rid of him. That's why he said he was going to foreclose."

Fred paced back and forth across the room. "That crook wants to take the ranch. He's as bad as the DWP. He needs a good beating."

"Fred, getting into a fight isn't the answer," Jake said. "Instead, let's get him where he's vulnerable."

Fred stopped his pacing and stared at Jake. "How do we do that? He owns half the valley and most of the people not already owned by the DWP."

"According to Grace's notes, he may be doing some sort of crooked stuff at his bank. If we can get the authorities to take a look, it could bury him."

Fred resumed his pacing. "Which authorities? I can't see Charlie Cole arresting him. I doubt he knows any more about banking than I do."

"No, not him. I mean banking authorities. There's a state agency that regulates the banks. Maybe they'll take a look."

"I can't wait around until some state inspector decides to do something," Fred's voice rose. "He's going to take our ranch."

"It takes a while to foreclose," Jake said. He turned to Alice. "Has he started the foreclosure process?"

Alice nodded and spoke scarcely above a whisper. "Yes, he sent a registered letter."

Fred practically exploded. "He sent a foreclosure letter and you didn't tell me?"

Alice stared at her plate. "I was afraid what you might do and get yourself into trouble."

Fred shook his head in disbelief and slumped back down in his chair. "Jesus, we could end up just like the Schaffers and have to move away."

"You need to prove you've made the payments," Jake said. "Do you have receipts for your payments?"

"I never missed a payment, and I'm sure I have all the receipts," Alice said.

"That ought to put you in the clear. Gather them up. Does the letter say how much time you have?" Jake asked.

"It said we had ninety days to clear it up. With time already elapsed, we have a little over two months left—till mid-August."

Jake looked at his hands and counted on his fingers. "In that time, maybe we can get the state banking office involved. I'll make some calls this week."

"Just do it carefully," Grace said. "I like my job and want to keep it."

"I've also been thinking about the sale of Grace's ranch," Alice said. "She's never received any payment, so she must still own the ranch."

"You've never been paid?" Jake asked. The look of shock on his face matched the surprise in his voice.

"No. At the settlement, Mr. Magon gave me a check, but Mr. Watson said I should endorse it to him and he would see that our mortgage was paid off and put the balance in my savings account at the Inyo Bank."

"That sounds fairly normal," Jake said. "A lot of sales are handled that way."

"But I never received anything."

"But you signed a lot of papers at the settlement, didn't you?" Jake said.

"Yes, of course."

"Undoubtedly, those documents transferred the title. Did you read them?" Jake asked.

"Not really. I don't know any of that legal stuff, and Mr. Magon said they were the same forms the DWP uses for all its purchases. Also, Mr. Watson was there."

Fred absent-mindedly pushed some of his half-eaten pie around his plate with his fork while he thought it over. "So, you signed the papers and Magon gave you a check that you endorsed to Watson. Maybe Alice is right. Maybe since you never received the money, you didn't actually sell the ranch."

"No," Jake said. "She received the check, and the DWP can say they paid her with the check, and what she did with the check afterward is not their concern."

"Still, it's worth checking to see if the transaction was recorded," Fred replied. "I think they record all the property transactions at the courthouse. It can't be that hard to look it up in the county records. Maybe we can check tomorrow."

"Hi, Eleanor," Alice said as she and Fred entered the county recorder's office.

The spritely lady looked up from a large ledger. "Alice, Fred, I haven't seen you since I don't know when. What brings you in?"

"We want to check some property sale records," Fred said. "But you'll have to show us how."

"Of course. It's easy once you get the hang of it. Which property?"

"Grace Berks' ranch sale," Alice said.

"It's here. I remember recording it," the woman said as she slid a large volume from a shelf and thumbed the pages. "Berks, Berks. Here it is. Oh, yes, I remember, this was one of those Mr. Magon came in himself and registered with a different company name."

"What do you mean, 'registered it with a different company name'?" Alice asked.

"I guess the DWP changed the way they registered the deeds on a few of the properties." She pointed to the page. "Here's the property that Grace sold. It was conveyed to 'DWP, Inc., a California corporation'." She turned the page. "Now look at this other sale. This one conveys the property to 'The City of Los Angeles, a municipal corporation of the State of California'. That's the name they've been using since they began buying valley properties in the early years of the century."

"What difference does that make?" Fred asked. "DWP means Department of Water and Power, and it belongs to the City of Los Angeles. The sale is still valid, isn't it?"

"Yes, of course, it's valid, and Mr. Magon registered the Berks property and a few others to this different entity."

"I don't understand," Alice said. "Aren't they just two different names for the same company?"

"They have to use the correct name for the title," Eleanor replied. "The DWP may have created a different entity to hold some properties and use the older name for others."

"Are they still using the old name for other recent purchases?" Fred asked.

"Yes. That one I showed you registered to the City of Los Angeles was about the same time as the Berks sale."

"You said there are others that were sold to this DWP company. Which ones?"

"The recent ones I remember were the Boyd and Stevens properties out by you that sold some months ago. There were some others, but I don't remember which ones."

Fred's eyebrows furrowed. "Berks, Boyd, and Stevens are all on our ditch. Where are the other properties that were sold to the DWP?"

"I think they were up around Big Pine and Bishop. I have to get back to work, so you'll have to look them up yourself." She handed him a volume. "Here's the index. They are organized by names of seller and buyer, so you can look for transactions involving DWP, Inc."

Alice and Fred set to work finding the DWP property purchases. An hour later, they sat looking at their list. Alice ran her finger down her notes. "Okay, we know which ones were sold to DWP, Inc., but I don't see what that tells us."

"Did you notice what they all have in common?" Fred asked.

Alice shrugged. "They're all ranches?"

"More than that. The DWP name was used only when the ranch was on a ditch, but the properties sold to the City of Los Angeles didn't include ditch shares."

"I still don't see what difference it makes," Alice said.

"I don't either. Maybe none." Fred called across the room. "Eleanor, we got a question. How can we find out the difference between ownership by DWP and the City of Los Angeles?"

Eleanor set her work aside and thought for a moment. "Mr. Magon probably knows. I could ask him for you. He's taking me to dinner in Bishop Wednesday evening."

Fred's mouth dropped in surprise. Going to dinner with Magon? Somehow, it was difficult to picture him eating in a civilized manner and even harder to imagine this lady having anything to do with the thug. Before he could say anything, *Wump*! Alice kicked his ankle under the table and gave an almost imperceptible shake of her head that said to hold his tongue. He glared at her but said nothing.

"Oh, no, don't do that," Alice said to Eleanor. "We wouldn't want to bother him."

"It wouldn't be any bother. He's very nice. We've been out to dinner several times, and he's always a perfect gentleman."

Fred and Alice glanced at each other, shock written across both faces.

Eleanor filled the uncomfortable silence. "Oh, I know some people don't have a high opinion of him, but when I'm with him, I have such a good time. You know, a woman my age doesn't get many invitations."

"Isn't there another way to find out about these companies rather than disturbing Mr. Magon?" Alice asked.

Eleanor thrummed three fingers on her chin as she gave it some thought. "Yes. If you want to know about different corporate entities, the starting point is to look at their articles of incorporation."

"What would that tell us?" Fred said.

"Facts like when it was formed, where it's headquartered, who set up the corporation, how many shares, and sometimes who owns them."

Alice looked puzzled. "I can't see that any of that would really tell us much."

"It's only a start," Eleanor said. "But knowing when a company was created and who set it up and owns it might answer some of your questions. Anybody can register a corporation and call it anything they want."

Fred looked at the list of ranches bought by DWP. He had never given any thought to how companies got their names or who named them. He realized anybody, even himself, could create a company called DWP, Inc., and everyone would think it was the Department of Water and Power. "Where do you keep those records?"

"We don't have them here," Eleanor replied. "They're kept in Sacramento at the Secretary of State's office."

Alice's face brightened, and she spoke quietly to Fred. "Ok, let's go to Sacramento. I've never been there. We could leave on the train Thursday and get back this weekend. If Grace went with us, we could kill two birds with one trip."

"What do you mean, 'two birds'?" Fred asked.

"Grace could talk with the state banking people about the problems she found at the bank, and we can investigate the registration of this DWP company."

Before heading home, Fred and Alice called on Grace at her cottage after she got off work. She agreed to ask for Thursday and Friday off and go with Alice and Fred.

CHAPTER 41   SACRAMENTO

Fred and Alice, accompanied by Grace Berks, boarded the train Thursday morning for the three-hundred-mile trip to the state capital. With a train connection in Reno, they arrived in Sacramento that evening and checked into two rooms in a hotel near the capitol building. First thing Friday morning they went to the State Banking Department on the fifth floor of the state office building.

After they had introduced themselves, Clarence Lowell, the head bank examiner, dressed smartly in a tweed suit, said, "Mr. Shapiro called and made the appointment for you, but he didn't give much detail. How can I help you?"

Fred looked at Grace, waiting for her to speak. She mutely clutched her purse. After a brief pause, he gestured toward her. "Grace, here, works at the Inyo Bank. She thinks she found evidence of crooked dealing at the bank. Grace, go ahead, tell him."

Grace straightened her shoulders like she was girding for battle and spoke hesitantly. "You see, Mr. Lowell, I recently began working at the Independence branch of the bank that's headquartered in Bishop. I don't know much about accounting, so I am probably wrong about this, but I found what I think are discrepancies."

"That's okay. Tell me what you found."

"I didn't notice any problems at the local branch in Independence, but when I spent a week covering for Margaret Collins at the main office in Bishop, I found a lot of strange things that don't make sense." She took her diary from her purse and set it on the desk. "I noted them in this diary."

"Did you ask the manager about them?" Lowell said.

"No, Margaret said I should keep them to myself. She never explained why, but I think she's afraid of Mr. Watson. Also, I am brand-new and worried about my job."

"Let's take a look at your diary."

Grace pushed the small notebook across the desk so he could see it as she explained each entry.

When she finished the list, the examiner leaned back in his chair, contemplating Grace. "This is shocking if it's true. Are you sure you didn't get the numbers wrong?"

"I tried to be careful." She nervously folded and unfolded her hands. "Also, I didn't tell you about my check because it never appeared in the bank's accounting."

"Your check?"

"Yes, I sold our ranch property to the City of Los Angeles. They gave me a check. At the settlement, Mr. Watson had me endorse the check over to him and said he would put the difference between the sale price and the loan balance in my bank account. I found out he deposited it in his personal account in Los Angeles, and I have never received a cent."

The examiner stared at her skeptically. "I have a hard time believing that. Surely, he gave you a receipt and has accounted for the money. Maybe he set up a different account for you."

Grace's voice rose. "No! He never set up anything."

He frowned and jotted notes on a paper.

As he was writing, Alice spoke. "Mr. Lowell, when Grace explained her diary, she mentioned our loan payments. I made payments on our loan every month. I paid cash at the Independence office and kept all the receipts." She laid a stack of small papers on the desk. "Here are my receipts for the last two years, but Grace said none of my payments were listed for several months."

"It looked to me like the payments had been listed in the ledger and were erased later," Grace added.

Lowell glanced through the receipts. "Did the bank send you delinquency notices?"

"None," Alice replied. "But recently, they sent us a notice that they were going to foreclose."

The examiner stood up. "I will have to talk to my boss to see what we do next. I think it would be best if you say nothing about this to anyone else, especially Mr. Watson." He picked up the diary. "May I keep this?"

Grace hesitated and looked questioningly at Fred and Alice.

Lowell watched their faces. "On second thought, if you folks have time, I can have my assistant copy the entries and return the original this afternoon. I'll give you a receipt to acknowledge that I have it."

"That would be okay," Fred said. "We're going to another office to look at articles of incorporation and we can come back later."

"That makes it easy," said the inspector. "That office is on the third floor."

"Do you think it will do any good?" Grace asked as they descended the stairs to the third floor.

"He seemed to believe you. We just have to wait to see what happens." Fred replied .

At the office of the Secretary of State, Fred asked to see the articles of incorporation of DWP, Inc. After a brief wait, the clerk returned with file folders. "There are three companies with that name. Which do you want?"

"Can we look at all three?" Fred asked.

The clerk laid the folders on the counter and spoke officiously. "Read them here. Don't tear them or get them out of order."

Fred read the company name on each folder. "Duffel Wirth Products, Inc., (dba DWP), Redding, California; Dungy, Wagner, and Pickering, (dba DW&P), San Francisco; and DWP, Inc., Los Angeles."

"The last one," Alice said.

Fred opened the folder and spread two sheets on the counter. There were three simultaneous gasps.

Fred's mouth dropped, and his eyes widened. "I'll be damned."

Alice's hand covered her mouth. "Oh, good grief."

"Holy Mother of God!" Grace cried.

Alice read aloud the first page showing the corporate details: "Agent: Earl Magon; 3107 Council St., Los Angeles; Business: Land Investment; Directors: Earl Magon; Principal Shareholders: Earl Magon."

Fred ran his finger across the page as though his touch would reveal whether it was true. "All those properties now belong to Magon's company."

"And everyone thinks they belong to the real Department of Water and Power," Grace said.

"That's why he goes to such lengths to buy them," Alice said. "He gets them instead of the City of Los Angeles," Alice said.

"But why wouldn't everyone find out?" Grace asked.

"Because it all appears normal," Alice replied. "Everybody assumes DWP, Inc., refers to the Department of Water and Power, and this is just a different way to register the sale, just like Eleanor did. Some clerk records the purchase--money paid and land acquired, and everybody goes about their business. All that the Department of Water and Power employees know is that the DWP bought the land to get the water. Their crews use the land and water as if it's theirs, and Magon never says otherwise."

"But if they use the land and water, then why does he do it? What good does it do him?" Grace asked.

"Who knows? He's sure to have some sort of angle in mind." Fred gazed at the ceiling as he thought about it. "My guess is that, at a later date, when the time is right, he will claim his properties and sell them." After another moment of contemplation, he added, "Or maybe it's sort of like a kidnapping. He takes title and tells the Department of Water and Power they can have the property back if they pay ransom."

"Somebody at the real DWP is bound to notice," Alice said. "It's got to be against some law, and he'd lose his job and probably be arrested if anybody figures it out."

"Yeah, but he's the boss of property acquisitions. He's a thug, and nobody wants to cross him," Fred said.

Grace's voice cracked with anger. "The Department of Water and Power gave me a check, but Magon took title, and Watson took the check for himself. I'm left with nothing." Her voice rose. "I'd like to kill them all."

"You can't kill them, or at least you shouldn't," Alice said.

"If it's a crime, I imagine Mr. Magon would pay to keep it a secret," Grace said.

Fred stared at her. "You're talking blackmail!" He chuckled. "I never thought I'd hear such a thing from you."

"Me neither," Grace replied. "But then I never had everything stolen before."

"But it's Watson who stole from you, not Magon," Alice said.

"Either way, a little revenge would be sweet," Grace said.

"We have to be careful," Fred said. "A thug like Magon is capable of most anything, including murder."

"I wouldn't put it past Watson, either," Alice added.

Saturday evening, the Southern Pacific train pulled into the Independence station where Jake waited to take them home.

"Thanks for meeting us," Fred said as he and the two women stepped off the train onto the boarding platform.

"Glad to do it," Jake said as he took the ladies' small valises. "The car's on the other side of the station. You find anything interesting?"

"A lot," Alice replied. "Anything interesting happen here while we were away?"

Jake smiled like he had a great joke. "Just two more dynamite attacks on the DWP."

Fred stopped walking and stared at Jake. "Seriously? You're not joking? Where this time?"

"Thursday night, somebody hit the intake of the power plant above Big Pine. Then, yesterday, there was a huge blast of the siphon down at No Name Canyon. That pipe is nine feet in diameter, and they blew the whole thing apart. I hear water is flowing all over the desert south of Little Lake."

Fred chuckled. "Bet they're having cat fits in L.A. The city cops up here yet?"

"Yup. A couple of carloads of cops and Pinkertons got here Friday afternoon. They came to the store asking lots of questions. I don't think they have any idea who did it."

CHAPTER 42   SWIMMING TO L.A.

After Jake dropped Alice and Fred off at their ranch house, Alice prepared a quick dinner of ham and eggs.

At the table, Alice looked pensive as she stirred her tea. "You think that man in the bank department will actually come over here?"

Fred shrugged. "Don't know. He seemed to take it seriously. We'll have to wait and see."

"Yeah, I hope they decide to go over the bank's books."

"Magon's the one that has me stumped," Fred said. "He's a thug, but I doubt that creating a company named DWP breaks any laws. But sure as shootin' he can't take title to something the real DWP has paid for."

"Whatever it is, I'm sure it's crooked."

Fred pointed with his fork. "You want that last piece of ham?"

"Go ahead … I worry that we talked too much about Magon and property titles in front of Eleanor. I never imagined that she might go out with somebody like that. No telling what she might say to him about our checking property records or going to Sacramento."

"I don't see that it would make much difference," Fred said. "He hasn't bothered us for a while. I guess he's busy buying up other properties. So many folks are giving up and moving away that he's too busy buying their ranches to bother with this place. Who knows, maybe Eleanor will civilize him."

"I doubt that. I just hope she's okay. She's too naive to get involved with the likes of Magon."

"Well, I got involved with you and I lived to tell the tale."

Alice pointed her finger at him like a pistol. "Talk like that and it'll be the last tale you tell."

He laughed and they talked a while longer. After cleaning up, they turned in for the night.

Fred had no trouble falling asleep as soon as his head hit the pillow, but his slumber was filled with nightmares of poisoned cattle and being locked up in jail. Long after midnight, he was in the midst of a dream with Tinker barking at Watson and Alice holding hands, when a voice pulled him from his fitful sleep.

Alice was shaking him. "Fred, Fred, wake up. Tinker's barking his head off."

What now? It seemed like he had just nodded off. "Probably just a coyote," he mumbled. "It'll be okay. Go back to sleep."

"No. This is different. You better go check."

"Damned dog," Fred muttered as he dragged himself out of bed. He slipped on his pants, struggled into his boots, and headed out the front door to see what was bothering the dog. The dog's growls sounded like they came from the back of the house. As he rounded the corner, the pungent, sulphury stink of gasoline struck him, and in the faint moonlight he saw his dog snarling at a dark lump of a man bent down at the side of the house, trying to light a match in the light breeze.

"Hey, what the hell?" Fred shouted.

The man reached into his coat and pulled out a pistol as he straightened up. With the gun pointed at Fred, he growled, "Lukin, on the ground…Now! That stupid Eleanor said you knew about my DWP. But you're not going to get a chance to tell anybody about it."

Fred recognized Magon's deep, threatening voice. "Tinker!" he shouted as he dove to the ground and rolled to the side.

Magon's shot hit the ground where Fred had been. Before he could get off another shot, the snarling dog had the man's wrist in his jaws. Magon yelled in pain as a second shot exploded, followed by a brief whine. The dog dropped to the ground. Magon shook his hand and took a step toward Fred.

Suddenly, a bright flash and the simultaneous sounds of a deafening boom and breaking glass filled the night from the window. Magon flew back like a train had hit him and sprawled on the ground next to the dog.

Fred stood up, and as he stared at Magon's body, Alice rushed around the corner from the front door, carrying a shotgun. "You okay?" she asked in a shaky voice.

He looked himself up and down, checking for damage. "Think so."

She knelt down by the dog and stroked his fur. Blood oozed from his head. "Poor Tinker. Poor old dog." He feebly wagged his tail. She looked up at Fred. "He saved your life. He's a hero."

"So are you."

She looked back at the dog. "I think he's gone now." She bent over and put her cheek on the top of his head and ruffled his fur. "What'll we tell Carl?"

"I dread telling him anything. He doted on that dog." Fred stood by Magon's body and watched a dark spot spread across the sand that otherwise looked white in the moonlight. At such a short range, the shotgun had mangled the left half of Magon's face.

"Is he dead?" Alice asked.

Fred softly prodded Magon's body with the toe of his boot. "Gotta be."

"What'll we do now?"

"You go inside. I'll go into town and get the sheriff."

"No, don't!"

"I've got to. He's going to find out, and it's better to tell him now."

"Why?" Alice asked. "Don't make things complicated."

He looked at her and shook his head. She never failed to surprise him. "It's already complicated."

"Not if nobody finds him. Nobody knows he's been here. Let's keep it that way."

"Why try to hide it? You shot him trying to burn our house down—with us in it. It's good that you shot him."

"I don't want people to know about it. They already talk too much about me shooting at people. I don't want any more gossip." She turned and looked toward the black profile of the Inyo Mountains to the east. "It's a huge desert and there are lots of mountains. There are Paiute grave mounds all over the desert. Who'd know the difference?"

"The coyotes will dig him up."

"That's why the Indians covered theirs with boulders, to keep the coyotes away."

"What? Are you an expert on Paiute graves now?" Fred asked.

Alice smiled.. "Sort of. When we were kids, Betty and I started to dig one up out in the sagebrush. Our dad caught us and whipped the dickens out of us with his belt. We never got to see what was in there."

"Good thing. Otherwise, its ghost would still be haunting you." He glanced at the eastern sky. "We got maybe a little more than four hours till daylight. You got an old blanket we can wrap him in? Gotta keep the blood out of the pickup."

"I'll find something," she answered as she turned toward the house, and Fred headed to his truck parked by the barn.

After considerable cranking and coaxing, the truck came to life and Fred backed it up to the body as Alice came from the house with a blanket. She climbed onto the bed of the truck and spread out the blanket.

Fred grabbed the body by the armpits, hefted it, and then set it down. "Damn, for a short guy, he's really heavy. Bet he outweighs me by fifty pounds."

Alice took hold of his feet. "Try it now."

Together, they wrestled the heavy cadaver onto the truck. Fred put a shovel by the body as Alice tugged and pushed the body and rearranged the blanket to keep blood off the truck bed. As he watched her, Fred wondered how many couples worked as a team to dispose of a body in the middle of a warm spring night.

Fred glanced around the farmyard for anything he'd forgotten or any obvious giveaways. He looked at Tinker and figured he'd bury him when they got back. He picked up Magon's gun lying on the ground and put it under the blanket wrap. He would bury it with Magon. What about the window Alice shot out? He couldn't fix that now, but, at least, being at the back of the house, it wasn't visible from the front, and he could fix it later. He noticed Magon's gas can and decided to put it with the others he had in the barn. Nobody would notice, but that reminded him of the major loose end: Magon's car. How did he get out here? Surely, he didn't walk from town carrying a can of gas. His car must be somewhere close. "I need to find his car," he said to Alice. "Can't be too far away."

"He didn't drive past the house," Alice said. "We would have heard it."

"Yeah, maybe back toward town. His keys are probably in his pocket," Fred said as he climbed onto the truck bed. During the war, he'd seen men on both sides searching the pockets of the dead, but he'd never done it. Now it was his turn—disgusting. As he reached into the front pockets of the pants, he struggled to keep last night's dinner down. He was in luck — he found the key on the first try. He hopped down and started walking down the road. It didn't take long. About a quarter mile closer to town, he found Magon's Chevy parked a few yards off the road amid the sagebrush. In the driver's seat, he felt the upholstery and looked around. It was a nice car, and unlike his pickup, it started on the first try. He couldn't very well leave it out in the open. The barn seemed like a sure way to get trapped, but he didn't see a better alternative for the moment and drove the Chevy into the barn.

Fred started his pickup with Alice at his side and Magon's blanket-wrapped cadaver in the back. With his hands on the steering wheel, he stared silently into the night with the truck idling.

"What's wrong?" Alice asked.

"Hadn't thought much about it, but I don't know where to bury him where nobody can find him."

Alice slapped the dashboard. "Fred Lukin, we got a thousand square miles of desert around us. We just pick a spot and dig a hole. It'll get light soon, let's go!"

"It's not that simple. I figured we'd take him into some canyon in the Inyo Mountains. But I overlooked that there's no way to cross the river without going way north or south to reach the nearest bridge and somebody might see us. So we're stuck this side of the river, and it's too near town. Plus, with no roads through the brush, we'd leave tire tracks leading right back here."

"Nobody'll find the grave in the middle of the sagebrush and cactus."

"You'd be surprised how many people roam around hunting jackrabbits or just wandering. A fresh mound would be like a magnet."

"Well, then, how about Los Angeles?" Alice asked with a wry smile.

"That's a long drive."

"Let him swim."

He shook his head. "We can't just dump him in the aqueduct. People drink that water."

"Yeah, Los Angeles people. Besides, think how many animals fall in and drown in the aqueduct every day."

He slapped the steering wheel. "Okay! Let's do it." He shifted into gear and drove out of the farmyard.

About three-quarters of a mile from the ranch, the road to Independence crossed the aqueduct with its maintenance road along the bank. Fred turned south on the service road and, with his headlights off, drove until he thought he was far enough from the ranch and well south of town.

"This looks like as good a spot as any," he said as he pulled close to the edge of the big ditch. "Stay there. I can handle it."

He let the tailgate down and was reaching for the body when headlights appeared on the service road coming from the north. He slammed the tailgate shut, got back in the cab, and slowly started forward. In a few minutes, a pickup caught up with them, and its lights flashed. Fred stopped and waited. The other driver got out and walked to Fred's window.

"Oh, it's you, Fred," the man said as he looked in the cab. "Hi, Alice. What're you guys doing out at this hour?"

"Hi, Leon," Fred greeted the DWP watchman. "A young steer got loose. A white-face yearling. Darned thing's been making a habit of it. I don't know how he finds his way through the fence. He went down this way last time. Thought we'd look down here again."

"Hope you find him. We're always havin' strays fall into the aqueduct. There's no way out, and they eventually drown. Not sure I'd want to drink this water when it gets to L.A."

"Nah, me neither. I'll take the fresh water up here. No tellin' what people drink or eat down south. But what're you doin' out here now?"

"The DWP's got me and some other guys patrolling the ditch at night. All I ever see is a few jackrabbits and coyotes." Leon glanced at the truck bed. "What ya got there? Looks almost like a body all wrapped up."

Fred laughed nervously. "Yeah, for sure. I shot old Bill Mulholland for buildin' this ditch. Nah, actually, it's a little runt calf that died. I'll take her out in the brush and bury her."

The DWP patrolman shook his head. "Too bad. This time of year, in the heat, they start stinkin' right away, so ya gotta do it quick. Well, I gotta go — keeping the City's ditch safe." He walked back to his pickup and drove around Fred and Alice and continued down the aqueduct service road.

As the patrolman drove away, Fred leaned his head against the steering wheel and gripped it to steady his trembling hands. *Damn, why did I let Alice talk me into this? It would have been so much simpler to report it to the sheriff.*

Alice patted him on his shoulder. "I was scared to death. That was good. I think maybe you could write pulp westerns."

Fred laughed. "Yeah, me 'n Zane Grey. Call it *Riders of the Purple Aqueduct.*"

Alice looked back at the truck bed. "Leon's gone. Let's dump him now."

"Nah. We gotta get further down so it doesn't float past Leon."

Fred watched the DWP patrolman's taillights recede down the service road. When he saw the taillights turn west, he shifted into gear and continued south. When he passed where the patrolman had turned off, he eased to a stop. "Time for his swim to L.A."

While Alice waited, he got out and stretched as he gazed at the spring sky. Looking at the stars calmed him. When he was a kid, his dad had taught him the constellations, but there weren't many he could still identify—his favorite, Orion, with its bright, three-star belt wasn't showing this time of year, but of course, there were always the big and little dippers to help him find his way. He shook his head. *Gotta quit daydreaming and hurry before it gets light.* He pulled the heavy body off the truck bed. It hit the ground with a hollow-sounding 'whump'. He pulled Alice's blanket off the body and struggled to drag the thug to the edge of the aqueduct. In the moonlight, the right side of his face was pasty white and the left side was dark mush from Alice's close-up shotgun blast through the window. Fred guessed there must have been as much broken glass as buckshot in him. Fred smiled. *Don't get on the wrong side of Alice.*

"What are you waiting for?" Alice whispered from the truck and hopped out to help.

Fred scanned the desert landscape to be sure they were alone. While he stalled, Alice bent down and gave a push. With a splash, the DWP acquisitions manager disappeared into the dark water flowing south to the thirsty city. She straightened up and brushed her hands together, signifying the task's completion. "Maybe we should have weighted him down."

"Too late now," Fred said as he climbed into the truck.

When they pulled into the farmyard, Fred checked his pocket watch--a little before four. "Still time to get rid of his car," he said to Alice.

"What'll we do with it?"

"Hide it in plain sight," he replied. "I'll drive into town the back way from the south side. You drive our pickup on our regular road and wait for me behind Jake's store."

Magon's car started easily and Fred returned to the aqueduct service road. He followed it to the westbound track that took him to the south edge of town near the DWP compound. He didn't see anybody around and drove into the DWP equipment yard and parked alongside the trucks, tractors, and equipment. What would he do with the keys? Hide them in almost plain sight. He got out and slid the key ring under the floor mat. What about his footprints? It would be hard to get rid of all of them, but he yanked a branch off a sage bush at the edge of the lot and swirled it around the sand to get rid of his prints near the car.

Did he forget anything? He didn't think so and started walking. Crossing the highway, he skirted around the east edge of town and walked the three-quarters-mile length of town to the north end, then doubled back and hurried down the street to meet Alice waiting behind Jake's store.

CHAPTER 43   PEACE AND HONESTY

It was almost five Sunday morning when Fred and Alice got to bed after sending Magon floating down the aqueduct toward Los Angeles. Fred usually woke about six thirty, even on Sunday, but today, he slept late. About nine, the aromas of brewing coffee and frying bacon persuaded him to get out of bed. After the bathroom, he dressed and headed into the kitchen, where Alice had breakfast almost ready. He helped himself to a cup of coffee and took a seat at the table. Alice hummed an unrecognizable tune as she flitted around the kitchen, putting the finishing touches on Sunday breakfast.

He watched her as he sipped his coffee and finally asked, "What are you so chipper about?"

"Why not? It's a nice spring day. I just got back from an interesting trip to the state capital, and I'm fairly sure that we are not going to be bothered by Mr. Magon anymore. Only thing to spoil it is poor old Tinker."

"Yeah, I gotta bury him. I'll do it after breakfast. Then I think it would be best to forget about Magon and never mention his name again."

Alice laughed and pantomimed buttoning up her lips with her fingers.

"And don't forget we still have to deal with Watson foreclosing," Fred said.

"I have all the receipts. Like Jake said, that ought to settle it."

When Fred finished breakfast, he sat back with his long legs stretched out under the table. He was going down a mental list of chores for the day when the sound of a car pulling into the farmyard interrupted his thoughts. He opened the door to check who was showing up on a Sunday morning. Damn, it was Charlie Cole. He couldn't have found Magon's body this soon, could he? Fred knew he should have gone to the sheriff right off instead of dumping the body. That was stupid. He thought of the dark blood stains on the ground at the back of the house and the dog still lying nearby. There was no way to show it was self-defense and not straight-out murder.

Fred stood in the doorway and waited as Cole walked up. He strained to keep his voice from shaking. "Morning Charlie. What brings you out here so early? Come for Sunday breakfast?"

"No breakfast. I figure you know why I'm here."

Fred struggled to speak normally in spite of his mouth feeling as dry as the desert. "If you're not here for Alice's fine Sunday breakfast, I have no idea."

"Two dynamite blasts this last week and you have no idea why I might want to talk to you?"

Fred stared at Cole with a bit of relief. Worrying about Magon's body, he had forgotten all about the blasts that Jake mentioned when they got back from Sacramento. Cole's visit had nothing to do with Magon. "Oh, yeah. Jake told me about them."

"Know anything about those blasts?"

This wasn't about Magon's body, but to be accused of another blast was enough to piss a person off. "What? You think I did that? Somebody blasts the aqueduct, and you don't have enough sense to think of anybody else to frame, so you come here."

"No need to get insulting. Just doin' my job."

"So far, you haven't done it very good. Every time something happens, you come trottin' out here with your trained goons from L.A."

"Dammit, Fred, I'm keeping them away from you. As soon as the Big Pine power plant was hit, Magon started ranting that it was your doing. Then, when the No-Name siphon got blown on Friday, he demanded your arrest. He brought his L.A. cops out here Saturday morning. You weren't around. He insisted you had skipped town and that was proof you were guilty. I told him to lay off and I'd talk to you."

"Okay, you've talked," Fred said as he started to close the door. "Now leave."

Cole jammed his foot in the doorway. "Hold on. You didn't say what you were doing Thursday and Friday."

"Get your foot out of there unless you have a search warrant."

"Ahh, so now you're a lawyer."

Alice joined Fred and glared up at Cole. "Charlie, we were together Thursday and Friday, which, we've been told, was when the two blasts occurred."

"And I told you before that a wife's testimony isn't worth beans."

"And you were wrong then, too," Alice replied. "We have been out of town since Thursday morning and got back Saturday evening."

"You have any evidence or witnesses to back you up?"

"I don't have to prove my innocence," Fred said.

Alice stepped between the two men. "Would you two stop acting like children? Of course, we have proof and witnesses. Jake dropped us off at the S.P. station on Thursday morning. Grace was with us, and the three of us took the train to Sacramento. We have ticket stubs and a hotel bill. We talked to people in the state government in the capital. Jake picked us up at the station when we got back Saturday night. Any more questions?"

"Thank you, Alice," Cole said. "That clears it up. And dammit, Fred, you could have told me that right off and avoided all this nonsense."

"You arrested me when Magon beat on me, then framed me for that other blast. I see no reason to tell you anything."

"Okay, okay," Cole said. "I didn't frame you. Someone else did, and you got released. That's done. But aside from that, we've been friends for a long time. It's time to make peace."

"I never made any false arrests or accused anybody. Peace depends on you."

"I'll work on it. Meantime, you want to tell me why you went to Sacramento?"

Fred glanced questioningly at Alice. She nodded agreement. He gazed skeptically at Cole. Men like Watson were potentially dangerous, and even though he'd known Cole for many years, he didn't know for sure where the sheriff stood and needed to find out. "What do you think about Mark Watson?"

"What do you mean?" Cole asked.

"Do you trust him?"

Cole looked at the ground for a moment. "No, I don't trust him…and you shouldn't either."

"I don't. He's one reason we went to Sacramento."

Cole's eyebrows rose. "Now you really got me curious. Care to tell me more?"

They had been standing at the door as they talked. Now, Alice pulled the door open. "Come on in. I'll fix some more coffee… in the interest of peace and honesty."

Cole removed his hat, and the three sat down at the kitchen table. Fred and Alice explained some of Watson's financial misdeeds uncovered by Grace and how Magon had created his own DWP corporation to take title to properties nominally bought by the DWP.

When they finished, Cole whistled. "Holy Jesus!" He swirled the coffee around in his cup. "So the only ones who know are you two and Grace?"

"No," Alice said. "Jake, and by now, probably Betty."

"And the bank examiner said they'd come and look into things?"

"He said he'd talk to his boss," Fred replied. "I think he believed us and thought it was serious enough to keep digging."

Cole stood to leave. "Until the state banking office acts, we need to keep this under wraps. Tell the others not to say anything."

"Before you go," Alice said, "there's another problem you should know about."

"What's that?"

"We've made all our payments on time, but Watson's trying to foreclose on our ranch."

"That's a little out of my bailiwick, but I'll mention it to Walt Hess, but my advice is to get a lawyer." He carefully placed his hat on his balding head. "Thanks for the coffee."

Fred walked outside with Cole, talking the whole time about the trip to Sacramento to divert the sheriff's attention away from the back of the house where the dog still lay. As soon as Cole drove away, Fred headed to the barn to get a shovel. He'd find a nice place to bury Tinker.

CHAPTER 44   MISSING

After talking to Fred and Alice, Cole couldn't get Magon and his DWP company out of his head. Maybe it was a legitimate arrangement with the Department of Water and Power, but that seemed unlikely. It had to be some sort of scam. If it was, it was hard to see how he could get away with it. If the real DWP paid for land and water rights, surely, they could assert their ownership. He'd leave that to them. Magon had always seemed to be a thug. Maybe he was also a con man. It was long since time to check him out.

When he got to his office Monday morning, Cole stuck his head through the doorway into Daggett's tiny office. "Hey, got a job for you. We've never checked to see if Magon has any sort of police record. How about running a check on him and see what turns up."

"Sure thing, boss. I've always thought he seemed more like a street tough than a property acquisitions man."

"Yeah, me too. But isn't that what robbers and thieves are, just property acquisition guys?"

Daggett laughed. "Yeah. For sure. That's what they do—acquire property—other people's property."

"While you're doing that, I'll go over to the DWP office and talk to Laird."

"Good afternoon, Hazel," Cole said to the elderly lady at the front desk when he entered the DWP office building.

"Hi, Sheriff. What brings you in today?"

"Just a normal social call."

"Sure thing," Hazel responded with a knowing smile. "When you show up, it's never 'just a social call'. What can we do for you?"

"I'm here to see Paul Laird."

"Okay. This way," Hazel said as she led Cole down a hall.

District Superintendent Laird rose slowly and walked around his desk with his hand extended. "Charlie, good to see you. What brings you here? Please don't tell me another blast. That one at No-Name Siphon was a doozy. It'll be hell to fix. Have a seat."

Cole took his hat off and set it on a vacant chair in front of Laird's desk. "No, Paul, no fresh attacks on your ditch since last week — at least not that I know of. No, this is about Magon."

Laird frowned. "Magon? He's a good man. I know he can be a bit rough and should be a bit more diplomatic, but it's hard to get that job done without stirring up a little resentment. So what's the problem?"

"A little resentment?" Cole said, his voice rising with exasperation. "He's a thug and you know it. But what I'm trying to find out is whether you authorized him to register ownership of the properties he acquires in his own corporation called DWP, Inc.?"

"His *own* corporation? What are you talking about?"

"Did you know that several of the properties where Magon arranged the purchase and your department paid, he titled to a company named DWP, Inc., that he owns?"

Laird stared silently at Cole for a moment.

Was Laird part of the swindle? Cole wondered. Was he just deciding how to play it?

Finally, the district boss broke his silence. "That sounds crazy."

"Apparently, he created a company called 'DWP', with him as the principal stockholder. When he arranged the purchase of some choice properties with water rights, he registered the owner as DWP, Inc., instead of the Department of Water and Power of Los Angeles. His company now holds title to those properties."

The superintendent rubbed his chin. "That still doesn't make sense. We paid for them, so they belong to us."

"No, they belong to whoever holds title—which in this case is Magon's DWP, Inc."

"I'll need to talk to our lawyers and Magon. Which properties are you talking about?"

"I don't know them all, but the Berks ranch is one. I'd suggest you check titles in the county records office and contact Sacramento."

"Yes, yes. I will look into it." Laird slowly stood. "Thanks for letting me know."

Cole also stood. "Before I go, I'd like to talk to Magon."

"I don't think he's in. He spends most of his time in the field. I'll talk to him about it when he gets back to the office."

Cole lightly slapped the edge of Laird's desk. "Okay, keep me posted. I know my way out."

As Cole walked out of the building, he ran the possibilities through his mind. It was pretty clear that it wasn't a legitimate arrangement with the DWP. Was Laird in on it? He acted like he didn't know about it, but maybe he was putting on an act—and a bad act, at that. It was odd that the man didn't seem surprised or outraged. If this was news, you'd think the DWP district boss would ask more questions. But no, he just said he'd look into it. It was hard to believe that the superintendent was part of it. But it was even harder to picture Magon pulling it off without others knowing about it and maybe providing cover. Laird was the DWP's top dog from Mono Lake in the north to Mojave in the south. If Magon was trying to steal choice pieces of land from the DWP, he'd sure want the top man on his side.

"Curiouser and curiouser," Cole muttered to himself. He didn't know all the ins and outs of DWP property transactions, but this just didn't make sense. If it was a fraud, it didn't fit Magon. In spite of his high-sounding title as Manager of Property Acquisitions, boil it down and he was mostly a strong-arm thug. It should be interesting to hear what Daggett found out.

When Cole got back to his office, Daggett was waiting. He looked ready to burst with news.

"I checked with Sacramento like you said and got some stuff on Magon you should find interesting. You'll never believe it."

"These days, I'd believe almost anything. What ya got?"

The deputy's face lit up like he had won the lottery. "In his younger days, Magon was a professional boxer. Had a reputation that he could punch like a locomotive but had a glass jaw and lost more than he won. He quit boxing and worked here and there as a bodyguard and all-around tough hombre. He was convicted of beating a man to death and served time in San Quentin."

Cole was perplexed. "How in the world did he end up working for the DWP?"

"I asked the man I talked to in Sacramento. He didn't know either. He said after Magon served his time, he faded from view and, a few years later, showed up working for the DWP.

Cole ran his hand through his thin, wispy hair. "We need to keep pushing him about this DWP thing. I think maybe it will be his glass jaw."

"Wanna pick him up now?"

"No. Not yet. We don't really have anything on him, and we need to let Laird and the DWP deal with it first. We can let it percolate for a while."

Late Wednesday afternoon, Cole sat at his desk, absent-mindedly going through the mail, not paying attention to any of it. He pushed the stack of envelopes aside and figured he might as well go for a coffee at the cafe. This time of day, the place would be empty, and Doris could sit down with him and get off her feet. He grabbed his hat from the rack and was heading for the door when it opened and Paul Laird stepped in. *Damn, I almost made a getaway, and Laird shows up.* The sheriff placed his hat back on the rack. "Paul, welcome. What brings you in?"

"Looks like you were on your way out," the district superintendent said. "Sorry to bother you. I'll only take a minute of your time."

In Cole's experience, whenever somebody said they'd take only a minute, it always seemed to turn into an hour. "Come in, Paul. Have a seat. What can I do for you?"

Laird pulled a chair in front of the sheriff's desk. "I hate to bother you with this, but I'm getting a little concerned about Earl Magon. You see, whenever he's out of the office, he leaves word where he's going. Monday, when you came to our office and wanted to talk to him, he wasn't there, and he didn't show up or leave word yesterday. I wouldn't normally think much of it, but this afternoon, one of the guys from the equipment yard told me his car has been parked in the yard since the weekend. He never parks there, yet it's been there for a couple of days. It seems strange and not like him."

Cole leaned back with his arms folded. "Any ideas about where he went?"

Laird shrugged. "No idea. That's why I came to you. I hoped maybe you'd look into it."

"I'm not clear about what I need to look into. He's absent, but you tell me he frequently works in the field, arranging land and water purchases." Cole silently amended his sentence with '*and running people off their land and stealing their water*'.

"Yes, he's usually out of the office, but he's supposed to let us know, and the fact that he left the car in our lot is unusual."

"Have you checked his house?"

"Yes. I sent a man over to check. No one answered his knock and the door was unlocked, so our man looked around. No one was there."

Cole shook his head and said with an ironic smile, "You're not supposed to tell the sheriff about your trespassing."

"A-ah, I was worried about him, and it wasn't really trespassing. Like most of the property in town, we, the DWP that is, own the house and Magon rents it."

"Forget it. I was just joking. Anyway, if he's gone and doesn't have a car, he might have gone on the train or gotten a ride with someone."

"We already checked with the SP stationmaster. He didn't remember Magon buying a ticket."

Cole tapped his pencil on the edge of his desk. "The gossip mill says he's been seeing Eleanor Rice over at the county records office. I can ask her if she knows anything. Unless she knows something, without more to go on, all I can do is keep my eyes open and wait till something develops."

"Okay, I guess that's all I can expect. If he doesn't show up pretty soon, I'll have to get somebody else to take over his job." The DWP superintendent headed out the door, then turned back. "Let me know if you find out anything."

"Sure thing," Cole replied. He glanced at the wall clock. There was still time to check with Eleanor before the records office closed. That sure messed up having a peaceful coffee with Doris. He yelled down the hall, "Daggett, I'm going upstairs to the records office."

As he trudged up the stairs to the second floor, he groaned and muttered to himself, "Dang it, it shouldn't be this hard to climb a few stairs." At the top, he paused to catch his breath. It seemed like everything was getting harder as the years passed, but he really didn't want to admit he was getting too old to keep up with the job. When his gasping slowed, he continued down the hall.

"Sheriff Cole, how nice to see you," Eleanor said when he entered. "I hardly ever see you. Mr. Daggett is usually the one to come to check our records. What can I do for you?"

"Good to see you, Eleanor. I just have a quick question. Have you seen anything of Earl Magon in the last few days?

"I had a very nice dinner with Earl last week, but I haven't seen him since. Why do you ask?"

"He hasn't checked into his office this week. Paul Laird is concerned and asked me to look into it."

With a quizzical expression, she cocked her head as she thought about it. "Goodness gracious, I hope nothing has happened to him. He seems like such a self-sufficient gentleman, and I can't imagine anything occurring that he couldn't handle."

Gentleman? She must be the only person within two hundred miles who would call him a gentleman. "Yes," he said, "I'm sure he must be okay. But let me know if you hear from him."

"Of course, Sheriff."

Walking back to his office, Cole wondered if maybe Magon had heard about Fred and Alice's discovery about DWP, Inc. and decided he'd skip town before the law caught up with him. He wouldn't be the least disappointed if Magon had hightailed it out of the valley.

CHAPTER 45   AUDIT

On a sunny Monday morning, two months after Fred and Alice's trip to Sacramento, the moment the doors opened at the Bishop headquarters of the Inyo Bank, four men dressed in dark suits and carrying briefcases marched through the door and asked to speak to the bank manager.

A tall, well-dressed man rose from his desk in the back of the lobby. "I am Mark Watson, the proprietor and manager of the bank. How may I help you gentlemen?"

The oldest of the visitors extended his hand. "I am Clarence Lowell of the California State Banking Department. We are here to audit your bank. As you know, California banking regulations require you to provide complete access to your operations and accounting."

The color faded from Watson's face, and his voice wavered. "I welcome your visit. We will provide whatever you ask. I am sure you will find everything in order. Where would you like to begin?"

"You can explain the operation of your bank to me while my assistants begin with your accounting records. They will need your financial statements, journals, ledgers, and statements from your correspondent banks for the last two years. They will ask for additional material as they proceed. Show them where they may work, and you and I can talk at your desk."

Later that week, Sheriff Cole was busy at his desk with paperwork when a man entered the office and extended his hand. "I am Clarence Lowell, the head auditor for the California State Banking Department."

Cole stood and extended his hand. "I am Sheriff Cole. Please have a seat."

"You have undoubtedly heard that we are performing an audit of the Inyo Bank," the bank examiner said. "I know that in a small town, everyone knows about our arrival within hours."

"Yes. I heard you have been working at the head office in Bishop, and that your agents visited each of the branch offices. Just the other day, one of your men was down here at the Independence office. How can I help you?"

"Whenever we do an audit, it is standard practice to introduce ourselves to local law enforcement. We are in the same business. You enforce the law among the citizenry, protecting them from criminals, and we enforce the regulations relating to the banking industry, protecting people from financial criminals."

"I hadn't thought about it that way before. I can't imagine that you need the local police very often."

"Not often, but it happens. Someone gets their money stolen from their pocket and they call you. They get it stolen by a bank, they call us. Depending on what we find, we occasionally need the help of the local police."

Cole figured this fellow was saying the bank had stolen somebody's money, and he recalled Fred's trip to Sacramento and Grace's diary. "Interesting. Someone must have reported some pretty serious problems at the bank to bring you all the way from Sacramento with a team of investigators. Are you finding anything to make the trip worthwhile?"

Lowell gazed at Cole as though he were trying to decide how much he could say. "We are finding that the audit is warranted."

"What do you want *me* to do?"

Lowell leaned forward in his chair. "This is most confidential."

Cole nodded. "Understood."

"We have found evidence that the proprietor of the bank, Mark Watson, has been embezzling from his own bank and from his customers. We will charge him with that and other banking-related crimes. We would like you to be present when we arrest him and provide aid in case there is trouble."

Cole whistled. *Holy God! Mark Watson? Embezzlement?* Just a few months ago he had talked to Watson about the connection to Barr, but he never imagined embezzlement. "When will that be?"

"Eight tomorrow morning before the bank opens. Whenever people suspect a bank might be forced to close, there is a rush to withdraw their money. To be fair to everyone, we close the bank to give us time to sort things out before there is a run. Consequently, we have to close it without warning. It is crucial that we keep this under wraps until the last minute. People will be understandably furious. Sometimes there is a riot and a mob breaks into the bank to get their money. We have to be prepared for that."

"So, you need me to control the crowd," Cole said.

"Exactly," Lowell replied. "Also, when we tell Mr. Watson of the charges, he may react violently. We may need assistance."

"Do we jail Watson?" Cole asked.

"Violators are seldom jailed. Usually, they are booked and then granted bail."

"Why not jail?"

"Typically, they are respected members of the community who we handle gently."

"Have you talked to Walt Hess, the county attorney?"

"Not yet. He's my next stop."

"You need anything else from me?" Cole asked.

"As soon as we get there at eight, we will post a sign on the door that the bank is closed. We also need a sign posted on the doors of the three branches in Big Pine, Independence, and Lone Pine at precisely the same time. Can you arrange that without revealing it beforehand?"

"All at the same time? That will be tough, but I can try. I have part-time constables in each town. I'll have them stand by without telling them why until the last minute. Just before eight, I'll call with their orders."

Early the next morning, Lowell faced Watson across his desk. "Mr. Watson, we have determined that your bank's liabilities exceed the assets by at least eight hundred thousand dollars, and your bank is insolvent. You must close your doors immediately. You are prohibited from allowing customers to withdraw from their accounts or to make deposits. Every aspect of your business is frozen as of this moment."

Watson's mouth dropped, and he was momentarily speechless. He stood, leaning forward with both fists on his desk, he thundered, "You and your incompetent minions know nothing about banking. This is the strongest bank in the state. I have customers to serve and refuse to close." He pointed to the door and shouted, "Now get out of my bank!"

Lowell slowly got to his feet. "Mr. Watson, I feared you might react this way so I requested the sheriff's assistance." He turned and nodded to his three assistants standing at the door. They opened the door and Sheriff Cole entered, followed by Daggett, and Dan

Nichols, the sheriff's constable for Bishop. The auditor turned back to Watson and announced his coup de grâce. "In addition to insolvency, we have found substantial evidence of embezzlement, and you are charged and under arrest for that crime. You must surrender your keys and the vault combination."

Watson stood straight with his head back and spoke through bared teeth as he poked at Lowell's chest. "I have done nothing wrong. It is your illegal and unethical examination that is wrong. I have taken nothing. You're the crook. You want me out of my bank so you can steal from the hardworking folks of this valley."

Lowell slapped Watson's stabbing hand away and nodded to Cole. "Sheriff, please take Mr. Watson into custody on the charge of embezzlement for the unlawful taking of clients' property with which he was entrusted."

Cole stepped forward and spoke curtly. "Mark." He pulled handcuffs from his belt and held them up. "We use these on all prisoners. Please put out your hands."

The banker looked around the bank lobby with desperation in his eyes. Cole wondered if he was looking for an audience or an escape route.

At the back of the lobby, Margaret Collins stood wide-eyed with her fingers over her lips, and the teller stood beside her with tears streaming down her cheeks.

Watson looked at his audience of the two young women and held out his hands, declaring, "I am not a crook!" as Cole snapped the cuffs shut.

"Post the notice and lock the door," the examiner directed his assistants. He turned to Margaret and the teller. "The bank is now closed. We would like both of you ladies to remain on the job to help us with the records. Until further notice, you will be employees of the State of California."

As soon as the closure notice was posted, a crowd began to gather in front of the bank. So, when Cole and Daggett escorted Watson out of the bank in handcuffs, people crowded around, yelling questions and demanding their money.

"What's going on, Charlie?"

"Where are you taking Mr. Watson?"

"That sign says the bank is closed until further notice. What does that mean?"

"You can't close the bank. I need my money."

And so it went, with more citizens joining the crowd and pressing close to find out what was happening.

Cole wasn't sure how to respond. He thought of what Lowell had said about riots. He had heard about other bank closures—people fighting and rioting to demand their money, attacking the police who were duty-bound to protect a bank. Protect it? His own savings were deposited in the Independence branch, and by now, it was supposed to be closed as tight as this one. He spread his arms wide, and waving them downward, he shouted words he did not believe. "Calm down, calm down. Everything will be okay. The banking authorities did a routine audit and closed the bank until they can clarify a few items. The bank will open as soon as they get this ironed out."

The crowd quieted momentarily, and he took the opportunity to lead Watson through the cluster of spectators to his black and white Nash police car. He guided the prisoner into the back seat while Daggett got in the driver's seat.

Cole leaned through the car window. "Get him outta here, Daggett. When you get to Independence, call an auxiliary deputy to stand guard. I'll handle things here."

When Daggett drove away, the crowd resumed their hollering.

"Why'd you take Mark Watson away in handcuffs?" a woman yelled.

"Open it up, Charlie. I have to get some cash for my business," hollered the man who ran the clothing store.

"Come on, please open up for a few minutes," a man pleaded. "I have to take my wife to the doctor in Reno today, and I need money for gas."

"Go home," Cole shouted. "I have money in the bank just like you, and I won't be able to get it either. You'll just have to wait. Maybe tomorrow."

A man shoved the sheriff aside and pushed on the door. "It's closed on Saturdays. I need it today."

Cole grabbed the man by the back of his collar and pushed him toward the street.

People crowded tightly around the sheriff, shouting, shoving, and even a few trying to punch him.

Charlie heard the door open behind him. Lowell stepped out and pointed a pistol into the air. Blam! With the blast that close, the sheriff knew his ears would be ringing for hours.

"Stand back," the bank examiner shouted. "We're performing an audit as required by law. We will finish as soon as possible so you can get back to your business. In the meantime, you must be patient. Please disburse and go home."

Swearing and grumbling, the sullen crowd released the sheriff and drifted away from the bank entrance.

With the closing notice posted and Watson on his way to jail in Independence, the phone wires ran hot the length of the valley. By the time Daggett had driven the forty-five miles to Independence, a crowd was waiting in front of the sheriff's office.

When Daggett helped his prisoner out of the car, Watson waved his cuffed hands in the air and shouted, "I am innocent. Those idiot bureaucrats from Sacramento trumped up false charges to stop me from fighting Los Angeles on your behalf."

Angry shouts to free him erupted from the gathered citizens.

Daggett gingerly guided his prisoner into the sheriff's office. "Please be seated, Mr. Watson," he said deferentially. "I have to book you and put you in a cell. I imagine you will be granted bail and can leave as soon as that is taken care of."

As Daggett got going on the booking papers, District Attorney Walt Hess came through the door.

Watson shot up from his chair with his cuffed hands outstretched. "Walt, this is an outrage! I've done nothing wrong. My bank is the strongest in the state, and that stupid state auditor claims it's insolvent. I demand you release me immediately."

"Calm down, Mark," Hess said. "Charlie called and asked me to see that Judge Daley was available for a quick bail hearing. Normally, we jail an arrestee before bail, but the judge is waiting upstairs, so as soon as Deputy Daggett books your arrest, we can get it ironed out."

Daggett finished the booking, removed the handcuffs, and released the prisoner to Hess's custody.

Hess escorted Watson upstairs to the judge's office, with Watson protesting his innocence with every step.

Judge Daley motioned them in. "Take a seat, Mark. You too, Walt."

Watson remained standing. "I won't be here long enough to sit. I have done nothing wrong, and you have no right to hold me."

"Sit your ass down, Mark," the judge thundered.

Watson's face paled. He gaped at Daley like a rabbit watching a hawk and obediently took his seat.

Daley turned to the district attorney. "Walt, you talked to the bank auditor. Please explain the charges."

Hess thumbed through a stack of papers. "Mr. Lowell from the State Banking Department provided this list of charges." He handed the papers to the judge. "The overall offense is embezzlement from a state-chartered bank. As you can see, there is a list of contributing crimes and a summary of the evidence. He states that they are still examining the records and there may be additional charges."

Daley scanned the papers, grunting, making tsk-tsk sounds, and looking up at Watson with each new offense on the list.

"Those are all lies," Watson exclaimed. "Fabrications by incompetent toadies paid off by the City of Los Angeles who know nothing about banking."

The judge finished with the papers and handed them back to Hess. He gazed somberly at Watson. "Mark, those are serious charges. Embezzlement of a bank carries a sentence of five to ten years in the state penitentiary. Of course, you are innocent until proven guilty, but when this goes to trial, ranting about your innocence won't be sufficient."

Watson folded his arms and glared at Daley. "I am not ranting. Never in my life have I cheated or embezzled. Any evidence that I have has been made up from whole cloth."

Walt Hess shook the folder of papers toward Watson. "Mark, this looks pretty damning — names lots of folks that were cheated.

If half of it's true, you're in for a tough battle. However, since you're a respected citizen with deep ties to the community, I will recommend you be granted bail and released until trial. I'd suggest you get busy preparing your defense with your attorney."

Watson exploded. "If half of it's true! If half of it's true! You know damn well none of it's true!"

"That's why we have trials," the judge said, "so a jury of your peers can judge the evidence."

CHAPTER 46   CLOSED

With his ears still ringing from Lowell's shot, Cole stood in front of the Inyo Bank, nervously watching the crowd as Daggett drove away with the prisoner. News of the bank's closure had flashed through town like a telegraph and people rushed to the bank, hoping to withdraw their money before their neighbors. The throng spilled into the street, shouting pleas and threats. Cole realized he hadn't taken Lowell's warning seriously enough. He'd heard about riots when banks had failed elsewhere, but thought surely, it wouldn't happen here. He should have called the sheriff's posse to help stand guard. But when he spotted a couple of posse members in the crowd shouting they wanted their money like everyone else, he realized the posse probably wouldn't have done much good.

These people were worried about their money. The Inyo Bank and its branches were the only banks in the valley, and their closure wouldn't spare anybody, not even the county sheriff. The only money he had was in his bank account at the Independence branch and what was in his pocket. He reached for his back pocket to feel his wallet. At least he had that, but it wouldn't last long. Hopefully, the bank would reopen pretty soon. He'd be in real trouble if it didn't, and he couldn't get anything from his bank account.

So far, the people were only yelling, but what if it got out of hand and someone provoked a riot? He imagined the mob breaking in, ripping the bank apart, and beating him and the auditors. God, what a mess. How much longer till the examiners finish? He checked his pocket watch—twenty after nine. The bank normally closed at three, but the auditors would likely work longer. This was going to be a really long day.

The hours lagged as he and Constable Nichols took turns standing guard to keep the mob from breaking down the door. Once, when Nichols was gone and Cole needed a break, he called on one of the young examiners to help. That only enraged the crowd. Someone threw a rock, luckily it was off target and did no damage. Cole feared that a riot was imminent. But others in the swarm turned on the offender and told him to lay off. Cole wanted to give medals to the peacemakers.

By four o'clock, the crowd had thinned. Shortly after five, auditor Lowell stuck his head out the door, motioning for Cole to come inside.

The auditor took a seat at Watson's desk and motioned for Cole to sit. "We're finished for the day, but we'll return tomorrow morning. We may have to work through next week."

"What have you found?" Cole asked.

"It's much worse than I imagined," Lowell replied. "Cash is short by over thirty thousand dollars. Other assets, like loans, are overstated by hundreds of thousands. Watson used funds held in trust to pay bills for his other businesses and diverted payments borrowers made on their loans to his own personal accounts. Over several years, Mr. Watson submitted fraudulent reports to our agency that overstated his assets and understated his liabilities, and the list goes on."

"What happens next?"

"As in all cases like this, nothing good," Lowell replied. "The bank will have to be liquidated to pay off the depositors and other creditors. We'll have to sell the bank's assets and maybe Watson's other businesses. I don't know yet if we will get enough to give depositors full value."

Cole was frustrated. "I'm a cop, not a businessman. What does all that mean?"

"Very simply, if you have a thousand dollars in your savings account, the most you might get back would be, for example, three hundred dollars. We won't know how much depositors might get until we chase down and liquidate the assets, and that could take several weeks or maybe even months."

Cole glanced through the window at the few people still milling in front of the locked bank. "What about them?"

"As long as the bank's closed, they won't have access to any of their funds until it's sorted out."

"None?"

"None."

Cole ran his hand across the top of his head. The full magnitude of the disaster was sinking in. "Holy God! This is the only bank in the valley. If it's closed, no one can get any money. For some, like me, our savings accounts are all we have—our life savings, and you say we can't get it?"

"That is correct," the examiner said.

"You can't do this. It's not right."

"I have no choice. Like I said earlier, we're both lawmen, and that's the law I'm sworn to follow."

"No one will be able to buy anything, not even food. This will bring the valley to a standstill. Isn't there anything we can do?"

"You need another bank in the area—quick. Our state banking office can work with your people to find a healthy bank to open an office here."

"How long will that take?" Cole asked.

"Can't say. Anything from a few weeks to a year or more."

Even though the Independence branch was closed, Grace worked through the day on Friday. In the afternoon, as she wrapped up her work and prepared to leave, Mr. Lowell phoned and asked her to work an additional week at the Bishop main office to help tie up loose ends. She would work with Margaret Collins, who said Grace could stay with her. That sounded good. Another week of work before she was out of a job, and she liked working with Margaret.

Early Monday morning, as she drove out of Independence on her way to Bishop, Grace felt like she was shedding her shackles. In Independence, people had shunned her after the bank closed. When she walked down Main Street, long-time friends gave her hostile looks and avoided speaking to her. It was as though they blamed her because they couldn't get their money. She wanted to scream that it wasn't her fault, that she didn't have any money either. She knew they felt cheated and helpless and needed someone to blame. She was a target. They didn't know about Watson's offenses. They knew he had been arrested, but they didn't know why. After all, he was a respected banker and surely wouldn't have committed any serious crimes. Those officious state auditors were just out to get him, and she was part of it.

When Grace got to the Bishop headquarters, Lowell had her team with Margaret, searching for discrepancies in the documents and ledgers. As she worked through the accounts, the number and size of the inconsistencies and misstatements stunned her. Cash was missing, the bank's debts were understated, and its assets were exaggerated. She gazed at the latest statement from the Pacific National Bank, the Los Angeles correspondent where Margaret's friend worked. Their statement showed the Inyo Bank's month-end balance of $13,970. The balance shown on Watson's report to the state banking department was $23,500, an overstatement of more than nine thousand dollars.

That same Pacific National statement said that the Inyo Bank owed it $42,000, and Watson's reports showed no such debt. They found similar discrepancies for the correspondent banks in Reno and San Francisco. Margaret said Watson had always insisted on preparing the state bank reports himself and didn't permit the employees to see them. It was clear that, for years, he had been lying to the banking authorities, other banks, and his customers.

Grace's next task was to examine customers' loan accounts. Her insides felt ready to rebel every time she thought of the mortgage loan on the ranch and her missing check.

She pushed the loan ledger across the table toward Margaret and pointed to her own account. "I don't understand why Mr. Watson arranged it so it's still on the books. Wouldn't it have made more sense to mark it as paid, even though he kept my money?

Margaret tapped her fingers on the table as she thought. "My guess is he wanted to show the bank as stronger than it really is, with more assets and fewer liabilities. Your loan is an asset for the bank, so he wants it on the books."

"But if the loan were still outstanding with no payments being made, shouldn't it be shown as delinquent?"

"Yes," Margaret said, "but showing it as delinquent would count against the bank. This way, he keeps your loan on the books, making the bank look healthier."

"Then why did he show the Lukin's loan as delinquent when we know they made their payments each month? That would make the bank look worse, wouldn't it?"

"Yes. But maybe that has nothing to do with the bank's condition. Everybody in the valley knows about his fight with Fred Lukin at Alabama Gates. That shamed Mr. Watson. My guess is that he wanted to set up Fred's loan to foreclose on the property."

Grace shook her head in disbelief. "He must think we're all stupid. Now he's finding out we're not so dumb."

Margaret stared steadily at Grace. "Is that what prompted the audit? Were you the one who reported it to Sacramento?"

Grace hesitantly nodded.

Margaret shook her head sadly, as though in mourning, and spoke quietly. "You shouldn't have. We could have worked something out. You not only killed the bank, but you killed our jobs."

"Work something out?" Grace said, her voice rising in exasperation. "When? You've worked here for a while now, and you know he's a crook. He's taken all my money. Should I live as a pauper while he cheats more people?"

Tears filled Margaret's eyes. "But what am I going to do? When this audit is over in a few days, I won't have a job. Nobody in the valley has any money except what's in their pockets, and they blame us. People won't speak to me. Even with what Mr. Lowell is going to pay me, I may not have enough to pay my way home to my family in the San Joaquin Valley." She wiped her tears with a handkerchief. "Shh, here comes Mr. Lowell."

"Is anything wrong?" the auditor asked.

Margaret looked at the floor. "No, nothing."

Grace raised her chin and glared at Lowell. "Yes. That crook took the check that was supposed to pay for my ranch. When can I get my money?"

Lowell folded his arms and took a deep breath. "Not soon, Mrs. Berks. Any funds in Mr. Watson's personal accounts will be combined with other assets to settle claims by depositors and creditors. By law, your claim is inferior to that of depositors, who must be paid first. If there is anything left, then you will be paid along with other creditors."

Grace's lips quivered as she struggled not to cry. "I don't have a cent to my name except that check. I've worked here helping you sort it all out. I ought to get some consideration for that."

Lowell's voice remained calm. "I'm sorry, Mrs. Berks. My hands are tied. We have to pay claims according to the rules of priority, and you are further down the list than the depositors."

Grace slumped into a chair and wrapped her arms around as though she was holding herself together. The image of Slim lying on the floor flooded her mind. Then, she saw Slim shake his head in disapproval as she handed the check for the ranch to Watson. She couldn't hold herself together any longer. She bent over and sobbed uncontrollably.

CHAPTER 47   REPERCUSSIONS

Jake sat at his cluttered desk in his store's back office, shouting into his phone at his wholesale supplier in Los Angeles. "What do you mean, you can't ship to me unless I pay cash first?"

"Just that," the man on the other end said. "And don't holler at me! We got word that the state banking authorities shut down your bank two weeks ago. My boss said we can't accept checks drawn on the Inyo Bank. Business in the Owens Valley will be cash-only from now on unless you have a checking account with another bank."

"You know darned well everybody in this valley uses the Inyo Bank and there aren't any other banks up here."

"Yes, Jake. I know. That's the point. Any check you write to me on the Inyo Bank can't be cashed. They're worthless."

"But I need to restock. My shelves are practically bare. I have money in the bank and will pay as soon as the bank opens again."

"And when will that happen?"

Jake was certain it would be soon. Everything — the businesses, the ranchers, everybody — depended on the bank. It just *had* to open up. "Probably by next week," Jake replied with growing doubt.

"That's not what we're hearing down here. Our bank notified us that the Inyo Bank is dead."

That can't be, Jake told himself with fading conviction, and said, "Nah, it'll open back up. But what'll I do with nothing to sell in the meantime?"

"I'm sorry. But with no bank, the only way to buy something is with hard cash. You folks up there will have to find some."

Without another word, Jake slowly placed the phone back in its cradle. He felt weak, like someone had drained his blood and energy. His only cash was the change in his pocket, a few bills in his wallet, and whatever was in the cash register. He punched the key on the cash register and the drawer sprang open. He slowly counted sixty-eight dollars in bills and three dollars and eighty-seven cents in change. He'd never given much thought to how much he depended on the bank. Use checks to buy merchandise and accept checks when customers pay their tab. Normally, at the end of the week, Betty deposited the extra cash or withdrew from the bank when they needed more. Whatever they had put aside over the years was in their savings account at the bank. If the bank never reopened, their life savings were gone. He sat down on the bentwood chair behind the counter and resisted the urge to cry.

The sound of the door opening interrupted his funk.

"Hey, Jake, you hidin' there behind the counter?"

Jake slowly stood and replied to his long-time customer. "Nah, just resting. How you doing today, Phil?"

"Awful, and you look worse than I feel."

"Thanks. I feel a lot worse than I look. What brings you in?"

"Groceries." He unfolded a paper that looked like the dog chewed it up. "Here's Thelma's list."

The shopkeeper looked at the list and shook his head. "Not much of this stuff left in stock."

"Gimme what you have. I'll need to cash my paycheck to pay for it."

Jake set the list on the counter. "Phil, I can't cash your check. I don't have enough cash to cover a paycheck."

"I know the Inyo Bank's closed, but this is my DWP check drawn on an L.A. bank. I've bought stuff from you for years. You know I'm good for it."

"I know, but you don't understand. I don't have enough cash, and with the Inyo Bank closed, I can't get any more. I can't accept checks because I have nowhere to deposit them, and I can't pay with checks because my bank's out of business. I can only deal in cash."

The man snatched his list. "Fine, dammit. I'll go to Lone Pine and buy at the Morris store."

Jake watched his customer storm out the door. It was unlikely John Morris's store in Lone Pine would do much better. He knew John used the Inyo Bank too and would probably face the same problems—no merchandise, no cash, and ultimately, no customers. He gazed around his store. The shelves were getting bare, and there wasn't much left in the storeroom. He shook his head in discouragement. With so little merchandise left to sell, there was hardly any point in staying open. But what else would he do if he weren't in the store? He shrugged and sat back down where Phil had found him. Closing the store just took too much energy he didn't have.

That same day, Henry Olivera sat slumped in his chair, counting the bills and coins spread out on his kitchen table. He leaned back and stared at the money—eighteen dollars and thirty-seven cents—all the cash he had left. His insides were queasy as he considered his situation. Working on the ranch was all he had ever done, and it had provided a good living. Now, except for the cash on the table, every dollar he and Isabel had saved was gone— locked in the dead Inyo Bank. All they had now were these eighteen dollars and the ranch, and they couldn't spend the ranch unless they sold it. He stood and looked out the window without seeing. "I'm all rung out. It's like I don't care about nothin' no more. The DWP's killin' the valley and the bank's gone."

Isabel walked to his side and put her arm across his shoulders. "It's time to sell. I know you don't want to sell to the DWP, but they're the only buyers and they've paid good prices for some of the other ranches. We could get out with enough for a small place in town and pay our living expenses for a while. There are a lot of houses for sale or rent in town with so many families giving up and moving away."

Henry turned and faced his wife. "It's those livin' expenses that's the problem. I can't figure how we'd get enough to keep us goin' very long. I'd have to find work. I don't know nothin' else besides ranchin', and I'm too old to start somethin' new."

Isabel gently chuckled. "I hate to tell you this, but you're too old to be doing all this ranch work. There's sure lots of things easier than ranching."

"Yeah, maybe you're right. God, I hate to face Fred and Murph and tell them I'm sellin' out."

"Darn it all, Henry, it was Fred that caused all this when he brought those state banking people over here. If it wasn't for that, we coulda hung on against the DWP. But with the bank closed and our money gone, we don't have anything. We gotta sell."

"If we sell, it will be the final straw for them. The DWP will have four of the seven ditch shares—a majority. They can close it down and dry out Fred and Murphy."

"But it don't make no sense for us to be broke just to keep those other guys going," Isabel said.

Several days later, Fred stood with his mouth open, trying to think of something to say. Sure, Henry and Isabel had been having a hard time since the bank closed, but so were he, Alice, and everyone else he knew. He had figured Henry would fight to the bitter end to hold on to his ranch. But his friend was saying they had already made a deal with the new acquisitions manager who had replaced Magon. After a long pause, Fred found his voice. "But Henry, you should have talked to Murph and me before you did this. Maybe we could have worked something out."

"That's what we all said to Boyd and Stevens when they sold," Henry answered. "And the same when Grace sold. But none of us were in a position to buy then, and for darned sure, it's worse now. None of us even has a bank account and we're all counting our pennies. That's all any of us have left—pennies. Everything Isabel and me had was in that bank. Now, it's gone. I decided to sell when I counted out all the money I had. Eighteen dollars!" Henry's voice rose. "Fifty-six years old, and all I had left was *eighteen dollars!*"

"Only ones left on the ditch is Murph and me, three shares, and the DWP will have four," Fred said. "We may as well walk away. They don't even need to buy us out. All they have to do is use their majority to shut the ditch down and we're goners."

"Damn it, Fred, you ain't got no reason to complain. You're the one that brought it down on us. You got those state auditors to come over here and close the bank. With the bank dead and everybody's savings gone, they're all sellin' out. All along, you said we had to fight the DWP, but because of you, we have to throw in the towel and sell out to the DWP."

Fred looked at the ground as he made patterns in the sand with his boot toe. "But Henry, I didn't know they'd shut it down like that."

Henry spit on the ground in disgust. "If you didn't know what you were doin' or what would happen, you had no business doin' it." As he walked away, he turned for a parting word. "With all that's happened, you might as well a been workin' for the DWP."

CHAPTER 48   SCUTTLEBUTT

Fred removed the old cigar box from his dresser drawer. He set it on the dresser and took out his stash of bills—what Alice called their mad money. He set the bills down on the dresser and looked at the eclectic collection of mementos at the bottom of the box. There was a tie clasp he had worn to some occasion years ago, but he couldn't remember what or when. For that matter, he couldn't remember when he had last worn a tie. There were two nearly identical rings. One was his father's Masonic ring, and the other his own. He picked up his father's and examined it in the morning light of early fall. His father had loved being in the Masons and never missed a meeting. On the other hand, even though Fred belonged, he only wore his ring on those rare occasions when his friends talked him into attending. He set the lodge rings back in the box and picked up one of the French coins from his time in France during the war. The two-franc piece was dated 1915, two years before he was over there. He would have liked France if those damned Germans hadn't been shooting at him. His shot-up leg was his major memento. It still hurt, especially in cold weather.

He put the coin back and picked up some bills. Not much left. Everything they saved over the years had been in the Inyo Bank. Unless the bank reopened, this was all they had to show for all their years of struggle and scrimping. He shouldn't touch it, but Alice wanted him to pick up some groceries. He counted out four dollars. That should be enough for groceries, with a bit left for coffee at the Inyo Cafe. He wondered who would be there. He thought about Henry's hostility and hoped he wouldn't face more of the same from other old friends who might blame him for the disastrous demise of the Inyo Bank and the loss of their savings. He took the bills and a few coins and returned the box to the drawer.

After struggling to get his temperamental, ten-year-old war-surplus pickup started, he drove to town, parked in front of Jake's store, and crossed the street to the cafe. The only customers were George King, the druggist, and Ed Walters, the proprietor of the feed store, who were sitting together at the window table.

"Hey, stranger, haven't seen you for a while," George said when Fred walked in.

Before Fred could respond, Ed Walters slammed his coffee cup down and stormed out the door.

Fred knew Ed was one of those who saw him as the cause of the bank's demise, but he asked, "What's eatin' him?"

George held both hands out, palms up as he shrugged. "We were just now talking about the bank situation. He says you brought it about when you reported to Sacramento and you're worse than the DWP."

"Yeah, I guess a lot of people think that. I did what I thought was right. Besides, it was Grace who reported Watson's crimes."

"That's what I told Ed, but he's pretty bull-headed and not about to change his opinion."

Doris approached with her pot in one hand and a cup in the other. "You ready for coffee, Fred?" Without waiting for an answer, she put the cup in front of him and began pouring. "Anything to eat?"

He shook his head, and she headed toward the kitchen.

"I haven't been to town much recently. You got any new scuttlebutt?" Fred asked.

"Yeah. Some interesting stuff going on," George replied. "First, the good. It looks like we might get a couple of new banks in the valley. Word is a Bakersfield bank called Security Trust is going to open a branch in Lone Pine soon."

"That's great news. Just in Lone Pine?"

"I don't know if they'll have other branches. But it's a start for getting back to normal."

Fred tapped his fingers on the table as he thought about it. Too bad Henry hadn't known about it. He might have hung on longer with a new bank moving in. "Yeah, with a new bank, maybe more people will stick it out. You think the new bank will help us recover our money from the Inyo Bank? Alice and me are like most people around here— all of our savings were in Watson's bank. Unless we can take it out of this new bank, we still won't have but what's in our pockets."

George shook his head. "I doubt the out-of-town banks will make up for the shortages at the Inyo Bank. But the new bank's bound to help put some money in circulation. And it's not just the bank from Bakersfield. I also heard the Bank of Italy is looking to open a branch in Bishop."

Fred looked puzzled. "Bank of Italy? Why would a foreign bank move in? I wouldn't want to send what little money I have to Italy."

"It's not really from Italy. It's owned by an Italian from San Francisco named Giannini and serves the Italian people up there. I heard it's in the process of changing its name to Bank of America."

"Yeah, America sounds better, and with more than one bank, we'll have some choice and won't have to be beholden to somebody like Watson. You're just full of good news. What else you got?"

Ed shrugged. "Don't know if this is good or bad, but you might find this interesting. Stan Parker said he saw someone that he was sure was Earl Magon driving through Lone Pine the other day."

The image of Magon flat on the ground with a pool of blood spreading in the sand flashed through Fred's mind. He hardly wanted to say he had launched Magon's body in the aqueduct. "You sure? Nobody has laid eyes on him in quite a while."

"I'm only sure I heard it, not that it's true. Over at the drug store, I must hear two wild stories a day about Magon. One day he's dead, and the next, he's living in Reno with a girlfriend."

Fred chuckled. "A girlfriend, eh?" He blew on his steaming coffee and took a sip as he thought about Magon. "You know, he took Eleanor Rice to dinner a while back. But it couldn't be her in Reno 'cause she's still working in the county records office."

George tilted his chair back. "I don't believe any of those wild stories, but it's sure a mystery how he was here one day and gone the next. Apparently, he has title to a bunch of ranch properties. Maybe he's hiding out at one of them. I heard the D.A. said since he got them through deceit, he doesn't have clear title and can't sell them."

Fred put his cup down. "I understand the DWP replaced Magon with a new man. He's taking up where Magon left off, buying up any property and water he can find."

"But the word is, he's not a thug like Magon," George said. "Now, the DWP only takes its proportional share of the water instead of shutting down the ditch and taking it all. If you don't sell, you keep your share of the flow without Magon strong-arming you."

"That's the way it should'a been from the start."

George nodded agreement. "I guess the new man's going door-to-door with offers for the ranches still holding out. A few days ago, he showed up at Leo Ruiz's place north of Lone Pine offering some cash and the rest deposited in an account in an L.A. bank."

"Leo didn't take it, did he?"

"Sure did. He's been ready to throw in the towel for a while. He told me that with the Inyo bank closed and his savings gone, the only thing left was his ranch. The DWP arranged to settle next week. And it's not just the ranches the DWP's after. Now they're buying town property. I heard they offered to buy Etta Julian's property in Lone Pine."

"She sell?"

"Not sure. She's a widow now and may want to move. Her son lives somewhere over in the San Joaquin Valley. But I don't see why the DWP wants to buy property in town."

Fred absentmindedly stirred his coffee as he thought about it. "The houses in town have water rights just like the ranches. The DWP wants every last gallon. With people desperate for cash, the DWP probably thinks they can wrap it all up."

"It's sure looking like they'll succeed," George said. "It's almost like the state banking guys are working with the DWP. That's what Ed Walters said—the bank auditors close the Inyo Bank so nobody has any cash, and immediately the DWP shows up offering cash and speeds up their buying."

"The DWP and the banking guys aren't in cahoots. It's just that the DWP wants all water and property, and with the bank closed, this is their chance."

George frowned. "Well, dammit, even if they're not workin' together, the results are the same and they're destroying this valley. That's one thing Watson's been right about. You hear he's holding a rally Saturday night up in Bishop? Imagine that. He's out on bail and holding a rally. Lots of people are going."

"You goin'?" Fred asked.

"Thinkin' about it. I can't stand Watson, but it might be interesting to see what he says. You want to go?"

"Not me, for sure. I'm not on Watson's welcome list." He stood. "I gotta go across the street. Alice wants me to pick up a few things at the store. I'll mention it to Jake. He might be interested in seeing what's going on."

As he crossed the street, Fred took a paper out of his shirt pocket and ran his eyes down Alice's grocery list. Not much stuff, and a good thing, too. He knew Jake was practically out of merchandise. When he went in, a glance at the mostly empty shelves showed the situation was worse than he expected. Short as his list was, Jake might not have even that much.

Jake stood by the cash register, explaining to a woman he was out of canned hominy and couldn't get more until his L.A. supplier resumed shipments to the valley. The woman grabbed her shopping bag and huffed out of the store, almost crashing into Fred.

Jake looked at Fred and shook his head in frustration.

Fred gave a sympathetic smile. "You have to take the bad with the good."

"But there isn't any good these days." Jake turned and pointed. "Just look at these shelves. Empty! Every housewife is mad at me like it's all my fault."

Fred handed his list to Jake. "To add to your happiness, here's Alice's list."

Jake glanced down the list. "I don't have most of this stuff."

"Give me what you have."

Jake walked back and forth behind the counter, talking as he grabbed a few items and set them by the cash register. "I guess Watson's holding a rally Saturday night up in Bishop."

"Just had coffee with George King. He mentioned it. I told him you might want to go."

"I might," Jake said. "At least it might keep me up to date about Watson's next move."

CHAPTER 49   RALLY

Following Fred's suggestion, Jake and George King drove together to Watson's rally on Saturday night. When Jake walked into the Bishop High School auditorium, the size of the audience surprised him. He hadn't expected such a turnout. A subdued murmur floated through the hall as the crowd waited for the program to start. Few seats remained, and Jake and George squeezed down a row near the back. Jake nodded to a man he didn't know in the next seat and quietly waited.

The murmur died and a rotund man clad in a red flannel shirt and Levi's, with his belly hanging over his belt, walked onto the stage. He gazed at the audience for a moment, then spoke. "Most of you know me, but in case you don't, I'm Aubrey Smith. I run a cattle spread down by Lone Pine. I've lived there all my life and my ranch has had its ups and downs — lots of downs. But through all the good and bad, I've been helped along by the support of the Watson family. They and their bank have been doing splendid work in our valley for over twenty years. Now, they need our help. As you all know, while the City of Los Angeles has been doing everything it could to destroy our way of life, Mark Watson and the Inyo Bank have stood firm to resist the thirsty monster. Now, the DWP has teamed up with the state bank regulators to get rid of Mr. Watson. We can't let that happen. Mark Watson needs our support so that he can continue to keep the DWP from taking every last drop of water and our way of life. Mark is here tonight to tell us what is going on with his bank and explain how we can help fight the voracious octopus. So here he is, Mark Watson, President of the Inyo Bank."

The audience stood and welcomed the banker with enthusiastic applause and whistles as he walked to the middle of the stage.

He waited until the ovation quieted. "Thank you for coming. I know all of you are wondering how we got into this mess. That is what I am here to tell you."

More cheers and applause filled the hall.

When the cheering abated, Watson continued. "As Aubrey just said, my family has been serving this valley for over twenty years. I am privileged to be the latest Watson to serve. But the survival of our valley has never been as threatened as it is now. Since the early part of this century, the City of Los Angeles has been working to take what is ours. They now control most of the water and land in our beautiful valley. To top that off, the California State Banking Department is helping them take the rest. I have resisted them, and as a result, they declared my bank insolvent and closed me down. I've been charged, unjustly and without a shred of evidence, of embezzlement. They say I embezzled your money. I want you to know, right here, right now, there is not a shred of truth to that accusation. Everything I have done has been to protect you and your money from the hands of those thieves."

He paused for the cheering, then resumed.

"I want to assure you my bank is one of the strongest in California. Your money is safe with the Inyo Bank. We have plenty of reserves. Those auditors don't understand banking. What they call a shortage is not a shortage at all. Those funds have all been invested here in the valley to help you. But that investment has stopped since the crooked state auditors walked into my bank without warning and closed it down. They won't even let me into my own bank, much less allow you to get your money when you need it."

He gazed sadly at the audience and shook his head in sympathy, then continued, his voice breaking with emotion. "You want to know what those government blood suckers do? They joke because you don't earn a state salary like them and paid for by your taxes. They laugh that you have no cash and can't even buy food."

"They have no business doing that," someone in the audience shouted.

"Absolutely," Watson shouted back.

"They're fat pigs eating at the public trough," another yelled.

Watson pointed at the man and hollered. "You're right. They're pigs and shouldn't be here poking their noses into my business or yours. My bank and this valley were doing just fine 'till they came to interfere. And you want to know who told them to come here and team up with the DWP?"

He paused to let the mystery build. "I'll tell you who," he shouted. "It was that traitor, Fred Lukin down in Independence! He went to Sacramento and told lies to get these bloodsuckers to come and destroy my bank. He even took Grace Berks, one of my own employees, with him to tell more lies. An evil man, who was born here, has forsaken his sacred marriage vows to his beautiful wife and taken another woman and turned on his lifelong friends and family for his own gain and carnal pleasure."

"He needs to be taught a lesson," a man yelled.

"Yeah, get him," another hollered.

Watson spread both arms with both hands open. "Now, now. I don't want to encourage violence. But… well… "

Jake leaned over and whispered to George. "I think it's time to get out of here."

"Go ahead," George whispered back. "I can get a ride back with somebody else."

"Nah, I'll wait," Jake said as he settled back.

For the rest of the evening, Watson gave more assurances he had done nothing wrong, that their money was safe, but the City of Los Angeles and the state banking auditors were devils bent on their destruction. The auditorium erupted in cheers and applause when the banker concluded, and people filed out of the hall.

"Whew," Jake said when he got into the car to head home to Independence. "The way it was going, I thought they might get around to me and call for a lynching 'cause I'm related to Fred."

"That's all just talk," George said. "I wouldn't worry. When we get some money circulating again, things will settle down."

"Sure hope so. It seems like everybody blames Fred. I'm afraid Watson will send his hounds after him." Jake glanced at George. "We better warn him and maybe post some guards at his place."

"It won't go that far."

"I wouldn't bet on it."

CHAPTER 50   INVASION

It's a lot cooler today, Fred thought as he examined his calves for disease. It had been a hot fall, and it was nice to finally get some relief. He ran his hand along a calf's ribs, checking for signs of weight loss. Some of the ranchers up around Bishop had calves showing signs of shipping fever, with breathing difficulty, coughing, and weight loss. So far, there was no evidence of it in this south end of the valley, and this calf felt just fine. The last thing he needed was a bunch of sick cattle. As he absentmindedly patted the back of the heifer, he glanced toward the barn and saw Jake getting out of his car. He waved and waited while his brother-in-law walked out to the field.

"What brings you out here?" Fred asked.

"George and I drove up to Bishop for Watson's rally last night."

"What happened?"

"Watson mentioned you as the one who brought the bank examiners over here to close the bank. And get this, he said you abandoned your wife and took Grace with you to Sacramento for your carnal pleasure."

Fred spat on the ground. "He's less than dirt. The best thing to do is ignore him."

"Hard to ignore when he's riling up his followers to get you. You need to watch out. I think we should get some men as guards."

"Nah. He's just talk. I can take care of myself. And, I have Alice." He chuckled. "Somebody comes out to make trouble, she'll take 'em all on."

Jake's voice rose. "Fred, this is serious! Watson has a bunch on his side, including those Klan guys. They're just dumb enough to do whatever he says. You can't fight them alone."

"You worry too much. We'll be okay."

"At least consider staying with us a while."

"I gotta be here, especially at night. That's when somebody might try something."

"But you just said they wouldn't do anything. Be sensible. You're putting both yourself and Alice at risk."

"Jake, thanks for your concern, but I'm stayin' here to defend the place. Don't worry."

Jake shook his head. "Okay, but keep your guns loaded. I gotta get back." He turned and walked to his car.

After Jake drove away, Fred examined the last few calves and then headed to the house for lunch.

"I saw Jake talking to you. What did he want?" Alice asked when Fred walked into the kitchen.

"He went to Watson's rally in Bishop last night and gave me an update."

"Anything interesting?"

"The same stuff we've been hearing all month about how innocent Watson is."

Alice stared at him for a moment and spoke an octave higher in that voice he knew signaled exasperation. "Fred Lukin! How many times have I told you you're no good at lying? Now tell me what you're trying to keep from me."

He smiled to himself. He should know, after all these years, that she would see through any of his deceptions. "Okay. Watson said I was the one who brought the bank auditors who closed things down, and I had taken Grace to Sacramento to satisfy my carnal lust. He's encouraging his followers to get me."

"Carnal lust? With Grace?" She laughed and grabbed a large knife from the counter and held it up. "You better not have carnal anything with Grace!" Her smile disappeared. "What did he mean, 'encouraging his followers to get you'?"

"Don't know. Jake wants us to go stay with them. But that would leave the ranch open, so I need to stay here. I want you to go stay with Betty and Jake."

"Absolutely not," Alice insisted. "If you stay, I stay. You can't face a bunch of them alone."

"I can handle it, and you'd just get in the way."

"Get in the way?" she questioned loudly. "Who was it that rescued you from those L.A. cops when they were taking you to the city? This is my ranch, too. I'm not going anyplace!"

Fred frowned and shook his head. He knew better than to try to change her mind. He hadn't managed it yet. "Okay, but if anything happens, I'll handle it."

"We'll do it together," she insisted.

"Dammit, can't you ever just be a regular housewife?"

"If I was just a regular housewife, I'd probably be just a regular widow by now."

She always seemed to have a quick answer that stymied him.

That night, before bed, Fred loaded his guns. He couldn't sleep and got up several times, stepping out on the porch, checking for intruders. Everything was calm, and he went back to bed, only to stare at the ceiling and wonder what might happen. He was dragging the next morning, feeling like he had a hangover even though he'd had nothing to drink.

All day Monday, he went through the motions of work, feeding the cattle and tending to his chores. He kept thinking about Watson riling up his followers. He tried to put on a brave face for Alice, but he couldn't hide from his own anxiety. He was exhausted when he went to bed that night. Tossing and turning, he played a dozen worrisome scenarios through his mind but finally fell asleep not long before the eastern sky began to lighten over the Inyo Mountains.

The rest of the week unfolded with no disturbance, and worry about Watson's threats faded into the background.

Then, Sunday night, shortly after midnight, the sounds of a crash and breaking glass brought him instantly awake.

Alice bolted upright. "What was that?"

Fred was already slipping into his pants. "Stay here. I'll go check." He grabbed his shotgun, leaning against the wall, and crept down the hall toward the kitchen, where the sound of the crash emanated. As he rounded the corner into the dark kitchen, dim forms of men in white robes and tall pointed hats filled the room.

"What the hell?" Fred shouted as he leveled his gun on the strangers. "Get out. All of you!"

The hooded figures spread across the kitchen with shotguns and rifles trained on him. A man who seemed to be the leader spoke. "Fred Lukin, you're charged with treason against the Owens Valley Water Protective Association. Hand over your gun."

Fred stepped back, slammed the door, and retreated down the hall. A crash and the sound of breaking glass came from the bedroom, followed by Alice's screams and the sounds of a struggle. "Ow, ow. Stop it, bitch," followed by more screams from Alice. Dim forms spilled out of the bedroom into the hall. A man in Klan costume held Alice off the ground with an arm around her throat. Blood poured from her nose, running down her thin nightgown. She kicked, writhed and struggled. When they got close, her captor let go and pushed her into Fred. A second hooded man held a rifle to Alice's head and growled, "Drop the gun, Lukin."

He didn't have much choice. Dammit, he wouldn't be in this position if she had gone to town to stay with Betty instead of insisting on staying. He leaned his shotgun against the wall. The man opened the door and herded the couple at gunpoint into the kitchen, where the rest of the coven waited.

The same man who had charged Fred with treason moments earlier stood in front of him and spoke as though he hadn't been interrupted. "The charge for treason is death. You will be hanged by the neck until dead."

"You sonofabitch," Alice screamed and kicked the hooded judge in the crotch. He howled. Holding his crotch with one hand, he slugged her with the other, knocking her to the floor.

Fred cocked his arm back and swung at his wife's attacker, knocking him against the kitchen table. At his side, someone shouted, "Bastard." Fred turned and the last thing he saw was the butt of a rifle flying toward his face.

On her hands and knees, the room swirled around Alice. There were dark blotches spreading on the floor. She didn't remember any spots on her kitchen floor. The front of her face hurt. She touched her nose and looked at her hand. It was red. It took a moment to realize the red spots were her own blood. It was coming back now.

A man had hit her. That was why her nose was bleeding. She looked to her left. A man was lying next to her with blood spreading from his head. It took her a moment. Then she recognized him. "Fred," she shouted.

A vicious voice sounded as though it was echoing down a tunnel. "Shut up, bitch," and the speaker kicked her in the ribs. She screamed.

Other voices came in a wavering jumble. "What'll we do with him now?" someone asked.

"Tie his hands and load him up. Then we get outta here."

Alice struggled to stand up. A man gestured at her and asked, "What about her?"

"Tie her up."

"Here's some rope," another white-robed vigilante said.

Two men slammed her back to the floor. They tied her hands behind her back and bound her ankles. "Do we leave her here?"

The leader pointed toward the door. "Take her outside, then we'll torch the place."

A man grabbed her tied wrists and dragged her into the yard. Her shoulders felt like they were being ripped apart. She screamed in agony.

Outside, the leader pointed toward a big cottonwood. "Tie her up. Wrap her up good so she can watch."

Two men held the petite, middle-aged lady against the tree, and a third wrapped the rope around her from shoulders to feet, completely immobilizing her.

"Light it up," the leader shouted.

Men splashed gasoline on a wall and poured it along the foundation. They stepped back and others touched torches to the freshly applied gas. The wall blazed up with a whoosh, and the vigilantes whooped. A few danced a joyous jig, their pointed hoods swaying and bouncing to an unheard rhythm.

Alice helplessly watched in despair as the house she and Fred had shared for so many years was engulfed in flames. Tears rolled down her cheeks.

The arsonists watched and howled approval as part of the roof flamed up.

"Okay," the leader shouted, "load up so we can take care of the traitor."

The hooded men pushed Fred into the back of a pickup, and piled into their cars and trucks, shouting and hooting like they were headed to a carnival.

Alice closed her eyes so she wouldn't have to watch the house burn. But she couldn't close out her image of Fred being carried like a side of beef in the back of a truck to a fate only God knew. Overwhelmed with anguish, her sobs turned to hopeless moans.

After what seemed like a lifetime, a car drove into the farmyard. Tied as she was, she couldn't see who drove up, but the car door slammed, and in seconds, Murphy stood before her.

"Bastards! Sonsabitches!" Murphy swore and quickly untied her. Freed, she collapsed to the ground. He picked her up and hugged her close for a moment and then, with hands on her shoulders, held her at arm's length. "What happened?"

She pointed at the burning house. Her mouth quivered. "Fred … they … they … " She turned and pointed down the lane. "They … he … " She stared blindly at the ground. Convulsing with sobs, she howled, "Fred, oh, Fred."

Murphy gently guided her toward his car. "There's nothing we can do here. We'll get Cole and find Fred."

He seated her in his car and was getting in when he heard a siren in the distance. He stood, waiting.

It took a while, but finally, the town firetruck, followed by Sheriff Cole and a string of cars, barreled into the farmyard. George King, the chief of the volunteer fire department, jumped from the truck and shouted instructions to others as they poured from their cars. They quickly ran a hose from the firetruck to the water ditch and began spraying the blazing house.

Cole joined Murphy by his car. "What happened?"

"Not sure, probably Watson's Klan," Murphy replied. "From my house, I heard some yelling and saw smoke. Drove over to see what was going on. They were gone when I got here." He nodded toward Alice, sitting in the car. "She was tied to the tree and the house was in flames."

"Somebody in town saw smoke and the glow of a fire and raised the alarm." Cole looked toward Alice. "I'll see what she can tell me."

"I'm not sure she can say anything. She seems pretty far gone." Murphy said.

Cole walked around the car and opened the door on the passenger side. She stared straight ahead as though she saw nothing. He gently touched her on the shoulder. "Alice, what happened? Can you tell me anything?"

She slowly turned her head and stared blankly at the sheriff as if he were a block of wood. Her mouth quivered, and more tears rolled down her cheeks.

Cole rejoined Murphy. "I don't think she can even speak right now. When we're through here, I'll take her to Jake and Betty's house so she can be with her sister."

"Yeah, maybe Betty can help her. Charlie, you gotta know this was Watson's doing. According to Jake, at that rally last week, Watson as much as told his guys to get Fred. They do whatever he says."

Cole rubbed his chin, rough with a long-since-five-o'clock shadow. "You're probably right. I heard about Watson's meeting.

But there's not much I can do without some evidence, and the main witness is so traumatized that she can't talk."

George King walked over from the fire that was gradually being beaten down. "Sheriff, one of our guys found something you should see."

Cole and Murphy followed King to the side of the smoldering house. King pointed at a sooty patch of ground. The sand was blackened with the letters, KKK.

Cole stared briefly. "Looks like they poured gas on the ground and lit it to leave their initials."

"Hard to say we don't know who did it," Murphy said.

"Yeah, we know the group, but no proof about individuals," Cole said. 'We all know Watson's driving this, but it'll be tough to pin it on him. His embezzlement trial starts tomorrow. Maybe that can bring something out. But what's more important right now is what they did with Fred. We gotta find him before it's too late."

CHAPTER 51   CAPITAL PUNISHMENT

Fred's only thought as he regained consciousness was that his head might explode with pain. He tried to reach up and touch it, but something held his hands behind his back. Everything was a fog, but he remembered a rifle butt careening toward his face. He heard men's voices sounding like they were echoing through a long tunnel

"You can't hang an unconscious man," one voice said.

"Why not?" another asked. "What difference can it make? Let's get it over with and go home."

"But he's got to know what's happening and why he's being punished. Otherwise, what's the point of doing it?"

"So what if he knows or not? He'll be dead. Come on, let's go."

Fred felt someone shake his shoulder and he realized he was lying on his side with his hands bound behind his back. He saw sideboards. He must be in the bed of a pickup. He looked up at the stars, bright in the night sky.

"Hey, I think he's awake," said a nearby voice.

"Get him up."

A hand grabbed his feet and pulled him over the edge of the tailgate. He screamed in pain when he crashed with a thud on the hard desert ground.

"See, I told you he was awake."

Two men grabbed his arms and yanked him to a standing position beneath a half-dead cottonwood. Another man threw a rope over a branch of the tree and quickly slipped a noose over his head and pulled it tight around his neck.

Men in white robes with tall, pointed hoods gathered around. He scowled with hatred at his Klan captors. He looked at each one, trying to figure out who was hiding under the hoods. The only parts showing were the eyes and the hands. In the dim light, he couldn't make out the eyes behind the roughly cut eyeholes, but he could discern their hands and, beneath their robes, their sizes and builds. Maybe if he could identify them, he'd have an idea how to talk them out of it. If he didn't, in a few minutes, he would be nothing but a cold piece of meat hanging from a pathetic tree in the desert. But even if he couldn't stop them, he wanted them to know that he knew some of them. Maybe it would haunt them.

He eyed the tall one standing on the left. By his size, Fred was sure that it was Jack McIntyre under the hood. He worked odd jobs around Bishop and had always seemed okay, but a little dim. The man standing next to him wasn't as tall, but even the robe couldn't disguise his ample belly. His Masonic ring showed prominently on his hand. That had to be Asa Plummer, who worked at the Bishop post office and was a deacon in the Bishop Masonic Lodge. Fred didn't know him well but thought he had always seemed a decent sort. A decent sort ready to lynch him? Then he noticed that the other men, maybe half of the vigilante gang, clustered close around Plummer, all wore Masonic rings.

"Asa," Fred loudly asked, "that you hiding under that robe?"

The man pulled his hood a little tighter and mumbled something.

"What? I can't hear you. Aren't you a senior deacon in the Bishop Masons?"

The pudgy man stepped back as though to disappear among his henchmen.

"The rest of you there with Asa, all Masons, eh? All sworn to brotherly love and fraternal ties to your fellow Masons."

"Somebody shut him up," one of the men growled.

"He gets some last words," another insisted.

"Yeah, last words," Fred said. Then it hit him. Watson was the top dog of the Bishop Lodge. That was why there were a bunch of Masons here, dressed in Klan get-up, doing their lodge leader's bidding. He figured he had to keep talking to delay the inevitable. "You've sworn to relieve the distress and misfortune of other Masons. But you hide under your hoods and do whatever Mark Watson says. You're even willing to lynch me, a fellow Mason, because Watson tells you to. Me, a Mason? That's right. I belong to the Independence Lodge, and I know the principles you swore to uphold. Is this how you do it?"

"I said shut him up," a man shouted. He stepped forward and grabbed the end of the lynching rope strung over a cottonwood branch. He jerked it tight around Fred's neck. Fred went on his tiptoes as he choked. Before his feet left the ground, another man grabbed the rope from the would-be executioner. Fred collapsed to the ground, gasping for breath.

"We can't do this," his rescuer said.

"He's a traitor, and Mark said to hang him," someone else responded.

Fred sat up, gasping for breath. "Not traitor," he croaked. "Watson's cheating all of you and lying about it."

The man who released the rope stood beside Fred. "This has gone far enough. We can't do this to a fellow Mason." He kneeled down and removed the noose but didn't untie Fred's hands. "Let's all go home," he told the lynch mob.

"What about him?" a man asked.

"Leave him here. He can walk home. We'll all be long gone by the time he reaches town."

Fred struggled to stand, but his rescuer pushed him back to the ground. "Stay there till we're gone."

Lying on the ground, Fred listened to the coven of hooded men get in their vehicles and drive away. When they were all gone, he attempted to stand, but with his hands still tied behind him, it took several tries. Finally, upright, he looked west at the towering mountains silhouetted black against the star-filled sky. Despite his throbbing head and aching body, he was alive, and everything looked more beautiful than ever. He gazed at the sage and rabbit brush down the slope. He took a deep breath. The pungent aroma of sage filled his senses. His neck still stung from the noose, but, God, it was good to be alive.

The lynch mob would probably be back to Bishop before he got to town. *Better get started.* Walking through the brush with his hands still tied behind his back, he watched the desert's nighttime personality: rabbits chewing on sage leaves, coyotes stalking the rabbits, and nighthawks and owls, sailing silently above it all, searching for their next meal.

Picking his way through the brush in the dark, it took almost an hour to reach the highway, where he turned south toward Independence. Up ahead, three cars slowly approached. Were they part of Watson's gang, coming back to finish the job? He backed away from the road and crouched behind a bush, waiting for them to pass. As they got closer, he recognized Cole's black and white Nash, followed closely by Murphy's car. He trotted toward the road to intercept them.

When Fred stepped onto the road, Cole screeched to a stop and sprang out of his police car. "Damn glad to see you. We all thought you were a goner."

"So did I," Fred replied. "How'd you find me?"

"Somebody called Jake's house and told where to find you. We were looking for the turnoff when we saw you," Cole explained as he untied the rope binding Fred's hands.

"One of those guys must've called from town after they let me go, but I think most of them were Klan from Bishop."

"They're probably home by now," Cole said.

"Is Alice ok?" Fred asked.

Cole hesitated and looked at Murphy. "Ah … ah, well … "

Fred's voice rose with anxiety. "Where is she? Did they hurt her?"

"She's ok, but really upset. We took her to Jake's house to be with Betty," Murphy replied.

Fred relaxed a little. "Okay. Take me to pick her up, and we can go home."

Cole grimaced. "Now, about your house …"

CHAPTER 52   MUCKING UP

Driving back to town, Cole explained as best he could what he knew about Alice and the fire. When they pulled up to Jake and Betty's place, Fred sprang out of the car and bolted into the house. The front room was dark, and he banged into a chair and noisily stumbled around, not knowing where to find Alice.

Betty sleepily entered the room, struggling to tie the belt on her robe. "Fred, you look terrible."

"Where's Alice?

"Shhh," Betty said, putting her finger to her lips. "She's asleep in the extra bedroom. I put her to bed when Murphy brought her. She was so upset that she was barely able to speak. Don't wake her."

"I won't." He said as he rushed past her, banged open the door, and barged into the bedroom.

Alice sleepily opened her eyes. "Fred," she cried, instantly wide awake.

He sat on the edge of the bed, gently brushed her hair back, wrapped his arms around her and hugged like he would never let go. After a few minutes, he pushed her back and gazed at her. Dark as it was, he could see the red and purple bruises on the side of her face. He gently touched her swollen jaw.

"Ow."

"Does it hurt a lot?"

"Of course. But I bet I don't look as bad as you," she replied as she reached up and brushed the blood-matted hair on the side of his head. She laughed. "Aren't we a pair? What a sight we must make. Me with a bashed-in jaw and you with bloody hair. I was terrified I might never see you again."

"Me too you. They threatened to hang me, and what bothered me most was that I would never be with you."

She hugged Fred with her head on his shoulder. "What happened?"

They continued talking about their night and what came next.

After a while, Betty rapped on the door and stuck her head in. "It's almost five o'clock. You better get some sleep. Watson's trial starts this morning."

"They won't need me," Fred said. "I gotta see about the ranch."

Alice held Fred's shoulder for support and stood unsteadily. "I may as well get up 'cause I sure can't sleep. Mr. Hess said he might call me as a witness, but not on the first day. I'll go with Fred to check the ranch." She looked down at her nightgown, blood-stained and torn in the struggle with the KKK men. "I think I just might need some clothes. Can I borrow some of yours?" she asked her sister.

"Of course. But Fred, I don't know what we can do about you. You won't fit into Jake's clothes and can't wear mine."

Fred laughed. "I don't need a skirt. I still got my pants on. All I need is a shirt and shoes, and I'm set."

Betty pointed in the general direction of their store. "We ought to be able to find something at the store. There's hardly any groceries left, but there's still some clothes on the shelves."

"Can we borrow your car to go out to the ranch?" Fred asked.

"I'm sure that would be okay," Betty replied. "We won't need to go but a couple of blocks to the courthouse."

Alice and Fred each bathed and doctored their cuts and bruises. Alice dressed in Betty's loaner clothes while Fred chose from a selection of shirts and a pair of boots Jake fetched from his store in the early hour. After a quick breakfast, with a mix of anxiety and eagerness, they headed out to their ranch in Jake's car.

Alice sat in the car to take it in. Whisps of smoke rose from blackened studs of the walls on the part of the house torched by the KKK arsonists. She fought back tears as she gazed at the remains of the house they had lived in for so many years. It was almost like she had lost a close friend. So many good times – good days, good nights. Carl was born there, friends visited, and all the meals and stories that had been shared.

Her moment of mourning was interrupted when Fred opened the car door. "You coming?" he asked.

"Not sure I want to. It hurts to see it."

"Yeah, it's a mess, but it looks like the firemen saved most of it." He took her hand. "Let's see what's left."

They walked into the kitchen between charred studs where the front door had been. One wall of the kitchen was gone, but the rest was mostly intact. Peels of wet wallpaper hung from the unburned walls, and puddles of water covered the floor from the soaking the firemen had applied.

Alice scrunched up her face. "God, it smells awful – wet charcoal and the laundry — already mildewing." She ran her hand over the stove and opened the icebox like they were injured friends.

Fred pushed at a still-standing wall. "I think we can rebuild."

"But can we ever get rid of this horrid smell?" Alice asked.

"Don't know. We'll have to see what it's like after it dries out. I hope our insurance will pay for it. But I think maybe our insurance agent was one of the guys in the Klan gang."

In the bedroom, Alice pushed on the bed and water oozed out of the mattress like a wet sponge. She scrunched her lips and shook her head in frustration. "It's all gone. No house, no furniture." She opened the closet and held up a dress. "Look at this – drenched. We don't even have anything to wear. They may as well have let it burn."

Fred put his arms around her. "It'll be okay. We're still here. Last night when I got loose, I realized how lucky I was to be alive. We can get through this. Most of the furniture will dry out and we can wash the clothes. I think we can rebuild the house."

"What'll we do in the meantime? Camp out?"

"We have the barn." He paused. "The barn! The horses! I hadn't thought about them. I need to check on them."

They both hurried across the farmyard. Their three horses were waiting in their stalls for their morning oats, and the car was still there.

"Thank God they left this much," Alice said.

"See. It's going to be okay. We can fix this up and stay here in the barn while we work on the house."

Alice laughed. "Yeah. That's what I said – camp out."

"The faster we clean it up, the quicker it'll dry out. I'll let the horses out and check the cattle, and then we can start mucking it out."

"I joked about camping," Alice said. "I hope we can stay with Betty and Jake for a while. It'll be easier when we go to Watson's trial."

CHAPTER 53   TRIAL

That evening, Fred and Alice returned to Jake and Betty's house, dirty and dog-tired.

Over dinner, Alice described what they had accomplished at their burned house. "Now tell me what went on at Watson's trial."

"It seemed really strange to start on Halloween. But at least it finally got going," Betty replied.

Fred slapped his fork down on the table. "It's all a waste of time. They aren't goin' to do a thing to Watson. He'll walk away and laugh at all of us."

"No, you're wrong. He's going to get his comeuppance," Alice replied.

"You never know, but my money's on a conviction," Jake added.

Fred picked up his fork and took a bite of ham. "Hope so. If Watson walks and gets his bank back, he'll try to revive his foreclosure on us."

"Even if he's acquitted, I don't think he'll get the bank back," Jake observed. "Today's testimony by the state bank examiner showed that the bank is a bust. It will have to be liquidated to pay off the creditors, including us. Watson's out of the banking business."

"I don't just want him out of the banking business," Alice said. "I want him locked up in a small, dark cell." She paused for a moment. "What else happened?"

"First, they picked a jury," Betty explained. "Most of the jury pool was rejected because they knew Watson or knew about the case. Most of the ones picked were from outlying districts like Death Valley. After they picked the jurors, the district attorney questioned a guy from the state banking office. He explained their audit and the charges against Watson. There were a whole bunch of charges, but the main ones were that Watson had embezzled funds from his own bank and lied to the authorities."

"I know it's some sort of cheating, but what does embezzlement really mean?" Fred asked.

Jake wiped his mouth with his napkin. "The bank auditor said it was when a person dishonestly takes money that has been entrusted to them. In this case, Watson took money from the bank and the bank's clients."

"Did Grace testify?" Alice asked.

"Not yet," Betty replied. "I think she's on tomorrow."

"Was anything said about Watson's Klan coming after us?" Fred asked.

"Not a word," Jake replied. "When we left the court, I asked the DA about that. He said it was not related to the bank failure and not part of these charges. Separate charges could come later, but it would be hard to prove anything because the players couldn't be identified. The only way to prove anything would be if one of those KKK guys snitched and testified. That's probably not going to happen because being an informer is practically a death sentence. Also, it would be almost impossible to tie it to Watson."

"So that worm's going to get away with it?" Alice fumed. "They burn our house down, beat us up, and almost hang Fred, and nothing happens to them?"

"Seems likely unless somebody squeals," Jake replied.

"I'd like to make a pistol squeal in Watson's ear," Alice growled.

"Please don't say that in court. You already did that to an L.A. cop." Jake said.

The next morning, Fred, Alice, Betty, and Jake walked together to the courthouse for the second day of Watson's trial.

Fred's head throbbed as he limped up the steps. He paused and rubbed the bandaged side of his head where the Klansman had bashed him with the rifle butt. He squirmed in the coat borrowed from Jake's store, a size too small. "I don't know why I'm doing this. I still think it's a waste of time."

"I told you before, they'll find him guilty," Alice mumbled through her swollen lips and bruised jaw. Rather than covering her bruises with make-up for the trial, she wore them like medals so people could see what Watson's Klan vigilantes had done.

Fred rubbed his neck where the rope burns showed and looked back at the stream of people following them into the courthouse. "Looks like everybody in the county is here."

"I hope we can get a seat and there are no fights," Alice said. "Half the people think Watson's a hero, and the other half want to see him in prison."

"It went okay yesterday," Betty commented.

They passed through the tall doorway into the courtroom and a murmur spread through the room as spectators turned and watched. Had everybody already heard about his abduction and close encounter with a vigilante noose? For sure, everybody would know about the fire. Fred tried to ignore the looks as he scanned the crowded courtroom for seats. On the right, a guy quickly turned away as though to avoid Fred's gaze. That had to be Asa Plummer, one of the Sunday night vigilantes. What a temptation to grab him out of his seat and beat him senseless. Were those other respectable-looking men seated around Plummer also part of Watson's KKK vigilantes?

On the left, near the front, Murphy stood and waved. He had saved some seats. Alice and Fred pardoned themselves as they squeezed down the aisle. Alice and Betty sat side-by-side between Fred and Jake. The sisters talked quietly and Fred nodded to acquaintances. Everyone waited for the second day of the biggest show in the Owens Valley.

The low drone of conversation died, and the bailiff announced Judge Lambert, the visiting judge from Bakersfield. The judge welcomed the jurors and spectators and then reminded them about court rules and decorum. The judge whacked his gavel. "Call your next witness, Mr. Hess."

District Attorney Walt Hess stood. "I call Clifford Hanchett."

A paunchy man of late middle age stepped forward and was sworn in.

"Mr. Hanchett, please tell the court where you work and your present position."

"For the last four years, I have been working as a self-employed accountant serving businesses in towns from Reno to Mojave."

"And you work with the Inyo Bank?"

"Yes. Most of my work is with small local banks. On a rotating schedule, I bring their accounting up to date, check their accounts, and prepare financial statements for the state banking department."

Hess handed a paper to the witness. "Mr. Hanchett, please identify this sheet."

"This is a list of payments from the Inyo Bank to various correspondent banks during the month of November of 1926 that Mr. Watson told me to record."

"How many different transactions are shown on the sheet?"

Hanchett examined the sheet. "Thirteen for the month."

"Please read the first one."

"Fifteen thousand dollars deposited at Wells Fargo Bank of San Francisco on November 1st."

"A year ago," Hess observed. "How was this payment made — with a check or cash?"

"He told me it was a check drawn on the Inyo Bank paid to the order of Wells Fargo Bank for deposit in the Inyo Bank's correspondent account at Wells Fargo."

"Such a check would transfer money from the Inyo Bank to the Wells Fargo Bank?"

"Yes," Hanchett replied.

"Did you see the check or other confirmation that the payment was made?" Hess asked.

"No. All the transactions shown on this page were ones that Mr. Watson ordered me to record but showed me no checks or deposit confirmations."

"I understand you and Mr. Lowell examined these various transactions. Please tell the court what you found regarding this particular transaction."

"No such payment was made to Wells Fargo. Instead, $15,000 was deposited in Mr. Watson's personal account at the Pacific National Bank of Los Angeles."

Hess gazed at the jury. "So, Mr. Watson was taking money from the Inyo Bank and paying it to himself, but recording it in the bank's records as a deposit in the Inyo Bank's correspondent account at Wells Fargo?"

"That is correct," Hanchett replied.

"Does the Inyo Bank or Mr. Watson have an account with Wells Fargo Bank in San Francisco?"

"No. The man I spoke to at Wells Fargo said they had no record of a checking or other deposit account for the Inyo Bank or Mr. Watson."

"Very well," Hess said. "Let's look at another transaction. Please explain to the court the transaction dated November 26th."

Hanchett ran his finger down the paper, then looked at Hess. "It shows a check for $7,000 drawn on the Inyo Bank for deposit at Wells Fargo."

"Did Wells Fargo confirm such a deposit?"

"No," Hanchett replied.

"Did you and the auditors trace the money? And if so, what did you find?"

"Yes, we traced it and found that $2,000 went to Natural Soda Products, $1,000 to Tungsten Products Company, $750 paid to

Coso Hot Springs, and $3,250 to Mark Watson's personal account at the Pacific National Bank of Los Angeles."

"Please tell the court what these companies are," Hess said.

"Natural Soda Products is a company that processes soda ash from Owens Lake for sale to other companies for manufacturing cleaning products, glass production, and paper manufacturing. Tungsten Products is a mine west of Bishop, and Coso Hot Springs is a resort down by Little Lake."

"Who owns these companies?"

"Mark Watson owns all three."

"So, in this case, Mark Watson told you to record a check as a deposit in Wells Fargo, but it never went to Wells Fargo. Instead, the money went to three companies owned by Mr. Watson, with a big part going to Mr. Watson personally?"

"Yes."

"The sheet I handed you lists other transactions. When you total all the transactions for the month, what does it show?"

Hanchett glanced at the sheet. "For November of last year, the deposits allegedly made to Wells Fargo Bank totaled $97,000. However, none of that money actually went to Wells Fargo."

The sound of a collective gasp from the spectators and jury echoed through the courtroom.

The judge rapped his gavel. "Silence! ... Please continue, Mr. Hess."

"Can you summarize where this $97,000 actually went?" Hess asked the witness.

"We traced this money and found the totals of $44,000 going to National Soda, $5,000 to Tungsten Products, $1,000 to Coso Hot Springs, and $47,000 to Mr. Watson's personal account at Pacific National Bank."

"Thank you, Mr. Hanchett," Hess turned to the judge. "That's all I have for this witness for now."

The judge glanced toward the defense table. "Your turn, Mr. Carey."

Watson's defense attorney stood. "Thank you, Your Honor." He scanned the list of transactions about which Hanchett had just testified and shook his head. He looked up and glared at Hanchett. "Mr. Hanchett, when you began your testimony, you said you had worked as an independent accountant for *only* four years. Given that bank accounting can be quite complex, that doesn't sound like much experience. Isn't it possible, with your limited work with the bank, that you don't understand the figures and could have made errors in examining these transactions?"

A slight smile crossed Hanchett's face. "It is true I have worked as an independent accountant for a relatively short time. But prior to that, I spent seventeen years as an accountant at Merchant's National Trust in Los Angeles. I moved to Bishop to enjoy the more peaceful life of this beautiful valley." He laughed. "Boy, was I wrong about the peaceful life. Anyway, when I left

Merchants, I was their chief accountant, supervising a staff of seven. As for errors, I worked with Mr. Lowell, the chief examiner for the state banking department, and his three assistants. We checked those figures several times and I am sure they are correct."

Carey cringed and shook his head like a fighter trying to shake off a punch. "No more questions for this witness."

The judge glanced at the large clock on the wall and whacked his gavel. "It's lunchtime. We'll recess and resume at one-thirty."

As Fred, Alice, Betty, Jake, and Grace filed out of court together, Walt Hess's familiar voice waylaid them. "Grace, Alice, wait." The group stopped as Hess hurried down the hall to catch up. "I wanted to see you before you went to lunch. Grace, we talked about this earlier, and I know you don't want to be revealed as a source. But as far as Watson's concerned, it's unlikely he'll be back in the bank. So there's not much to lose if you testify. You still willing to do it?"

Grace hesitated, and before she could respond, Fred spoke. "Walt, you know Watson's got his gang. He may not do anything, but his followers might. Even if you aren't afraid of them, after Sunday night, I am, and Grace should be."

"Aaah… I don't think they'd go after a woman."

"Dammit, Walt, Watson's Klan gang beat up Alice and almost lynched me."

Grace reached over and gently patted Fred's arm. "It's okay. I'll do it. Slim would've, and I can't do less."

"You sure?" Hess asked.

"Yes. They can't lynch us all, and this stuff has to be brought to light. If people know about it, those snakes wearing hoods will crawl back into their holes."

Hess looked at Alice. "What about you, Alice?"

"If Grace can do it, I can't refuse. Let's kill them with our testimony."

Hess smiled. "Alice, I'd rather you didn't put it that way, but this afternoon, you're on."

CHAPTER 54   GRACE AND ALICE

After lunch, court was declared back in session, and D.A. Hess called Grace Berks to the stand.

Rising from her seat, Grace squeezed down the row and Hess guided her toward the witness stand. Standing straight in her tailored, blue serge Scars Rocbuck suit, she swore to tell the truth and took her seat.

Walt Hess smiled and began his questions. "Mrs. Berks, I understand that you and your husband owned a ranch near here. Please tell the court the disposition of that property."

Grace's eyes were wide with terror at being in front of the audience, and her voice shook. "Slim and I lived there ever since we got married when I was nineteen, goin' on forty years ago. I worked at home, but never anywhere else."

"Yes, Mrs. Berks," Hess said. "And what happened to the ranch?"

She nervously folded and unfolded her hands. "Everybody here knew Slim. Well, after he died in January last year, I knew I couldn't take care of the place by myself, so I decided to sell. 'Course, nobody was buying except the Department of Water and Power, so I sold to them in February and moved into town. Now I live in a nice little cottage over there by the school."

"Who handled the settlement?"

"Mr. Magon. He handles most of the DWP's acquisitions."

"Did you get paid?"

"Well, sort of. Mr. Magon gave me a check from the Department of Water and Power. Mr. Watson was there, and he said to endorse it to him. The bank held the mortgage, and he said he'd see that the mortgage was paid off and he'd put the difference in my bank account."

"Did he put the money in your account?"

Grace's voice rose. "*NO!*" She pointed at Watson sitting at the defense table. "That, that… that man stole it."

Whispers and comments from the spectators rumbled through the courtroom.

"What do you mean, stole it?"

"He told me it would take time before the money appeared in my account at the Inyo Bank. I waited and waited and the money has never appeared."

"So, here it is, November, and you still have not seen any of the money?"

"Not a cent. I found out he had deposited my check in his own personal account at the Pacific National Bank in Los Angeles."

"Why have you waited this long to say anything about it?"

"I didn't. Several times, when I asked Mr. Watson about it, he said to wait just a little longer, that these things take time."

"For the last several months, you have worked for Mr. Watson at the Inyo Bank. Did you have occasion to check the records for your ranch property?"

"I worked here at the Independence office. Those records were kept in Bishop, so I didn't get the chance to see them until May, when I worked a few days in the head office. I saw bank records showing that I still owed the same balance as when the ranch was sold."

Hess handed a paper to Grace. "Mrs. Berks, please tell the court what this document is."

"It's the bill of sale that transfers my spread to DWP, Inc."

"So, in February, you signed your property over to DWP, Inc. At that time, did you know what DWP, Inc. was?

"I thought it was the Department of Water and Power of the City of Los Angeles. Everybody refers to it as the DWP."

"To the best of your knowledge, does the Los Angeles Department of Water and Power now own your ranch?"

"No! I just recently learned that Mr. Magon owns it."

Hess glanced at the jury with a puzzled look. "Mr. Magon? But you said the property was sold to DWP, Inc., meaning the Department of Water and Power."

"People refer to it as the DWP, but that is not its legal name. There is another company with the legal name, DWP, Inc."

"And what company is that?" Hess asked.

"It's a company that Mr. Magon owns. When Mr. Magon arranged for the Los Angeles Department of Water and Power to buy our property, he had the deed of sale show DWP, Inc., as the purchaser. So by arranging the sale to DWP, Inc., he ends up as the owner of my property through his company."

A collective gasp, followed by the murmur of conversation, swept through the courtroom. The judge pounded his gavel and the people quieted down.

"How did you find this out?" Hess asked.

"I went to Sacramento with Alice and Fred Lukin to check the corporate records. Fred and Alice were the ones who uncovered DWP, Inc., with Earl Magon as the owner."

Another hum of conversation spread through the courtroom, and as one, the spectators turned and stared at Alice and Fred. The judge pounded his gavel again and ordered, "Silence, silence … Please continue, Mr. Hess."

Hess folded his arms and looked at the jury with a baffled expression. "Let me get this straight. The real Department of Water and Power paid for your ranch with a check made out to you. You signed your check over to Mr. Watson, who kept the check for himself, but Mr. Magon, by way of his own corporation, DWP Inc., has title to the property, and you have neither your ranch nor the money."

Grace dabbed her eyes with her handkerchief. "That is correct."

"Besides your own ranch, did you find other irregularities in the accounts at the Inyo Bank?

"Yes. I listed them in the diary I gave you."

Hess handed her the diary and questioned her about her entries, most of which related to the problems already discussed by the state auditor and Hanchett. After she had explained her entries in the diary, Hess had it introduced as evidence and then finished questioning Grace.

The judge glanced at the defense table. "Your turn, Mr. Carey."

Carey approached the witness stand. "Mrs. Berks, you have never worked outside your home until last spring when you joined the Inyo Bank. Where did you get training to qualify for bank duties?"

"On the job. The people at the bank showed me what to do."

"What part of that training gave you the knowledge to understand the complex workings of a bank?"

"All of it was helpful, and I watch and learn," she said with a quick nod. "And, I have enough common sense to notice when something isn't right."

"You stated that Mr. Watson deposited your check in his personal account in a Los Angeles bank. How do you know that?"

"A friend who knows someone who works at the L.A. bank told me. Then the auditors traced the check and confirmed the deposit."

Carey turned to the judge. "Her answer is hearsay. Please strike it from the record."

"Counselor," the judge replied, "you asked the question, and the witness answered how she knew. The testimony will remain."

Carey grimaced. "Very well." He glanced at a paper he held and then addressed the witness. "How do you know it was a personal account and not simply another correspondent account for the Inyo Bank?"

"Mr. Lowell said the account was in Mr. Watson's name with no mention of the bank, and no checks were written on that account for bank purposes."

The defense attorney asked a few more questions and then indicated he was through with the witness.

Hess stood. "My next witness is Alice Lukin."

Knowing full well everyone in the courtroom would focus on her badly bruised face, Alice rose and paused to let them see the damage. The cheery yellow of the dress she borrowed from Betty was in stark contrast to the black and blue splotches on her face. She held up the hem of her skirt as she walked past the bar, and the clerk swore her in. She demurely took her seat in the witness box, and after the preliminaries, Hess began his questions.

"Mrs. Lukin, do you and Mr. Lukin have a mortgage loan on your ranch from the Inyo Bank, and are you the one who handles the payments on the loan?"

Alice sat straight in the witness chair as she answered. "Yes, we have a loan, and I handle the monthly payments. Every month, I go to the Inyo Bank and pay with cash from our savings account."

Hess lifted a stack of paper slips from his table and handed them to Alice. "Are these the receipts for your payments?"

"Yes. I've kept all of them and have more at home showing that I paid every month, on time."

Hess thumbed slowly through the slips of paper. "I would like to have these receipts admitted as evidence." He handed them to the court clerk. "Please number these as exhibits and allow counsel for the defense to examine them." He turned back to Alice. "Surely, you've been a little late and received a late notice at one time or another."

Alice's brows furrowed. "Absolutely not. Never! I am very careful."

"The auditors noted the bank listed your loan as in default for several months. How would you explain that?"

Alice's voice rose. "I can't. I made all our payments on time." She pointed at Watson sitting at the defense table. "Ask him why he lists them that way."

"We will do that. Meantime, why do you think they were listed as delinquent?"

Before she could answer, a shout came from the audience.

"I'll tell you why -- because *he* was after my wife."

Everyone in the court turned to see Fred standing and pointing at Watson at the defendant's table.

The judge pounded for order. "Quiet! Sit down, sir, or you will be escorted from the courtroom."

Jake, sitting next to Fred, grabbed him by the belt and pulled him into his seat.

Alice glared at her husband and turned back to the district attorney. "What was your question, Mr. Hess?"

"Why do you think the bank listed your loan as delinquent?"

Alice turned toward the jury. "When Fred was put in jail, unjustly, I might add, Mr. Watson came out to the ranch and told me he would help with Fred's legal issues if I would, as he put it… ah…be generous with him. He said he was very attracted to me and asked me to go into the house with him. When I told him to leave, he said we were delinquent on our mortgage payments and he would foreclose. I said I had all my payment receipts. He insisted they were forgeries."

"He asked you to go into the house with him? What did you understand that to mean?"

She turned toward the jury. "It was quite clear that he…" she hesitated and looked back at the judge, "he…ah…ah…he wanted me to … ah." She looked at the floor, and her lips quivered as she tried but failed to speak.

"Take your time, Mrs. Lukin," the DA said. "Take your time."

She fumbled in her purse for her handkerchief and wiped her teary eyes. She stared at her lap for a moment. Then, sitting ramrod straight, with a shaky but strong voice, she declared, "He wanted me to go to bed with him, and if I didn't, he would foreclose."

Gasps, whispers, and a few snickers flowed through the audience. The judge whacked his gavel. "Silence!"

After the spectators quieted down, the D.A. continued. "Did he examine the receipts for your payments?"

"No."

"So, without looking at your receipts, he declared them to be forgeries?"

"Yes, that is correct."

"Mrs. Lukin, when you told Mr. Watson to leave your ranch, did he?"

"Yes."

"Did you hear from Mr. Watson after that?"

"Yes. The next week, we received a registered letter from the bank saying they would foreclose on our ranch."

Hess took a piece of paper from his table and handed it to Alice. "Is this the letter you received?"

"Yes."

"Did the letter give a deadline to bring your loan current before it foreclosed?"

"Yes. August ninth."

"August ninth has passed. Did the bank foreclose on your property?"

"No. I guess with Mr. Watson's arrest and the bank closed, it was… sort of… ahh… forgotten."

Again, soft laughter and tittering wafted through the courtroom.

"Thank you, Mrs. Lukin." The D.A. turned to the judge. "I am through with this witness."

"Mr. Carey," the judge said.

Watson's defense attorney stood. He looked at a paper, then glared at Alice. "Mrs. Lukin, I understand that in two instances, you shot at Los Angeles policemen. First, you shot at their car on your ranch, and later, you shot Lieutenant Dodson's ear. As a result, he lost his hearing and was forced to leave the police force. Is that true?"

Subdued applause rippled across the courtroom. The judge pounded his gavel. "Order. Stop that clapping."

"I know nothing about Mr. Dodson's job," Alice said softly.

"But did you shoot at the police?"

"No. The men I shot at were not policemen here in Inyo County. They were private citizens threatening other private citizens. They may have been policemen in L.A., but not here.

When I shot at Mr. Dodson, he was holding a gun to my husband's head in the act of kidnapping him, and he tried to shoot me. In the other instance, those men were trespassing on our property, threatening us with their guns."

Quiet applause echoed through the room again. The judge pounded his gavel. "Order, order, or I will clear the courtroom."

Hess rose. "These questions do not relate to the witness's testimony and are irrelevant."

"Sustained," the judge said. "Mr. Carey, confine your questions to the issues before the court."

"Yes, Your Honor. Mrs. Lukin, you testified that Mr. Watson said he would help with your husband's legal issues if you would be generous with him. Isn't it possible that he meant simply that you should be a good bank customer or some other form of generosity?"

Alice raised her chin and spoke confidently. "No. Both of us knew exactly what he meant. He wanted me to go in the house and go to bed with him, and he made it clear that if I didn't, he would foreclose on the ranch."

"But he never foreclosed, did he?"

"He began the process but got arrested for embezzlement first," Alice replied.

Carey retreated behind his defense table. "I'm through with this witness."

After Alice stepped down from the witness stand, Hess called several more witnesses and then rested his case. Court was adjourned until the next morning.

CHAPTER 55   VERDICT

The next morning, it was Carey's turn to mount his defense. He had Watson recount the development of the Inyo Bank and explain how it had helped finance the growth of local businesses and ranches. Then, he asked Watson to explain the many transactions that were at the heart of the charges against the banker. "The prosecution contends you used bank funds to support your other businesses, such as your soda ash business, and paid funds into a secret, personal bank account in Los Angeles. Please explain those transactions."

"All of that was entirely above board," Watson said. "My bank's main business is to lend money to other businesses. The bank lent money to my own businesses just as it did to other firms. As for the bank accounts in my name at other banks, I put funds there to pay bank expenses in the city."

Carey faced the jury. "Sounds reasonable to me."

He asked Watson more questions about the bank's operations to show that Watson's actions were normal and that the bank was the well-run savior of the valley. Without mentioning Watson's attempts to conquer Alice Lukin, he concluded and said he was through with the witness.

District Attorney Hess stood for his turn at cross-examination. "Mr. Watson, you said your bank's payments to your other businesses were normal. Please explain to the court why, if they were above-board payments, you disguised them as deposits to a non-existent account at Wells Fargo Bank?"

It was a rare occurrence for Mark Watson to be speechless, but this time, his mouth opened and closed like he was trying to say something, but no sound came out. He looked at Carey as though to be rescued. The defense attorney stared at the floor without saying anything.

Hess faced the jury. "I guess that question was too difficult. I'll ask an easier one." He turned back to face Watson. "Mrs. Berks testified that you took the check when she sold her ranch. Yet, she has never received any of the money, and her loan is still shown as active in your bank's accounting. Why has the bank never shown her loan as being paid off?"

"That must be a simple oversight by the staff. When I got that check, I'm sure I gave it to Miss Collins in order to make the proper entries in our books. I had not realized she failed to make the proper accounting entries."

Hess looked at a paper he held, then at Watson. "That same check was deposited in your personal account at the Pacific

National Bank in Los Angeles. How did that happen if you gave it to your staff?"

"I guess Miss Collins misunderstood my directive and deposited it in the wrong account. I will correct it as soon as I am permitted to resume control of my bank."

"So, your bank staff have access to your personal checking account in L.A.?"

"It is an account for the Inyo Bank, not a personal account."

"The state bank auditor, Mr. Lowell, testified that that account was in your name, not the bank's, and was never used for Inyo Bank business. Is that incorrect?"

Watson was silent for a moment before answering. "Yes. The auditor does not understand banking. That account was a reserve."

"The auditor found that last year, you used funds from that account to pay for a hunting trip to Canada. Is that the kind of expense that the bank has reserves for?"

Watson stared at the district attorney. After a substantial delay, Hess asked, "Mr. Watson, can you answer my question?"

Watson looked at the ceiling and then at his hands. "Of course. That was a legitimate business trip to cultivate clients."

"Which clients?"

"I don't remember. It was a long time ago."

"A long time ago? You can't remember clients you took on an expensive business trip just last year? Very well. Let's turn to another issue. Mrs. Berks testified that every Friday she phoned to report the cash balance at the Independence branch office. She said she always spoke to you and thinks you changed the numbers to show a smaller balance. Why did you change them?"

Watson had regained his composure and spoke with assurance. "I have never changed any numbers. In fact, I have never spoken to Mrs. Berks about the Friday balances. As president of the bank, I was always too busy to handle such minor tasks. I believe it was usually Miss Collins who tended to that. She may have changed the figures. I have suspected for some time that she might be skimming some cash."

"Did you talk to her about it?"

"Yes. Of course. She was upset and denied it. I didn't have the heart to terminate her employment."

"You must be very kind."

"Yes, I am. As an important leader in this county, I feel an obligation to help everyone, especially my employees."

"Does that generosity extend to the bank's borrowers?" Hess asked.

"Yes, of course. Especially the borrowers."

"Earlier, Mrs. Lukin testified she made payments on their mortgage loan on time every month. But your bank records show no payments for the last eighteen months and classified the Lukin loan as delinquent. Was it your generosity that stopped you from foreclosing on the loan?

"Yes. That I did not foreclose earlier shows how charitable I am with our borrowers."

"But I understand you have begun the foreclosure process. What prompted you to proceed?"

"I can afford to be charitable only so long. When a borrower misses that many payments, we are almost forced to foreclose."

"Which months did she miss her payments?

"Several over the last year. I would have to check our books, but I have not been allowed to enter my bank."

Hess picked up a stack of receipts and handed them to the witness. "Here are bank receipts for her payments for the last two years, showing that she paid every month."

Watson fanned the papers like a deck of cards but did not examine them. "These are forgeries."

"All of them?"

"Every single one."

"But the bank's records show only eighteen months of non-payment. Did she forge the ones for the months she paid?"

"Yes. That woman cannot be trusted."

Subdued laughter spread through the courtroom, and the judge whacked his gavel. "Silence!"

"You didn't look at them very closely. How could you tell they were forgeries?"

"I don't need to look. Years of experience at the bank enables me to detect such things by the feel and weight of the paper and the type of ink, and I am positive they were forged."

"They feel forged? How do forged documents feel?" He paused. "No, please disregard that question. Please turn the stack of receipts over so you cannot see the writing on the front side. Now, from the bottom of the stack, count out ten receipts and set them aside."

Watson counted the slips as instructed.

"Now, without looking, feel and heft receipts numbered eleven through twenty from the bottom and tell the court whether or not they are forgeries."

Watson ran his fingers over the sheets. "Yes, I am sure they were forged."

"Please turn them over and look closely at those receipts. Tell the jury whose loan account they apply to and which bank employee signed them."

Watson glanced at the receipts. His face fell and he stared at the D.A.

"Please tell us whose account and who signed them."

Quietly, almost in a whisper, Watson said, "They are for your loan account, and I signed them."

Chuckles, snickers, and loud guffaws echoed through the courtroom.

"Silence!" the judge ordered.

When it quieted, Hess asked, "Do you think they were forged?"

"No," Watson mumbled.

"Thank you, Mr. Watson." Hess turned to the judge. "Your honor, in view of this testimony, I request that the court stipulate there is no evidence that the Lukin's mortgage is delinquent and therefore should not be foreclosed."

"I will take that under advisement," the judge said.

"I am through with this witness," the district attorney said.

The judge excused Watson and said, "Mr. Carey, call your next witness."

"Yes, Your Honor. I would like to recall Clarence Lowell of the California Banking Department."

Lowell rose from his seat at the back of the courtroom and made his way to the witness stand. After he was reminded that he was still under oath, he took his seat.

Carey stood at the defense table. "Mr. Lowell, now that you completed your audit of the Inyo Bank, what tasks remain?"

"After auditing, we usually supervise a restructuring so the bank's finances are healthy and it can resume business. If the bank is not viable, we supervise its liquidation so we can return as much value as possible to the bank's depositors and creditors. We are now in the process of liquidating the assets of the Inyo Bank, as well as Mr. Watson's other businesses."

"What do you mean by other businesses?"

"To make up for shortages, we will sell Mr. Watson's other enterprises to raise funds to pay the bank's creditors. These other enterprises include the vanadium mine west of Bishop, the hardware store in Bishop, the soda ash plant on Owens Lake, and his Little Lake resort."

"Will that generate enough cash so those groups get all their money back?"

"Our estimate is that we will be able to pay off about eighty percent of the bank's liabilities. In other words, an average creditor who is owed one hundred dollars might get eighty dollars back."

A low rumble echoed through the courtroom as the spectators commented on the testimony.

"Is that true for the depositors? Each one will get eighty cents on the dollar?"

"All bank clients of the same class will be paid on a prorated basis, but clients of lower priority may get less. We are confident that we will recover enough to pay the depositors all or most of what they are owed. Other creditors with lower priority will get something, but less than the depositors, and the stockholders will probably get nothing."

Applause and a few cheers interrupted the testimony when people heard they would recover the money they had generally given up as lost.

Another whack of the judge's gavel.

Carey asked a few more questions and then rested his case.

The District Attorney rose. "Your honor, I would like to call Margaret Collins as a rebuttal witness."

"Proceed. But limit your questions to issues relating to previous testimony."

Margaret was sworn in and Hess began his questions.

"Miss Collins, Mr. Watson said that you took those Friday calls from the branches about their cash balances and recorded them in the bank's books. Did you usually take those calls?"

"Absolutely not. Mr. Watson was very insistent that he take those calls himself. He also recorded the numbers."

"Mr. Watson said you were skimming the cash. Did you *ever* skim the cash?"

"Certainly not. My job was bookkeeper, and I didn't usually handle the cash. That was the teller's job. When cash was submitted to us, the teller counted and recorded it, then put it in the vault.

"Did Mr. Watson ever speak to you about skimming the cash?"

"Never."

"Mr. Watson said that he gave you Mrs. Berks' check and you deposited it in his account at the Pacific National Bank. Did you process that check?"

"No. I never saw it."

"I am through with this witness," Hess said.

"Your turn, Mr. Carey," the judge said.

"No more questions," Carey said.

The judge ordered a break, and then each side summarized its case. The judge gave the jury instructions and sent it to its deliberations. Late in the afternoon, they announced they had reached a decision.

As Fred watched the jury file in, he figured they were solidly in Watson's corner. He glared at Watson sitting at the defendant's table with a self-satisfied smile, as though he were certain to be found innocent. Once he was back in his bank, he would find a way to foreclose on the ranch. Fred had worked on his ranch all his life, and that jackass would take it all and laugh while he was doing it. He leaned over and whispered to Alice, "This has all been a waste of time."

Alice took Fred's hand and whispered back, "You said that before. Wait and see."

"Have you reached a verdict?" the judge asked.

"Yes, your honor," the jury foreman answered. He handed a paper to the bailiff, who handed it to the judge.

The judge looked at the sheet and read the verdict. "We, the undersigned members of the jury, find the defendant, Mark Watson, guilty as charged on all charges."

Watson's eyes bugged and his jaw dropped in surprise. The rest of the courtroom erupted in pandemonium. Watson's opponents cheered, and his supporters stood and shouted about his innocence.

The judge pounded his gavel and shouted, "Order! Order! Silence!"

One of the men Fred had pegged as a Klansmen jumped over the bar as though to rescue Watson. But then he stood in apparent indecision and confusion, gaping at the judge.

"Stop that man," the judge shouted at the bailiff. At the same time, Sheriff Cole, who had been sitting in the gallery adjacent to the jury box, ran and seized the invader's arms and slammed him face-first to the floor. In an instant, the sheriff had the man's hands behind his back with handcuffs locked around his wrists. With the help of the bailiff, Cole lifted the man to his feet. At the sight of blood gushing from the man's nose and mouth where he had collided with the floor, the crowd quieted, and Cole pushed the man out the door.

With the courtroom totally silent, the judge whacked his mallet. "Well then … I guess we can continue." He then read the charges one by one:

"Embezzlement, guilty."

"Theft, guilty."

"Perjury, guilty."

"Violation of California state banking regulations, guilty."

"Abuse of the legal processes, guilty."

"Extortion, guilty."

Fred couldn't believe his ears. Maybe it was his imagination, like one of those flashbacks he had about the war. A soft wind of whispers wafted through the courtroom. Was everybody else as shocked as he? Fred had never figured a jury of local residents would find Watson guilty. He turned and hugged Alice.

Alice whispered. "See, I told you. Now we won't have to worry about foreclosure."

"Yeah, I guess we'll get our savings back, too," Fred said.

The judge said he would announce the sentence the next day, then thanked the jury for its service and excused them.

People filed out of the courtroom and gathered in small groups to discuss the verdict. Most of the discussions were subdued, but the Watson partisans filled the hall with loud denunciations of the judge and jury. Most of the spectators ignored the noisy Watson faction, and the hall outside the courtroom slowly emptied.

The next morning, the courtroom was filled to capacity with people eager to hear what would happen to the banker.

The judge told the defendant to stand. "Mark Watson, the court sentences you to ten years of confinement in the California State Penitentiary at San Quentin." He pounded his gavel and announced, "This court is adjourned."

CHAPTER 56   SAINT FRANCIS DAM

On a pleasant spring day in 1928, Fred entered the Inyo Café. He whacked his hat against his thigh to get the dust off, as was his habit even when it wasn't dusty. He nodded to the morning coffee regulars and pulled a chair up to the accustomed table by the window.

Without a word, Doris set a cup in front of him and poured steaming coffee.

"Thanks, Doris."

"How's your rebuilding going?" George King asked.

"Slow. We've got enough fixed up to finally move out of the barn, but I've still got a long way to go. God, I wish I could get some of those Klan guys to pay for it."

"You're never going to get anybody to admit they were involved," George said. "You get anything from the insurance?"

"Not much. The agent in Bishop sabotaged the claim. I think he was one of the Klan gang that went after me. That's why it takin' so long to rebuild—damned little insurance money." Fred stirred some sugar into his coffee. "Speakin' of Klan and stuff, what happened over at the trial for Watson's accomplices yesterday? Any of you go?"

There was a unanimous shaking of heads, and Jake spoke. "I heard Perry Sexton gave a full account of his aqueduct blast at Cottonwood Creek last April. He said Mark Watson offered to forgive his debt to the bank if he would do it. He implicated several others in the plot."

"It's strange that they haven't charged Watson with any of those blasts," Fred said. "He's the one who was directing it all along."

Jake laughed and added, "That is, after the first one that got it all started, sort of like the Boston Tea Party."

A nervous chuckle echoed around the table.

Murphy swirled the coffee in his cup. "I guess since Watson's already doing ten years for his banking crimes, they figured they'd go after the others. You know, there hasn't been a single blast since Watson was sent away."

"Yeah, things have been pretty quiet," George agreed.

"Well, quiet no longer," came a familiar voice from the door.

They all turned to see Sheriff Cole standing in the doorway.

"What do you mean, Charlie?" Fred asked.

Cole grabbed a bentwood chair while the others scooted aside to give him room. He glanced around the table, making sure he had everyone's attention. "Just got word that Mulholland's dam in the

San Francisquito Canyon north of L.A. burst Monday night. The details still aren't clear, but apparently, the whole thing failed, and a wall of water over a hundred feet high roared down the canyon. Wiped out farms and towns all the way to Ventura on the coast."

Everyone at the table stared at Cole, too stunned to speak.

Fred broke the silence. "What do you mean, wiped-out farms and towns?"

"Just that. The flood followed the canyon of the Santa Clara River. The little towns nearest the dam were washed away, and farms and houses all the way to the ocean were flooded."

"What about the people?" Fred asked.

"It was in the middle of the night when everybody was in bed. There was no warning. People didn't have time to escape. They're still finding bodies clear up in the tops of trees. That's how deep the water was. The guy who phoned me said they even found a little girl asleep at the top of a tree like the water carried her there from her bedroom in the middle of the night."

The men at the table were silent as they digested the news.

"That dam was Mulholland's pet project," George said. "The papers said he had a major hand in the design."

"Musta been some design," Murphy responded. "They just finished filling it, and it busts. God knows how many people might've died. Isn't that some sort of murder, Charlie?"

Cole drummed his fingers on the table. "I doubt it. But here's the catch. Mulholland said it was radicals from up here who sabotaged the dam. That's why one of the L.A. cops called me. He said nobody else believes it was sabotage, but he had to ask if I thought anybody in this area was involved. Our folks might be guilty of some things, but I don't think that was one."

"It's one thing to blast the aqueduct," Fred said. "Nobody was hurt in any of those. But it's a whole 'nother thing to build a bad dam that kills a bunch of innocent people." He slapped the table. "Dang it, they should charge Mulholland with a crime, the same as some guy who blows up the dam."

"People like him never get charged with their crimes," Jake observed.

"That's for sure," Murphy said. "He was noted for saying that all the people in the Owens Valley should be hung, but there weren't enough trees. What about him? Think of the families that were drowned and washed away in the middle of the night because of him."

Fred sat somberly, imagining a hundred-foot wall of water hitting his house in the middle of the night. He put a dime by his empty coffee cup and got up. "I know nothing like that's happened around here, but I feel like I need to go home and see what little we've got left is still there."

Friday morning, four days after the St. Francis dam broke, Fred had finished breakfast when Sheriff Cole drove into the farmyard, stirring up a cloud of dust.

Fred walked out to meet him. "Charlie, you know if you stir up that much dust, you will be on Alice's hunting list."

"Tell her I'm sorry. I was in a hurry."

"Sorry about what, Charlie?" asked Alice, now standing in the doorway.

"The dust when I drove in."

She fanned her hand in front of her face to swish the dust away. "I hope someday we can get the roads paved."

"What brings you today, Charlie?" Fred asked.

"I got a call from the L.A. police about a body they found in the flood from the dam break."

Fred's face fell. When the police came calling about a body, it couldn't be good. He couldn't think of anybody he knew who might have been in the path of the horrible flood over two hundred miles away. "Who did they find? Somebody from here?"

"Sort of," Cole replied. "They found a body that had washed up in the flood. It wasn't in good condition, but they're pretty sure it's Earl Magon."

Fred stared at Cole. Magon had to have been dead when he dumped him in the aqueduct months ago. The thug's face was half gone. No way he could have lived through that.

Alice was the first to respond. "Magon? Didn't he disappear sometime last fall, about the time of the bank failure?"

Fred looked at his wife with admiration. She seemed so smooth and unflustered about the body of the man she had shot.

"Yeah," Cole answered. "He hasn't been heard from since before Watson's trial. Now he shows up dead."

"Poor man. Did he drown in the flood?" Alice asked with a sympathetic voice.

That was almost more than Fred could stand and it was hard not to laugh.

Cole stared at Fred for a moment, then replied. "Not likely he drowned recently. The L.A. cops said his body was in terrible condition. Decomposed like he'd been dead and in the water a long time. One side of his face was gone, like maybe the fish ate it. The only reason they could identify him was that he still had some of his clothes with identification in his pocket."

Alice shook her head with deep concern. "That's awful. Maybe he fell in that lake and drowned before the dam broke."

Cole looked at the ground and traced a pattern in the dirt with his boot. "Could be. Could be. But not many people up here will be sorry he's gone. Certainly not me, and I can't imagine you folks will mourn him either."

Fred watched Alice, curious what she'd say next.

She didn't disappoint. "Oh, it's so sad when anyone passes, even a man like that. Imagine drowning in that big reservoir. So lonely. But he must've been a lonely man, all those years living by himself, with so few friends."

Cole shrugged. "Yeah. Not many friends here, for sure. And since he gave you such trouble, I thought you'd want to know. Well, I gotta get back to town."

As Cole drove slowly out of their farmyard, Alice clapped her hands. "That calls for a party. We haven't had a good one in a long time, and we can hold a wake for Mr. Magon."

Later, when Fred went into the house for lunch, he found Alice sitting at the table looking downcast. "What's the matter?"

She looked up with teary eyes. "This party. When I started making the guest list, it reminded me of how many of our friends were gone. The Schaffers lost their ranch and moved away. The Stevens and Boyds gave up and sold to the DWP. Grace had to sell after Slim died, and then Henry and Isabel threw in the towel and sold out. So many other families sold out to the DWP and moved away, so there are not even enough kids to keep all the schools open. They closed the grammar schools in Aberdeen, Keeler, and Laws, and there's barely enough kids left to keep schools open here and in Big Pine. It's like the whole valley's empty. So few of us left. Makes me feel like crying."

"Yeah, a lot of abandoned ranches." Fred paused as he thought about the struggle and all the people no longer there. "I heard that the DWP now owns over ninety percent of the land and water in the valley. And, Henry still won't speak to me 'cause he blames me for bringing the bank down."

"He'll come around. Just give him time. Most everybody's getting their money back in the bank liquidation."

Fred smiled. "Well, at least we still have our land and water and a few friends who hung on. We have Betty and Jake, Murph and Anna Mae, Charlie and Doris, and a few others. Enough for a party—just a bit smaller."

Alice laughed and clapped her hands. "And we don't have Magon or Watson."

***************THE END **************

Appreciation and Thanks

I want to thank my family. They have made my life a joy:

Judith, whom I have loved since I first saw her in high school, and have enjoyed every minute of being with her for more than sixty years. With respect to this book, my thanks to her for her encouragement and ideas, especially for suggesting the title and designing the cover.

Suzanne, who is always an inspiration of courage and drive.

Karen, who always has great judgment and is constantly trying to take care of Judy and me.

Wyatt, our grandson, who reveals additional talents and abilities every day.

Nick, who is always interesting. Thanks to Nick and Karen for helping me with the book cover.

****

My thanks to the many friends who provided helpful comments and criticisms of my many drafts:

Alan Iannacito, who provided suggestions and encouragement through several drafts and seasons.

The Rocky Mountain Fiction Writers Critique Group of southwest Denver, particularly Bill Brinn, Cathy Clark, Rick Duffy, Tom Farrell, Sue Hinkin, Still Kallil, Mel Lake, Merrie Need, Susan Schoolman, and Brendan Smiley.
And many others, to whom I apologize for not naming.

About the Author

I was born and raised in the Owens Valley. I earned BS, MBA, and PhD degrees in finance from the University of California, Berkeley, and taught finance at the University of Pennsylvania, the University of Houston, and the University of Colorado, Denver, where I retired as a Professor Emeritus. I live in Denver, but a part of me will always belong to the Owens Valley.

Even though my academic training and career were in finance, I have an enduring interest in history, particularly the history of California. As a child, I listened to the stories of the people who experienced the events fictionally portrayed in this novel. I have enjoyed translating some of those accounts into what I hope is an interesting and fun-to-read story.

 I hope you, the reader, will forgive the liberties I have taken with reality to paint a picture of the conflict over water in the early 20th Century.

---- Jim Morris

References

To learn more about water conflict in the Owens Valley and other parts of the state, the following books will give you a good start:

Mark Arax. *The Dreamt Land*, Alfred A. Knopf, 2019.

Mary Austin. *The Ford*, University of California Press, 1917.

W.A. Chalfant. *The Story of Inyo*, revised edition, Community Printing and Publishing, 1933.

Frances Gragg & George Putman. *Golden Valley*, Duell, Sloan & Pearce, 1950

Abraham Hoffman. *Vision or Villainy*, Texas A&M University Press, 1981.

William L. Kahrl. *Water and Power*, University of California Press, 1982.

Catherine Mulholland. *William Mulholland and the Rise of Los Angeles*, University of California Press, 2000.

Remi A. Nadeau. *The Water Seekers*, Forgotten Books, 1950.

Robert A. Pearce. *The Owens Valley Controversy & A.A. Brierly: The Untold Story*, Robert A. Pearce, 2013.

Marc Reisner. *Cadillac Desert*, Penguin Books, 1986.

Les Standiford. *Water to the Angels*, Harper Collins, 2015.

Jane Wehry. *The Owens Valley*, Arcadia Publishing, 2013.

Jon Wilkman. *FloodPath*, Bloomsbury, 2016.

www.ingramcontent.com/pod-product-compliance
Lightning Source LLC
Chambersburg PA
CBHW070154120726
47909CB00001B/104